HIGH PRAISE FOR AMANDA HARTE!

CAROUSEL OF DREAMS

"A plot-driven, high-energy, fast-paced tale. Ms. Harte's work never fails to impress. "

—*Romance Reviews Today*

"An emotional tale [with] plenty of mystery, passion and riveting characters. "

—*Reader to Reader*

RAINBOWS AT MIDNIGHT

"*Rainbows at Midnight* is a page-turner . . . a fine tale that will never disappoint. "

—*Romance Reviews Today*

MIDNIGHT SUN

"*Midnight Sun* is a beautifully written story. . . . Amanda Harte breathes such life into her settings and characters!"

—*Romance Communications*

"A terrific read by Ms. Harte. . . . This is a fresh setting, a can't-put-down-novel."

—*The Belles & Beaux of Romance*

"A must read."

—*CompuServe Romance Reviews*

NORTH STAR

"*North Star* is thought-provoking, poignant, and a very satisfying read. Don't miss it!"

—*The Belles & Beaux of Romance*

"*North Star* is a well-written and intelligent read, with depth and richness that is extremely satisfying."

—*Romance Communications*

AN UNFORGETTABLE KISS

The sheer arrogance of the stranger's statement made Susannah laugh. "Spoken like a man whose ego is as large as his muscles."

"And what's wrong with muscles?"

"Nothing." Particularly when they were attached to a man who looked like a Greek god. "They're preferable to oversize egos."

His blue eyes twinkled, as if her words amused rather than annoyed him. "Why do you think my ego is oversized?"

He really was the most attractive man she had ever seen. He might be bold and brash, but he was also almost impossibly handsome. "Let's start with that boast about an unforgettable kiss."

"That was not a boast. It was a simple statement of fact."

So swiftly that she had no way of anticipating his action, he wrapped his arms around her and drew her close. Susannah caught her breath in amazement. What had she said about muscles? His were even more developed than she had thought. And, oh, how they felt!

Susannah raised her eyes to his, memorizing the curve of his brows, the faint crinkles at the corners of his eyes, the way his lashes rested on his cheeks when he blinked. He stared at her for an instant . . . or was it an eternity? . . . and then he slowly lowered his mouth to hers. She could have pulled away. She should have pulled away. And yet she did not.

CAROUSEL OF DREAMS

AMANDA HARTE

LEISURE BOOKS   NEW YORK CITY

For Jean Ellen Mayer,
who brought sunshine to a rainy semester in France.
Merci beaucoup!

A LEISURE BOOK®

August 2002

Published by

Dorchester Publishing Co., Inc.
276 Fifth Avenue
New York, NY 10001

ISBN 0-8439-5039-0

Visit us on the web at www.dorchesterpub.com.

CAROUSEL
OF DREAMS

Chapter One

Late March 1908

"This is the most ridiculous thing I've ever heard." Charles Moreland stared at the letter that had been delivered that morning. If he hadn't recognized the handwriting and known that the author was not inclined to practical jokes, he might have believed it to be a hoax. "Anthony is off his rocker."

The man on the opposite side of the desk leaned back, propping his feet on the shiny surface, his relaxed posture as eloquent as the words that had raised Charles's hackles. "I say, old man, aren't you overreacting?"

Old man! The blood that pounded in Charles's head sounded louder than the thump of the looms next door. He clenched his fists, barely restraining himself from wringing Brad's neck. "Just because I'm six months older than you doesn't make me an old man." Charles spat the words at his friend. His friend. Hell, with friends like Anthony and Brad, it was no wonder his life was in such a mess.

There had been a time when . . . Charles shook his head. That

1

time was gone like so much else in his life. Now his days were spent in this office, confined as surely as if he were in a jail cell. That the room had been his father's only made Charles hate it more.

Brad shrugged, unaffected by his friend's anger. "It's not your age," he said smoothly, "it's your attitude. Face it, Charles. Ever since you came back, you've been acting like an old man." Brad ran a hand through his fiery red hair. "Anthony used to say that you were the daredevil one of us. What happened?"

As if Brad didn't know. Everyone in Hidden Falls knew about the fire that had changed the Moreland family's lives. If it hadn't been for the fire, Charles would still be in New York, not stuck in this godforsaken backwater of a town burdened with more problems than any one man should have to solve. If it hadn't been for the fire, his father would be reaping what he had sowed instead of leaving Charles a legacy of debts and lies. But Charles had no intention of discussing his problems with Brad or Anthony or any of the well-meaning citizens who had offered advice. Advice wasn't what Charles needed. Miracles were. Unfortunately, no one in Hidden Falls seemed to be doling out miracles this year.

"I can't picture Anthony with a wife," Charles said, once again staring at the letter. Insanity. Certifiable insanity. The bell in the clock tower rang, signaling the start of the dinner break. Charles knew that if he looked out the window, he would see hundreds of mill workers scurrying home for the noon meal. That was insanity of a different type, the fact that all those people were dependent on him for their livelihood. Charles wouldn't think about that. Not now. Instead he focused on Anthony's announcement. That was better than looking at the potted plant in the corner, remembering the day he'd helped his mother smuggle it into the office and the way his father had laughed, declaring it to be exactly what he wanted. That had been a lie, just like all the others.

Charles started to crumple Anthony's letter, then shoved it at Brad. "It seems to me Anthony has been on the verge of marriage at least a dozen times." Charles noticed that Brad's eyes narrowed as he spoke.

"On the verge is one thing." When the three of them had been at college together, Anthony had been in and out of love more times than Charles could count, while he and Brad had had longer-term romances. "Putting a ring on a lady's finger is something else."

Lowering his feet to the floor, Brad stared at Charles. "You didn't really think we'd all wait until we were thirty, did you?"

He had, and that was part of the problem. In a world where almost everything else had changed, Charles had hoped that at least one thing would remain constant. "I figured that was one of the ABC pacts that we'd keep."

When the three of them had arrived on campus, someone—Charles couldn't remember who—had dubbed them the ABCs, not just for their first initials but also because the trio had insisted on being first in everything. The nickname had stuck and had become a matter of pride for the three men. Though they had pursued different studies, they had pledged the same fraternity, and it was well known that one did not invite one of the ABCs to a party without the others.

During their four years together, the trio had made a number of pacts, the two most memorable being lifelong friendship and bachelorhood until at least thirty. Now it appeared that one of those promises was in serious jeopardy.

Brad shook his head slowly, as if he had put no credence in their agreements. "I reckon when a man gets to a certain age, he starts to think about settling down."

Something in his tone made Charles blink. "Not you, too." Was he the only one who knew that matrimony was not the answer to all problems?

As if unwilling to meet Charles's gaze, Brad rose and stared out the window. The sounds of footsteps and voices had diminished. By now the mill hands would be eating, fortifying themselves for another six hours' work. After a week of gloomy skies, the sun had finally emerged. If they'd been at school together, Charles would have persuaded Anthony and Brad to play hooky. Instead, he was sitting in a room that he loathed with every fiber of his being, discussing marriage.

"If I could convince that gorgeous sister of yours," Brad said calmly, "I'd be a wedded man before summer's end."

"Jane?" Charles stared at his friend's back. Brad fancied Jane? What other surprises did the day hold in store?

"Who else but Jane?" Though his tone was calm, the way Brad ran a hand through his hair told Charles he was more disturbed than he wanted to admit. How odd to think that normally calm Brad was so infatuated that his hands shook.

If Brad was upset, so was Charles, though for different reasons. He closed his eyes, trying to keep the pain at bay. A year ago Brad's answer to Charles's question might have been different, but now there was only one Moreland daughter anyone would describe as gorgeous. The twins were no longer identical.

Charles inhaled deeply, trying to slow the pounding of his pulse. "Then I guess it's lucky for Jane that she's still in Switzerland." To his relief, his voice sounded normal, as if the memories Brad had unleashed no longer had the power to wound him.

He opened his eyes. A ray of sunshine spilled onto the floor. A year ago Charles might have considered it a good omen; now he no longer believed in omens, at least not good ones. He rose, shoving the chair beneath the desk.

Brad leaned against the wall, his posture once more casual. "When are Jane and Anne coming back?"

Too soon. Not soon enough. But Charles said only, "The end of August. If I'm lucky, their ship will dock a week or so after the carousel is finished. Of course," he added, his lips twisting into a wry smile, "with my luck . . ." He picked up a paperweight and tossed it from hand to hand.

"I'll say this much for you." Brad pointed his finger at Charles in a parody of accusation. "You're giving the town plenty to talk about."

"Like the fact that the prodigal son stayed in Hidden Falls." When he most definitely hadn't wanted to. When every instinct had told him to put as many miles as possible between himself and his childhood home. When only a deeply instilled sense of duty had kept him from fleeing.

Shaking his head, Brad said, "That's old news. No, the carousel's what everyone's talking about now." Brad narrowed his eyes again in that assessing look that made Charles uncomfortable. His friend had always had an uncanny ability to see beneath the surface. "I've got to admit that I don't understand why a man with your financial problems would go to that kind of expense," Brad said.

The answer was easy. "I want Anne to have something special when she comes home." Charles stared at Brad, daring him to refute his logic. Though he had intended to say nothing more, the words tumbled out. "Someone in this family deserves happiness."

For a second Brad looked surprised. Then a satisfied smile crossed his face. "So, you've got a kind streak, after all."

Charles shrugged. Let Brad think what he liked; Charles had no intention of discussing his motives. "Hard to believe, isn't it?" He pointed toward the door. "Now, get out. I need to figure out how I'm going to pay the carousel carvers."

Susannah Deere closed her eyes and took a deep breath, savoring the air in the small forest. The calendar hadn't lied. Spring was coming. The scent of mud was beginning to replace the crisp, snow-laden air, and the fallen pine needles were losing their pungency. Susannah opened her eyes and lengthened her stride, suddenly anxious to put distance between herself and the house. Though she would pay the price tonight by sleeping in a dusty room, she needed to escape. If only for a few minutes, she would think about spring's advent, not what she had left behind.

You couldn't tell that winter was ending by looking at the ground. It was still brown and dotted with the icy remnants of the last snowstorm. But the sky that peeked through the treetops was blue, and the leaf buds were noticeably larger than they had been at home. Susannah stopped, startled by the thought that this was now home. This was where Dorothy wanted to be, and—God willing—it would make a difference.

Though few birds had returned, squirrels chattered to one another, and in the distance Susannah heard rhythmic pounding. Despite the cool air, she stripped off her gloves and touched the bark of a birch tree, feeling the slightly nubby texture as she assessed the best way to interpret it. Neither charcoal nor pen and ink would be effective. If she were using oils, she would dab dark brown on the trunk, creating a three-dimensional effect. With watercolors, she would have to rely solely on shading to capture the tree's beauty. Her fingers curled, longing for the feel of a brush between them. But for the next few days at least, there would be no time for painting.

Please, God, Susannah prayed as she slid her hand along the tree trunk, *help Dorothy.* It had been a difficult decision, uprooting them from the only home Susannah had ever known in the hope of making Dorothy happy. But maybe, just maybe, it had been the right one.

It hadn't seemed that way at first. Though Susannah had written a letter, directing that the house be opened and cleaned, somehow that message had been lost. Instead of the cheerful home she had expected, they were greeted by years' worth of dust, furniture still shrouded in cotton covers and musty drapes. Susannah had sneezed; her mother had frowned. But, with one of the mercurial changes of mood that had become so common, Dorothy's frown had soon turned into a radiant smile.

"Look, Susannah," she said as she climbed the stairs with more energy than Susannah had seen in months, "here's my room." Dorothy had flung open the door, acting as if only a week and not forty years had passed since she had lived here. Seeing her mother's happiness, Susannah knew it would be futile to suggest they find a room in the hotel until the house could be cleaned. Dorothy would not rest well anywhere else.

Though it had taken hours of dusting and scrubbing, as soon as the room was livable, Dorothy had climbed into the four-poster bed and fallen asleep, a contented smile on her face. It was worth it. This was where Dorothy wanted to be. Surely now the healing would begin.

Susannah tipped her head, listening. The pounding was closer. She looked at the sky, assessing the sun's position. She had been gone less than an hour. If she hurried, she could discover who was making the noise and still be back before Dorothy wakened.

The small forest, Dorothy had once told her, extended to the edge of their property. On the other side was the Moreland estate. When Susannah emerged from the trees, she saw an expanse of formal gardens that held the promise of beauty, a stable and, at the far edge of the clearing, a man wielding a sledgehammer against a small building.

He was tall, and though the day was cool, he had shed his hat and coat, revealing sandy hair and muscular arms. For a second Susannah stared, wishing she had her oils. Neither watercolor nor charcoal would do justice to this man's power. It was more than physical. Even from a distance, there was something about the tilt of his head and the way he held the hammer that caught her attention and made her want to capture his essence. She squinted, trying to etch the image onto her memory. Was there a Greek god of destruction? If so, this man must be his modern incarnation.

She moved closer, and as she did, he turned to face her. Though Susannah doubted he could have heard her approach over the sounds of the hammer and splintering wood, something had alerted him to her presence.

"Are you lost?" His voice was slightly harsh, as if he were unaccustomed to the effort involved in demolishing a building. Susannah gave him another appraising look. Could she have been mistaken? No, his clothes and the calluses on his hand proclaimed him to be a worker.

She shook her head in response to his question. "I live on the hill," she said.

The stranger was magnificent, his broad shoulders and rippling muscles far different from the men she normally met. Scholars rarely wielded anything heavier than an unabridged dictionary, and they never divested themselves of their coats and cravats in public.

Susannah took a deep breath in an effort to slow her racing pulse. The man's eyes were darker blue than she would have expected, given his sandy hair. She made a mental note to use cerulean when she painted him. Right now those cerulean eyes were moving from the top of her head to her toes, as if he were assessing her the way she had him. Susannah blushed. Men of her acquaintance were rarely so bold.

"That's right," the stranger said. "I heard folks was movin' into the Ashton mansion this week." His words were drawled, the dropped consonants and poor grammar negating Susannah's original suspicions that he might not be a workman. This man was most definitely not a professor or a scholar. His surprisingly intelligent eyes sparkled with what appeared to be amusement. "Looks like the old place needs a bit of cleanin'." He gave a meaningful glance at her face.

As color flooded her cheeks once more, Susannah brushed her forehead. She wasn't sure what startled her more, finding a cobweb on her fingers or realizing that this man believed she was a servant. She lowered her gaze as she considered her options. She could tell him who she was, but that might make him uncomfortable. Why do that when there was no harm in pretending to be a maid? The truth was, she had performed more physical labor today than many servants.

"There's nothing up there that some honest labor can't cure," she said. *Tarnation!* The perfect diction she had been taught did not sound like a scullery maid's speech.

But the man did not appear to notice. "Honest labor?" he asked, his left eyebrow raised in a quirk. "That's an odd choice of words." He glanced at the sun, as if to tell the hour. "Shouldn't you still be workin'?"

Susannah shrugged. "I could ask you the same question." She looked at the building that she guessed had once been a gazebo, then back at the hammer that he'd dropped to the ground. " 'Pears to me you're slackin' off." There. She had managed a colloquialism. Though her parents would have shuddered, the man only smiled, as if amused.

"I reckon no one will know, unless you tell 'em."

A light breeze stirred the air. Though Susannah shivered, it was more from excitement than cold. There was something oddly liberating about the charade she had begun. She couldn't remember the last time she had indulged in such levity. As the only child of elderly parents, she had had few childhood companions, and the games she and her parents had played had been sedate, more akin to the college classes they taught than a typical youngster's pastimes. Since she had become an adult,

Susannah's life had been filled with worthwhile activities, not frivolous conversations with strange men.

"So what will ya give me to keep yer secret?" This was turning into fun. Reality would intrude all too soon, but for just a few minutes longer she would pretend that she had no cares or responsibilities.

The man tipped his head to one side, setting the sinews of his neck into relief. She would have to remember how they looked when she painted him. "Let me think a minute." He gave her another appraising look, then said, "I reckon a kiss would be about right."

A kiss. The shiver that made its way down her spine owed nothing to the breeze. Susannah's cheeks flamed again. "My silence is worth more than that," she protested. It was all a game. He wouldn't kiss her. Of course he wouldn't.

His laughter surprised her. If his gaze sent shivers through her, his laughter was like a warm blanket, wrapping itself around her. "You kin say that, but you ain't never experienced one of my kisses," he declared.

As his lips curved into a smile, Susannah found herself wondering if they were as firm as they looked. She took a step backward, then stopped. The man wasn't intimidating her. No, indeed. It was simply that she was unaccustomed to this type of banter. "I reckon I don't plan to start now." Kissing, that was.

"Why not? What do you have to lose?" Surely it was her imagination that he had lost his drawl.

"The real question is, what do I have to gain?"

He shrugged and moved a step closer. She could feel the warmth of his breath on her cheek. It was a comforting feeling, like the smile he had bestowed on her.

"You'd gain an unforgettable experience."

The sheer arrogance of his statement made Susannah laugh. "Spoken like a man whose ego is as large as his muscles."

"And what's wrong with muscles?"

"Nothing." Particularly when they were attached to a man who looked like a Greek god. "They're preferable to oversize egos."

His blue eyes twinkled, as if her words amused rather than

annoyed him. "Why do you think my ego is oversize?"

He really was the most attractive man she had ever seen. He might be bold and brash, but he was also almost impossibly handsome. "Let's start with that boast about an unforgettable experience."

The man took another step toward her. This time Susannah did not move. "You're mistaken," he said slowly. "That was not a boast. It was a simple statement of fact."

"I see."

He shook his head. "No, you don't. But you will."

So swiftly that she had no way of anticipating his action, he wrapped his arms around her and drew her close to him. Susannah caught her breath in amazement. What had she said about muscles? His were even more developed than she had thought, as firm as the marble statues she had studied. And, oh, how they felt! It was one thing to admire his arms from a distance. It was far, far different to be held in their embrace.

Why had she never realized how well a man's body fit with a woman's? Where she was soft, he was hard. Where he was angled, she was curved. Apart they were pieces; together they formed a perfect whole. Dimly Susannah was aware of a blue jay's raucous cry and the hint of moisture in the air. But nothing mattered save the wondrous way the stranger made her feel.

Susannah raised her eyes to his, memorizing the curve of his brows, the faint crinkles at the corners of his eyes, the way his lashes rested on his cheeks when he blinked. He stared at her for an instant . . . or was it an eternity? . . . and then he slowly lowered his mouth to hers. She could have pulled away. She should have pulled away. And yet she did not.

It was the softest of touches, a fleeting brush of his lips on hers. Susannah closed her eyes for a second, savoring the taste of spring and sweat and sweetness. Someone sighed. She wasn't sure who, any more than she was certain whose heart was pounding. All she knew was that she had never imagined a moment like this. She opened her eyes and stared at the stranger, watching his eyes darken with emotion.

And then his lips descended again. This time there was nothing soft about them. This time there was nothing fleeting. Instead, his mouth was fiercely demanding. He splayed his hands across her back, pulling her more firmly against him, while his lips coaxed hers to part, and his tongue set her blood to boiling. In the distance a carillon began to play, the bells' pealing forming a counterpoint to the ringing in Susannah's head.

It was wonderful! She wrapped her arms around the stranger's neck and drew him closer, not wanting the kiss to end. He was right. It was unforgettable. But it was more than that. This was magic. It was so much more glorious than anything she had ever experienced. Not even Anthony's . . .

Anthony!

With an anguished cry Susannah wrenched herself from the stranger's arms and ran toward the house on the hill.

What a woman! Charles started to follow her, then shook his head. Something had spooked the lovely dark-haired wench, and as far as he could tell, that something was his kiss. It figured. Today had been that kind of day. First Anthony's announcement that he planned to marry, then Brad's calling Charles an old man, now a woman fleeing his kiss. Charles didn't want to imagine what would be next.

He picked up the sledgehammer and pounded the side of the gazebo. Damned gazebo! He should have turned it into kindling a year ago. Maybe then he would have been able to forget. Though Charles scowled at the building, he couldn't stop himself from smiling when he thought of the woman who had been in his arms only minutes ago. While there were many memories he wished were not imprinted on his brain, he had no desire to forget her or her kiss.

She was pretty. More than that, she was beautiful, if you could look beyond the smudges on her face and the old clothing. Charles's sisters would never have appeared in public in such dated clothing. But, then, his sisters weren't in the habit of cleaning houses. Nor were they in the habit of engaging strange men in verbal sparring.

It had been fun. The stranger had the quickest wit and most acerbic tongue he had met in a long time. Combine those with an undeniably attractive face and the warmest brown eyes this

11

side of the Hudson, and it all added up to unforgettable.

When Charles chuckled as he swung the hammer again, his laughter had nothing to do with the satisfaction of splintering the fancy latticework. The bubble of mirth that showed no sign of bursting was caused by the thought that the stranger had believed him to be a simple workman. That much was clear from the way she had looked at him and the tone of her voice when she'd addressed him. There was none of the servility that he heard from the mill workers. Instead, she had treated him as an equal. In her eyes Charles Moreland, owner of the famous Moreland cotton mills, was nothing more than a laborer. And, oh, how good that had felt.

Charles couldn't remember the last time he had felt so free. For the few minutes that the stranger had been here, he had forgotten the fire, the mill, the debts, even his sisters. For a few minutes, nothing had mattered but the lovely dark-haired woman with the smudge on her cheek and the prettiest smile he'd ever seen. Life with a woman like that could be fun.

Charles's arm stopped, midswing. Where had that thought come from? He wasn't thinking about living with a woman. Damn that Anthony! It had to be the news of his engagement that had twisted Charles's mind and made him dream of brides. He didn't want one. He didn't need one. Hell, he couldn't afford one. He had no business entertaining such thoughts.

Charles wouldn't think about a wife. Indeed, not. He had much more important things to occupy his mind. He had a mill to run, a fortune to rebuild; he even had a carousel to construct. There was no time for nonsense.

But, oh, how sweet the stranger's kiss had been.

Chapter Two

"Sure and you won't regret it."

Susannah raised an eyebrow, wondering why the maid she had just hired had mentioned the specter of regret. The only thing Susannah was likely to rue was the kiss that, try though she might, she could not forget. It was sheer insanity, of course, to be thinking about how good it had felt to kiss a strange man. It was even crazier to have lain awake last night, replaying those magical moments when he had held her in his arms and nothing had mattered except the wonder of being with him in a world that had suddenly shrunk to encompass only the two of them.

Susannah tugged the drapes open, sneezing at the cloud of dust her action had produced. Never again. She would never again kiss a stranger, and if luck were with her, she would never again have to see that particular stranger. Though Hidden Falls might be a small community, it was unlikely her path would cross a worker's, especially if she took care to avoid the Moreland estate.

"I'm certain I won't regret hiring your family, Megan." Susannah turned back from the window and smiled at the dark-haired

13

woman whose green eyes were almost as arresting as the stranger's cerulean ones. *Stop it!* She would not think about him.

This morning Susannah had put Anthony's ring back on her finger. It had probably been a mistake removing it yesterday, but when she had seen the magnitude of the cleaning effort, she had hesitated to put her only piece of jewelry into dirty water. Today, however, the diamond was once again on her left hand, a talisman reminding her that she was sensible Susannah Deere, engaged to marry Anthony Borman.

And sensible Susannah had a house to clean, starting with this dining room. Though she would have been content to eat in the kitchen, Dorothy had been horrified by the suggestion, which was why Susannah now stood here, trying to decide what to tackle first. The windows were so coated with grime that even had the sun been shining, little light would have penetrated the dirt, and it was difficult to discern the carpet's original color.

Three feet away Megan stood, one hand propped on her hip, her head tilted slightly. She was, Susannah noted, a strikingly beautiful woman.

"Me da is the best horse trainer in these parts," Megan said, her voice devoid of any hint of boastfulness. She was quite simply stating a fact. "As for Mam—one taste of her bread and you'll think you've gone to heaven."

"Heaven will be getting the house clean." Though Susannah and her mother had worked for hours the previous day, they had managed to finish only the room where Dorothy would sleep.

Megan grinned. "Sure and we can do that, too. I'm not afraid of hard work." There was something infectious about the young woman's smile that made Susannah doubly grateful Megan and her family had appeared at her front door early this morning, offering to work for her. Not only had they saved her the trouble of advertising for help, but they had also saved her valuable time. With extra hands, the house would soon be habitable, and if the mouthwatering aromas wafting from the kitchen were any indication, she and Dorothy would be dining well, starting today. Perhaps fate was indeed smiling on Susannah. If so, it would be a welcome change.

Susannah turned at the sound of footsteps on the hardwood floor. Her mother stood in the doorway, a perplexed expression on her face. Though of only average height, Dorothy Ashton Deere had such a regal bearing that people frequently believed her to be much taller. Her silver hair was always perfectly coifed, and while her clothing was simple, the tailoring was impeccable. On a good day, she could have posed as a member of royalty. Today, it appeared, was not a good day.

"Norma?" she asked. "Where's Norma?" Dorothy stared at Megan. "You're not Norma." Her lips turned down, and for a second Susannah thought she might cry. To Susannah's dismay, though Dorothy had seemed her old self at breakfast, she now wore the distant, disoriented look that so worried her daughter.

"Norma's not here today." Susannah crossed the room and put her arm around her mother's shoulders, squeezing gently as she tried to reassure her. Though she had never heard the name before, Susannah guessed that Norma had been a maid or cook when Dorothy was a child and that her mother had somehow confused Megan with her.

"This is Megan." Susanna gestured toward the newly hired maid, who sketched a brief curtsey. Heavens! Susannah hadn't thought anyone curtseyed except at debutante parties, but judging from the smile on Dorothy's face, her mother appreciated the gesture. "Megan's going to get the house sparkling again." When Dorothy did not offer to help, apparently having forgotten that she had swept floors yesterday, Susannah made a show of sniffing the air. "I think Moira is baking some of those sugar cookies you like. Shall we go see if they're ready?"

Dorothy smiled again and led the way to the kitchen. "Norma," she cried at the sight of the apron-clad woman rolling out cookie dough. "You're here!" One small mystery was solved. Norma, it appeared, had been the Ashtons' cook.

Moira O'Toole turned. "What can I do for you, milady?" she asked. Like her daughter, Moira had dark hair and full red lips. The resemblance ended there. While Megan was slender, Moira's ample curves suggested that Megan had exaggerated neither her mother's prowess as a cook nor the fact that she enjoyed sampling her own concoctions.

Amanda Harte

Susannah looked around the room, pleasantly surprised by the progress Moira had made in a few hours. The work surfaces and floor had been cleaned, and someone—perhaps Moira's husband Brian—had arranged for a delivery of staples. Moira stood next to a long counter, her flour-coated hands mute testimony to the task Susannah and Dorothy had interrupted.

Dorothy took a step forward, an eager smile on her face. "Susannah said you had baked some of those . . ." She paused, searching for the word. "Those . . . you know." While Moira O'Toole stood patiently, Dorothy frowned. Then a smile lit her face again. "Those sweet things."

"Sugar cookies," Susannah said quietly.

Moira nodded. "Yes, milady. You just sit right there, and I'll make you a nice cuppa tea to go with them."

"This room looks better already," Susannah told Megan a few minutes later when she rejoined her in the dining room. With Dorothy settled in the kitchen, Susannah could return to the day's major task: ensuring that at least one more room was habitable.

Megan rose, clenching and unclenching her fingers as if to work out the kinks that dusting the deep crevices in the chair legs had caused. "I should hope it's better." She gave the still grimy crystal chandelier an assessing look. "I reckon this'll be prettier than the Moreland place when it's all done."

Susannah reached for a dust cloth. "I imagine you know the Moreland house well," she said to Megan. Moira had explained that she, her husband and Megan had worked at Fairlawn for several years.

Megan bent down and began to wipe another chair leg. "It was nice before the curse."

Susannah looked up from her own dusting, startled. "I don't believe in curses," she said flatly. Her parents were too practical, too grounded in everyday realities, to encourage belief in anything that could not be touched or seen.

Megan continued polishing the furniture. "Beggin' your pardon, ma'am, but that's what everyone calls it. The Moreland curse." When she glanced at Susannah, there was no denying the sincerity on her face. Megan O'Toole believed what she had

16

been told. "How else do you explain the fire that destroyed half the house, killed Mr. and Mrs. Moreland and left one of the daughters disfigured?"

As Megan delivered the litany of the Morelands' misfortunes, the blood began to drain from Susannah's face. "What a tragedy!" She swallowed deeply, trying unsuccessfully to block the images that Megan's words had conjured. "But curses don't cause fires."

For a long moment, the only sounds were Dorothy's soft laughter spilling from the kitchen and the pounding of Susannah's blood. Then Megan shrugged. "Maybe so," she said, "but how do you explain all the accidents at the mill? They started right after the fire."

"Coincidence."

"Yes, ma'am." So softly that Susannah barely heard her, Megan muttered, "A curse."

He didn't need any more problems. Indeed, he did not. Charles frowned as he climbed the final flight of stairs. Unfortunately, whether he needed them or not, problems kept multiplying faster than the goldfish had in the back pond. The pond was empty now, yet another casualty of the last year, but his problems remained.

As he yanked open the door to the carding room, Charles tried to repress the memories of the night that had changed all their lives. It was futile to think of that. He couldn't undo the past. All he could hope was to make the future better. And to do that, he had to solve the problems at the mill.

Nothing appeared to be amiss. The women who were combing the cotton into slivers were working steadily, though their conversation had ceased the moment they had become aware of his presence. That was to be expected. The mill hands were always uneasy when he visited. Charles greeted them, then moved on to the roving and spinning rooms. Everything was running smoothly there. As it should be.

In the aftermath of the fire, he had believed the only challenges he would face were financial ones, figuring out how to increase the mill's profitability enough that he had a prayer of repaying the shockingly huge debts his father had managed to incur. He hadn't anticipated dealing with accidents like this morning's.

Charles visited the other floors. In each case there was nothing out of the ordinary, no clue as to what had occurred. Somehow—and no one seemed to have the slightest idea how it had happened—someone had spilled a container of red dye onto the bolts of toweling for the new Catskills resort.

It made no sense. Since this fabric would not be printed, there was no reason for it to have been moved into the room with the vats of dye. Unless this was no accident. Unless this was like the other inexplicable incidents that had plagued the mill.

Charles returned to his office and grabbed his umbrella. Though he had an endless list of tasks to be accomplished, he needed a break from the mill and its problems. At first they had seemed minor. One morning the loom girls had discovered that all the plants they had so carefully nurtured had fallen from the windowsills. Though smashed crockery, dirt and broken leaves had sullied the otherwise immaculate floor, it had taken only a few minutes to clean the mess. By the next morning, the plants had been repotted and reinstalled on the sills.

As the months had passed, the damage from the accidents had increased, culminating in this morning's destruction of the toweling. That was disastrous. Everyone at Moreland Mills knew how important this shipment would be. The resort owners had made no secret of the fact that they wanted one mill to supply all their linens and that the intricately woven two-color toweling was a trial. If the resort was happy, they would order more. Much more.

This wasn't coincidence. Someone had deliberately sabotaged the mill's most important product and had waited until it would be virtually impossible to recreate it.

Charles strode down Mill Street, anxious to put several blocks between himself and the ruined fabric. Tonight he would figure out a way to produce the towels. Right now, he needed to clear his head. When he reached Bridge Street, he started to turn left. The carousel carver was due to arrive today. Maybe talking to him would help Charles forget the sight of the red blotches on otherwise perfect weaving.

"I'd ask what kind of day you're having," a familiar voice called from the opposite direction, "but I suspect I don't want to know."

Charles stopped, unsure whether he was pleased or annoyed by Brad's interruption. His friend crossed the street, his habitual grin creasing his face. Why shouldn't Brad smile? His father owned the railroad, and while Brad would one day inherit it, he had few responsibilities other than attending an occasional board of directors meeting. Brad wasn't plagued with broken pots and spoiled fabric.

"You don't want to know," Charles conceded at last. As the church bells chimed the hour, he clapped his friend on the shoulder. "Let's have a drink."

Though they were in the middle of the street and a wagon was approaching, Brad made a show of stopping and pressing his hand to his chest, as if assailed by a sudden pain. Charles started to laugh. "Now you've shocked me," Brad declared, his voice making a mockery of his words. "Drinking before sunset. What would your father say?"

The laughter that Brad's antics had provoked died abruptly as his question wrenched Charles back to reality. "In case you haven't noticed," he said, not bothering to purge the bitterness from his voice, "my father's not here." *And I wouldn't listen to him, even if he were.*

The wagon rumbled by, flinging mud in its wake. Brad stepped back. "Well, then, what are we waiting for?"

What, indeed? Charles had wanted a break to clear his head; Brad's humor might be just what he needed, if he could keep him from talking about John Moreland.

When they were seated in the tavern, their first glasses of whiskey half empty, Brad leaned forward. "I suppose you've heard that old Mrs. Deere moved back into the Ashton place." Though they had taken a table in the back, far enough from the bar that few patrons could overhear them, Brad spoke more softly than usual.

Charles nodded his assent. "I doubt there's anyone in town

who doesn't know that." He would have to pay a social call at some point, since his mother had told him that Dorothy Ashton, though years older than Mary, had befriended her.

Brad took another swallow, then lowered his voice again. "Did you also know that her daughter is the woman Anthony plans to marry?"

Charles stared at his friend. He hadn't known that Dorothy Ashton Deere had a daughter. All his mother had said was that she taught German at a private girls' school in Boston and had married a Harvard history professor.

"What makes you think that? Anthony just called her his angel."

Even in the dim light of the tavern, Charles saw that Brad's eyes twinkled with amusement. "Never underestimate the power of love. We don't hear from Anthony for months on end, and then he writes two letters in two days. Yes"—he nodded, raising his voice to be heard over the heated argument that had broken out at the bar—"I got one from him today. He said her name's Susannah, and she's moving here with her mother." Brad placed his glass back on the table and nodded to the bartender, who had quieted the dispute through the simple expedient of refilling glasses. "I reckon we'll get to see Anthony more often now that he has a reason to come to Hidden Falls."

When they'd ordered another round of drinks, Charles turned back to Brad. "If he does visit us, it'll be the first good thing I've heard of Anthony's engagement."

Brad traced the gouges that an impatient patron had put in the table. "I told you marriage wasn't so bad."

"And I told you I'm not ready to concede that point."

Shaking his head in mock disgust, Brad said, "You're the most obstinate man I've ever met."

"Surely that's not news. And I suspect it's not the reason you wanted to talk to me this afternoon. The gleam in your eye says you've some other announcement you want to spring on me."

Brad had the grace to look abashed. "Am I that obvious?"

"Yes. Now, what's tickling your tongue?"

When the bartender had deposited their drinks on the table,

Brad leaned forward, lowering his voice again. "Have you heard that Mrs. Deere hired the O'Tooles?"

"What did you say?" Blood rushed to Charles's face.

"You heard me—all three of them. Brian was bragging to anyone who'd listen when he came in to pick up an order at the mercantile."

"Damn it all!" Charles jumped to his feet. Though he had thought it impossible, his day had just gotten worse. Pulling a coin from his pocket, he tossed it onto the table and turned toward the door. "She can't do that!"

Brad swallowed hastily, then grabbed Charles's arm. "Where are you going?"

"To talk some sense to Mrs. Deere. Alone!"

By the time he reached the gray house on the hill, Charles's initial anger had faded, replaced by the conviction that as a newcomer Mrs. Deere had no way of knowing about the O'Tooles' problems. Once he explained the risks, she would be certain to dismiss the family that no one in Hidden Falls dared hire.

Charles strode up the front walk, idly noting that the house had been repainted recently. Though his own home was constructed of rose brick and Brad's was a stately redbrick Georgian, the Ashton home—Pleasant Hill as they called it—was a frame house. Big and square, its porches and the tower room perched on the roof like a decoration on a cake kept it from looking severe.

Charles knocked on the front door, then waited for what seemed like an eternity. Even with only one servant in his residence, his own door was opened more quickly. Surely Mrs. Deere had staff besides the O'Tooles. Hadn't he met one of the maids yesterday?

"Good afternoon, Char . . . er, Mr. Moreland." Megan O'Toole greeted him with a smile that went beyond simple courtesy. She ushered him into the wide entry hall, then stood a few inches closer than custom dictated, her smile warm and welcoming.

Charles had to admit that in her black uniform with the ruffled white apron, Megan O'Toole was a comely greeter. But beauty was not the reason he was here. "Good day, Megan. Would you tell Mrs. Deere that I'm here to see her?"

"Sure and I'll do that." Megan made a little curtsey that somehow shifted her skirts so that her shapely ankles were visible. "If there's anything else I can do for you . . ." She licked her lips in a blatantly sensual gesture.

Charles pretended not to notice the invitation. He had been a fool to flirt with Megan when she'd worked for his parents. At the time, even though Megan had offered more, they had never passed beyond a few stolen kisses. Though she had had the allure of being forbidden fruit, soon after he'd returned to New York, Charles had lost interest. Unfortunately if Megan's behavior was any indication, she had not.

"Right this way, sir." The saucy tilt of Megan's head and the sway of her hips were meant to be seductive. He was as certain of that as he was that her kisses would never again tempt him. Though she had been willing, her lips held none of the attraction of the stranger he'd met yesterday. If he wanted to dally with a servant—which, of course, he did not—he would choose the brown-eyed woman with the sweetest kisses on earth.

Refusing the dusty chair that Megan suggested, Charles remained standing in the parlor and studied the room. Though he and his sisters had occasionally peeked through the windows, this was the first time he had come inside the house that had been empty since soon after he was born. The years of neglect had not been kind to it, but at least there was none of the permanent damage his own home had sustained. A few weeks of labor would restore the Ashton mansion to close to its original beauty; it would take many months and far more money than he possessed to recreate the south wing of his house.

Though the windows were still coated with grime, Charles saw a flash of lightning, followed by the deep rumble of thunder. Seconds later, raindrops pelted the glass. Today would not be a good day for working on the gazebo.

"What can I do for you, Mr. Moreland?"

Charles turned, incredulous. The sound of the rain had masked her footsteps, but even had he been warned of her approach, nothing would have prepared him for the sight of the woman who now stood only two feet from him. Her face bore no smudges. Her hair was carefully groomed, her expression calm. Though her dark green gown was the plainest he had ever seen, devoid of the ruffles and furbelows his sisters preferred, it was clean and perfectly pressed. She was not a servant; that much was clear from the way she regarded him.

"You're . . ." For a second his mind refused to make the connection.

Her lips as tightly pursed as the spinster schoolteacher whose displeasure he and his sisters had dreaded, the beautiful stranger said, "I'm Susannah Deere, and you're obviously Charles Moreland. Since my mother is resting, perhaps I can help you."

Susannah Deere! Charles fought back the bile that rose to his throat. The woman he had kissed, the woman who had haunted his dreams last night was Anthony's fiancée. Was this some kind of cosmic joke, or was it a curse, the sins of the fathers being visited on the sons?

The wind lashed rain against the windowpanes, the storm's fury mirroring the tumult inside Charles. He was an idiot! How could he have thought this woman was a servant, even for an instant? No servant he had ever met had had that imperious tilt to her head, and none had the aristocratic features that spoke of generations of fine breeding. Charles's glance fell to her left hand where a large diamond solitaire sparkled. She hadn't been wearing it yesterday; he was certain of that. If he had seen the ring, he would have realized that she was not a scullery maid. And then he would not have made the colossal mistake of kissing Anthony's betrothed.

What an idiot he was! Kissing another man's affianced bride. Kissing *his friend's* fiancée. Charles wished he could pound his head against the wall. Maybe that would knock some sense into it. Dear God! Despite everything he had vowed, it appeared he had learned nothing in the last year.

Though Charles's thoughts roiled, Anthony's bride-to-be seemed unruffled by his appearance. Perhaps she had known who he was. Perhaps yesterday had been a game for her, a modern version of Marie Antoinette's playing shepherdess. Lord help Anthony if that was true!

Her shoulders rigid, her head tipped ever so slightly upward, Susannah crossed the room and sat in one of the Louis XV chairs that flanked the marble fireplace. She gestured Charles toward the other. Perhaps she was not as calm as she appeared. Not only had she not extended her hand in greeting, but she seemed to be avoiding any contact with him. A full three feet separated their chairs.

"Was there a reason besides neighborliness that brought you here today?" Her voice was cooler than the river in winter, and like a splash of ice water after a sleepless night, it dispelled Charles's confusion, reminding him why he'd climbed the hill.

"In point of fact, there was." Thank goodness, his voice sounded as calm as hers. While he couldn't undo yesterday's insanity, he had no intention of letting this woman see that he remembered how sweet her lips had tasted. They were forbidden lips, and he would never, ever taste them again.

She nodded slightly, her gesture as regal as her speech. "Shall I ring for tea? I'm told Mrs. O'Toole's scones are delicious."

It was the opening he needed. "That's why I'm here."

"To sample the scones?" She raised a brow. "I should have thought you would have had more important things to do." Surely her voice hadn't held that sharp tone yesterday. And if this was the way she normally spoke to guests, why would Anthony want to marry her? Charles could not picture his fun-loving friend saddled with a woman who acted as if she had vinegar in her mouth.

"Not the scones, per se, but I did want to discuss the O'Tooles. Brian O'Toole, to be specific."

As she inclined her head slightly, Charles noticed that a lock threatened to come loose from her pompadour. Miss Susannah Deere would not be pleased if her hair refused to do her bidding; he was certain of that.

"Brian is my groom and horse trainer. I can't imagine what there is to discuss."

Charles paused for a moment, marshaling his anger. He would accomplish nothing by shouting at her. "I realize you're new to the neighborhood, Miss Deere." It sounded so odd to call her that. In his dreams last night, she had been nameless.

24

"Are you aware that the O'Tooles used to be employed by my family?"

She nodded again, and this time the lock slipped from its mooring, bouncing on her neck, reviving traitorous memories. Charles thought of how soft her skin had felt beneath his fingertips and how sweet her kiss had been. There was nothing soft or sweet about her today. Her voice was liquid ice, and those sensuous lips had yet to curve into a smile. "Moira O'Toole told me that when I asked for references."

"Are you also aware of the circumstances of their dismissal?" She couldn't be, or she wouldn't have hired them.

But she nodded again. "Certainly." Though her expression seemed imperious, Charles noticed that she gripped the chair arms so tightly that her knuckles whitened. "Mrs. O'Toole explained that you were forced to reduce the size of the staff after your parents died," she said.

Half truths. He should have expected that. The O'Tooles were unlikely to admit what had actually happened. "While that may be true, it's not relevant here. Did Moira O'Toole tell you that my father had fired Brian a week before his death?"

This time Susannah shook her head, then raised one brow, silently encouraging Charles to continue.

"I'm sorry to be the one to tell you this, but Brian O'Toole is a chronic drunk. To be fair, he's an excellent trainer when he's sober. Unfortunately that's not very often." A slight widening of her eyes was the only reaction Charles saw. "Brian's carelessness when he's drinking endangered the horses. He doubled their medicine one time and almost killed one of them. Another time he set the stable on fire." An involuntary shudder rippled through Charles. Would he ever be able to think about fire without remembering the odor of charred wood or the sight of his sister's face and hands? Taking a deep breath to steady his voice, Charles continued, "In the end, my father had no choice but to let Brian go. He couldn't risk having him anywhere on the estate."

As the rain subsided, Charles heard the sound of voices in the hallway. Though he could distinguish no words, he recognized Moira and Megan O'Tooles' distinctive lilts. If Brian was in the house, he was staying out of sight. Wise man.

Susannah was quiet for a long moment. "I see," she said at last. Was there a hint of sadness in those lovely brown eyes? Charles knew he was a fool to care, but he hated the thought that he had caused that sorrow. He seemed to have turned into a Jonah, bringing trouble everywhere he went.

"Would you like me to recommend another trainer?" It was the least he could do for a neighbor and Anthony's wife-to-be.

"That won't be necessary."

Her reply surprised Charles. "But I understand that you asked Brian to buy three horses for you."

"That's true."

"Even if you don't need a trainer, you'll need a groom."

The sun burst through the clouds, lighting the room for a few seconds before it hid again. Susannah stared at Charles, her dark eyes serious. "I have a groom," she said firmly. "His name is Brian O'Toole."

"But—"

"Mr. Moreland, I heard what you said." Only the way she continued to grip the chair arms told Charles that Susannah Deere was not as calm as she wanted him to believe. "Brian O'Toole made a mistake, and he's paid for it." She rose, clearly indicating that the visit was over. "I believe in giving people second chances. Until such time as I find him to be incapable of handling his duties here, Brian O'Toole will remain in my employ."

He couldn't let her do this. He owed it to Anthony to keep his fiancée safe. What if the next time Brian dropped a smoldering cigarette it set Susannah's house on fire? "I think you should reconsider. You could be endangering yourself and your mother if you choose to dismiss my warnings."

"You misunderstood me." She stared at him, sadness still visible in her eyes. "I didn't dismiss what you've said. I heard your concerns. I simply came to a different conclusion than the one you obviously wanted me to reach." When they reached the front door, Susannah stopped. "You raised some accusations about Brian O'Toole's intemperance and how that made him unfit for employment. What conclusion would you like me to draw from the fact that I smelled liquor on your breath this afternoon?"

Charles's eyes widened as her barb hit. How had he ever been so mistaken as to think Susannah Deere was sweet?

"Are you sure you don't mind about the windows?"

Charles looked at the man who—if all went according to plan—was going to solve one of his problems. With his golden blond hair and blue eyes, Rob Ludlow was a fine-looking man. Not that his appearance mattered to Charles. It was the beauty Rob could create that was important, and if he needed more windows to create that beauty, so be it.

"Do whatever's necessary," Charles said. "I want this to be the finest carousel my sister has ever seen."

The carousel carver walked around the stable, his even stride telling Charles he was measuring the space. "There's plenty of room," Rob said when he completed the circuit. "I just need more light."

"Fine." It wasn't as if Charles had any horses to consider. There had been none in over a year, and there were no prospects of any in the future, unless a miracle occurred. The stable that had been the envy of the county was empty and, since miracles were in short supply, was likely to remain that way.

Charles gestured toward the loft. "Your quarters are upstairs. They're simple, but they should be adequate." When the O'Tooles had worked here, they had lived in the loft apartment. "You'll take your meals in the main house."

Rob nodded. "I have two helpers arriving next week. As long as we've got the right supplies, we don't need luxury."

There was a quiet confidence about Rob Ludlow that reassured Charles. Rob had come with the highest of recommendations. Not only had he worked with Illions and Dentzel, two of the premier carousel carvers in the nation, but his careful blending of styles and his own special elements had given Ludlow horses a cachet. While not everyone had heard of him, those who had viewed his work had been impressed. And that included Charles.

"Let me show you where I plan to put the carousel."

27

The rain had stopped soon after he had returned home, and the sun was once more shining. From force of habit, Charles slid the stable door closed behind them, though there were no horses to keep inside. The two men walked across the wet grass, discussing Rob's ideas for the carousel animals.

"I've never carved a menagerie," he told Charles. That had been one of the reasons Rob had accepted Charles's commission. He had been looking for a new creative challenge, and the opportunity to carve a variety of animals besides horses had appealed to him. "You've got enough open space for the pavilion," he said as he surveyed the lawn.

Charles shrugged. "That's why my grandfather named the place Fairlawn." Charles had always believed the house itself, which he considered a poor imitation of a European castle, little short of a monstrosity, but even he admitted that the lawns and gardens were magnificent.

He led the way toward the gazebo, stopping when the half-demolished building was visible. There was no reason to go any closer. "That's the spot I had in mind. What do you think of it?"

Rob nodded his approval.

"The building will be gone within a week."

Rob grinned. "Don't rush on our account. I told you we worked fast, but it'll take us a hell of a lot longer than that."

When they turned back toward the stable, Charles thought he saw a flash of color in the gazebo. He swung around, hoping he was mistaken. There was no reason for anyone to be in the gazebo. Perhaps it was only a bird. Charles stared. The flash reappeared. For a second he stood immobile. It was not his imagination or even a bird. It was worse, much worse. A woman, her hair covered by a hooded cloak, darted out of the small building and began to run toward the trees.

Charles caught his breath in horror as images of the day he had fought so hard to forget unrolled before him. *No! Dear God, no!* It couldn't be *Jezebel*.

Chapter Three

"I hate to tell you this, son." The portly, gray-haired attorney leaned forward, his grayish blue eyes radiating sincerity.

Charles tried not to flinch. It wasn't Ralph's fault that just the word *son* brought back memories he had spent a year trying to obliterate. Charles took a deep breath, forcing himself to relax. There was no reason to take out his frustrations on the older man. Ralph Chambers had always been a friend, and since Charles's father's death, he had provided more than legal counsel. He'd been one of the two men in Hidden Falls whom Charles had felt he could trust to give him good advice. That was why he had come to Ralph's office today, to see whether he had any suggestions. Ralph was his last recourse, for Charles's other advisor, Philip, had been unable to help.

Ralph steepled his fingers, then propped his chin on his fingertips, his gaze fixed on the wall behind Charles, as if he found the elaborate wallpaper fascinating. Though late morning sun streamed through the window onto Ralph's desk and appeared to be reflecting into his eyes, the attorney seemed oblivious of everything except his study of the wall. It was not an auspicious sign. Judging from the fact that Ralph would not look at him, Charles suspected he would not like whatever he had to say.

"The most prudent course of action might be to sell the house and the mill," the attorney said. "You could repay the majority of the debts with the proceeds of the sale."

Charles gritted his teeth. His intuition had not failed him. He did not like the advice. If only Ralph knew how often Charles had considered selling the mill and how attractive that alternative had appeared. He would waken in the middle of the night, convinced that it was the only rational choice. For an instant, Charles would be filled with a sense of relief that made him almost light-headed. Unfortunately, all too soon reality would return, and he would remember that any decision he made affected more than himself.

"I can't do that to Anne and Jane," he said, wishing there were another answer. "It's their inheritance. If I sold the house, where would they live?"

Though Ralph did not meet his gaze, he nodded, as if he had expected Charles's response. "With what you could earn in New York, you could provide your sisters with a comfortable home either here or in the city."

Charles had thought of that. He leaned back in the chair and crossed his ankles. Maybe if he relaxed, something would inspire him. Something other than flocked wallpaper and shelves crowded with more law books than any one man could possibly read. "It wouldn't be the same."

This time Ralph looked directly at him, his expression so stern that Charles felt as if he were a witness Ralph was cross-examining. "Would that be so bad?"

"Maybe not for Jane." Although as a child the younger of the twins had been shy and had declared that she would never leave Hidden Falls, Charles could tell from her letters that the months she had spent in Switzerland with Anne had changed her. Jane could probably survive another move and even thrive in a new environment. "It's Anne that I worry about." So much in her life was different now; surely she deserved some stability.

Ralph's secretary opened the door to remind him that he had an appointment in fifteen minutes. "Thank you, Gertrude."

Though Charles had often believed Ralph to be stodgy, he had surprised the townspeople by hiring Hidden Falls' first female secretary. "If women can work in your mill," he had told Charles, "they can work in my office." It was logic Charles could not refute.

Ralph leaned across his desk. "What about you, son? What's best for you?"

Charles shook his head. His best interests were no longer a factor. "You know how I feel about New York. I'd move back tomorrow, if I had only myself to consider." It would be wonderful to escape this cursed town and the albatross of a mill that his father's will had decreed he should manage. Manage? The mill needed a magician or a miracle worker, not a manager.

The sun went behind a cloud, momentarily casting gloomy shadows into the room. Behind his spectacles, Ralph's expression was equally grim. "I'm not saying you have to sell tomorrow, but it may come to that if you're unable to raise the money."

"I don't understand it." That was part of Charles's frustration. "Those damned bankers won't lend me another dollar. It makes no sense. They know how good I am at improving profits." When he had lived in New York, Charles had quickly established a reputation for being able to evaluate companies to determine how they could be made more efficient and—what was even more important to the owners—more profitable. His analyses had been so accurate that soon even companies that were doing well had requested his services, hoping to keep ahead of their competitors.

"I cannot imagine anyone disputing your talents," Ralph agreed. "But there must be a reason they're reluctant to extend credit. What have the financiers told you?"

"That I've already achieved all possible improvements here." Charles jumped to his feet and strode to the window, his eyes fixed on the five-story brick building that was Moreland Mills. It dominated the town more than just physically. If the mill closed, which was a real possibility, given its current financial state, the town would die, for there was no other industry to sustain it.

"It's not true that I've done everything I could. If I had hydroelectric power, I'd be able to increase the output. I could drive the looms faster." That was part of Charles's frustration. He knew what had to be done; he simply didn't have the money to make it possible. "The mills in Lowell are already using hydroelectric. That's why they produce more tonnage than any of the other cotton mills in the country." And Charles wasn't content being in second place. He wheeled around. "I need money to build the generator."

Ralph stared at the wallpaper again, the expression on his face telling Charles he was uncomfortable with what he was about to say. "You know I'd help you if I could. I shouldn't be burdening you with my problems, but the truth is, I haven't fully recovered from some bad investments."

Ralph was too polite to vocalize what both he and Charles knew, that those investments had been the same ones that had destroyed the Moreland fortune and that it had been at John Moreland's urging that his friends had sunk substantial sums in what had proven to be a scam. The young companies that had held so much promise on paper had turned out to be mere fabrications by a few enterprising con men who had managed to win his father's trust. Even in his most cynical moments, Charles did not believe his father had set out to ruin his friends, but—regardless of his intent—the result was the same.

Though he had no way of confirming it, Charles suspected that some of the bankers he had approached for loans had been part of the venture that had come close to bankrupting his father. Blaming John Moreland could be one reason they were so adamant about not lending Charles a cent.

"I wish my father hadn't encouraged you to join him."

"So do I, my boy. So do I. But it's water over the falls, as they say." Ralph tapped the bridge of his spectacles with his forefinger, pushing them back on his nose. "Do you have any other source of financing?"

"Just one," Charles admitted. He frowned as he glanced out the window again. "If the insurance company would settle the claim, I could repay some of the debts and put in the new generator." The insurance adjuster's delays had proven to be a source of frustration rather than financing.

"There is still no decision?"

Charles sank into the chair and stretched out his legs. Staring at the mill only reminded him of how much was wrong with his life. "He tells me they're investigating. Hell, Ralph, shouldn't a year be long enough for an investigation?"

Gertrude tapped on the door, then handed Ralph a stack of papers. "Your next client's file," she said with a pointed look at Charles.

"We'll be done in a moment," Ralph told his secretary. He turned back to Charles. "One thing you learn when you reach my age is that time goes quickly. A year isn't very long."

"It hasn't seemed short to me." If anything, the last year had been the longest of his life.

"You young people are so impatient. Why, take your friend Matt . . ."

Charles looked up, startled. "Matt Wagner?" Why was Ralph talking about Matt?

"He came to see me earlier today." Ralph polished his spectacles. "I would not be betraying a confidence if I told you that Matt plans to settle here. He asked if I would consider taking him on as a junior partner, now that he's passed the bar."

Charles tried not to frown. He had never told Ralph how deep the enmity ran between him and Matt. It was bad enough that he'd made Ralph privy to his financial problems; there was no reason to burden him further. Still, Ralph's words raised unpleasant prospects. Matt planned to live in Hidden Falls. Was there no end to the bad news? "Did you agree?" Charles was pleased to note that his voice was as calm as if he were discussing the health of Ralph's potted palm.

The attorney shrugged. "Matt has an impressive record. He graduated in the top one percent of the class at Harvard." Ralph's eyes clouded, as if with pain. "The boy made something of himself. I can't deny that. But . . ." This time there was no doubt that Ralph's expression was one of pain. "I have to consider my clients. I believe that to them he will always be the

Matt Wagner they knew ten years ago. I cannot take the chance of alienating them."

Thank God! Charles closed his eyes for a second as relief flowed through him. Matt would not remain in Hidden Falls. Charles would not be forced to encounter him regularly. But as he leaned back in the chair, Charles heard Susannah Deere telling him that she believed in second chances. Matt wouldn't get one. No matter what he said or did, neither Ralph nor anyone else in town would let him start anew.

Charles opened his eyes. That was good. It was just. Matt didn't deserve a second chance. Not after all the trouble he had caused.

"If it isn't the robber baron."

Charles was two blocks from the attorney's office, heading toward the mill, when he heard the familiar voice. Had it been only minutes since he had thought he had been reprieved and would not encounter this man? The bad luck that had plagued him for a year showed no sign of abating. Though the sun was shining, Charles felt as if a cloud had settled over him.

He stopped, turning to face his childhood nemesis, who ap-. peared to have emerged from one of the boardinghouses. Matt had changed little in the five years since Charles had seen him. His dark brown hair was still unkempt, as if he hacked it with scissors rather than visiting a barber. His brown eyes were as penetrating as ever, seeming to look beneath the surface. His features were the ones Charles remembered, finely chiseled and oddly aristocratic for a man of decidedly humble birth. Only his clothing had changed. Gone were the slightly tattered garments that he had once worn proudly, despite the church matrons' attempts to provide newer clothing. In their place was a suit that announced more clearly than the arrogant tilt of his head that Matt Wagner was a man to reckon with.

"I heard you were back," Charles said, trying to keep his voice low. The street was crowded with mill workers returning from their dinner break. Charles saw no point in advertising to everyone in Hidden Falls the fact that he and Matt were once again at loggerheads. "I cannot say that I was pleased by the news."

Apparently unfazed by the woman who jostled him, Matt raised an eyebrow in the expression Charles remembered so well. "I cannot say that I was pleased"—his tone was a mocking imitation of Charles's own words—"to hear that you followed in your father's footsteps."

Charles stared down Rapids Street at the river, refusing to take the bait. Matt had always known how to raise his hackles. That was one more thing that time had not changed. "My family is none of your business." Though he kept a smile on his face because they were in public, Charles's voice was steely. "Despite what you may think, it never has been and never will be."

A condescending smile lit Matt's face. "Some things never change," he said coolly, "like your pigheaded attitude."

Two could play the same game. "Some things never change." Charles echoed Matt's phrase. "Like your meager vocabulary. I would have thought that all those years at Harvard would have improved it at least a modicum." Charles continued walking. He had a mill to run. If Matt had something to say, he could do it walking. Charles nodded a greeting as half a dozen mill hands crossed the street in front of him.

"We can engage in verbal sparring all day." Matt kept pace with Charles. "That won't accomplish anything, and it's not the reason I came back."

"Just what was the reason?"

For the first time, a shadow of hesitation marred Matt's apparent composure, reminding Charles of the boy he had once seen peering through a set of iron gates, a wistful expression on his face. "Would you believe me if I said it was to help you run the mill?" His ironic tone made Charles doubt the flicker of hesitation he'd seen. Perhaps it had been nothing more than a trick of the light.

"Absolutely not!" Matt had never been one to help others, and most definitely not Charles. Though Harvard might have awarded him a diploma, Charles was certain it had not turned renegade Matt into a philanthropist.

The street was almost empty now as the last of the workers scurried to be inside the mill before the bell rang.

Shrugging, as if Charles's vehement rejection bothered him

not a whit, Matt said, "That's what I thought. The truth is, I came to make sure you didn't kill any more innocent people."

Though Charles hadn't believed Matt still had the power to hurt him, he was wrong. Matt's words were like a blow to the solar plexus. Charles took a deep breath, fighting the urge to lash out at the man who had always known where to strike for maximum impact.

"It was an accident," Charles said, his voice amazingly calm, even though the memory of Matt's father's mangled body still sent ripples of horror through him.

"So you say."

"You know it was an accident."

Matt's eyes darkened with something that might have been remembered pain. "Then I'm certain it won't bother you if I ensure there are no more accidents."

Charles stopped to confront Matt. "I run the safest mill in the state." Not only was it a matter of personal pride, part of Charles's innate need to be the best, but it was also good business sense. Accidents decreased production. No mill owner, particularly one facing Charles's financial difficulties, could afford that.

Matt appeared unconvinced. He extended one of his hands and stared at it. "Last week two men suffered severe lacerations of their right hands." He clenched and unclenched his fist, as if to emphasize his point. "In addition, the tip of one woman's left index finger was severed." Matt's voice was solemn, intoning the litany of minor incidents that had plagued the mill recently. For a man who had been back in town for less than a day, he was remarkably well informed.

"I see you're still meddling in things that are none of your business."

Matt tipped his hat, ending the conversation. "Be careful, Charles. Those accidents just may be my business."

It was not a comforting thought.

Susannah stared out the window, narrowing her eyes as she studied the trees. Even from a distance, the burgeoning buds were visible, proof that spring was imminent. This was the scene she wanted to capture in her painting: the weeks before the leaves unfolded and the flowers burst through the ground. She would call it *Promise of Spring*.

She turned back to her easel, her brush flowing smoothly over the canvas as she brought the trees to life. With windows on all four sides, the tower room had more light than any other part of the house. That was one reason Susannah had chosen it for her studio. Equally important was the fact that the room was far enough removed from the rest of the house that Dorothy might not find it. And if she did not discover Susannah's garret, she would not be disturbed by the fact that her daughter was once again indulging in a frivolous pastime.

Susannah mixed a little more yellow into the green. That was better. Now she had captured the hint of verdant beauty beneath the gray exterior. Perfect. The feeling of pure delight that swept through her was one Dorothy would not understand. Neither she nor Susannah's father had approved of their daughter's artistic endeavors.

As a child when Susannah had shown them the pen-and-ink drawing of a woodland sprite that had fired her imagination, they had chastised her for wasting time that should have been spent conjugating German verbs. Each year, though she had dreamed of watercolors or a real palette for her oils, her Christmas gifts had been sturdy boots and stockings or neatly hemmed handkerchiefs. "You must be practical, Susannah," her mother had told her. "Painting is self-indulgent. It brings no good to others. You must remember why we are placed on this earth."

It was a lesson Susannah learned well, and for years she had been a dutiful daughter, studying history with her father and German with her mother, spending her free time first knitting socks for the poor, then—when she grew older—helping to teach them to read. It was, as her parents had told her, a fulfilling life. She could take pride in the fact that she was useful to others. But though she never spoke of it again, she knew that the emptiness deep inside her could only be filled by painting.

And so she had found ways to steal moments for herself. The long rides that her parents approved because they enriched her health were shorter than they ever knew once Susannah discovered a meadow where she could spread a blanket and sketch. Later she had enlisted a friend's help, storing her supplies in Lucinda's attic, being careful to wash all traces of paint from her hands before she returned home. Though she had hated the deception, Susannah knew that she could no more stop painting than she could breathing. It was part of her.

She stepped back and studied the canvas. This was the first time she had put a human in a landscape. He hadn't been planned, but when she had begun filling in the trees, she had reached for a dark brown. Almost without her volition, she had found herself adding a centaur, the half-man, half-horse figure from Greek mythology. In her painting, he was emerging from the forest, an expression of wonder on his face, as if he were surprised by the promise of spring. It was, she knew instinctively, the detail that turned the painting from ordinary to special.

With his powerful shoulders and arms, the centaur made a dramatic contrast to the softness of the trees and grasses. His nose was strong, his chin firm, his eyes cerulean. Susannah blinked. Why were the centaur's eyes blue? She had planned to give him Anthony's face, and Anthony had gray eyes. Anthony's features were not this firm, and he most definitely did not have arms and shoulders like that.

Susannah felt the blood drain from her face as she studied the painting. The centaur looked like Charles Moreland. How on earth had that happened? It wasn't as though she admired Charles. Oh, it was true that he was an attractive physical specimen and that his shoulders and arms did belong on a centaur. It was also true that she had been unable to obliterate the memory of how good it had felt to be held in those arms and how wonderful his kiss had been.

All that was superficial. Under the undeniably handsome exterior lay a man who would make an entire family suffer because of one man's mistake, a man who wanted her to dismiss Brian O'Toole. Charles Moreland was rigid and unforgiving. Those were not characteristics Susannah admired. Why, then, had she made him the central figure in her painting? How annoying!

She reached for her brush, determined to obliterate those blue eyes and soften the contours of the face. She was mixing grays, trying to find the right shade to match Anthony's eyes, when she heard the tower door open.

"Oh, Susannah," her mother called. "There you are." As Dorothy stepped into the room, Susannah felt a band constrict around her heart. She had tried so hard to keep her mother from knowing about her painting, and now here she was. As a child Susannah had feared her parents' censure. When she grew older, she had kept her artistic endeavors secret because she had not wanted to hurt her parents. They would never understand how important it was to her, and so it had seemed best to pretend that the hours she spent in the stable loft were devoted to reading. If her parents had ever guessed how she passed some afternoons, they had never mentioned it.

Now Dorothy was here, and there was no way to camouflage Susannah's activity. The most she could hope was that her mother would not be too distressed.

"I looked for you everywhere," Dorothy said as she stepped into the room, her smile eager and surprisingly girlish. Since they had returned to Dorothy's childhood home, she had seemed happier and more relaxed than Susannah had seen her since her father's death two years earlier. "Do you know that the trees are starting to open?" Without waiting for a response, Dorothy continued, "I wanted to go for a walk and thought you might come with me."

"That's a good idea. Why don't you get our cloaks?" Susannah steered her mother toward the door, hoping that she wouldn't notice the easel. But Dorothy was not so easily deterred. She walked across the room and studied the painting.

"Oh, what a pretty . . ." A frown crossed her face as she stared at the easel. "It's a pretty . . ." Again, she hesitated, visibly struggling to find a word.

Susannah tried not to frown. It wasn't her imagination. Her mother's vocabulary had diminished. Although she had once been equally fluent in English and German, it had been weeks since Dorothy had addressed Susannah in German, and now her conversation frequently faltered as she searched for common English words.

"Pretty *thing*." Dorothy's smile was triumphant.

"It's a painting," Susannah said softly, waiting for her mother's reaction.

Instead of the criticism she expected, Dorothy merely smiled again. "Yes, of course, dear. That's what I said. A pretty painting."

Susannah's hands shook as she began to clean her brushes. She ought to be happy that Dorothy had not objected to her painting. Wasn't this what she had sought all her life, her mother's approval? But Dorothy's words had brought only pain. Somehow her mother had forgotten not just the word for painting but the fact that she had always disapproved of Susannah's artistic efforts.

Blinking rapidly to keep the tears at bay, Susannah descended the back stairway. She had been so confident that the move would help Dorothy. Ever since Susannah's father had died, Dorothy had spoken of returning to her childhood home. When she had become increasingly forgetful, Susannah had thought her mother was simply preoccupied with thoughts of moving.

Susannah gripped the railing and brushed the tears from her eyes. Though Dorothy seemed happier now that they were settled, there had been no miracles. The changes had been subtle at first, but now there was no denying them. Her mother was ill, and her condition seemed to be worsening.

Susannah took a deep breath, trying to quell the horrible dread that clutched her heart. There had to be something she could do. Perhaps Dorothy needed a tonic. Susannah had heard the faculty wives discussing the efficacy of liver tonics, claiming they were little short of miraculous. That was what Dorothy needed. Susannah forced her lips into a smile as she reached the bottom of the stairs. Her course was clear. She would consult a doctor tomorrow. Surely he would have a tonic to cure her mother's forgetfulness.

Chapter Four

"This is mighty fine horseflesh." Brian O'Toole grinned as he flicked the reins. "Mighty fine."

Susannah smiled. "You found the horses." Though she didn't claim to be an expert, she couldn't fault Brian's choices. The two mares he had selected for her and Dorothy to ride appeared to be gentle, and the gelding that pulled the shiny new carriage was a beauty.

It was a wonderful day to be outdoors. The afternoon was unusually warm, with only a few puffy white clouds scudding across the sky, and before they reached the end of the drive, Susannah had seen two robins squabbling over a fat worm. It was a lovely spring day, one that would be perfect, if only Dorothy had agreed to come with her. But she had not.

"I'm not ill," she had insisted when Susannah suggested they consult a physician. "I don't need to see a doctor." Though Susannah had raised the topic several other times, her mother had been steadfast in her refusal. Susannah was equally steadfast in her determination to visit him, although she told no one her destination. Rather than raise speculation, Susannah had asked

41

Brian to take her into town, ostensibly to mail a letter to Anthony and to visit the shops. That wasn't a lie, except by omission. She had written to Anthony as she did each day, telling him the myriad details of her life in Hidden Falls.

Though they were poor substitutes for the daily conversations she and Anthony had had in Boston, letters were all she had. While Anthony's came less frequently and tended to be brief and matter-of-fact, Susannah tried to make hers amusing. She told Anthony virtually everything that happened, painting him a picture with words as surely as she did with watercolors. The only things she did not mention were her worries about Dorothy and the way she had met Charles Moreland.

Susannah's cheeks burned as she remembered that day. How could she have been so mistaken as to believe him a common laborer? There was nothing common about Charles, including his kiss. Especially his kiss. It was absurd to remember the way his lips had felt and even more ridiculous to regret that Anthony's embraces had never stirred her the way that one stolen kiss had. She would not think about kisses, and she most definitely would not think about Charles.

Turning her head to the right, Susannah studied the row of evergreens that lined the road. "The falls truly are hidden, aren't they?" she asked Brian. Though she could hear the roar of the water in the distance, the trees blocked the view of the river.

"Yes, ma'am," he agreed. " 'Tisn't the fault of those trees, though. The falls are farther upstream. Folks here say Mother Nature hid the falls, but she had nothin' to do with these trees. They were planted by the first Moreland." The curl of Brian's lips told Susannah how little regard he held for Charles's grandfather and his botanical efforts.

She couldn't disagree completely. Though the towering spruces were magnificent, Susannah would have preferred them in another location.

"Why would anyone want to hide the river?" she asked. When she and Dorothy had first arrived in Hidden Falls, Susannah had been impressed by the beauty of the rapidly flowing water and had wished the river were visible from Pleasant Hill rather than being obscured by the trees.

"I reckon 'twas the mill old man Moreland was seeking to hide." Even his Irish lilt couldn't soften the contempt in Brian's voice. "That mill changed everything. Before it was built, folks used to go swimming in the river. Afterward, it wasn't the same. Even the fish died." Brian lifted the whip handle and gestured toward the Moreland mansion. "I reckon that's why old man Moreland had that swimming hole dug—so his son and his friends had a place to cool off on a hot day. Sure and they didn't invite the rest of us."

"But the mill provides work." Though Susannah didn't like the picture Brian was creating, in all fairness she had to remember that he might not be impartial in his judgment of the family that had fired him.

" 'Tis true," Brian admitted. " 'Tis also true that the Morelands cheat everyone who works for them." Brian turned to look at Susannah, his green eyes filled with what appeared to be sincerity. "I don't mind tellin' you, ma'am, that there's plenty of folks who reckon the fire was God's way of punishing the Morelands."

"Mr. O'Toole!" The thought was so appalling that Susannah's stomach began to roil. "If you value your employment with me, you will not repeat such dreadful lies."

Though Brian nodded, the creases that formed at the corners of his mouth told Susannah he, like his daughter, was among those who believed the tale.

They rode in silence. While the day was still beautiful, some of Susannah's joy had faded, destroyed by the knowledge that at least a few of the townspeople harbored such strong resentment of the Morelands.

As they crossed the bridge spanning the Cranberry River, Susannah gazed at the town that was going to be her home until she married Anthony. The five-story redbrick building that was Moreland Mills dominated the river's edge. There was no denying that. But rather than being an eyesore that cried out for camouflage, it was an attractive building with gently arched windows and a hexagonal bell tower. As she looked up the hill at the large houses, she wondered if the first Moreland's objective had been to keep the workers from staring at his home rather than to hide the mill. Perhaps the man had had more sensitivity than Brian gave him credit for and hadn't wanted to flaunt his success and his neighbors' before the townspeople.

"Thanks, Brian," Susannah said as he helped her climb out of the carriage. "I'll walk home when I'm finished." That way fewer people would know where she'd gone.

She gave the center of Hidden Falls an appraising look. It was a surprisingly pretty town. Though it had no central square the way many New England villages did, Main Street was attractive, lined as it was with trees. Many of the buildings were of gray native stone, while a few were constructed of redbrick like the mill. The sole frame building appeared to be the church, its graceful white spire towering above its neighbors.

Though at this time of day there were few pedestrians on the street, those she passed greeted Susannah warmly. On another day, she would have stopped to speak with them, to introduce herself, as the friendly but curious faces told her people were interested in the new town resident. But today Susannah had only one thought: seeing the doctor.

Her hands grew moist as she turned onto Rapids Street. There it was, the small stone building where Hidden Falls' only doctor practiced. Megan had described the structure and the town physician—a Dr. Kellogg—as she told Susannah all about the town.

Susannah swallowed deeply, willing her heart to cease its wild pounding. Dr. Kellogg would be able to help her. Of course he would. All Dorothy needed was a tonic, and the doctor would have it. Susannah reached for the doorknob, then stopped, dismayed. The doctor was not at home. Though a lamp lit the window, a small card announced that he was making house calls. Susannah clenched her fists as she tried to bite back her disappointment. The day was not over yet. Perhaps if she ran her few errands, he would have returned by the time she was finished.

Retracing her steps onto Main, Susannah entered the Hidden Falls Mercantile, one of the town's redbrick buildings. Though as a child she might have lingered, staring through the big plate-glass window at the displays, today she was too distressed by her mother's refusal to visit the doctor and the doctor's absence to window-shop. She would buy the thread she needed, visit the post office and then return to the doctor.

The air in the mercantile was redolent with spices and perfumes, and the sound of women's voices drifted from the back of the shop. As Susannah approached the rear counter, she saw two gray-haired women studying the display of lace collars. Their conversation ceased abruptly when they heard her footsteps.

The taller of the women raised her head, looked at Susannah for a second, then said, "Good day, my dear. You must be Dorothy Ashton's daughter." Her voice was soft and sweet, her smile equally so. "Welcome to Hidden Falls. I'm Henrietta Morgan." She turned to the woman at her side. "This is Leah Schwartz."

"I'm pleased to meet both of you," Susannah said truthfully. It was to be expected that the townspeople would know her identity, since in a town as small as Hidden Falls, new residents were as conspicuous as palm trees would have been in Boston. What encouraged Susannah was the fact that Henrietta Morgan had referred to Dorothy by her maiden name. These women were old enough to have been Dorothy's childhood friends. Perhaps renewing their friendship would be part of the healing process.

Leah took a step forward and stared at Susannah for a second. There was, Susannah realized, nothing rude about the stare. Instead, it appeared that Leah was nearsighted and, unlike Henrietta, wore no spectacles.

"Why, we haven't had this much excitement in months," Leah said with a chuckle. Her voice reminded Susannah of a bird's chirping. Perhaps that was why her bonnet was adorned with a bird. "Between you and your mother, and Matt Wagner coming back and then the carousel—"

"A carousel?" Though she had admired pictures of them, Susannah had never ridden one. As with painting and jewelry and ruffles on clothing, her parents had considered carousels to have no redeeming value.

"Oh, yes, my dear," Henrietta chimed in. "Charles Moreland has commissioned one. It's all anyone can talk about."

As Leah nodded, the sparrow that embellished her hat tipped forward, reminding Susannah of a bird drinking from the birdbath in her parents' backyard. "We heard he hired one of the best carvers in the country. I haven't seen the carver yet, but the tale is that he arrived a few days ago."

"It's all so exciting," Henrietta said, her face flushed with pleasure. "Everyone is speculating on where Charles will place the carousel. Some say the park, others the mill yard."

"It's good for all of us to have something happy to look forward to," Leah continued. "Especially after that dreadful fire."

Susannah wondered if she had misjudged Charles Moreland. A man who would commission a carousel for the town couldn't be as unfeeling as she had believed. Perhaps the afternoon at her house had been an aberration, the result of what appeared to be a deep-seated conflict between the Morelands and the O'Tooles. Perhaps Charles was the warm, amusing man she had met near the gazebo, the one who had . . . No, she would not think about his kiss.

Something of Susannah's discomfort must have shown on her face, for Henrietta took a step toward her and laid her hand on Susannah's arm. "I'm so sorry, my dear. Here we are chattering like birds in a cage, when you must have things to do. But tell me, how is your dear mother?"

"Happy to be home." That much was true.

Leah nodded, setting the bird to bouncing again. "I don't mind telling you I was surprised as could be when I heard that Dorothy was returning. Don't misunderstand me. I'm glad she's back. It's simply that I thought she'd decided Boston was her home." Leah bobbed her head. "I beg you to give Dorothy my regards and tell her she must come for tea soon."

"Yes, indeed." Henrietta squeezed Susannah's arm gently, then released it. "It would be like old times having the three of us together again. Why, when I think of the scrapes we got into . . ."

Leah gave her friend an admonishing look. "Now, Henrietta, don't shock Dorothy's daughter. You know how young people are. They think we were born old and stodgy."

"Speak for yourself." Henrietta's eyebrows rose an inch. "I don't consider myself either old or stodgy."

The way Leah bristled at Henrietta's tone told Susannah that the two women had had this conversation many times. "I'm sure my mother would enjoy visiting with you," she said to diffuse the tension. Since Dorothy had resisted leaving Pleasant Hill, Susannah continued, "Perhaps you would like to come to our house for tea. Shall we say in a fortnight?"

When they had set a date, Susannah purchased thread, mailed her letter, then returned to the doctor's office. He was still gone. She glanced at her watch. She would walk back to Bridge Street, then circle back here once more. If Dr. Kellogg was still gone, she would have to return tomorrow.

This time as she made her way down Main Street, Susannah paused to greet other pedestrians. The women were as friendly as Henrietta and Leah had been, welcoming Susannah and asking whether she knew anything about the carousel. Henrietta had not exaggerated. The carousel was the town's favorite topic.

"No, I haven't seen the plans," she told one woman.

The unmistakable sound of an automobile startled Susannah. Though they were becoming more common in Boston, this was the first she had seen in Hidden Falls. According to Moira O'Toole, only three people in town owned one. Brad Harrod, Philip Biddle, and Ralph Chambers were regarded as real mavericks for buying the vehicles.

Susannah turned back to the woman. "Yes, I think the park would be an ideal location for it."

The people who had ventured onto the street to watch the automobile's progress went back inside, and Susannah continued on her way.

When she reached the intersection of Main and Bridge, Susannah looked at the buildings that anchored the four corners. The bank, with its imposing facade and tall columns, stood opposite the white-framed church, while the other two corners were occupied by the town's sole hotel and a tavern. The automobile that had caused a flurry of activity was parked near the tavern. Charles Moreland, it appeared, was not the only Hidden Falls resident who imbibed during the day. *Stop it!* Susannah chided herself. She had more important things to do than think about Charles. Like seeing the doctor.

Susannah turned right and climbed the short but steep hill that led away from the river. When she crested the hill, she turned and looked back, surveying the town from yet another vantage point. Deciding to take Forest Street, Susannah raised an eyebrow when she saw that the only trees lining the way were a couple of scrawny saplings. Perhaps the town's founders had had a sense of humor when they named this road.

But Susannah's smile faded as she approached the houses at the end of the block. While the other buildings in Hidden Falls had pointed to prosperity, the peeling paint and broken porches on Forest told Susannah that not everyone shared equally. Her eyes widened when she saw a dozen children of school age playing in the mud next to one of the dilapidated houses. Their clothing was threadbare, and one of the little girls wore no stockings.

Susannah bit the inside of her lip to keep it from trembling. No matter how often she encountered it, she had never grown inured to the sight of poverty. Still, she knew how to deal with it. Susannah's parents had spent years teaching her to help the less fortunate. A faint smile crossed her face. Perhaps some good would come from this. Helping the people on Forest was something she and Dorothy could do. It was something they *would* do. And maybe, just maybe, the work would be part of Dorothy's healing process.

Susannah strode briskly down the hill. Dr. Kellogg was still on his rounds, and it was time to return home. She continued along Rapids, turning onto Mill.

"Mr. Moreland," she said as she recognized the man who stood near the front gate. The bubble of happiness that filled her told Susannah that, deny it though she might, she had come this way deliberately.

The man who had disturbed so many of her dreams crossed the street and lifted his hat in greeting. "Miss Deere," he said, a hint of a smile crooking his lips. "I'm surprised you're speaking to me. I didn't think I was one of your favorite people."

"I want to apologize for my rudeness." No matter how much

she disagreed with him, she should not have criticized Charles the way she had. A lady would never allude to a casual acquaintance's imbibing.

Charles shook his head. "If there are any apologies due, they're mine. My actions were inappropriate."

Though his gaze had met hers, his eyes were now focused on her lips. Susannah felt the heat rise to her cheeks as she tried to guess which actions he meant. Was Charles speaking of his demand that she fire Brian O'Toole, or was he remembering the kiss they had shared? To cover her confusion, she said quickly, "You're causing a lot of excitement in town, Mr. Moreland."

As naturally as if they did it daily, he kept pace with her, walking slowly down Mill Street. "I seem to specialize in generating excitement or at least commentary. But, please, call me Charles. And do tell me what I've done to warrant the townspeople's attention this time."

"I'll call you Charles if you call me Susannah." As they walked, she continued, "All anyone can talk about is the carousel. I keep hearing about the one your parents rented for your sisters' birthday. Now everyone wonders whether this one will be more spectacular."

Those cerulean eyes that refused to be banished from her dreams twinkled. "I certainly hope so. My carver says . . ."

They paused as a wagon rumbled down the street, the pounding of the horses' hooves and the squeak of the wheels making conversation difficult. When the road was once more quiet, Charles said, "I never knew how much there was to learn about carousels until I started this project."

He took Susannah's hand and placed it on his arm as they crossed the street. Though she knew it was impossible to feel warmth through the layers of his clothing and her gloves, Susannah would have sworn that her fingers tingled.

"Rob Ludlow—he's my carver—told me more than any one man should have to know about carousel design."

As the train chugged into the station, Charles paused. It was futile to try to talk over the noise of the engine and the clacking of the wheels on the steel rails. When the train had passed, and he and Susannah started to cross the bridge, Charles asked, "Where was I?"

"Carousel design."

"Right. I told Rob all I cared about was that they were pretty, but he insisted on telling me about gold manes and jewels, and then he started talking about Coney Island and Philadelphia. In case you wondered," he added, "those are styles of carousel carving." Though he pretended to be annoyed, Charles could not hide his enthusiasm, and it was infectious. Or perhaps it was simply that being with Charles somehow managed to lift Susannah's spirits. Even when his views had disturbed her, their encounter had still left her feeling more alive than ever before.

"See what I mean? I feel like I took a course in carousel design." Charles's smile was rueful. "And to think all I wanted was a special gift to welcome my sister home."

The townspeople hadn't told Susannah that was the reason for the carousel. "She must be very fond of them, if you're going to all this trouble."

Charles gave Susannah a quick smile, wondering what his sister would think of the woman who—despite his efforts to forget her—still haunted his dreams. Her lips were curved in a smile, reminding him of just how tender they had felt, how sweet they had tasted. Why, oh why, could he not forget that kiss? It had been one moment out of a whole lifetime. Surely he could wipe it from his memory. Susannah Deere might be beautiful. She might have given him the most memorable of kisses. Neither of those changed the fact that she was engaged to Anthony, and—no matter what else he did—Charles would not betray a friend.

He wouldn't think about delicious mouths and kisses. Instead, he'd talk about his sister. "Anne was happier at that birthday party than any other time I can remember." Thank goodness, he sounded normal. At least those disturbing thoughts of forbidden kisses weren't reflected on his face or in his voice.

"The party was for both of the twins," Charles continued. "My sisters look identical, but they're two very different people." As soon as the words were out of his mouth, Charles flinched.

Though Anne and Jane might have been identical twins, they no longer looked the same. Thanks to him. If it hadn't been for him, his parents might still be alive, and Anne might still be beautiful.

"Jane has always been shy," he told Susannah as he tried to obliterate the memory of the day that the Morelands' world had changed so dramatically. "We had to coax her to ride one of the carousel horses. Anne was just the opposite. My father had to literally carry her off the horse when the party ended."

"How about you?"

Charles shrugged. "I told everyone I was too old to ride."

"But I'll bet secretly you wanted to."

"That's one bet you'd win."

As Susannah laughed, Charles pictured her on one of the painted ponies, with him standing at her side, his arm around her waist. *Damn it all!* It was Anthony who should be riding carousels with her, not him.

"I heard that your sisters are in Europe."

Though the subject she raised was an unhappy one, Charles was glad for the distraction. Anything was better than thinking about the one woman on earth he could never have. "It's ironic, isn't it? When I went to Europe on a grand tour with Anthony and Brad, my sisters were furious that I wouldn't take them with me. Now Anne and Jane are there, but it's about as far from a pleasure trip as possible. The only reason they went was that the doctors here couldn't help Anne." Charles clenched his fist in frustration. "Who would have dreamt that we'd all wind up in places we didn't want to be?"

As they passed Fairlawn, Charles saw Susannah glance at the house that had been both his father's most prized possession and the cause of his death. Though she had no way of knowing the direction his thoughts had taken, Susannah's brown eyes were filled with compassion. "I probably shouldn't pry, but where would you rather be?"

"Anywhere!" When she looked startled by the vehemence of his reply, Charles softened his words. "Actually, I want to be back in New York City, not stuck here running the mill." *Or living in a house filled with memories.*

51

Susannah laid her hand on top of his in a brief gesture of comfort. "I saw some of the Moreland toweling in the mercantile. It's beautifully made. I've seen nothing to match it in Boston."

Charles tried not to frown as he thought of that particular lot of toweling. "It may be well woven, but it wasn't supposed to be red. Someone spilled dye on it." Charles thought about the day he'd discovered the damaged fabric. After he'd persuaded his best mill hands to work through the night to weave another bolt for the Catskills resort, he'd tried to find a way to salvage the original lot. "My only recourse was to have it dyed solid red and hope someone would want red towels. So far there hasn't been a lot of demand."

Susannah tilted her head to one side, apparently considering his problem. "You could make some blue towels and offer red, white and blue sets for Independence Day."

He hadn't considered that. "It might work. The town is mighty patriotic." As she nodded, he tempered his original statement. "I'm not saying everything about the mill is bad. It's just that I never dreamt I'd be worrying about how to sell red towels." And he certainly hadn't thought he'd be dreaming about his friend's fiancée. "But, tell me, what is it you dream of?"

"That's easy." Her eyes sparkled with enthusiasm, and the smile that lit her face was almost incandescent. Charles felt his heart skip a beat as he waited for her to tell him what fueled her dreams. Anthony. Of course it was Anthony. Wasn't that what every woman dreamt of, marriage and children?

"Paris," she said, the word rolling off her tongue. "I've always wanted to live in Paris."

It was absurd to feel so relieved. "What would you do there?"

Though her eyes still sparkled, she hesitated before she said, "Paint." Susannah's steps slowed, and she looked directly at him, apparently waiting for his reaction. When he nodded, encouraging her to continue, the words tumbled out. "I love to paint, but I'm afraid I'm not very good at it. For as long as I can remember, I was sure that if I went to Paris, I could study with a master and become famous." She gave a self-deprecating laugh. "Now my dream is to learn whether I have any real talent."

Charles tried to mask his surprise. Though there was no denying Susannah's enthusiasm, he had difficulty picturing Anthony married to a painter. The truth was, he had trouble picturing Anthony married to Susannah. She was so different from the other ladies Anthony had courted. Though they hadn't been as pretty as Susannah, they all seemed frivolous compared to her, and not one could match her wit or intelligence.

Charles had always thought that when Anthony married, he would choose a woman who'd give him blind adoration, and Susannah was clearly not that kind of woman. Anthony had changed, though, for this time he appeared serious. The ring on Susannah's finger was proof of that.

"Perhaps you could have a few painting lessons on your honeymoon," Charles suggested.

"Honeymoon?" She looked startled by the thought.

"You know," he said, trying not to wince at the images his words conjured. "The trip newly married couples take."

"I know the term," Susannah said with a touch of asperity. "I'm simply not certain why you believed we were going to Paris. Anthony wants to honeymoon on Cape Cod." Charles's face must have reflected his surprise at the destination, for she continued, "As you mentioned, he's already been to Paris."

They began to climb the drive to Susannah's house. "I'm surprised that Anthony wouldn't take you to France." If Susannah were his bride, Charles knew he'd take her to Paris or even to the moon if it would make her smile.

Susannah shrugged. "I never told him I wanted to go there."

"Why ever not?" Charles could not mask his surprise that Susannah had confided her dreams to him and not to her fiancé, especially when it was something so obviously important to her.

"Anthony has his heart set on Cape Cod," she said simply.

"And your wishes don't matter?"

Susannah shrugged again. "His are more important."

She must love him very much. Though it shouldn't have mattered, Charles found it oddly disturbing that perhaps after all Anthony had found a woman who adored him.

"The carvers have started work," Charles said, deliberately changing the subject. "Rob told me they don't mind an occasional visitor, so if you're curious about the carousel, you'd be welcome."

As Susannah nodded, Charles told himself that he would ensure he was nowhere near the stable when she came. A wise man kept himself as far as possible from temptation, and Susannah Deere certainly qualified as temptation. Thank goodness she was almost home! Their discussion had taken far too many unplanned turns.

Charles opened the front door for Susannah, then followed her into the hall. Even to his untrained eye, it was apparent that someone had spent many hours cleaning the house. Gone were the cobwebs and the coating of dust he'd noticed on his first visit. In their place, he saw gleaming wood and a sparkling crystal chandelier.

He had seen Susannah home. There was no reason to linger and every reason to depart. As Charles started to turn, he heard footsteps. Seconds later, a woman emerged from the parlor. Though she looked older than he had expected, Charles knew this could only be Dorothy Deere, Susannah's mother. As she approached, he searched for a resemblance. Dorothy was several inches shorter than her daughter, and her hair was the shade of gray that suggested she had been blonde as a child, not a brunette like Susannah. Only the shape of their eyes was the same. Right now those eyes shone with what appeared to be recognition.

"Dorothy, I'd like you to meet . . ." Susannah began the introductions.

But Mrs. Deere shook her head. Holding out both hands in welcome, she took a step toward Charles. "Oh, honey, you don't need to introduce us," she said with an oddly girlish chuckle. "I'd know John anywhere."

For a second, Charles was too astonished to react. Then he felt the blood drain from his face. She was wrong. Dead wrong. He was not like his father. Not in any way.

Chapter Five

The sledgehammer landed with a satisfying thud. Charles raised his arm and swung again. Thud! Another section of the gazebo splintered. It didn't matter if the rain started and his feet began to slip on the grass. It didn't matter if it took him all night. All that mattered was destroying that cursed building. Today. Dorothy Deere's words had galvanized him as nothing, not even the fire itself, had done. He couldn't change what she had said. He couldn't change what had happened. But he sure as hell could demolish the scene of the crime. No matter what, he would not stop until there was nothing but kindling left.

If only the memories were so easily obliterated.

Though he was a grown man, today Charles felt like a schoolboy, playing hooky for the first time. It was unusual to be able to leave the city early enough to catch the train that arrived in Hidden Falls in the middle of the afternoon, but today everything had fallen into place, and here he was, whistling as he hurried across the bridge. What luck! A sense of pleasant anticipation swelled deep inside him. Now he'd have time to talk to Jane before they dressed for Brad's parents' silver wedding anniversary party.

Charles's lips curved in a smile as he thought of his sister. Shy Jane had managed to surprise him. "If you can't keep a secret," she had written in her last letter, "throw the next page away unread." But Charles was in the habit of keeping his sisters' secrets, and so he had continued reading. "Don't laugh, big brother, but I think I'm in love. He's the kindest, most wonderful person on earth, and I'm the luckiest person alive. No one else knows, and they won't until we're sure this is true love, but I'm so happy I was afraid I'd burst if I didn't tell you."

Charles wasn't sure what intrigued him more: his sister's exuberance or the identity of the man Jane thought she loved. It had to be someone from Hidden Falls, for Jane rarely left home. That narrowed the choices. The only person Charles could imagine was Brad, but surely—even though it was supposed to be a secret—Brad would have told him.

"You're early!" *Charles's mother brushed her hands and presented her cheek for his kiss. When he'd entered the house, the servants had told him he'd find his mother in the conservatory, tending her beloved flowers. She gave Charles a radiant smile, then tilted her head to one side.* "I hope it's not bad news that brings you home early." *His mother had always been a worrier.*

"No," *he assured her.* "Just some lucky schedules and a train that was on time." *Charles sniffed a gardenia, then feigned casualness as he asked,* "Do you know where Jane is?"

"Try the gazebo." *Of course. A woman who believed herself in love would be attracted to the fanciful building that Charles's grandmother had made her private refuge.*

As he approached the white structure, Charles heard a woman's laughter. It didn't sound like Jane, but perhaps Jane in love sounded different. A masculine laugh told Charles that Jane—if it was Jane—wasn't alone. Was this her mystery man? Charles grinned, imagining the couple's surprise when they saw him. A second later, his grin was replaced by a shocked frown. Though they stood in the shadows, there was sufficient light for Charles to see what had made them laugh. The woman had her legs wrapped around the man, her skirts hiked to her waist, her hands gripping his shoulders. There was no doubt what they were doing.

Oh, Jane! I hope you're not making a mistake. But as the couple moved from the shadows, Charles saw that the woman was not Jane. This woman was a brunette; his sister was blonde. Thank God! And then they turned, moving in the throes of passion. For a second Charles stood motionless, paralyzed by shock. Then bile rose to his throat as his mind registered what his eyes had seen.

"You bastard!" he yelled at his father. "What the hell are you doing?"

The man Charles had once idolized swiveled his head. "Get out of here!" he snarled, his face reddening with anger. Or was it embarrassment? The bastard ought to be embarrassed. If there were any justice at all, a lightning bolt should strike him and that whore. As Charles watched, his father turned, lowering the woman to the floor and shielding her from him. "I'm sorry, my darling," he murmured.

Charles stood, frozen in place, more shocked by his father's words than by the unspeakable act he'd interrupted. Not once in his life had he heard his father use that gentle tone toward his mother.

"Get out of here," John Moreland repeated. This time his voice was harsh, the tone of a man accustomed to commanding and to being obeyed.

In the past, Charles would have quailed before such obvious rage. Not today. Not ever again. "The hell I will!" he snarled. If John was angry, so was he. And he had right on his side. "I'm not leaving here until you tell me what you were doing with this floozy."

A vein in John's forehead bulged. "You may be my son," he said coldly, "but I owe you no explanation. Now get out of here. I'll meet you in my study."

Mercifully, no one saw Charles reenter the house. He wasn't sure he could have faced a servant, and the thought of seeing his mother filled him with dread. How could they continue to act the charade of a happy family when John—for he refused to think of him as his father—had destroyed the foundation?

Charles paced the floor, waiting. Where was the man? Had he and that woman left together? And who was she, the Jezebel who was wrecking his parents' marriage?

As John entered the room, he strode to the sideboard and poured himself a generous serving of whiskey. Only when he'd downed half did he turn to face his son. Though Charles had expected him to speak, his father merely stood there, glass in hand, as casually as if *he were greeting a guest at a party. Only the tightening of his fingers on the tumbler betrayed the older man's discomfort.*

"You bastard!"

John's eyes narrowed. "Be careful who you call a bastard." His steely tone reminded Charles that the use of the "B word," as he and his sisters had referred to it, had been forbidden in their household.

"You had me fooled." Charles spat the words at the man who'd taught him that and countless other lessons. "All those years when you talked about honesty and decency, I believed you." And that was what hurt, the fact that the man he had once believed to be a shining example of all that was good was a hypocrite.

John took another long swallow, draining the glass. "I've never been anything less than honest."

The effrontery of the man! Not only was he an adulterer, he was also a liar. "I beg to differ. What I saw was not just dishonest, it was despicable."

Though his hands appeared to shake as he placed the glass on the desk, John's voice was steady. "You don't know what you're talking about," he said in a tone that might have intimidated another man. Charles was beyond intimidation.

"I know what I saw," he countered. The sight of John and that woman was etched on his memory, an indelible image. Why had Father done it? Why? "What I don't know is how you could betray Mother and your marriage vows."

Fists clenched, John took a step toward Charles, and for a second Charles thought he would strike him. Let him try! The time for honoring this man had ended. "This isn't about your mother." John's voice rose.

Charles raised an eyebrow and pretended to study the velvet drapes. "I suppose you're going to try to tell me that she wouldn't care."

As John's eyes widened, Charles realized that he was looking beyond him.

"What is it I wouldn't care about?"

Charles spun and faced his mother. Oh, God! Could the day get any worse? Though they had closed the door, somehow she had heard the argument and had decided to intervene.

"It's nothing, my dear," John said. Though his words were directed

58

to his wife, he gave Charles a quelling look, demanding that he remain silent. "This is between Charles and me."

At another time, Charles would have acceded to the unspoken command. But that was when he had believed that fathers deserved to be honored and obeyed. This man deserved nothing, nothing at all.

"How can you say that Mother isn't involved?" he demanded. It took every ounce of self-control Charles possessed to keep his hands at his sides, when what he wanted was to smash John's face. "You betrayed her in the foulest way possible."

His mother gasped, and the blood drained from her cheeks. "Oh, John. I thought . . ."

The man who had vowed fidelity held out his arms to the woman he had wronged. "Come here, my dear." Without hesitation, Charles's mother moved to John's side. Wrapping his arm around her waist, her husband whispered something in her ear. As Mary Moreland nodded, a flush stained her cheeks.

"Leave us alone," John said.

"I won't leave her with you. You don't deserve her."

"Don't try my patience, Charles. I'm still your father, and this is still my house. Leave us. Now!" He pointed toward the door.

Charles refused to budge. Instead, he turned to his mother. Though her expression was sad, she nodded her agreement. "It would be best if you left us alone." She patted John's arm.

Charles felt as if he'd been kicked in the stomach. How could his mother stand there and let that man touch her, knowing what he'd done? Didn't she care? Had she no pride?

"I'll leave you alone," Charles agreed, his voice as steely as his father's. "Permanently. When I walk out the door, it will be for the last time." Though his mother gasped, Charles continued. He kept his eyes fixed on John, wishing he could skewer him with a knife, not simply his gaze. "If you think I'll stay in this house and be party to your hypocrisy, you're wrong. I have moral standards, even if you do not."

Mary Moreland's lips tightened in anger. "Charles, I forbid you to speak to your father that way."

"That man is not my father. He is an animal, nothing more."

John recoiled as if from a blow. When he clenched his fists and took a step forward, Mary laid a restraining hand on his arm. "Please, Charles," she said, her eyes filling with tears. "Don't be so rash. There are things you don't understand."

"I understand enough."

She shook her head. "You know what the Bible says about not letting the sun go down on your anger."

"The Bible also says—"

"Charles!" This time her voice brooked no argument. "Leave your father and me alone for a few minutes. But I will expect you at dinner with your sisters."

His sisters. They lived here every day. Did they already know about Jezebel? They couldn't, Charles decided. One of them would have told him.

"No, Mother. There will be no dinner. I will not break bread with that hypocrite. You and my sisters will always be welcome in my home. As for you, sir"—he turned to his father—"this will be the last time I set foot in your house."

But it hadn't been. When he had seen the twins, he had found himself unable to tell them the truth of what had happened. Instead, he had pleaded an emergency, claiming that was why he had to return to New York immediately and wouldn't be able to accompany them to the Harrods' party.

And then the nightmare that he had thought might end once he left Hidden Falls had only worsened. For when he reached his home, he had been greeted by a telegram, informing him that a terrible fire had swept through the Moreland mansion, killing his parents and seriously burning Anne, who had attempted to rescue them. Only Jane was untouched, for she had been absent from the house. Even now, a year later, Charles did not know where Jane had gone that night.

What he did know was that it was his fault that his family had been destroyed. Though no one could confirm it, he could picture what had happened. As surely as if he'd been there, he saw his parents arguing, heard the angry words, then saw the lamp overturn. Had it burst into flames immediately or smoldered for hours before igniting the room? Charles did not know. But he did know that he was responsible.

If only he hadn't come home early. If only he hadn't lost his temper with his father. If only . . .

There was no way to undo the past. All he could do was try in whatever way possible to create a future for Anne and Jane. That would have to be enough.

"This house is beautiful."

Susannah straightened and rubbed the small of her back. Megan was right; the house was beautiful. "It's taking a lot of work to make it that way," she pointed out.

The two women were in one of the second-floor bedrooms. They had finished cleaning the first-floor rooms and were now tackling what would be guest chambers. Though the furniture was all of excellent quality, the years of neglect had left mildew on cushions and had dulled the finish of the wood. Restoring its former beauty was strenuous if not backbreaking work. Still, the results were rewarding, and Susannah found herself surprised at how much she enjoyed living in a house that was unabashedly opulent.

Megan dragged a chair to the window. Climbing on it, she reached for the drapery hooks. "Where will you live when you marry?" she asked as she handed the first panel to Susannah.

Although she and Anthony had discussed many things, housing was one decision they had not made. "I'm not sure," Susannah admitted. "Anthony lives in a boardinghouse now, but we'll want something bigger." Particularly if Dorothy lived with them. That was another discussion they had not had. Though Susannah had hoped that being in her childhood home would cure whatever ailed Dorothy, she had seen no improvement. Only this morning her mother had gotten lost going from her bedroom to the kitchen, making Susannah doubt she could live alone. Anthony would understand. Of course he would.

"Perhaps we'll buy a small house." Though in Boston she had shared a three-room flat with her parents, now that she was in Hidden Falls, Susannah found that she enjoyed being surrounded by grass and trees. Buying a house with a yard wasn't just for herself and Anthony. It wasn't even because Dorothy would be with them. Susannah wanted her children to grow up in a more pastoral environment than she had.

She smiled, thinking of her children. The boy would have sandy hair and cerulean eyes. *Stop it!* Of course he wouldn't look like that. He would have Anthony's gray eyes and the dark brown hair they both shared. Her child would *not* look like Charles Moreland.

"Then there's no chance that you'll stay here after you're married." Megan's words brought Susannah back to reality.

She shook her head. "Anthony is a college professor. There's no work for him here." Susannah folded the drapery panel and placed it in a wicker laundry basket. When they were all down, she and Megan would hang them outside to air.

Megan unhooked another panel and handed it to Susannah. "I remember when Mr. Anthony came here for a visit. I was surprised. Begging your pardon, miss, but he wasn't as handsome as Charles."

Susannah couldn't deny Megan's assessment. Anthony was not as handsome as Charles. No man she had met was. But there were many things more important than an attractive face. Anthony was kind. He would never condemn a man for one mistake.

"Sure and Mr. Anthony had an eye for a pretty girl," Megan continued. "I reckon that's why he picked you. You'll give him pretty babies." Susannah flushed. Was Megan a mind reader that she knew Susannah had been thinking about babies? "Still," Megan mused, "I couldn't believe such a fun-loving man wanted to be a professor."

Susannah shrugged. "Professors aren't serious all the time." Although her parents had been. It was only since they'd come to Hidden Falls that Susannah had heard her mother laugh frequently. Anthony's quick wit and joking manner had appealed to Susannah from the beginning. Though he taught history as her father had, Anthony did not seem to find it as serious as Father had.

Megan grabbed one of the basket handles. "Sure and you're lucky to be marrying," she said as she and Susannah descended the back stairs. "A husband's what I dream of most."

What surprised Susannah wasn't the fact that Megan longed for matrimony but that she appeared to believe it would elude her. "A beautiful girl like you shouldn't have any trouble finding a husband." Susannah had heard that there were more men working in the mills now than ever before, and many of them were single. Megan should have her pick of eligible bachelors.

When they reached the clothesline, Megan grabbed a handful of clothespins. "I'm a wee bit particular," she told Susannah. "I've picked out the man I want, but he isn't ready."

Susannah had not faced that dilemma. From the first time she had met Anthony, he had pursued her, proposing marriage when she'd known him less than a week. "I'm afraid that I have no experience, but I've heard that some men need to be encouraged. Perhaps that's the case with your young man."

Megan tilted her head to the side, considering. "You might be right." She grinned. "I think I'll try a spot of encouragement."

"Philip." Charles looked up in surprise when his visitor was announced. He had been so engrossed in a book that he had heard neither the arrival of an automobile nor Philip's knock on the door. The hours after supper were the time of the day that Charles reserved for himself, and he frequently spent them in his library, surrounded by books and the comforting smell of leather chairs. Reading provided respite from the daily worries and those disturbing dreams that had begun after he had kissed Susannah Deere. But he would not think about those dreams or the horribly empty feeling when he awoke and realized he was alone. Dreams like that were best forgotten.

Charles rose to offer the older man a comfortable chair. "What brings you to this side of the river?" Though he saw the former banker and family friend often, they normally met either in Charles's office at the mill or in the hotel's restaurant. It was rare indeed for Philip Biddle to come to Charles's home.

"Do I need an excuse to visit you?" Philip settled in the chair, waving away Charles's offer of a drink. A tall, thin man, Philip's prematurely white hair made him look older than his fifty years. "The truth is," he said, "I worry about you, Charles. Even though I know you've done your best to hide it from me, I'm aware that

63

the past year has been difficult for you. Now I'm hearing rumors that your financial difficulties are worsening. And then there's the expense of the carousel." Though his posture was relaxed, Philip kept his eyes fixed on Charles, apparently waiting for his reaction, and there was an intensity to his gaze that Charles had rarely seen.

Charles shrugged as he took the chair opposite his friend. "I won't pretend all is well. You know it isn't." Far from it, although he did not plan to share that particular piece of information with Philip. "Still, the contract with the Catskills resort will help."

Philip nodded, his blue eyes serious as he settled back in the chair. "Excellent, my boy. Excellent." He pulled a pipe from his pocket and began to fill it. "I wish there were a way I could help you. You know I'd buy the mill if I could. Unfortunately . . ."

There was no need to say more. Everyone in Hidden Falls knew that Philip had retired early from his position as president of the bank so that he could be with his wife when her illness had confined her to a wheelchair and that even after Rosemary's death he had not returned to work. Though it was assumed that Philip was comfortable financially, no one believed him wealthy.

"I never expected you to buy the mill or even invest in it," Charles said truthfully. If he had once hoped that Philip would be able to exert enough influence over the bank's directors that they would grant him a loan, that hope had been dashed. Philip's principles, it appeared, would not permit him to lobby for a family friend.

Tamping the tobacco, Philip said, "I know you didn't expect it, my boy, but I feel that I owe you more than I was able to give. Rosemary and I always considered you and your sisters the children we weren't blessed enough to have."

"And you know that we looked on you as family." The childhood friendship Charles's mother and Philip's wife had shared continued after their marriages, and Philip and Rosemary had been invited to all the Moreland family celebrations.

The sun had set, and the sole lamp Charles had lit failed to chase the shadows from the room. He ought to light several more, and yet there was something comforting about sitting here in the semidarkness. He and his father used to . . . No! He would not think about that man.

"When are the girls returning?" Philip asked as he lit his pipe.

Charles seized the question, grateful for the distraction. "I'm not certain; perhaps August."

Philip nodded. "We need to plan a proper welcome home for them."

"That's why I'm building the carousel."

"Just so, my boy. Just so."

When Philip left half an hour later, Charles found that he could no longer concentrate on his book. Instead, he wandered around the library, pulling a book from the shelves, then replacing it when he realized that it would hold his attention no more than the one he'd been reading. He was looking for something, and yet he couldn't say what it was.

He was almost ready to extinguish the lamp when a slim volume caught his eye. As he leafed through it, a smile crossed Charles's face. The photographs of Paris were magnificent. Susannah would enjoy them. Charles glanced at his watch. It was too late to visit her today, but there was no reason why he couldn't go tomorrow afternoon.

"Good day, Charles." Megan flashed him a brilliant smile when he arrived at Pleasant Hill the next afternoon. The warmth in her voice made him feel that she had spent the day waiting for him. That was nonsense, of course. Megan was simply being neighborly.

"Good afternoon, Megan. Is Miss Deere home?" He would say nothing about Megan's informal greeting. Perhaps it was only a slip of the tongue that she had forgotten to call him mister.

"She went out an hour or so ago." Surely it was only chance that Megan's hand brushed his as she reached for his hat. "Would you like to wait?"

Unwilling to surrender his hat, Charles asked, "Did she say where she was going?"

"I can't say as she did, but she'll likely return soon. Why don't you come in?" Megan laid a hand on his arm, drawing him into the hallway. "I finished my chores," she said with an impish smile. "I'm sure you and I could find a way to pass the time." The tip of her tongue moistened her upper lip. It might have been an innocent gesture, but the way she stared at his mouth told Charles it was not.

"Another time, perhaps," he said firmly. "Is Mrs. Deere at home?" Perhaps she would know where Susannah had gone. It was foolish, of course, to place such importance on giving Susannah the book today, but Charles wanted to see her face when she opened the cover and saw the photograph of the Eiffel Tower.

Rather than answer his question, Megan countered with one of her own. "Are you sure you wouldn't rather take a walk or . . ."—her tongue flicked seductively over her lips—"or do something else with me?"

The generously proportioned hallway suddenly seemed claustrophobically small. Cursing himself for having ever kissed Megan, Charles said simply, "Another time."

She gave him a saucy grin. "Sure and I'll hold you to that promise. Now, wait right here and I'll fetch the mistress."

Minutes later Dorothy Deere appeared in a pale pink dress that even Charles, whose fashion sense was limited, knew was decades out of date and too youthful a style for a woman over sixty. Its ruffles and furbelows were so different from the austere lines of the frocks her daughter wore that Charles wondered which of them was the parent.

Dorothy smiled at him, her blue eyes seeming to recognize him. "Good afternoon, Charles."

Thank God. Charles let out the breath he hadn't been aware of holding. The last time had been an aberration; today she knew that he was Charles, not John.

"Susannah is not home," Dorothy continued, "but I would be pleased if you'd stay for tea."

Charles shook his head. "Thank you, but I need to return to the mill." It wasn't the truth; what he needed was to see Dorothy's daughter. "I wondered if you knew where Susannah went. I have something I'd like to give her."

The older woman's face mirrored her disappointment. "Are you sure you won't stay?"

"Another time." That phrase was becoming a refrain.

Dorothy closed her eyes for a moment. "Let me think," she said. "I know Susannah told me where she was going." She tipped her head to the side, then opened her eyes. "Now I remember. She's with the horses."

Charles lengthened his stride as he headed for the stable. Although he had never been inside it, he knew from childhood explorations where it was located, and town gossip had informed him that Susannah had purchased three horses and a coach.

Charles glanced at the old building. That was odd. The front door was closed. Charles knew from experience that stables were dark unless the doors were left open. Except at night, it was normal to open the top of the Dutch doors when someone was inside the stable. Perhaps her mother was mistaken and Susannah was not here.

"Susannah!" Charles called as he let himself into the building. Even with the door open, the stable was dim. Charles blinked as his eyes tried to adjust to the darkness. "Susannah." The only response was a horse's whinny and another's soft snorting. Susannah must not be here. Charles turned and prepared to leave when he heard someone stumble, bumping one of the walls.

A muffled curse was followed by a man's voice demanding, "Who's there?" The lilt and the slurred words told Charles two things: the speaker was Brian O'Toole, and he was drunk.

Charles muttered a curse of his own. Though Susannah might believe in second chances, it appeared that Brian did not believe in sobriety. "I'm looking for Miss Deere."

"S'not here. Nobody's here." As the horse trainer came closer, Charles saw that his face bore several days' growth of beard.

"I see." And he did. He saw that Susannah had taken a risk, hiring Brian O'Toole, and she'd lost.

"Got a match?" Brian laid his hand on Charles's arm.

Charles recoiled. "You never learn, do you? You almost burned down my parents' stable, and now you're starting on the Deeres'. Sorry, Brian. The last two things on earth I'd ever give you are a match and a glass of whiskey."

"So it's thinkin' you're high and mighty, is it?" Brian punctuated his words by spitting on the stable floor. Though the man could barely remain upright, his aim was so accurate that he missed Charles's boot by only a fraction of an inch. "Let me tell you somethin', Mr. High and Mighty. You Morelands are all the same." Brian swayed, then grabbed the door for balance. "You think you're better than the rest of us. That's what got your da killed." Brian spat again. "Watch out, laddie. You're next." His drunken laughter followed Charles down the hill.

Charles clenched his fists in anger. It was easy to dismiss Brian's threats as the rambling of a man who had overindulged in both whiskey and dreams of revenge. Charles had no fears for himself, but Susannah was different. Didn't she know how dangerous a drunk could be? She was risking not just her horses but her own life and her mother's.

Charles scowled. Susannah was so tenderhearted that she saw only the good side of people. Her optimism kept her from realizing that men like Brian had destroyed their good sides long ago. Susannah was innocent and naive and Charles had to protect her. He owed it to Anthony.

Chapter Six

"This is incredible!" Susannah looked around the converted stable. Other than the faint underlying smell of horses, which even the scent of fresh wood shavings could not obliterate, there were no traces of the building's former use. Sunlight streamed through large windows, and only the indentations in the packed earth floor showed where the stalls had once stood.

"What's incredible?" Rob Ludlow asked. He had shown no surprise when Susannah appeared at the workshop, but had greeted her as if he'd expected her. After introducing her to his two assistants, Rob had shown her his plans for the carousel. Sketches of the three horses they were now carving hung on the walls near the huge chunks of wood that would one day be painted ponies.

Though the other men's horses still bore no resemblance to the magnificent steeds in the drawings, Rob's was different. Susannah laid a hand on the block of wood that would soon be his horse's head. At this point, only the roughest outlines were visible, and yet Rob already seemed to have captured the stallion's arrogant pose.

"I'm amazed that you can take something as ordinary as a piece of wood and create such beauty from it."

Rob picked up a chisel and returned to work on the horse. Though Rob was about the same height as Charles Moreland and had blond hair and blue eyes, no one would mistake him for Charles. This man's hair was golden rather than sandy, and his eyes were a milky blue, not cerulean. Susannah felt the color begin to flood her cheeks. How annoying that she compared every man she saw to Charles! She would stop. Of course she would.

"From my view, the most amazing thing about carving is the amount of work involved." Rob closed an eye and stared at the wood, then tapped the chisel against one corner. The outline of an ear began to emerge.

Susannah heard a muffled curse from the other side of the room and guessed that Mark or Luke—she wasn't yet able to distinguish between the brothers—wasn't having Rob's success with his carving.

"It may require work," Susannah agreed, "but you also need talent, and that's a gift." A low chuckle told her the brothers concurred.

Rob slid the chisel along the side of the ear, smoothing a rough edge. "There were times when I was convinced being able to carve was a curse rather than a blessing." Susannah stared, not sure what astonished her more: Rob's confession or the fact that—though they had met only minutes before—she felt as if they'd been friends for years.

"When I was young," Rob continued, "the uncle I lived with thought I was wasting my time if I whittled. He wanted me to be a farmer like him."

Susannah's astonishment grew and with it a glimmer of understanding. Perhaps the reason she had felt an immediate affinity for Rob was that they shared experiences. Besides both wanting to be artists, they both had relatives who disapproved of their vocations. "But you're a carver now," she said, her voice warm with admiration, "so you must have convinced him that that was what you were meant to do."

Rob stroked the side of the horse's ear, as if searching for a splinter. "That's one way of describing it. The truth is, I realized that the only way I would be happy was if I were carving, and I wasn't going to let anyone stop me."

Susannah wondered if her parents might have viewed her painting differently if she had told them that was what she needed to be happy. Perhaps not, for happiness was not a subject often raised in the Deere household. When they were not discussing scholarly pursuits, her parents spoke of duty and service to others. Susannah had learned early that it was a sign of weakness to ask for anything. A strong person gave; she did not take.

"You're happy now," she said to Rob. It was an observation, not a question. Seeing the way he caressed the wood, the way his eyes lit with pleasure as the animal began to take shape, no one could doubt that this was what gave him joy.

"Indeed, I am!" Rob laid his chisel back on the table, then turned to Susannah. "Would you like to carve a piece?"

Susannah blinked in surprise. She had come here out of curiosity, wanting to view not just the horses but also an artist at work. Not once had she considered that Rob might teach her. "I've never carved anything," she said, even as her fingers itched to touch the wood, to see if she could transform it into a piece of beauty. "Don't expect miracles."

Rob's expression was solemn. "I don't, but I think you have a good eye. That's the first thing you need if you want to carve." He reached into a barrel and pulled out a small piece of maple that was obviously the discarded portion of one of the animals. "Close your eyes and hold this for a minute," he said as he handed it to her. "What do you feel?"

Though Mark and Luke had been talking while they worked, they grew silent. Her self consciousness did nothing to quell her excitement as Susannah laid the wood in her left hand and stroked it with her right, turning it until she had touched all four sides. "It's smooth on the underside," she said at last, finding a position that felt right to her, "but prickly on the others. It reminds me of a hedgehog."

Rob chuckled. "I was right. You have the eye and the touch." Mark—or was it Luke?—handed her a chisel and hammer as

71

Rob continued, "If the wood makes you think of a hedgehog, that's what it should be."

Susannah looked at the chunk of maple. Viewed from this angle, it resembled nothing other than a piece of wood. Though she suspected it would end up as kindling, she wanted—no, she needed—to try to bring to life her vision.

"Here's how you start." As Rob coached her through each step, Susannah made the first tentative chisel marks. The hammer and chisel felt awkward in her hands. The wood was a foreign substance, so different from her canvas and paints, and yet there was a sense of familiarity. She was creating something.

Susannah and Rob worked in silence for a few minutes; then she heard a soft creak as the door opened. She looked up. The stranger was about Charles's height, but whereas Charles had sandy hair and blue eyes, this man had hair and eyes as dark a brown as her own.

Rob rose and dusted his hands on his pant legs. "Hello, Matt. I didn't expect to see you so soon."

The man named Matt stared at Susannah, his eyes frankly assessing her. "If I'd known you had a beautiful lady here," he said without looking at Rob, "I would have come sooner."

Susannah felt the color rise to her cheeks. Would she ever become so accustomed to compliments that they did not embarrass her?

"Aren't you going to introduce us?" For the first time since he had entered the workshop, Matt turned to Rob.

Rob laughed, as if amused by the way Matt had stared at her. "Susannah, this rapscallion is Matt Wagner, Hidden Falls' newest attorney. Matt, I'd like you to meet Miss Susannah Deere."

Matt closed the distance between them and took Susannah's hand in his. Bowing low in a courtly gesture that she thought had disappeared with Regency England, he pressed a kiss on the back of her hand. *"Enchanté."*

Rob turned toward Mark and Luke. "Gentlemen, it appears that our visitor has a strong preference for female pulchritude." As the assistants began to laugh, Susannah tugged her hand out of Matt's grasp.

"I'm afraid your attempts to impress Susannah are for

naught," Rob said. "If you look at her other hand, you'll see that she's already spoken for."

Matt shrugged, though a wry smile crossed his face. "Perhaps I was simply attempting to prove that the years I spent at Harvard weren't all wasted."

It was an afternoon of surprises. First the camaraderie with Rob, now a connection to this man. Matt Wagner did not look like the students her father had brought home. Though he was as well dressed as those men, there was something about him—a sense of recklessness—that the others had not had.

"You were at Harvard?" She hoped her voice did not betray her skepticism. "Perhaps you met my father, Louis Deere. He taught history there. My fiancé . . ." why did it seem so awkward, referring to Anthony that way? ". . . Anthony Borman also teaches history."

Matt shook his head. "I'm afraid I never had the pleasure of meeting either of them."

Realizing that the men would not sit until she did, Susannah picked up her partially formed hedgehog and, settling on the stool, resumed carving. "What brings you to Hidden Falls?" she asked Matt.

It was Rob who answered. "He used to live here."

"So it was a homecoming." First her mother and now Matt. There must be something about being raised in a small town that made people want to return. Susannah doubted she would ever feel that way about Boston.

For a moment Matt said nothing, and Susannah wondered if he was going to answer her question. "You could call it that," he said at last. "The fact is, I know a lot—some might say too much—about the conditions in the mill."

Considering the reluctance with which he had spoken, Susannah hesitated to ask Matt to explain his enigmatic remark. She bent her head over the maple and chiseled another corner away. There was no doubt about it. This did not look like a hedgehog.

"What my friend is trying to say is that he's a crusader."

Susannah's head jerked up, and she stared at Matt. Though Rob's tone was joking, the description was appropriate. She could envision Matt in a coat of chain mail, tilting at a quintain.

"I prefer the word *reformer*," Matt said.

"In any case, he thinks he can better the mill workers' lives."

A flush of pleasure that had nothing to do with the way Matt was staring at her warmed Susannah's cheeks. "What a truly admirable goal!" Though Matt might not resemble the scholars who disputed obscure points of history with her father, her parents would have considered him a kindred spirit, for he wanted to help the less fortunate.

Rob chuckled. "Now you've hurt my feelings, Miss Deere," he said in a voice that made mockery of the words. "I thought you valued beauty."

"I do," she agreed. "But I also value justice." And justice was what Matt Wagner sought.

"She's not just beautiful; she's wise, too," Matt told his friend.

Susannah couldn't help it. She laughed at the men's light bantering. "Flattery will get you nowhere."

"But carving lessons might." As if to demonstrate, Rob laid his hand on hers and guided her as she formed the hedgehog's nose.

All three of them laughed.

Charles lengthened his stride when he reached the bottom of the hill, trying to forget what he had seen in the Deere stable. Brian meant nothing by his threats. They were simply the ravings of a man who had consumed far too much whiskey. And yet Charles found it difficult to dismiss everything Brian had said. Was it possible that there was a grain of truth in his allegation that John Moreland's death had not been an accident? Nonsense! Charles shook his head in disgust. It was ridiculous to put any credence in something Brian O'Toole had said when he was inebriated.

The unmistakable sound of a rifle shot caused Charles to stop. Damn it all! Though Brad had mentioned that he'd thought there were hunters in the woods behind their homes, this was the first time Charles had heard them. Didn't they know that the only animals out now were the old ones, enfeebled by the long winter, or newborn fawns? Surely even an inexperienced hunter knew better than to kill either of them. Charles clenched his fists, wishing it were the hunter's neck he was wringing.

Though he had made it a habit to stop in the stable each day to see the carvers' progress, between his encounter with Brian and the knowledge that hunters prowled the forest, Charles was in no mood for a detour today. He would return to the mill and let honest work help him push unwanted memories away. But as he approached the building that Rob and his men had converted into their workshop, Charles heard the sound of a woman's laughter. So this was where Susannah had come. Her mother was right. She was with the horses. It was simply that those horses were carousel animals.

Charles fingered the book that he had thrust deep inside his pocket. He could give it to her now. With a lighter heart than he'd had since Megan had opened the door at the Deere mansion, Charles entered his stable.

As his eyes adjusted to the relative darkness, he felt blood rush to his face. He had expected to see Rob and Susannah, but not the bastard who'd been the trial of Charles's childhood. What a tableau the three of them made! Rob knelt beside Susannah, his hand wrapped around hers, while Matt stood so close to her that Charles doubted he could slide a piece of yarn between them. Damn it all! What were they doing?

He took a step forward, clenching his fists as he tried to control his anger. For surely it was anger he felt, not jealousy. Susannah was engaged to one of his friends. The emotion that he felt—and there was no denying its strength—was anger on Anthony's behalf. It had nothing to do with the fact that Charles wished it were his hand that cradled Susannah's or that he longed to stand so close that he could hear her breathing.

They were so engrossed in whatever it was Susannah held in her hand that they did not hear his approach, and that angered Charles as much as their unseemly proximity to the woman who haunted his dreams.

"What the hell are you doing here?" Charles clapped a hand on Matt's shoulder and dragged him away from Susannah.

Rob jumped to his feet. Her brown eyes clouded with confusion, Susannah rose and stared at Charles. The two assistant carvers dropped all pretense of working. If his goal had been to attract attention, Charles had succeeded. But that had not been his intention. All he had wanted was to give Susannah the book and see her smile.

"It's a free country," Matt said. Though the words were civil, he shook off Charles's hand and glared at him.

"This is private property." How dare Matt set foot on his land? Charles had told him years ago, when they were both still boys, that he was forbidden to enter the estate. It appeared that was one of the many lessons Matt had not learned.

Matt's lip curled in disgust. "Ah, yes," he said, his voice dripping with sarcasm. "You wouldn't want to let the poor boy near your precious carousel horses, would you? His dirty clothes might sully the paint."

The barb hit home, as Charles realized that Matt was not speaking of the carousel horses that Rob and his helpers were carving. Though he and Matt had traded many insults over the years, this was the first time Matt had alluded to the day of Anne's and Jane's birthday party and the carousel their parents had rented.

Did Matt know that Charles had seen him standing at the gates, a wistful expression on his face as he heard the music and watched the horses move? Did he know that for one fleeting moment Charles had been tempted to open the gate and let Matt ride the carousel? He hadn't, of course. That would have been unseemly. But it was one of the few regrets Charles had.

Matt's voice was close to a snarl as he continued, "It might surprise you to know what those dirty clothes did touch that night."

He was baiting him, the way he'd done so often over the years. Charles refused to take the bait. "So long as you stay off my property, nothing you do interests me."

Matt raised one eyebrow. "I wouldn't be so certain of that. What I do may not surprise you, but I can virtually guarantee that it will interest you." He turned and executed a neat bow in front of Susannah. "Good day, Miss Deere. It was a pleasure making your acquaintance. Good-bye, gentlemen," he said to

Mark and Luke. "And you, Rob, know where I live. Come any time." Without another word or a backward glance at Charles, Matt left the stable.

Susannah spoke for the first time since Charles had arrived. "Since it seems that outsiders are not welcome on Moreland land," she said, looking steadily at Rob, "I had best be leaving." Though she kept her voice low, there was no disguising the anger that tinged her words. She held out an oddly shaped piece of maple and what appeared to be a chisel and hammer.

Rob took the tools, but he refused the wood. Susannah laid it on the table. "Keep the hedgehog," Rob said. "You carved it."

Charles felt a flash of annoyance. So that was why Rob had been holding Susannah's hand. He hadn't been flirting with her; he was teaching Susannah to carve. Not for the first time, Charles cursed his temper. He should have asked what they were doing, not leapt to the wrong conclusion. Charles thought he had mastered his temper, but something about this woman triggered the best—and the worst—in him.

Susannah backed away from Rob, refusing to touch the wood. "I wouldn't want Mr. Moreland to think I was stealing his property." This time she made no attempt to hide her contempt.

"For Pete's sake, Susannah, I didn't mean that."

For the first time, she looked at him, her eyes blazing with anger. "Just what did you mean?"

From the corner of his eye, Charles saw Rob motion to his assistants and lead them outside, leaving Charles and Susannah alone. She eyed him warily.

Charles ran a hand through his hair, trying to curb his frustration. Why was it that he so often managed to say the wrong thing to Susannah? He couldn't blame her if she believed him to be some sort of misanthrope. It was Charles's misfortune that Susannah sought to befriend the two people in Hidden Falls that he knew could not be trusted: Brian O'Toole and Matt Wagner.

"Matt and I've never gotten along," Charles said. "He was my childhood nemesis, and even though we're adults now, some things never seem to change."

Susannah shrugged, apparently dismissing his explanation.

She was wearing a dark green dress today. Somehow, though he knew her eyes to be brown, they appeared to be flecked with green this afternoon. "There's no excuse for rudeness, Charles. Matt wasn't harming anything."

She could be as prickly as the hedgehog she had been carving. "Maybe I see him from a different perspective," Charles suggested.

"And maybe that perspective is wrong. You appear to see the worst in everyone."

"And you're unreasonably optimistic." As she bristled, Charles continued, "Your faith in others would be touching if it weren't so dangerous."

Though he expected another quick repartee, Susannah's steady gaze faltered. "What do you mean?"

He heard the hesitation in her voice and gentled his own. "You didn't take my advice about Brian O'Toole. Susannah, I wish to God I didn't have to tell you this, but today I found Brian in your stable, drunk and ready to smoke." Charles shuddered as the images of flames and charred wood rose before him. "He could have set the place on fire."

Blood drained from Susannah's face, and she swallowed deeply. "I'll talk to him." The quavering in her voice told Charles she had heard his unspoken fear, that she and her mother might have been injured . . . or worse.

"I'm afraid talk will not be enough."

A wry smile crossed her face. "Don't underestimate my powers of persuasion, Charles."

"I don't." As she sailed out the door, Charles realized that he had forgotten to give her the book of photographs.

By the time he returned from the mill that evening, the sun had already set, and his house was empty. Charles could practically see his housekeeper's pursed lips as she had placed his dinner back in the oven. "If you can't come home at a reasonable hour, don't blame me if your supper is dried out," she had chided him more times than he cared to remember. "Your parents believed that food should be eaten when it was ready." But he, as he had told Mrs. Enke, was not his parents, and his responsibilities at the mill were more important than a perfectly cooked meal.

He switched on the lights in the dining room and settled at the table. The gravy that Mrs. Enke had left simmering on the stove helped camouflage the undeniably dry beef, but nothing could help the peas. They were hard pellets, as unpalatable as buckshot. Charles took another bite of meat, chewing slowly as he thought of the contract he'd negotiated with the Catskills resort.

As he had hoped, they had been sufficiently impressed by the towels Moreland Mills had woven that they had agreed to have the mill supply all their linens. Though the late-delivery penalties were steep, the pricing was good. If all went well, other hotels and even visitors to the resort would order towels and sheets from him. This one contract was far from enough to repay the mill's debts, but it was a start.

Charles reached for a piece of bread, then cocked his head. What was that noise? It sounded like an animal whimpering. Though there were deer and raccoons in the forest, they rarely approached the house. When the noise was not repeated, Charles buttered the bread and took a bite. It must have been his imagination. But seconds later, he heard soft scratching on the French doors followed by another whimper. It had not been his imagination.

Intrigued, Charles rose and flung open the door. There, huddled on the stoop, were two of the most bedraggled puppies he had ever seen. Their fur was tangled and matted with mud, their expressions woebegone. "Hey, fellas, what are you doing here?" Charles bent down and stroked one of the dogs' heads. The little critter tried to lick his other hand, then nipped a finger.

"Whoa, there. I'm not your dinner." But it was apparent from the plaintive cries that both dogs were hungry. It was equally apparent that they were too young to be away from their mother. Charles looked around. Where was she? Bitches rarely let their pups wander this far. Remembering the rifle shot he'd heard that afternoon, Charles frowned. Had the hunter wounded or killed the mother dog? It was too dark to search for her. It was also impossible to leave the pups on their own.

With a sense of inevitability, Charles picked up both dogs and carried them into the kitchen. "Okay, boys," he said as he placed them back on the floor, "we're gonna get you something to eat." Seen in this light, Charles realized that one of the puppies' fur was much lighter than the other's. Both, however, had outsized paws, floppy ears and such pitiful expressions that it would have taken a heartless man to turn them away.

Regardless of what Susannah thought, he was not a heartless man.

While Charles opened the icebox and studied its contents, the puppies explored the kitchen, sniffing, then licking the tile floor. When they realized that the strange surface was not edible, they hurled themselves at Charles, yipping frantically as their paws slid on the smooth tiles. Grinning, Charles patted their heads and guided them back toward the door.

He poured a small quantity of milk into two shallow bowls and sat them in front of the dogs. If luck was with him, they would know how to drink from a bowl. If not, he'd have to devise some other way of feeding them. The puppies sniffed the milk, gave it a tentative lap, then—apparently convinced that this was a substance they recognized—began to slurp noisily. Thank goodness!

When the darker pup had finished the bowl, he looked up at Charles and yawned as if asking where he should sleep. It was absurd. Charles already had more responsibility than he wanted. The last thing he needed was two helpless animals dependent on him. "Okay, fellas," he said as he opened the back door, "out you go." Instead of moving toward the door, the light-colored dog settled on top of Charles's boot, while his brother rubbed Charles's leg.

They were wild animals. Their place was outside. Charles reached for them, fully intending to put them in the yard. But then the dark one yawned again, and the look he gave Charles seemed to say that he trusted him.

"Okay. Okay. But it's just for one night." He arranged an old blanket next to the stove, then placed the puppies on it. They sniffed, circled three times and settled in. Seconds later, they were asleep. Success. Charles returned to the dining room.

His dinner was cold, the gravy congealed. Charles pushed the plate aside and helped himself to the stewed apples Mrs. Enke had designated as his dessert. That, at least, was palatable. He was emptying the bowl when he heard whimpering.

Despite himself, Charles couldn't help laughing. He opened the door and found two tiny balls of fur waiting for him. As light spilled onto them, their tails began to wag furiously. "I thought you were going to sleep," he said. They looked up at him expectantly. "Oh, all right." He brought the blanket from the kitchen into the library. They sniffed, circled and slept. He read. And if his attention strayed from the printed page to the puppies, it was only to be expected.

Charles yawned one final time, then moved the dogs back into the kitchen where they could do less damage. Still groggy, they protested only slightly when he put them inside a crate. They'd be safe there. But when Charles began to climb the stairs to his own room, he heard the sound of toenails clicking on the polished floor. Looking back, he saw the puppies standing at the bottom of the staircase, looking up at him. They whimpered. He glared. They scratched the stair. He glared. They cried. He glared. Then he shrugged his shoulders, accepting the inevitable.

"Just once."

Despite the fact that Salt and Pepper, as he had named the puppies, woke him countless times during the night, when he approached the mill the next morning, Charles's step was jaunty, and he found himself whistling under his breath. It was going to be a good day. He would visit Susannah again this afternoon. Not only would he give her the book, but he would also ask her advice on the puppies. She might know of a good home for them.

As he walked through the iron gates at the edge of the mill, a familiar figure hurried from the office. "Mr. Moreland! Mr. Moreland!"

The worried expression on the man's face told Charles that whatever the news was, it was not good. "What's wrong, Wilson?"

When Wilson's frown deepened, Charles knew he had been

mistaken. Today, it seemed, would not be a good day. "Someone got into the mill last night."

The sun was shining; the birds were chirping; it was only Charles's imagination that a dark cloud threatened to dump rain and hail on him. He took a deep breath before he asked the next question. "What happened? Did someone spill another vat of dye?" They had a critical shipment of linens for the Catskill resort due to be completed by the end of the week. If the newly woven bolts had been destroyed, it would be close to impossible to meet the shipment.

"Worse," Wilson said. "Begging your pardon, sir, but you need to see this."

The dread was now palpable. Had it been only twelve hours since he had felt encouraged by his progress at the mill? As they climbed the stairs to the weaving room, Charles tried not to imagine what Wilson might consider worse than the destruction of two days' work.

"There you are, sir." Wilson pointed toward the looms.

For a moment, Charles's brain refused to register what his eyes saw. The looms were operated by an intricate system of belts and pulleys. Surely he was only imagining that every one of the pulley belts was cut. Without the belts, there was no power to the looms, and weaving was impossible.

Wilson was right. This was worse than the loss of a thousand yards of fabric. Though Charles kept a few spare belts as a contingency, should one of them be worn beyond repair, he had two or three, not the hundred that he needed to return the weaving room to full operation.

"Does the watchman have any idea who did this?"

Wilson's answer was a formality. Charles already knew he would say, "No, sir."

As he strode to the storeroom, hoping that the supply of belts was larger than he remembered, one question kept reverberating in his mind. Who? Who would have deliberately destroyed the belts?

Charles clenched his fists as he thought of Matt's face and the way he had announced that whatever he would do would interest Charles. Was this what he meant? Or was it Brian, still smoldering over their argument, who had broken into the mill?

Unlike Susannah, Charles trusted no one.

Chapter Seven

"I don't know what to do." Though Ralph had urged him to sit, Charles continued to pace the floor of the attorney's office. His mother might have called it nervous energy. As far as Charles was concerned, it was anger, pure, distilled anger, that had him wearing a path in Ralph's carpet. Just as anger and the determination that nothing would prevent him from fulfilling his contract with the resort had helped him choose a course of action, the same fury had propelled him to Ralph's office, seeking a way to prevent further problems.

"Seems to me you've done the only thing you could," Ralph said. "You repaired as many looms as you could, got them started again and arranged to keep them running all night." Though the attorney nodded solemnly, his blue-gray eyes radiated approval. "I hope you won't object to my pointing out the obvious, but that's a not insignificant accomplishment for less than one day. Your father would have been proud."

Charles did not want to discuss his father. It was John's fault that he was in this predicament. He stared out the window, refusing to look at the mill. Though it dominated the river's edge, if he looked to the right he saw the train station rather than the building that imprisoned him as surely as a pair of shackles.

"What I did was simply react," Charles told Ralph through clenched teeth. "That's not enough. I want to do something to ensure that problems like this never happen again."

"I understand, my boy. Truly, I do." There was no doubting the attorney's sincerity. "Don't forget, though, that this is probably an isolated instance. Why not keep your attention focused on what's important, namely getting that cotton woven?"

His voice was so smooth and mellow that Charles could picture him in front of a jury, convincing them of his client's innocence. Charles did not want to be convinced. "It's not an isolated instance, Ralph." Charles wheeled and faced the attorney. "I might have believed that the smashed pots and the missing spindles were simply mischievous pranks, but it's gone beyond that. Way beyond. Someone's trying to destroy Moreland Mills, and I want to know who it is."

"Of course you do." Ralph peered over his spectacles. "But you need to be practical, too. Hiring an investigator and extra guards costs money."

And that was one thing Charles did not have.

"I'm sorry, Miss Deere." The doctor steepled his hands as he leaned forward. "I wish I could tell you otherwise."

Susannah closed her eyes, not wanting him to see the tears that had begun to well. She had considered it a positive omen when she had finally found Dr. Kellogg in his office. Though the doctor was younger than she had expected, she had been reassured by both his quiet smile and the intent way he listened. Susannah had been encouraged when he had consulted two different books, asking her to confirm symptoms. It was only when he had given her his diagnosis and—worse yet—the prognosis that Susannah's hope had turned to despair.

"I do not want to mislead you or hold out false hope," the doctor continued when she blinked her eyes open. She glanced at him, then stared at the wall, not wanting to see the creases that bracketed his mouth or the pity that radiated from his eyes.

"I have seen others with your mother's symptoms, and there is no cure."

Susannah's head jerked up, and she felt the blood drain from her face. That was unthinkable. There had to be a way to help Dorothy. "Surely a tonic . . ."

Dr. Kellogg shook his head slowly. "I can prescribe one if you insist, but it will make no difference."

"Are you certain?"

The doctor's expression was grim. Even if he had not uttered a word, Susannah would have known what he was about to say. "When a person has brain fever, there is nothing I can do to help." His lips thinned, and his voice was fierce as he added, "I wish to God my answer were different!"

Susannah blinked back her tears as she left the doctor's office. Perhaps he was wrong. Perhaps there was something that would restore her mother's memory. Perhaps if she worked with Dorothy, teaching her the way her mother had once taught young ladies, Dorothy would remember simple things, like what year it was. Just this morning Susannah had found her mother crying. When she had asked what was wrong, Dorothy had turned her tearstained face toward Susannah. "Oh, my dear, someone has killed President Lincoln."

But Abe Lincoln had been dead for over forty years. Her mother's sorrow over the former president's death, which seemed as fresh as if the assassination had occurred last week, had disturbed Susannah as much as Dorothy's insistence on wearing the ruffled frocks she had found in the attic.

Susannah straightened her shoulders and forced a smile onto her face. Crying solved nothing. She would think, and somehow she would find an answer. Dr. Kellogg did not know everything. If he did, Anne Moreland would not be in Switzerland. She would have had her burns treated here. Susannah would take her mother to Europe, if that would help. But first she would ask Charles whom he had consulted in the States.

The man had his rough edges, like the wood she had attempted to carve, but Susannah realized that there had been a reason for his apparent hostility: the fear of fire. That colored everything. It also explained why he'd been so rude to Matt, for he'd just come from his encounter with Brian, and fear—as Susannah knew—could linger. If Charles's emotions hadn't already been frayed, he might not have overreacted. At least that was what Susannah told herself. Perhaps he was right and she was an unreasonable optimist, but she didn't think so. Charles was an inherently good man. Why else would he be building a carousel for the town?

As she turned onto Mill Street, a familiar figure emerged from the gates. Charles! For a second Susannah's spirits soared as, despite her daily admonition, she remembered the day she'd met him and the wonderful kiss they'd shared. Then she saw that Charles's shoulders were stooped. The poor man! Susannah made a quick decision. Today would not be a good time to ask about doctors. That would only remind Charles of his sister's injury. She could wait. If Dr. Kellogg was right, a few days' delay would make no difference to Dorothy. She might not be able to help her mother today, but perhaps she could cheer Charles.

"Hello, Charles." Susannah noted with pride that her greeting sounded as carefree as if she'd just come from a party rather than consulting a doctor who'd dashed her hopes.

Charles crossed the street, tipping his hat when he stood at her side. "Susannah!" Though those cerulean eyes that haunted her dreams were still filled with pain, the corners of his mouth quirked up in a smile, and Susannah felt her heart begin to expand. Her parents were right. What was important was helping others. "What brings you into town?" Charles asked.

"I had a letter to post." It wasn't a lie. She had indeed mailed her daily missive.

"To Anthony?" Though they were only two words, the tone of Charles's voice set Susannah's antennae to quivering. It sounded almost as if he disapproved of her writing to Anthony. That was, of course, sheer nonsense.

"Who else?" she asked with a little shrug. "He says the letters brighten his days." She gave Charles a quick smile. "Maybe I should write one to you, too. You look as if your day could use some brightening."

Charles quirked an eyebrow as he matched his pace to Susannah's. "Are you volunteering? I thought you didn't approve of my perspective." Thank goodness, his tone was once more bantering.

"I may not have liked what you told me," Susannah admitted, "but you were right. When I got home, I discovered that Brian was drunk." Susannah frowned at the memory of the man who'd fallen asleep slumped against a stall, a cheroot still clutched between his fingers. By some miracle, it had been unlit. "That won't happen again."

"I hope you're right." The neutral tone to Charles's voice told her he was trying to hide his skepticism.

"Moira will ensure that Brian doesn't drink." Charles and Susannah passed the company store. Like the mill, it was a redbrick building. Unlike the mercantile, it boasted no plate-glass windows filled with merchandise. From the comments Susannah had overheard, the Moreland store's primary lure was its low prices.

"I don't know about you," she continued, "but I wouldn't want to cross Moira O'Toole. I'm betting that Brian doesn't either." As she had hoped, Charles chuckled. "Now, are you accepting my offer of a friendly ear?"

His chuckle turned into a full-fledged laugh. "You're as persistent as Salt and Pepper."

What was the man talking about? "I beg your pardon?"

Charles laid Susannah's hand on his arm as they crossed the street. On the opposite corner, a man apparently inspired by the unusually warm April day was raking leaves in the park. Megan had explained that the townspeople, rather than assess an additional tax to pay for maintenance of the park, had agreed that they would establish volunteer committees for its upkeep. Now that it was spring, the committees were once again active.

Susannah looked down. It was surely her imagination that Charles's hand had lingered on hers an extra second or two, as it was undoubtedly her imagination that she could still feel its warmth.

"Salt and Pepper are two puppies that adopted me last night."

Susannah blinked. Just when she thought she understood this man, he revealed new facets.

"You look surprised." The amusement in his voice lightened

the weight on Susannah's heart. It felt so good to be able to help someone, even if the only assistance she could provide was bringing a smile to his face.

"It was the phrase 'adopted you' that startled me," she dissembled. She would not tell Charles that she had difficulty picturing him with puppies. Charles was too serious for puppies. And yet, a small voice reminded her, the Charles she had met at the gazebo that first day had not been serious.

"I don't know how else to describe it. They appeared on my doorstep and wouldn't leave." His smile was wry. "To be honest, I don't need any more trouble, and I suspect they'll be exactly that."

Susannah, who had never had a puppy, could not agree. "I'd wager that they're the cutest things on earth."

"Well, now, I couldn't disagree with that. That's why I accepted the adoption." Charles grinned as if he realized the absurdity of the situation and was enjoying it. "Do you want to see the dogs? I imagine Mrs. Enke is ready to drown them about now."

"I'd love to. And while we're walking, you can tell me why you looked like Atlas, carrying the world on his shoulders."

Charles stopped in the middle of the bridge and glared at Susannah. "You *are* persistent." The lightness of his tone defused the accusation.

"I've been told that persistence is my finest virtue or worst fault, depending on your perspective."

"There's that word again."

"And you're stalling."

"Guilty as charged. The fact is, I hate to even think about what happened."

Charles resumed walking before he began his tale. As she listened to the story of the sabotaged belts, Susannah suspected that the simple act of putting one foot in front of the other helped him relieve some of his tension, for he seemed to have regained some of his jaunty stride by the time he finished.

How well she knew the therapeutic effects of walking! That as well as the desire to avoid discussion of her visits to Dr. Kellogg was the reason Susannah insisted on walking home whenever she came into town. She would ask Brian to drive her, but always returned on foot. The walks, she had learned, helped clear her thoughts.

"It sounds as if someone wants the mill to fail," Susannah said as they passed the Harrods' house. Charles had slowed his pace to a stroll rather than the forced march they had taken while he was reliving the morning's events.

"That's what I thought, too. My only question is who's behind it."

"You sound as though you suspect someone in particular."

"Indeed, I do. Brian O'Toole or Matt Wagner."

"Matt?" Though Susannah found it difficult to believe either man capable of sabotage, she could not imagine what motive Matt might have. "Why?"

"He hates me."

"Oh, Charles. Surely not."

"Why is that so difficult to believe? You saw Matt yesterday. Surely you can't deny that he hates me."

She shook her head slowly. "You'll probably accuse me of being overly optimistic again, but I don't think that's the case. I saw antagonism between you two, even animosity, but not hatred." Susannah stopped and looked at Charles. "You don't hate Matt. I won't believe it." The speculative look she saw in his eyes told her Charles was considering what she had said.

"Regardless of what has transpired between you two in the past, Matt is a self-described crusader," she continued. For reasons she couldn't quite explain, it seemed vitally important to assure Charles that Matt did not hate him. "Matt wants to improve conditions in the mill. He told Rob and me that yesterday afternoon." Susannah would not believe that Matt had been lying. "If that's true—and I think it is—why would he sabotage the looms? It could only hurt the same workers that he's trying to help."

The road was dappled here as the huge spruce trees broke the sun's rays. Though Charles turned so that she could see only his profile, Susannah watched his lips tighten as he considered her argument. "That's not completely true," he said at

90

last. "If Matt had simply weakened the belts and they broke in operation, the flying leather could have injured people. But this way the damage was so complete that there was no question of operating the looms. No one was in danger."

"No physical danger," she agreed. Whatever had caused the rift between Charles and Matt, it was clear that the enmity still ran deep, and unless she could find compelling proof to the contrary, Charles would believe that Matt deliberately sought to destroy his mill. "Don't you pay your weavers for the amount of fabric they produce?"

Charles nodded.

"Then they suffer for every hour the looms are idle. What would Matt have accomplished if he caused them to lose pay?"

"I hadn't considered that. You might be right."

Susannah smiled, sensing that it was difficult for Charles to admit that Matt was not a monster. "So my perspective isn't all bad?"

"I surrender!" Charles tossed his hands into the air in a mocking gesture of capitulation. Then, just as suddenly, his face darkened. "I probably should do exactly that—surrender. It's what my attorney advises. He tells me I should sell the house and mill and move back to New York."

"Why don't you do that? You said that was your dream." It was odd. Though Charles had told Susannah that he wanted to return to New York, when she pictured him, it was strolling along the Seine, not walking in Battery Park. It was silly, of course, to be confusing her dreams with his.

They were climbing the drive that led to Charles's house. Though Susannah had seen it from the road and the stable, this was the first time she had had a close view of the front facade. With its crenellated parapet and corner towers, the redbrick and stone building looked like the drawings of medieval castles Susannah had seen in her father's history books. Though this was far more fanciful, it appeared that the architect who had designed the Moreland mansion had also received the commission for the mill, for the mill had similar towers and, though its roof was more utilitarian, the dentil molding resembled the house's crenellations. There was no doubt that both structures had been envisioned by the same person.

"As much as I want to sell this albatross, I can't do that to my sisters, especially Anne. For whatever reason, she loves this monstrosity." Charles scowled at the house. "I want to preserve it for her and Jane."

Another facet of the man. Though he might want people to believe that he was a cold, calculating businessman, the truth was, he had a kind, compassionate heart . . . at least where his family was concerned.

Charles swung open the huge wooden door that in medieval times would have admitted men on horseback and led Susannah into the house. Since the leaded glass windows admitted little light into the massive hallway, gas lamps were lit to relieve the gloom. Susannah was surprised. She would have expected electricity. Though Pleasant Hill had yet to have it installed, that was understandable, given how long the house had been vacant. She wondered why the Morelands hadn't electrified their home.

"Cheerful, isn't it?" Charles made no attempt to hide his sarcasm. "Fortunately, some of the family rooms are a bit more inviting."

The kitchen was not one of those. Its dark wood cabinets and red tile floor only emphasized the absence of sunshine. It appeared to be the perfect setting for the scowling woman who greeted Charles.

"About time. I want those creatures out of my kitchen," she announced with a baleful glance at the two bundles of fur who tussled in the corner.

After Charles had performed quick introductions, he crouched next to the dogs and ruffled first one puppy's ears, then the other's. Susannah watched, amazed at the way Charles's face seemed to relax as he stroked the puppies. Even his shoulders seemed to have lost their rigidity, as if the dogs had drained the tension from his body.

"They are adorable," she said, her fingers itching to touch the puppies, to see if their fur was as soft as it appeared. Someone— and she doubted it was the dour Mrs. Enke—must have given them a bath.

"Beggin' your pardon, miss, but I reckon you wouldn't be thinkin' they were so adorable ifn it was your shoes they chewed." Mrs. Enke glared at the dogs. "You kin think those teeth are small, but they're sharp. My toes will never be the same again."

Susannah bit the inside of her lip to keep from smiling. Though she knew puppies enjoyed chewing on leather and appeared to have a particular affinity for boots, she had never heard of them gnawing on a shoe while it was being worn. Had Salt and Pepper sensed Mrs. Enke's dislike and decided to punish her?

"Perhaps they need to run off some of their energy," Susannah suggested. As Charles nodded his agreement and reached for Salt, Susannah picked up Pepper. The dog stared at her for a moment, apparently trying to decide whether she met his approval, then began to yip and squirm with pleasure. His fur was soft, and the way he gazed at her melted Susannah's heart. Was there anything on earth as sweet as a puppy?

She held him with both hands, her fingers stroking his back. Pepper whimpered and squirmed, his tail wagging furiously. Then Susannah heard the unmistakable sound of liquid hitting the floor. Though most of it had missed her, her skirt bore a telltale stain.

"See, what did I tell you?" Mrs. Enke crowed with satisfaction.

"It's nothing that cannot be cleaned." Setting the puppy on the floor once more, Susannah reached for a towel, wiped the worst from her skirt, then mopped the puddle. "Let's take them outside," she said to Charles as she picked up Pepper again. The puppy furrowed his forehead, then began to lick her fingers. "You're sorry, aren't you?" Susannah crooned to the tiny ball of dark fur. "You were so excited, you didn't know what you were doing."

After she and Charles deposited the squirming dogs on the grass, he led her to a wrought-iron bench on the rear patio. Although from the front of the house the destruction was not evident, from here scorched bricks and boarded windows stood as mute testimony to the fire that had changed the Moreland family's lives. Susannah had heard the townspeople say that

93

Charles was fortunate that the house had not been completely destroyed, but she thought that might be a mixed blessing, for the empty shell remained as a daily reminder of all that had been lost. Susannah wondered how Charles managed to live with it. *He has no choice,* she reminded herself. As she herself had no choice but to live with the knowledge of her mother's illness.

Oblivious of her dark thoughts, the puppies gamboled on the lawn, chasing each other, then chasing their tails; barking in apparent anger, then nuzzling each other, their differences forgotten.

"Typical siblings. Fighting one moment, best friends the next." Charles chuckled as he watched the dogs. He was sitting so close that she could feel the warmth of his arm on hers, even though they did not touch.

"Is that what it was like in your family?" Susannah seized the subject, eager to think of something—anything—other than how good it felt to be sitting here with Charles watching two dogs' silly antics. "I always wanted a brother or sister." She had often wondered how different her life might have been if she'd had a sibling and hadn't been the only child of elderly parents.

Charles gave her a long appraising look. "Trust me; sisters are a mixed blessing . . . especially now." The pain that filled his eyes told Susannah he had demons that needed to be exorcised and nothing, not even the puppy who jumped on his legs, clambering for attention, would do that. It was obvious that Charles considered his familial responsibilities to be a burden. Susannah understood that; what was unclear was why the burden weighed so heavily on him.

She bent down to ruffle Salt's fur. The puppy licked her hand, then raced toward the ruined wing of the house. "It must have been difficult, losing both your parents at the same time and in such a tragic way."

For a moment, Charles stared into the distance. When his gaze met hers again, his expression was carefully shuttered. " 'Difficult' is one way to describe it." Though his tone was faintly mocking, Susannah sensed that he was straining to maintain his casual pose. "It's amazing how one day can change everything so completely."

Susannah nodded. Though at first she said nothing, Charles saw that her hands were tightly clenched, as if she were fighting some strong emotion. Didn't she know that he didn't want her pity? When she had offered a friendly ear, he had hesitated to accept, fearing that his account of the sabotage at the mill would rouse nothing more than pity. What he craved was understanding. Susannah had given him that. Even more, she had provided helpful suggestions. Although they joked about it, she did provide a different perspective—and it was a good one.

Talking about the mill was one thing. Though difficult, he could do that. His family was far different. The anger that he felt when he thought of the destruction at the mill paled in comparison to the fury that memories of his father's betrayal caused. He would not discuss his family with anyone, not even Susannah.

But Susannah had no such hesitation. When Pepper whined, she settled him in her lap, then turned back to Charles. "I have no experience with dramatic changes like yours," she said. "For me, they've been gradual. As you know, my parents were older than most." A rueful smile crossed her face. "Most people thought they were my grandparents. The truth is, they were old enough to be. As a child, I didn't realize how different my family was." She stroked Pepper's head and smiled when the pup licked her hand. "Now that I'm an adult, I suspect my arrival was a surprise and that my parents weren't sure how to handle the infant who disrupted their lives."

Though her words were light, Charles wondered if Susannah realized how much she had revealed. Not once had he thought that his parents considered him or the twins a disruption. He tried to imagine what Susannah's childhood must have been like. It appeared to have been vastly different from his own. Charles could scarcely remember life without the twins, and once they had been born, the house had been filled with tears and laughter, angry squabbling and whispered secrets. Though the three of them had experienced the normal heartaches and joys of growing up, through it all there had been the stabilizing force of his parents' love.

"Since my father died," Susannah continued, "my mother has changed. She's relying on me more and more, to the point where it sometimes seems that I'm the parent, and she's the child. And then . . ." Susannah stopped abruptly. She scooped Pepper up and placed him back on the ground. As the puppy scampered away to play with his brother, Susannah looked up. Though she had forced her lips to curve into a smile, her eyes shone with unshed tears. "I cannot imagine Dorothy living alone," she said softly.

And that, Charles suspected, would cause some strain in Susannah's marriage, for he could not picture Anthony wanting his mother-in-law to live with them. Had Susannah considered that, or was this another problem she had not shared with her fiancé like the fact that she wanted to visit Paris?

Paris!

"Wait right here," Charles said. "I have just what the doctor ordered."

Chapter Eight

"That does not look like fun."

Brad pointed to the stacks of papers that covered Charles's desk. In an effort to reduce costs, Charles had dismissed his bookkeeper and now handled all the mill's paperwork himself, from paying bills to scheduling production and sending invoices to customers.

"It isn't fun. I hesitate to tell you this, Brad," he said with a mocking look at his friend, "but I've discovered that life isn't always fun." Although the past week had been considerably more enjoyable than the preceding year. The reason for the change wasn't hard to find. Each day when he returned from the mill, Charles would find Susannah at his house, playing with the dogs. It was, she insisted, the least a neighbor could do, especially a neighbor who was as thrilled by the pictures of Paris as she was.

She had told Charles that, though she wanted to devour the book, she was savoring it, looking at one new picture each day. If he didn't object, she'd like to talk to him about the places the magical book revealed. Object? Far from it. Charles looked forward to Susannah's visits. He told himself it was because every-one benefited. The puppies were able to dissipate some of their youthful energy. Mrs. Enke was glad to have the creatures, as she persisted in referring to them, out of the house, and Charles . . . Charles was happy to spend a few minutes tussling with Salt and Pepper, listening to Susannah's laughter and watching the way her eyes sparkled with delight. The respite was only temporary, of course. But while he and Susannah romped with the dogs, Charles was able to push the worries that were so much a part of his life to the darkest recesses of his brain. And when Susannah smiled at him, nothing mattered other than keeping that sweet smile on her face.

It was ridiculous, of course, to place so much importance on her smile. After all, the reason Susannah came down the hill each day was to play with the dogs and speak of Paris, not to see him. Though she had never said it, Charles assumed that her visits were at least partially motivated by a need to put aside her worries about her mother, just as he sought to forget the mill's problems. Susannah came for respite. He would do well to remember that and to stop wishing that he were the attrac-tion.

"Let's change that." For a moment, Charles stared at Brad, not certain what he meant. It was only when Brad said, "Let's have some fun" that Charles remembered what he'd told his friend. *Stop it!* he admonished himself. *Stop daydreaming about Susannah.*

"What do you propose?" There had been a time when Charles had instigated the ABCs' amusements. Unfortunately, since he had returned to Hidden Falls, his energies had been focused on far less pleasant things.

"We need a celebration," Brad announced. "Just this morning my mother reminded me that we've been remiss. We need to introduce Susannah Deere to Hidden Falls society." As Brad looked down his freckled nose in a parody of the town's ma-trons, Charles chuckled. Though it was short of a full-fledged laugh, it was the most mirth this godforsaken office had seen in the past year.

"I thought we could invite Anthony and make it an engagement party." Brad paused expectantly. "So, what do you think?"

Charles rose from behind the desk and clapped his friend on the shoulder. "You surprised me," he said with feigned solemnity. "I was wrong. Your brain hasn't atrophied, after all, if it can come up with an idea like that."

As Brad shook his head, a ray of morning sunshine turned his auburn hair to flame. "Atrophied, huh? I suppose that's preferable to what you're doing to your brain. It appears to me that you're trying your best to destroy it with excessive work."

"Touché." It was a familiar refrain. From their first semester at school, Brad had been convinced that Charles studied too much. By some ironic twist of fate, it had been Anthony with his apparent allergy to studies who had become a professor, while Brad, who had excelled seemingly without opening a book, was a professional dilettante. "Seriously, Brad," Charles continued. "A party for Susannah and Anthony is a good idea. Anthony keeps postponing his visit to Hidden Falls. If the party is in his honor, he'll have to come." And Charles would be able to see the engaged couple together.

As the mill clock chimed, Brad rose and walked toward the door. "You're not still angry that Anthony's getting married, are you?"

"Not angry, just puzzled." About so many things. It was difficult enough to envision Anthony married; imagining him married to Susannah was proving impossible. Though Susannah wore his ring and wrote daily letters, Anthony seemed to be far less engaged. Gossip reported that Susannah rarely received mail, and Anthony appeared to be in no hurry to visit his fiancée. Charles couldn't understand that. If he were betrothed to Susannah . . . But he wasn't.

Despite his efforts to keep his errant thoughts at bay, images of Susannah continued to intrude throughout the day. While he was juggling accounts, trying to find an extra hundred dollars to satisfy one of his creditors, he closed his eyes and saw her sitting on the grass, holding Pepper in her lap while Salt licked her fingers. When he inspected the new toweling, running his hand along the smooth fabric, he remembered the softness of Susannah's hand and how her lightest touch had set his blood to boiling. And when he bit his lip in sheer frustration over the length of time it was taking to get the pulley belts repaired, his mind conjured the way Susannah's lips had felt pressed against his.

Charles slammed the desk drawer shut and swore fiercely. *Thou shalt not covet.* How many times had he recited those commandments? How many times had he sat in church while the minister threatened fire and brimstone to those who did not obey them? He'd been so certain that obedience would pose no problem. And now, here he was, breaking one of the commandments. For, while Susannah was not yet his neighbor's wife, she would soon be. Charles clenched his fists in anger as he realized that he was little better than his father. What a legacy John Moreland had left!

Though his work was far from finished, Charles could remain in the office no longer. He was outside the mill gates striding down the street when he recognized the man on the opposite side. It was that kind of a day. Other than the clear sky and light breeze, nothing was going well. At least Charles didn't have to worry about Matt speaking to him. The way they had parted the last time left no doubt that neither of them desired the other's company. But, to Charles's surprise, Matt crossed the street.

"It's no secret I don't like much you do," Matt said without preamble, matching his gait to Charles's. "But I have to admit that I was impressed by how quickly you got the looms operational again."

Charles's surprise turned to shock at Matt's unexpected praise. The man had never approved of anything Charles had done. Charles looked around. There was no one else on the street, no potential client that Matt was trying to impress. Why was he literally going out of his way to compliment Charles? Unless the compliment was false, designed to needle Charles by reminding him that not all the looms were back in operation.

"You wouldn't have had anything to do with the damage in the first place, would you?" he asked, unable to avoid voicing his suspicions.

Though his hat shaded his face and made it difficult to read his expression, Matt appeared genuinely startled by the accusation. He stopped, then took a step toward Charles. "Why would I do that? It would hurt innocent people at least as much as you. Unlike you, they can't afford it."

He couldn't afford it, either, but Charles knew that particular fact would not trouble Matt. He nodded and resumed walking. The sooner he was across the river, the better. "That's what Susannah said." Susannah, the champion of the underdog, the defender of puppies and his best friend's fiancée. Surely that last description should not be so painful.

"She's a wise woman." Matt narrowed his eyes as he spoke, and for one horrible second Charles feared that Matt had read his thoughts and knew how Susannah haunted them. Then he said, "Don't worry, Charles. When I make my move, you'll know, and there will be no doubt of my involvement."

It was little more than a veiled threat, a reiteration of the promise Matt had made before. Another man might have been annoyed. Charles was simply relieved that Matt was no longer discussing Susannah. "I'm shaking in my boots." He made no attempt to hide his sarcasm.

"I doubt that. Of course," Matt said with one of those lightning-fast changes of subject that had annoyed their schoolteachers, "if you were a superstitious man, you might shake in your boots over accepting an invitation to another party at the Harrods', especially considering what happened the last time."

There was no point in asking how Matt knew about the party Brad's mother was planning. News had always spread quickly in Hidden Falls, and somehow Matt had always managed to be one of the first to be informed. "There's no similarity other than the location," Charles insisted. They were almost at Bridge Street. Surely Matt had no business on Charles's side of the river.

"For everyone's sake, I hope you're right." Matt shuddered, and this time Charles saw what appeared to be genuine pain on his face. "I don't think I'll ever forget the sight of flames shooting through your windows."

Flames? Charles stopped short and put a restraining hand on Matt's arm. "What do you mean?" he demanded. "You weren't here. You were in Cambridge."

If he hadn't known better, Charles would have said that the expression he saw flit across Matt's eyes was sympathy.

"I see your father didn't tell you."

"Tell me what?"

"That I had an appointment with him that afternoon."

Charles tightened his grip on Matt's arm. "What possible reason could you have had for meeting John?" He would not refer to the man as his father. John Moreland had lost that title along with his son's respect the same afternoon that Matt claimed to have visited him.

"If he chose not to confide in you, far be it from me to contravene his wishes." Matt shook off Charles's hand and strode in the opposite direction.

He was bluffing. This was simply more of Matt's needling. But, though Charles told himself that Matt had been lying, that he hadn't been in Hidden Falls that day and that he hadn't visited John, there was no denying the fact that Matt's words had rung true.

Why had he come home that day?

"Who died?"

Susannah laid her fork on the table and closed her eyes for a second, trying to muster her strength. Was Dorothy going to inform her that Abraham Lincoln had been assassinated? It had been several days since she'd mentioned that, long enough that Susannah had hoped the memory lapse had been an isolated incident. Dorothy had seemed so much better that Susannah had not asked Charles about doctors. Now, as she looked at a dinner that had lost its appeal, she knew she'd been wrong. "No one passed away," she said quietly.

Her mother shook her head in disbelief. "Someone must have," she insisted, gesturing toward Susannah with her knife. "Why else would you be wearing those ugly clothes?"

Susannah glanced at her dress. It was one Dorothy had seen dozens of times, but today the sober color and plain style appeared to have disturbed her. "What would you like me to wear?" For weeks now, though Dorothy had worn only the clothing from her youth, she had made no comment about Susannah's dress. Susannah had no idea what had precipitated her mother's sudden interest.

Her face brightening, Dorothy said, "Why not that pretty apple-green frock Mother had made last week? You'd look fetching in that, Susannah."

Susannah's heart plummeted and the chicken and dumplings that had tasted so delicious a few minutes ago lodged like a lump in her stomach as she realized that Dorothy was once again in another time.

"Aren't these dumplings delicious?" Susannah asked in a deliberate attempt to divert Dorothy's attention. She took a bite and made a show of savoring it, though she might as well have been eating wallpaper paste for all the pleasure it gave her.

"Indeed they are," Dorothy agreed as she ladled another serving of chicken and dumplings onto her plate. "It was a stroke of genius hiring Moira O'Toole. Her meals are one of the best parts of being home again."

Susannah took a deep breath, exhaling slowly as she tried to slow the racing of her heart. The diversion had worked. Though for the moment Dorothy was back in the present, Susannah had no way of gauging how long that would last. The lucid periods, as she had come to call them, were being overshadowed by the times when Dorothy was clearly living in another period. And, oh, how that wrenched Susannah's heart. It was horrible, watching her mother's memory fade.

Even worse was the feeling of helplessness. Nothing Susannah did appeared to have any effect. She had tried to interest Dorothy in the plight of the poor on Forest Street, but Dorothy seemed oblivious of their suffering. When that had failed, Susannah had asked for her mother's assistance translating a particularly difficult German book. Once again Dorothy had displayed no interest in something that had formerly been an important part of her life. With each failure, Susannah's despair grew. She, who had been so successful helping others, was unable to do anything for the person she loved most.

As soon as dinner was finished and Dorothy was settled for her afternoon nap, Susannah raced to her studio. Other than playing with Charles's puppies, painting was one of the few ways she had of relieving her tension, for when she stood in front of her easel, she could forget everything except the scene she was creating.

An hour later, Susannah took a step back and stared at the canvas. Unlike her normal pastoral scenes, this one depicted a violent thunderstorm. The sky was dark and foreboding; streaks of lightning threatened the figures that cowered under a tree. With a wry smile, Susannah realized that she had not managed to escape her dark moods, after all. She had simply translated them into paint. And yet, the act of painting had been cathartic. For when she looked at the figures, though they fled the storm and feared it, the tilt of the woman's head told Susannah she would not be defeated. Nor would she.

"Susannah, my dear, John is here to see you." Dorothy stood at the foot of the stairs.

"You mean Charles."

"Of course; that's what I said. Now, hurry. He's been here a long time. You don't want to keep your gentleman caller waiting."

Quickly Susannah cleaned her brushes and shed her smock. "Charles is not my gentleman caller," she said as she descended the stairs toward her mother. "You know I'm going to marry Anthony." But even as she pronounced the words, Susannah felt as if she were speaking of someone else. Anthony and the promises they had made seemed so far away. Though she wrote to him daily, his letters were less frequent, and it sometimes seemed to Susannah that the distance between them grew with each passing day.

"Who's Anthony?" Dorothy asked.

Susannah bit back a sigh. It had been her parents who had introduced her to Anthony and her mother who had insisted he was the perfect husband for Susannah. Now, it appeared, Dorothy had forgotten him, at least for the moment.

When she reached the parlor, Susannah apologized for keeping Charles waiting. He shook his head, clearly perplexed. "I just arrived."

As Charles settled into the chair across from her, Susannah studied him. His hair was a bit too long, as if he hadn't found the time to visit the barber, and it was slightly tousled by the wind. There was nothing unusual about that, nothing that should make her fingers want to bury themselves in his hair and smooth it from his brow. Susannah clenched her fingers, then forced them to relax. It was unseemly to even think about touching Charles.

Oblivious of the direction her thoughts had taken, Charles smiled at Susannah and her mother. "I'm here as an ambassador," he said. "Or maybe as a scout, to give you some advance warning." He shrugged, and once again Susannah was struck by the way not even his well-cut jacket could hide the power of his muscles. "You'll be receiving an official invitation, but I wanted to tell you that Mrs. Harrod is planning a party in honor of both of you." With a nod toward Dorothy, he said, "She wants to welcome you back to town and to celebrate Susannah's engagement."

For a long moment, Dorothy was silent. Then she nodded slowly. "Louis and I rarely attend social affairs, but we'll certainly make an exception for this one."

Charles shot Susannah a quick look, his expression mirroring his confusion as he realized that Louis was Dorothy's husband who'd been deceased for more than two years. Susannah shook her head and mouthed the word *later*. "Please thank Mrs. Harrod and tell her we accept with pleasure."

The party might be good for Dorothy. Other than the day she had had tea with Henrietta Morgan and Leah Schwartz, she had had little contact with the other residents of Hidden Falls, refusing all of Susannah's suggestions that she go into town. Dorothy had enjoyed her tea party; perhaps she would also find the Harrods' celebration pleasant. Though that was uncertain, there would be one undeniable benefit to the evening: Anthony would be there. Susannah managed a smile. It would be so good to see him again! They would laugh and talk and dream together.

She heard a muffled yip. Charles shrugged, then said, "I have two frisky puppies outside, and my housekeeper has threatened to stop feeding the carousel carvers if I don't keep the dogs away from her." He shrugged again. "I thought I'd take them on a long walk . . . maybe to the falls." Charles gave Dorothy a warm smile, and his eyes twinkled with mischief when he looked at Susannah. "Could I convince either of you lovely ladies to accompany me?"

"You go, Susannah," Dorothy said without hesitation. "I need to prepare a lesson." And she left the room, heading for the library as if she were still teaching school. Susannah tried not to sigh as she pinned on her hat.

When they were outside, she pulled two rags from her pocket and engaged in a short game of tug-of-war with the dogs. As they yipped and pulled, trying to wrest the rags from her fingers, she started to smile. Even more than painting, the dogs' antics helped her.

"I'm sorry, Charles," she said as she rose and brushed dust from her knees. "Today is one of Dorothy's bad days. She's not always so confused."

He handed a leash to Susannah. "You offered me friendship and a sympathetic ear," he said as they walked away from the house, Salt and Pepper pulling the ropes as eagerly as if they were sled dogs in harness. "My sisters used to say that I was a good listener, so I'd like to return the gift."

"Maybe another time." She should talk to Charles and ask him about doctors, but that would have to wait until her emotions were less raw. Today Susannah wanted nothing more than to forget. Deliberately changing the subject, she said, "Believe it or not, I haven't seen the falls yet." Susannah had lost count of the number of times she had suggested she and her mother visit the falls. That idea had been rejected as soundly as the proposition that they ride the horses that Brian kept so well groomed.

"Then you're due for a pleasant surprise."

They walked through the woods, the dogs leading the way, taking occasional detours as Pepper chased a chipmunk and Salt insisted on investigating its hole. The sight of two puppies with oversize paws trying to crawl into a tiny chipmunk burrow made Susannah laugh.

"You should do that more often," Charles said. "You're beautiful when you laugh."

Susannah blushed. There was no reason that the compliment

should warm every inch of her from her scalp to her toes. She didn't react that way when Anthony told her she was beautiful. But Anthony was not here, and the expression in his friend's arresting cerulean eyes made her skin tingle.

"Are the falls truly hidden?" Susannah asked, once again seeking to change the subject to something more innocent. The trees here were dense, taller than the spruces Charles's grandfather had planted, and crowded with underbrush. It was obvious that Nature had created this forest.

"Hidden? That depends on your perspective." Charles emphasized the last word.

She laughed again. "You won't let me forget that, will you?"

"Not if it makes you laugh. I told you that I like it when you laugh."

And, though it seemed vaguely disloyal to Anthony, Susannah liked it when Charles gave her one of those admiring looks that seemed to last an eternity at the same time that they ended far too quickly.

The sound of rushing water was louder, telling Susannah that the falls must be close. She quickened her pace as they followed the well-marked path. In most places it was wide enough for two, and so she and Charles walked side by side, following the puppies, whose enthusiasm did not appear to have dwindled despite the distance they'd come. The water was a torrent now, but though Susannah peered through the foliage, she saw no sign of the falls.

Afterward she blamed herself for being preoccupied with sighting the falls. She wasn't sure how it occurred, but before she knew what was happening, Pepper had wound his leash around her legs, and she started to tumble forward. An instant later, she was in Charles's arms, pressed against his chest.

She stood for a long moment, trying to still the pounding of her heart. That was surely the result of nearly tripping. It had nothing to do with the warmth of Charles's arms or the sweet scent of his breath as it fanned her cheek. The dogs raced ahead, reveling in their newfound freedom, the leashes trailing behind them. And still neither Susannah nor Charles moved.

They stood, their gazes locked, their hearts beating in unison.

He smiled. She smiled. His hand rose and cupped her cheek. She moved closer, glorying in the slightly rough texture of his fingertips. And when he traced the contours of her face, she sighed with pleasure. It was only a moment, but for that moment, Susannah felt safe and cherished.

All too soon the puppies returned. When they nipped at her feet, Susannah pulled away from Charles, suddenly conscious that they were in a public place and that it was more than unseemly for her to be in Charles's arms. It was wrong. But, oh, how wonderful it felt!

"Be careful. The path is slippery through here." There was a catch in Charles's voice, as if he'd been running.

Susannah did not trust herself to speak. Not yet. She needed to slow the racing of her heart before she tried to form a word. And to do that, she needed to put distance between her and Charles. She should move so that there was at least a foot between them. But when he took her hand in his to guide her along the trail, Susannah did not protest. The path was slick, she rationalized, and her legs felt oddly unstable. It would not do to fall and wrench an ankle.

They walked in silence for another few minutes, the sound of falling water growing louder with each step. Susannah wondered if he was remembering, as she was, the day they had met and the kiss they'd shared. Perhaps he had forgotten that day. It would be best if he had, if Susannah were the only one whose dreams were haunted by that stolen embrace. But something about the way Charles had looked at her made Susannah believe that he, too, recalled that day and that hers were not the only troubled dreams.

Charles stopped. "We're at the top of the falls," he said.

"I don't see it." Though she strained to look through the dense stand of evergreens, Susannah could see no sign of the river.

"That's why it's called Hidden Falls." Charles tightened the grip on her hand, and she felt a surge of warmth course through her veins. "It's only visible lower down."

The path descended sharply now, the mist from the falls turning the hard-packed dirt to mud. As the dogs led the way, they squealed in delight when they lost their footing and slid. Susannah couldn't help smiling at the thought of Mrs. Enke's reaction to having such filthy creatures in the kitchen.

And then the trees parted, and Susannah saw the falls. Though narrower than she would have imagined, considering the roar they generated, they were beautiful, tumbling straight over an embankment of perhaps twenty feet, then twisting to the right and falling again.

"It's magnificent!" She turned and smiled at Charles. Tiny lines crinkled the corners of his eyes as he smiled, but it was the fire she saw in those eyes that made Susannah catch her breath. He hadn't forgotten that first day. She could see the memory reflected in his expression along with something more, something even stronger. As Charles's lips parted, Susannah swayed, drawn to him like iron filings to a magnet. The roar of the falls was nothing compared to the roar of blood in her ears as her own lips parted and she raised her face for his kiss. His mouth was an inch from hers. She moved. He moved. And then Pepper hurled himself at Charles, barking frantically.

The spell was broken. The falls were nothing more than a pretty cascade of water. She and Charles were nothing more than neighbors taking a walk together. That was the way it should be. It was Anthony she was going to marry. It was Anthony she should be kissing. Only Anthony. But somehow the day had lost its sparkle.

By the time they reached Susannah's house, even the dogs were tired, and she and Charles had resorted to carrying them. Susannah looked down at her mud-stained dress. At least the fabric was serviceable, and the dark color helped camouflage the damage. Charles's white shirt had not fared as well.

She handed Pepper to him with a wry smile. He would have his hands full—literally—getting both dogs back to Fairlawn.

"I can't get much—"

Before Charles could finish his sentence, Megan flung the door open and cried, "Thank the Lord you're here!"

Susannah's heart began to pound with fear. "What's wrong?" Megan's normally pale complexion was deathly white, and her cap was askew, as if she'd run her hands through her hair.

"It's your mam. She's gone."

Susannah tried not to panic. This was one of the things the doctor had told her might happen, that Dorothy might begin to wander. He had also said she would probably return home of her own accord. But Susannah was unable to wait. She needed to find Dorothy and know that she was safe.

"She didn't go to the falls, or we would have seen her."

Charles nodded. "Perhaps she's visiting Mrs. Harrod."

That was possible. Dorothy might want to accept the invitation in person. "I'll take the buggy." And tomorrow, Susannah resolved, she would see about joining the telephone line. Though Dorothy had opposed what she called a newfangled notion, if she left again it would make it easier to find her.

"I'll check the woods on foot." Charles gave Susannah a reassuring look. "She'll be fine."

Susannah wished she were so certain. Despite everything the doctor had said, her mind continued to conjure images of Dorothy slipping on a steep path or falling into the river. Susannah climbed into the carriage. An hour later she returned, her face grim. Dorothy had not visited the Harrods, and no one in town had seen her. Susannah's only hope was that Charles had found her.

As she drove the buggy toward the house, she saw Charles in the open doorway. He was back! But where was Dorothy? Megan stood at Charles's side, her hand on his arm, her face tilted up toward his as if she were about to be kissed. A shaft of pure fury shot through Susannah. How dare she! Dorothy was lost somewhere, and all Megan could do was flirt.

Susannah leapt from the buggy and ran to the door. "Where is she?"

Before Charles could speak, Megan said, "Charles found her." Though Megan gave Susannah a swift glance, her eyes returned to Charles, and she smiled again.

Charles's expression was serious as he faced Susannah. "She had come down the hill and appeared to be looking for the gazebo."

"Where is she now?"

It was Megan who answered. "Me mam took her to her room to rest."

Susannah would check on Dorothy in a moment. First she needed to thank Charles.

"I already thanked him," Megan said, as if she could read Susannah's thoughts. "Properly," she added and stared at his lips.

Susannah could feel the flush color her cheeks. It was absurd. She didn't care whether Charles kissed Megan. Of course she didn't. After all, she would soon marry Anthony.

But that night Susannah dreamt of Charles. He stood in the doorway to the gazebo, his arms wrapped tenderly around a woman, his head bent toward her. In the moonlight, Susannah saw the woman turn ever so slightly.

No! she cried. *Not Megan!*

And then she woke.

Chapter Nine

Susannah couldn't help smiling. Today was the day, and what a day it was! The sun was shining, and the spring flowers seem to have burst into bloom almost overnight, as if they too were celebrating the fact that in just a few hours Anthony would be here. Humming softly, she slid open the pocket door to the dining room. Dorothy was already seated at the table, buttering her breakfast toast.

"Are you sure I can't convince you to go with me?" Susannah asked as she refilled her mother's coffee cup. "It's a lovely day for a ride, and you know you'd enjoy seeing Anthony." Susannah spooned some of Moira O'Toole's fluffy scrambled eggs onto her plate and took her seat across from Dorothy.

Dorothy sipped her coffee, then shook her head. "Why don't you bring him here for tea? Norma will make scones."

"Moira."

"Of course." Dorothy's face was intent with concentration as she placed her cup carefully on the saucer, almost as if it were the first time she had used a cup and saucer. When the cup was settled, its handle precisely aligned, she looked up and smiled.

"I'm glad to see you're wearing a pretty frock today. It's important when you have a gentleman caller."

Though the term was old-fashioned, Susannah couldn't dispute the fact that—unlike Charles—Anthony was her gentleman caller. When Anthony had heard about the party the Harrods were planning, his letters had changed. They became more frequent and brimmed with enthusiasm about his visit to Hidden Falls. He had even arranged to come two days before the party, a fact that filled Susannah's heart with joy.

It would be so wonderful to see Anthony again! They would have time to talk and to plan their future. They would take long walks; perhaps he would help her with the garden she was attempting to restore; most of all, they would be together, and that would break down the barriers that distance seemed to have built between them. Once he was here, those crazy feelings she had experienced when she was with Charles would disappear. They were nothing more than aberrations, caused by all the changes she had gone through. It was like the dizziness that was the inevitable result of twirling too long. Once she saw Anthony again, Susannah would regain her equilibrium. She was certain of it.

"Top of the morning to you." Brian O'Toole doffed his cap as she entered the stable. "Sure and that lad of yours is going to be glad when he sees you."

Susannah smiled, not simply at the compliment Brian paid her but also at the fact that he was sober. Since the day she had spoken with Moira and Brian, explaining the consequences if Brian endangered the horses again, Brian had not touched a drop of whiskey. "He's a good man," Moira had insisted, "and he can be strong when needs must." Whether it was necessity or Moira's watchful eye, Susannah did not care. What mattered was that Brian had kept his promise. Truly, it was a wonderful day. Susannah smiled again as Brian helped her into the carriage. Today she would drive it, for she wanted to be alone with Anthony on the return trip.

When she crossed the bridge and descended to hitch the horses in front of the train station, Susannah realized that her hands were trembling with excitement. Soon! Anthony would be here soon. The distant whistle set her pulse to pounding, and she fisted her hands to still their shaking. Two or three families crowded onto the platform and stared at the approaching train. As it squealed to a stop, Susannah hurried forward, looking for Anthony.

There he was!

"Anthony!" she called as he descended the iron stairs. "This way."

He stared for a moment, then gripped his bag and walked toward her. "Susannah?" His gray eyes widened. "I almost didn't recognize you," he said when he reached her side. "You look different."

The family groups surrounded the young couple who had descended before Anthony. Were they newlyweds? she wondered. Susannah gave Anthony another smile. Soon they would be the ones returning from their honeymoon.

"If I look different," she said, "it's probably the dress." Though Dorothy, Megan and even Brian had assured her that the apple green was flattering, after a lifetime of navy, dark green and brown, Susannah still felt self-conscious wearing lighter colors. It was only because Dorothy had insisted that she had asked Hidden Falls' dressmaker to make some fashionable clothing for her.

Anthony stopped, his eyes assessing her from the crown of her hat to her boot toes. "It's not the clothes," he said at last. "There's something else. I can't pinpoint it, but you're more beautiful than I remembered."

Susannah laughed. "You may think I've changed, but it's plain to see you have not. You're still a silver-tongued flatterer." In a world where so much had altered, it was reassuring that Anthony was the same. The coolness she had thought she'd detected in his letters was surely only her imagination.

Anthony helped her into the carriage, then tossed his bag into the back. When he was seated next to her, Susannah flicked the reins. "I'd give you a tour of the town," she said, deliberately turning the horses left to cross the bridge, "but you probably know Hidden Falls at least as well as I do."

The way Anthony stared at her flooded Susannah's cheeks

114

with color. "I could ride all day with you, sweet lady, but I would like to see the carousel. I still find it difficult to believe that Charles is building one."

Susannah gave Anthony a sidelong glance as she felt the first twinges of discomfort. Though she had known him for more than three years, she had never heard that light, bantering tone in his voice, and he had never called her "sweet lady." Was she wrong in thinking that he had remained constant when everything else had shifted around her?

"The carousel promises to be magnificent," she said in a voice that somehow managed not to betray her uncertainty. "I've never seen anything like the way Rob can turn an ordinary piece of wood into something almost magical."

Anthony leaned back against the seat. "It sounds as though I have cause to be jealous. How can a simple history professor compete with a sculptor?"

Unsure whether he was serious or sarcastic, Susannah decided not to ask. Instead, she said mildly, "You have absolutely no reason to be jealous of Rob."

"Of course not." Anthony laid a hand on top of hers. "Surely you realize I was only joking. I know you're an honorable woman. I wouldn't have asked you to marry me otherwise. You're my sensible Susannah," he added. "You'll keep me grounded."

Sensible Susannah bit the inside of her lip, trying not to care that he hadn't said he was marrying her because he loved her. Of course he loved her, just as she loved him. It was foolish to think otherwise. Still, Susannah was thankful that they were approaching the Moreland stable and could end this conversation that had taken such a disturbing turn.

"Susannah didn't exaggerate," Anthony said a few minutes later when he'd been introduced to the three carvers and had inspected both the sketches and the works in progress. He ran his hand over Rob's half-carved horse's head and nodded approvingly at him. "Your work is magnificent." It was surely Susannah's imagination that the compliment sounded more sincere than the ones he'd paid her.

Rob shifted the gouge into his left hand and reached for a

mallet. "We've had your fiancée for inspiration. She stops in almost every day to encourage us."

"Susannah as a patron of the arts?" Anthony raised one brow. "What other surprises do you have in store for me?"

Before Susannah could reply, the half door opened and Charles entered the workshop, bringing with him the scent that Susannah had learned was dye. Though the smell of sawdust was pungent, the mill's dye overpowered it. Charles tipped his hat to Susannah, then clapped Anthony on the back. "God, it's good to see you again!"

As Anthony pumped his friend's hand, a smile of pure pleasure unlike any Susannah had ever seen crossed his face. "Where's Brad?" he demanded. "I thought you two would have met the train just like old times. I can't tell you how much I've looked forward to the ABCs being together again for a few days."

Susannah tried not to let her dismay show. Of course Anthony wanted to see his friends. Only a petty woman would wish he'd shown the same enthusiasm for her. Anthony had never been one for public displays of affection, she reminded herself.

Though Susannah remained silent, trying to quell her rising discomfort, Charles did not. "What's wrong with you, old man? You had the best welcoming committee Hidden Falls has to offer." As if he were aware of the harshness of his tone, Charles gave Rob and his assistants a wry grin. "I don't know about you, but I'd rather look at Susannah than Anthony and Brad."

As the carvers chuckled, Charles continued, this time addressing Anthony. "Brad said he'll meet us tonight. It'll be like old times."

Mark and Luke resumed their carving. They were infinitely better craftsmen than Susannah would ever be, but their skills did not approach Rob's. That was, they explained, why although they would carve the bodies and legs, Rob remained the head man, the one who created the most important part of the horses.

"One thing won't be like old times." Anthony continued to address Charles, almost as if he'd forgotten Susannah's presence. He looked around the former stable, his gaze moving from one corner to another. "Rob's horses will be magnificent when they're complete, but I miss the real ones. I'd been looking forward to a ride."

Though he tried to mask the spasm of pain that crossed his face, Susannah saw that Anthony's words had struck a sensitive nerve in Charles, and she wondered why his friend had said anything. Surely Anthony knew that Charles had sold his horses long before he converted the stable into a workshop for the carvers. Susannah tried not to frown. The Anthony she had known would not have reminded a friend of something that was obviously painful. "We have two horses that would benefit from more exercise," she said quickly. "Perhaps you'd like to ride one of them."

For the first time since Charles's arrival, Anthony looked at her, his gray eyes warm with approval.

"You and Susannah can explore the area together." Though Charles spoke to Anthony, he flashed Susannah a quick smile, as if to remind her that she had admitted she wished she'd had more time to see her new home.

Anthony nodded his agreement. It was what she wanted, the opportunity to spend time with him. Why, then, did it disturb Susannah that it was Charles who had suggested it and that Anthony had not said, "Only if you ride with me"?

Rob turned toward Susannah. "If you're serious about the horses needing exercise, I'd like to ride them. As your friend pointed out, my steeds may be beautiful, but it's more fun to ride a real one."

"You'd be doing me a favor." Susannah looked at Rob's two assistants. "You're welcome to ride, too."

Mark and Luke grinned with pleasure. Charles smiled. Anthony gave the assistant carvers a look that could only be called supercilious. "That's our Susannah—egalitarian to a fault."

Susannah stared, astonished. In all the time she'd known Anthony, he had never been so rude. What was wrong?

What was wrong with the man? In all the years he'd known Anthony, Charles had never seen such inexplicable behavior. Anthony had always been the predictable one of the ABCs. Charles cast a sidelong glance at the man who was climbing the hill next to him. It had started in the carousel workshop. Charles couldn't understand why Anthony had stared at the wooden horses, not Susannah. Why would a red-blooded man who had been separated from his fiancée for over a month prefer to look at half-carved carousel horses instead of the beautiful woman who would soon be his wife?

And this. You'd think he would want to spend some time alone with Susannah. If so, why had he insisted on Charles's accompanying him to tea at Pleasant Hill? If he'd been Anthony, he would have developed an intense interest in the rose garden or something—anything—that would give him an opportunity to be alone with Susannah. Charles's presence changed the dynamics; now it would be difficult to find a reason for a romantic rendezvous. And then there was the fact that the invitation had not included Charles. He would be a gate crasher.

"Mrs. Deere won't mind," Anthony said, as if he could read Charles's mind. "She's used to having students in her home."

"This is different. She's not teaching here. She might not appreciate an unexpected guest." There were other differences, too. Charles wondered whether Anthony had noticed Dorothy Deere's increasing confusion when she had still lived in Boston or whether it had begun after the return to Hidden Falls.

"I still don't think this is a good idea," Charles said. It was not too late for him to turn around.

Anthony slashed the underbrush with his walking stick. "All right," he said. "I'll admit it. I don't want to face the dragon alone."

"The dragon?"

"Susannah's mother. You must have seen that disapproving stare of hers and the way it can make a man feel like he's six years old again."

Charles shook his head. "I can't say that I have. She's always been cordial to me." Charles wouldn't mention the times that she had mistaken him for his father. There were some things that were best forgotten.

"We must be talking about a different woman." Anthony slashed at the bushes again. "Enough about her. Where did you discover Rob Ludlow?"

Though Charles's voice was even as he explained his search for a carousel carver, he could not dismiss his uneasiness. If Anthony disliked Susannah's mother—and his comments seemed to indicate that he did—how would that affect their marriage? Susannah was clearly devoted to Dorothy and seemed to have accepted the fact that her mother would have to live with her for the rest of her life. If Anthony didn't agree or was grudging in his acquiescence, Charles wondered what strains that would place on their marriage.

"I have to confess that curiosity about the carousel is the reason I came to Hidden Falls," Anthony said when Charles finished his explanation. "That and the opportunity to see you and Brad again."

Charles's disquiet grew as he realized that Anthony had not mentioned Susannah. Surely she had been the primary reason Anthony had come.

"What about your engagement party?"

Anthony looked nonplussed. "Oh . . . of course." He stared at the white frame house as if he'd never seen it. Perhaps he had not. Since Pleasant Hill had been vacant on his previous trips to Hidden Falls, there would have been no reason to come this far down River Road.

Anthony shrugged, then said, "I can't wait to see Anne's face when she sees the carousel. It's the perfect gift for her."

"I hope so." They were too close to the house for him to confront Anthony, to ask why he seemed unwilling to even mention his future bride. "Jane's latest letter said that Anne's treatment is more painful than the doctors had led her to expect, and she cries a lot."

Frowning, Anthony kicked a stone. "I can't imagine sunny Anne crying."

Charles could. The first few months after the fire, the pain had been so severe that though he knew she tried, Anne could not help screaming. The memory of his sister's anguish was one of the things that haunted Charles.

"Jane says nothing she does seems to help. To be honest, Anthony, I'm worried about both of them. Anne's the one who suffered the most, but this year has been difficult for Jane, too. She's not used to having to be the strong one."

"Damn! I wish I could help Anne. If I thought it would accomplish anything, I'd go to Europe." Anthony's vehemence surprised Charles. It wasn't like his friend to react so strongly. But then, many things Anthony had said and done today were not like the Anthony Charles used to know.

"Anne doesn't want to see any of us until the treatments are done," he explained as they climbed the steps to Susannah's house.

"I understand that, but—damn it all—she deserves better."

"On that, my friend, we are in complete agreement," Charles said as he knocked on the Deeres' front door.

Unlike the times when Charles had been obliged to wait on the porch, today Megan opened the door so quickly that Charles wondered if she'd been standing in the foyer, waiting for their arrival. She ushered them inside, giving Anthony a sidelong glance and flashing a sultry smile at Charles. As she led the way to the parlor, Anthony gave her swaying hips an admiring look. "That's a mighty fine example of feminine pulchritude."

Charles raised a brow. "You're an engaged man."

"I still have eyes. My father always said there was no harm in looking."

And Charles's father had done considerably more than look. But he would not think about John Moreland or his sins. Hadn't he accepted that he could not change the past? All he could do was ensure that he did not make the same mistakes.

Charles smiled as they entered the parlor. Dorothy and Susannah rose to greet them, their skirts making a soft swishing sound, their perfume filling the air with a scent that was sweeter than his mother's roses in June. For the briefest of moments, Susannah's eyes met his, and Charles's smile broadened. Anthony might find Megan appealing, but only a blind man would deny that Susannah was the most beautiful woman in Hidden Falls, perhaps in all of New York State. And that beautiful woman was going to marry Anthony, Charles reminded himself as he turned toward Susannah's mother.

Dorothy extended her hand to Charles. "It's so nice to see you again, John. Who is your friend?"

If Anthony noticed the slip, he gave no sign, perhaps because he was still staring at Megan. It was Susannah who stepped forward. "Good afternoon, Charles," she said with a faint emphasis on his name. As her mother nodded, she continued, "Dorothy, you remember Anthony, don't you?"

For the briefest of moments, Dorothy's face clouded. Then she said, "Anthony. Of course. We met . . ."

When her voice trailed off, Susannah completed the sentence. "Anthony is the man I'm going to marry."

"A wedding. Of course." Apparently reassured, Dorothy took a seat on the long sofa and gestured to Anthony to sit beside her. "When did you say the wedding would be, young man?"

Anthony blinked in surprise. "Actually, ma'am, we haven't selected a date yet. That's one of the reasons I came to Hidden Falls, to discuss precisely that subject with your daughter." He sounded as formal as if he were delivering a lecture. Surely a man should show a bit more enthusiasm for his own marriage. It was difficult to reconcile this sober man with Charles's fun-loving friend.

"I always thought June was the best month for a wedding," Anthony's future mother-in-law said. "That's when Louis and I married."

"Anthony and I had been considering August," Susannah interjected.

Charles studied his boots, cursing the moment he had agreed to accompany Anthony. The last thing he wanted was to help plan Susannah Deere's wedding.

"June might also be nice, especially if you would prefer that," Anthony said in that oddly formal voice. He directed his smile toward Dorothy. "My grandmother always said the secret to a good marriage was to abide by the mother of the bride's wishes."

Hogwash. Though the sentiment made Dorothy glow with pleasure, Charles knew it was totally false. Since both of Anthony's grandmothers had died before he had been born, neither of them could have given him that advice. Besides, why would a man who had described her as a dragon want to please Dorothy?

Susannah looked skeptical. "I don't see how we could plan a wedding so quickly. Even late June would give us less than two months."

"Perhaps June of next year would be a better time," Anthony said smoothly.

Charles stared at his friend. If the man was willing to wait that long to make Susannah his bride, he was crazy. Totally, certifiably crazy.

Susannah took a deep breath, savoring the scents of the night air. Dorothy was safely asleep and she . . . she needed to think. The day had not unfolded the way she had anticipated. Although the weather had been perfect and should have filled her heart with gladness, Susannah's thoughts were troubled.

She walked quickly down the long drive, hoping that the simple action of putting one foot in front of the other would help clear her thoughts as it did so often. Something was wrong. Perhaps she was overreacting. Perhaps tomorrow would be better. But today reminded her of the day she had played a sonata on Lucinda's badly out of tune piano. Although she had pressed the correct keys, the music had been discordant, jarring her ear. Lucinda, who had cheerfully admitted she was tone deaf, had applauded when Susannah played the final chords, just as Dorothy had been brimming with excitement at supper, announcing that she thought Anthony was a fine man for Susannah to marry. But Susannah had known that the music was wrong, just as she had realized that something was bothering Anthony.

Perhaps it was fatigue from the journey. Perhaps it was eagerness to spend the evening with his friends. Either of those could have been the reason Anthony seemed so different today. Susannah wanted to believe that. Oh, how she did, for the alternative was almost unthinkable. She did not want to believe that the time that she and Anthony had spent apart had changed them, that they had grown in different directions. Surely that had not happened. Susannah wasn't sure. All she knew was that the Anthony she had met at the train station today did not seem like the man she had left in Boston. And that was not a comforting thought.

When she reached the road, she turned right, heading away from the other houses. Though it was unlikely anyone would be out, she was taking no chances. Tonight she wanted to be alone with her thoughts.

"Susannah!"

She turned, startled by the sound of Charles's voice. Her momentary annoyance that her solitude had been disturbed faded, replaced by a question. "Where are Anthony and Brad? I thought you three were spending the evening together." That was part of what had disturbed her, the fact that Anthony had been more anxious to spend the evening with his college friends than with her. But the evening, it appeared, had been cut short.

In the moonlight, she saw Charles shrug. "I'm a working man, and the mill opens mighty early."

Though the explanation begged the question of why, if he needed sleep, he was headed in the opposite direction of his house, something in his expression kept Susannah from asking. Instead she said, "It's a beautiful night for a walk." A crescent moon had risen, and the sky was dotted with stars.

Charles pointed toward the heavens. "Mother used to call that a lover's moon. I never knew why."

"What a lovely image!" Susannah felt as if a weight had dropped from her shoulders. It was nothing Charles had said, but somehow the fact that he was here, walking by her side, had managed to chase the cobwebs from her head. For the first time since Anthony had stepped off the train, she felt as if the world were once more spinning on the right axis.

She took a deep breath. "Lover's moon. That's the perfect title for the painting I just started. I'll put the moon in the corner, so it's beaming down on the couple, and maybe I'll have some nocturnal animals and . . ." She broke off, embarrassed. "I'm sorry. I was babbling."

"Don't apologize. I was enjoying listening to your creative process." He sounded sincere. "Will you show me some of your paintings?"

Her steps slowed. "I'm not sure." No one other than Dorothy

had seen her work, and then only by accident. It was one thing to paint, quite another to show her efforts to someone. It would be like revealing her soul, and Susannah wasn't certain she would ever be ready to do that.

Charles nodded, as if he understood her reluctance. "I can't—and I won't—insist, but I would be honored if you would let me see your paintings."

There was something deeply humble about his words, and that humility touched Susannah more than she had dreamt possible.

"Perhaps," she said. "Perhaps."

Chapter Ten

"Come back here, you scamp!" Susannah was indulging in her favorite pastime of playing with the dogs, but today Pepper was being friskier than usual. It amazed her how different the two puppies were. Though they were littermates, their personalities were as varied as their coloring. While Pepper was the smaller of the two, he made up for his size in feistiness and was normally the one who instigated rough-and-tumble play. Today he had apparently decided that chasing squirrels was more exciting than tussling with Salt. When his quarry eluded him by climbing a tree, Pepper began yipping as he tried to scramble up the trunk after the squirrel. Salt sat next to Susannah, studiously ignoring his brother's antics as he chewed on a rubber ball.

"Pepper!" Susannah forced a stern tone into her voice, though it was admittedly difficult to be angry at the puppies. "Come back!" While the black dog continued to feign deafness, Salt jumped up and raced toward the house, a barking ball of fur.

Susannah turned, her eyes widening in surprise. The only thing that would excite Salt this much was Charles's arrival, but he wasn't due home for another hour. For the briefest of moments, Susannah considered that the reason Charles had left the mill early was that Anthony was with him. One look at Charles told her that was not the case. Though he bent down to ruffle the puppy's fur the way he did each evening, his movements seemed slow and deliberate, as if something had leached his energy, and he barely seemed to register her presence.

More than a little concerned, Susannah rose and hurried toward him. Though a stiff breeze heralded the approach of a storm, it paled next to the tumult she saw on Charles's face. His brow was furrowed, and his eyes radiated pain. "What's wrong?" she demanded. Charles had been visibly distressed the day the pulley belts had been cut, but that seemed insignificant compared to this.

He shuddered. "There was an accident at the mill." The words came out in a staccato rhythm, as if he had to force them past his lips. "A young girl lost two fingers changing a bobbin."

Involuntarily Susannah glanced at her hands. "Oh, Charles. How awful!" Susannah knew that accidents were a fact of life at textile mills, but since she had come to Hidden Falls, this was the first that had involved personal injury.

"Was something wrong with the equipment?" She didn't want to use the word *sabotage*.

Charles shook his head. "It appeared to have been simple carelessness. The mill hand next to her said she was daydreaming."

As Charles shuddered again, Pepper scampered to his side, jumping to gain his attention. When Charles did not immediately pat his back, the dog redoubled his efforts. Susannah bent down and scooped him into her arms to quiet him, but Pepper continued to yip and strain toward Charles. Bowing to the inevitable, Charles took the dog, recoiling only slightly when Pepper began to lick his face.

"He wants to comfort you," Susannah said, rubbing Salt's belly so that he would not feel neglected.

Pain clouded those cerulean eyes that, try though she might, Susannah had been unable to banish from her dreams.

"I wish it were that easy." Charles stroked the puppy's head as he continued, "The girl came to Hidden Falls to earn money

126

for her wedding. Now there may be no wedding."

"Why ever not?" Susannah tossed Salt's ball, then watched as Pepper squirmed to be set down so that he could chase it, apparently realizing that he had provided Charles with all the solace he could.

"I heard her young man say he wouldn't marry a cripple."

Susannah blanched. How could any man be so cruel? If she had been the one injured, Anthony would still want to marry her. Wouldn't he? "The man was probably in shock," she told Charles. "Surely he didn't mean it."

In the distance, thunder rumbled. Charles frowned. "I think he did." Charles was silent for a moment, his expression bleaker than Susannah had ever seen it. When he spoke again, his voice reflected the pain she'd seen in his eyes. "Do you have any idea how it feels to know that my mill may have ruined this girl's life?" Charles closed his eyes, as if trying to block the painful images.

"It was an accident." Susannah spoke as calmly as she could. Somehow she had to find the words to comfort him. "You know you run one of the safest mills in the country."

"Not safe enough." He laughed bitterly. "I know this may sound selfish, but the worst part of what happened today is that it made me fear that my sister will never marry."

"Anne?"

Charles's eyes were so filled with pain that Susannah's fingers ached to smooth the lines between them. "Yes, Anne. The doctors have warned us that she'll never regain her beauty. All they can do is hide the worst of the scarring." As the dogs barked, demanding attention, Charles tossed a stick as far as he could. "Don't you see, Susannah?" he asked when Salt and Pepper had raced toward the woods. "When I heard that young man, I couldn't stop thinking of Anne. I'm afraid men will see her face and turn away in revulsion."

"Surely not. All men aren't that shallow." Susannah could not believe that Charles—or Anthony, for that matter—would turn away from the woman he loved because of a physical infirmity.

"Why not? A scarred face is more serious than missing fingers." Charles clenched his fists, then slowly released them.

"Anne has always wanted children—lots of them. I can't bear the thought that she may never have them, and it'll be my fault."

Blood drained from Susannah's face. Though she had not thought that Charles could shock her further, he had. "What do you mean? You didn't start the fire."

The thunder was closer now, the air pregnant with rain and the tension that preceded a violent storm. Charles's expression was as dark as the thunderclouds. "I may not have set the fire," he said, "but I was responsible, just the same."

Susannah gasped, horrified by his words and by the look she saw in his eyes. Charles was a man facing unbearable sorrow. His reaction to the young mill hand's injury told Susannah that, though he could not have prevented the accident, Charles shouldered the burden. She understood why he assumed responsibility for the mill and everything that happened there. It *was* his mill. But why, oh why, did he believe he was to blame for the fire?

"Why?" When Susannah took a step toward Charles, compelled by the same need to comfort that had led the puppy to lick his face, he held up a cautioning hand. "Don't ask anything more, Susannah. There are some things you're better off not knowing."

"But . . ."

He shook his head. "You once offered me friendship. If you want to be a true friend, you'll forget everything you just heard."

Charles's lips were pressed together, and she knew he regretted having said as much as he had. What he was asking was impossible. She could not forget. But she would also do nothing to deepen his pain. "All right," she lied.

As the sky darkened and the rain approached, Susannah hurried home. The storm would pass in a few hours, leaving in its aftermath fresh, clean air. Unfortunately, the storm Charles's words had unleashed would not subside so quickly. When morning broke, the question would still remain: What had happened the night of the fire that made Charles believe he was responsible?

*   *   *

"I'll be the envy of everyone at the ball," Anthony said as he helped Dorothy into the carriage. Though Brad Harrod had offered to pick them up in his automobile, Susannah had believed Dorothy would be more comfortable in a horse-drawn carriage. "No one else will have two beautiful women on his arm," Anthony continued.

Susannah watched her mother smile with pleasure as she arranged her skirts. "Oh, Anthony, you're such a flatterer," Dorothy said with a flick of her fan. Susannah wasn't certain whether it was the smile or the new gown that made her look younger, but there was no denying the fact that her mother was glowing tonight. Ever since she had received the Harrods' invitation, Dorothy had seemed less forgetful. She had spent days planning her gown and helping Susannah choose hers, then had searched through the trunks in the attic, looking for the perfect accessories. It was, Susannah hoped, a sign that the doctor was wrong. Perhaps Dorothy did not have brain fever. Perhaps rejoining Hidden Falls society was the tonic she needed.

Anthony shook his head. "It's not flattery when it's true." Though she was seated and Susannah still stood on the ground waiting for him, Anthony did not release Dorothy's hand. "Will you grant me the honor of the first dance?"

Susannah blinked in surprise. Tonight's celebration was in honor of their engagement. Surely she and Anthony should have shared the first dance. Wasn't that traditional? She shook herself mentally. It was absurd to be annoyed by such a trivial thing. What was important was that Dorothy was pleased by Anthony's gesture.

It was the perfect night for a party. The previous day's storm had ended; the puddles had even dried; and tonight the sky was clear, spangled with stars and what Charles had called a lover's moon. Charles. Somehow she would have to pretend that she had not lain awake for most of the night, disturbed not by the rain lashing against her windows but by the memory of Charles's face when he'd said, "I was responsible."

She forced her lips into a smile. An hour later, Susannah wondered whether her face would crack from that smile. She and Dorothy and Anthony had stood in the receiving line with the Harrods, greeting guests, accepting congratulations and smiling more than she could remember. It seemed that half the town had been invited. While Susannah had known that what Dorothy referred to as "society" would attend the gala, she had been startled to see Rob and his assistants mingling with the other guests. Though Rob was an undeniably skilled craftsman, Susannah doubted he would have been invited to a similar event in Boston.

Rob was engaged at present in what appeared to be a serious discussion with Dr. Kellogg. Susannah tried not to frown as she thought of her own discussions with the doctor. Instead, she glanced around the room, looking for Charles. She'd seen him briefly as he'd gone through the receiving line, but then he'd disappeared. There he was, in the far corner, talking to a man whose name Susannah could not recall.

On the opposite side of the room Brian O'Toole, who was here with the rest of his family, working to supplement the Harrods' staff, carried guests' wraps to a spare bedroom. Susannah noted with pride that he walked steadily. To her knowledge, there had been no relapses with Demon Alcohol.

As the front door opened again, Susannah tried to mask her surprise. She had not expected to see Matt Wagner here tonight. She wasn't sure what surprised her more: that Brad's parents would invite him, knowing of the animosity he and Charles shared, or that Matt would accept.

After Matt had made his way down the line, Mrs. Harrod turned toward Dorothy and Susannah and nodded, indicating that the reception had ended. "Anyone rude enough to come later will simply miss the opportunity to greet you," she said, her smile belying the harsh words. "It's time to see if these frightfully expensive musicians are as good as my son claims."

Anthony gave his arm to Dorothy, then offered the other to Susannah. They moved slowly into the ballroom, pausing to speak to several guests. Though the Harrods' house was electrified, tonight hundreds of candles illuminated the ballroom, their flickering sending soft shadows dancing, while the scent of wax mingled with the fragrance of the flowers that Mrs. Harrod had massed in the corners, the ladies' perfumes and the pungent smell of cheroots.

As a cool breeze stirred the room, Dorothy turned toward the doorway, where two men stood. "Look, Susannah, isn't that . . ." Confusion clouded her eyes, and Susannah realized her mother had forgotten the men's names.

Susannah looked at them. Although both appeared to be about her mother's age, one man was tall and thin, almost ascetic in appearance, while the other was of shorter than average height and bespectacled. Even impeccable tailoring could not disguise his portly form. Though they moved with the assurance that said this was not their first visit to the Harrods' home, Susannah had seen neither of them before tonight.

"I don't know them," she told her mother.

"Nor do I," Anthony said.

Dorothy frowned; then with one of the mercurial mood changes that still mystified Susannah, she smiled, apparently having forgotten the men as the musicians began to play.

Anthony bowed slightly. "Are you ready, madam?"

As Dorothy moved into his arms, Charles appeared at Susannah's side. "I never imagined I'd be so fortunate," he said, his raised eyebrows telling Susannah he was surprised that Anthony was with Dorothy and not her. "May I have the honor of this dance?"

The song was a waltz, lilting and romantic. As Susannah placed her hand in Charles's and they began to glide across the floor, she almost sighed with pleasure. Not even in her dreams had she imagined that it would feel so wonderful, being held in a man's arms, her steps matching his, their eyes locked together as they whirled in time to the music. Though they had never danced together, the movements felt instinctive, as if their bodies were attuned to each other, as if they were two halves of the same whole, reunited for the space of a waltz. It was marvelous! For a few moments, nothing mattered save the joy that she found in Charles's arms. It was wonderful. Almost as wonderful as the kiss they had shared.

What was wrong with her? She was at a party to celebrate her engagement, and she was thinking of another man. Susannah felt blood rise to her cheeks at the memory of the kiss that should never have happened and the one she wished would have, the one that caused her to waken feeling bereft. To hide her confusion, she nodded toward the two strangers who were now standing near the doors to the terrace. "Do you know them?" she asked.

Charles bent his head and spoke softly, as if he were confiding a secret. His breath tickled her ear, sending little shivers of pleasure through her nerve endings. "The tall one is Philip Biddle, the other Ralph Chambers. They're old family friends."

The words were ordinary, but the way Susannah felt was not. *Stop it!* she admonished herself. Charles was a friend, nothing more. Anthony was the man she was going to marry.

"Ralph's my attorney, and Philip used to be a banker," Charles continued. "Why do you ask?"

"Dorothy recognized them but couldn't remember their names." It was amazing. Her voice sounded perfectly normal, giving no sign that her thoughts were in a turmoil.

"She probably danced with them when she was growing up."

The warmth of Charles's hand sent tingles up her arm. Trying to ignore it, Susannah said, "It's difficult to imagine Dorothy's childhood here. It appears to have been so different from the way we lived in Boston."

Charles seemed surprised. "In what ways?"

"For one, we never attended balls or receptions."

"Never?"

"Never. This is the first time I've danced."

"Now I know you're telling me a tale. You dance beautifully."

Another of the blushes that seemed so common when she was with Charles stained Susannah's cheeks. "I learned from a friend," she admitted. Then, concerned that he might have misinterpreted her words, she added, "I don't want to mislead you. My childhood was happy; it simply wasn't the same as most." Susannah spoke softly, for her mother and Anthony were only a few feet away.

"I didn't realize it at the time," Susannah told Charles, "but I think my parents were so in love with each other and so involved in their careers that they didn't have a lot of time left to spend with me."

His hand tightened on her waist, and his eyes darkened. "Then you missed an important part of childhood. My mother spent most of her days with my sisters. I'm not sure what they did together other than that she taught them to garden and do needlework."

Susannah smiled. "Dorothy taught me German."

It was Charles's turn to smile. "Let me retract my statement. You didn't miss out. It appears your mother did what mine did and taught what she knew." Charles grinned. "I imagine my sisters would tell you that being able to speak German is more important than pruning roses or making seat covers, especially now that they're in Switzerland."

From the corner of her eye, Susannah saw the two men—Ralph and Philip, Charles had named them—go onto the terrace. As the door opened, she caught a glimpse of another man. Her eyes must be mistaken, for there was no reason Brian should be outside. He was supposed to be carrying trays of food now.

"I imagine you'd have preferred to learn French."

Susannah nodded. "Ultimately I did learn it." Although she doubted she would ever go to Paris. The lovely book of photographs Charles had given her might be the closest she got to the City of Light.

"What did you do when you weren't in school?" she asked Charles. "Did your father take you to the mill with him?"

Though he erased it almost immediately, Susannah saw Charles frown. "I went to the mill at an early age and was taught every step of the process. Of course," he said with a short laugh, "like most young people, I thought I knew more than my elders and insisted there was a better way to weave cotton. He let me try out my ideas."

"Did they work?"

"Some did," Charles admitted. "Fortunately, the rest didn't cause any permanent damage."

"Your father sounds like a very enlightened parent." Susannah felt Charles's arm stiffen in what seemed like denial. It was not

133

the reaction she had expected, for surely he did not regret those experiences.

"Enlightened is one way to describe him." There was a bitterness to Charles's voice that surprised Susannah, but this was not the place to question him, particularly since the waltz was ending.

When the music died, Charles released her. For a second Susannah felt bereft, as if her source of warmth and comfort and something else, something she did not want to investigate too closely, had been taken from her. Then Anthony and Dorothy approached.

"May I have this dance, sweetheart?"

Susannah tried to mask her surprise. This was the first time Anthony had called her that, and though it felt good, she couldn't help wondering why he'd chosen tonight to use the endearment. Surely it wasn't because Charles and Dorothy could hear him.

Charles executed a small bow. "Would you do me the honor?" he asked Dorothy.

Instead of agreeing, Dorothy looked around the room, obviously searching for someone. "Where's Lucy? I thought you would dance with her."

Anthony opened his mouth, but Charles shook his head. Though he spoke to Dorothy, Susannah suspected the gesture was meant for Anthony. "You and your daughter are the only ladies I want to dance with tonight." Apparently mollified, Dorothy moved into Charles's arms.

As the music began, Susannah put her hand on Anthony's and let him draw her closer. This was her first dance with her fiancé. It was supposed to be special.

"Your mother seems to be in her element tonight," Anthony said as he and Susannah began to move to the music. "But who's Lucy? I didn't know Charles had a girlfriend. What else has he been hiding?"

Susannah stumbled ever so slightly. What would Anthony think if he knew of the kiss she and Charles had shared? He'd understand that it was a mistake. Of course he would. She forced herself to concentrate on the steps. This was another waltz, but for some reason, it seemed more difficult than the first one. Perhaps she was simply tired from standing, and that was why she felt awkward dancing with Anthony.

"Dorothy is certainly enjoying the ball." Susannah deliberately addressed only one of Anthony's comments. "It was so thoughtful of the Harrods to plan it."

Anthony guided them to the center of the room. It was, Susannah suspected, a move designed to draw attention to them. There was no reason she should feel uncomfortable. The evening was, after all, a celebration of their engagement. And yet Susannah could not easily put aside a lifetime of self-effacement.

"Why wouldn't Brad's parents want to host a party? It's not every day that two beautiful women come to a town this size. Surely that deserves a celebration." This was the old Anthony, the man with the silver tongue.

"Hidden Falls is very different from Boston," she agreed. Just as dancing with Anthony was very different from dancing with Charles.

On the other side of the room, Dorothy was laughing at something Charles had said.

"I like Hidden Falls." As Anthony twirled Susannah in a step that was not part of the waltz, Susannah tried not to stumble. "It reminds me a bit of my family's summer home on the cape. There's the same small-town closeness." Anthony's gray eyes sparkled with enthusiasm as they always did when he spoke of Cape Cod.

"The cape sounds beautiful."

"That's why I want us to honeymoon there. It will be the perfect place to begin our life together—so much nicer than a city like London or Paris." He twirled her again in a flamboyant gesture. "Don't you agree?"

Susannah started to nod. Then she remembered Charles asking why she hadn't told Anthony that she longed to visit Paris. This was the opening she needed.

"I've always wanted to see Paris," she said softly.

Anthony's handsome features hardened as he frowned. "It can't compare to the cape. They don't even speak English there."

"I think that would be part of the charm."

"You say that because you've never been there. Trust me." Susannah felt as if she were a student and he the professor, lecturing her. She stiffened. As if he understood her reaction, Anthony continued, and this time his tone was conciliatory, "Let's not argue about this. You'll enjoy the ocean. Besides, it's too nice a night to spoil with a disagreement."

On that point, they were in complete agreement.

Charles stood in the far corner of the room, watching the dancers. There was Susannah, flitting around the room, her peach-colored gown gleaming against her partner's dark clothing. She hadn't missed a single dance. Not that he had thought she would. As a guest of honor, she would have been virtually guaranteed a full dance card, even if she had been as homely as a mule and clumsy. But Susannah was not homely, and she danced divinely.

Charles felt his pulse race as he thought of how she had felt in his arms. It was only a dance. That was all. There was no reason to remember how they had moved as if they were two parts of a whole, reunited. There was no reason to remember how soft her skin had felt or how sweet her perfume had been. It was only a dance. That was all.

Charles started to frown at the thought that he should be dancing again. Brad's mother was as bad as his had been and would chide him about his social duties. To hell with duty! After Susannah, all the other women had seemed insipid. When Ralph came in from the terrace and headed toward him, Charles's mouth curved into a grin. Now he had an excuse for not dancing.

"I hate to admit these bones are old," the attorney said with a rueful glance at his legs, "but I need to sit down. Will you keep an old man company?"

"You're not an old man." Though Charles protested, he saw that his friend's face was flushed, and he pulled two chairs into the corner, then commandeered two drinks from Brian O'Toole. What were the Harrods thinking, letting Brian serve liquor? But, Charles was forced to admit, Brian seemed sober.

Ralph sank onto one of the chairs, his groan telling Charles that he had not been exaggerating his fatigue. "I don't want to confess how long it's been since I last danced with Dorothy Ashton. Dorothy Deere," Ralph corrected himself. "We may not be as spry as we were then, but holding her in my arms brought back a host of memories."

Charles took a sip of his whiskey before he spoke. "For me, being here has raised memories that should have been left buried." The only good part of the evening had been dancing with Susannah. The waltz he'd shared with Dorothy had been far different, for once again she appeared to have confused him with his father.

Charles looked at Ralph, debating whether he should ask him if he recognized the name Lucy. But, though he did not consider himself a coward, Charles knew there were some answers he would prefer not to know, especially if as he feared Lucy was the dark-haired woman his father had met in the gazebo that horrible day. Charles took another swallow. Though whiskey solved no problems, it did provide momentary relief from pain. Was that why Brian drank? Did he have secrets he wanted to forget?

"I understand, my boy." Ralph polished his spectacles with his handkerchief. "It's only natural you'd remember the last party, but your parents would not have wanted you to continue to grieve. You're doing the right thing, keeping the mill running."

Charles looked at Ralph, surprised. "I know, my boy," the attorney continued. "I haven't always believed that, but you were right. Your place is here in Hidden Falls."

"It's not as if I had a choice." Charles could not hide his bitterness. This was not the life he wanted.

Ralph slid the spectacles back on his nose, then peered at Charles. "Oh, but you did. There are always choices. And right now our choice should probably be to dance." Ralph lurched to his feet, his whiskey untouched. "I wouldn't mind dancing with Dorothy again."

While Ralph led the older guest of honor onto the floor, Charles offered his arm to Brad's mother. Half an hour later, as a dance ended, Charles heard a man calling his name. He turned and saw Philip Biddle nodding at him. Though he had seen Philip arrive at the same time as Ralph, this was the first Charles had spoken to him.

"I beg you to excuse me," Charles said with a bow to his partner.

When Charles joined Philip, the former banker gave him an appraising glance. "You look as if you need some fresh air," he said, opening the door to the terrace and gesturing to Charles to follow him. Once outside, Philip said bluntly, "You don't need fresh air any more than I do. I simply wanted to ensure that we weren't overheard."

Charles took a deep breath. Though the evening air was pleasant, he sensed that whatever Philip was about to say was not.

"I want to give you some advice. I hope you'll take it in the spirit it's offered." Philip clenched and unclenched his fists, the nervous gesture deepening Charles's sense of foreboding.

"I know you've always had my best interests at heart."

"Quite so. That's why I was concerned when I saw you deep in conversation with Ralph Chambers."

Charles stared at the sky. The night was calm; perhaps if he counted stars, he could absorb some of that tranquillity. Tonight was supposed to be a festive occasion, a celebration of Susannah's engagement. It was not meant to be a revival of unhappy memories or a discussion of the unplanned—and unpleasant—turn Charles's life had taken. Had Matt been right? Was there something sinister about the Harrods' parties?

"I don't understand, Philip. You know that Ralph's my attorney, and—like you—he's a longtime family friend."

"Quite so." Philip cleared his throat. "But I would be remiss if I did not tell you that I've heard some unsavory rumors about him."

"Ralph?" Charles made no effort to hide his incredulity. He swung around to face Philip, then glanced back at the house. Though the music was muffled, he could see the guests as the steps of the dance brought them near the window. There was Dorothy, waltzing with Ralph again, and that peach gown could only belong to Susannah. Who was her partner? As she moved,

Charles clenched his teeth. Matt Wagner had no right to hold Susannah in his arms.

"Ralph's as honest as the preacher," Charles said, forcing his thoughts away from Susannah's partner.

"Perhaps," Philip agreed, "although I heard that he's had some financial setbacks." Philip lowered his voice to a conspiratorial level. "All this is highly confidential, but the story is that he's breached his fiduciary responsibility with some clients."

Would the dance ever end? Now Susannah was laughing with Matt. "In plain English, what are you saying?"

Philip cleared his throat again, as if he were uncomfortable with what he was about to say. "That he's swindled some of them."

Charles shook his head. "I can't believe it. Ralph wouldn't do that."

"How do you know?" This time Philip's voice was as smooth as Ralph's. "People in desperate situations will do unexpected things. Perhaps Ralph's situation was worse than you knew."

Charles was silent for a moment, remembering Ralph's confession that he had not recovered from the bad investments he had made at John Moreland's suggestion. Was it possible there was a grain of truth in Philip's accusations?

"I still can't believe it."

Though the light was dim, Charles saw Philip nod slowly. "Just think about what I've said and be careful. I wouldn't want to see him take advantage of you."

Charles shook his head again. He wouldn't believe that Ralph was guilty of malfeasance. Ralph was honest. But, Charles reminded himself, he wouldn't have believed his father capable of infidelity if he hadn't seen the evidence. Perhaps Charles was not a good judge of character.

"Let's go back in." He strode toward the door, unwilling to pursue that line of reasoning.

"Good idea. The ladies will want to dance with you."

"What about you, Philip? Have you danced with our guests of honor?" Though he hadn't thought about it consciously, Charles realized he had not seen Philip on the dance floor.

Philip stopped. Turning to Charles he said, "No, and I shan't.

I may sound like a foolish old man, but when she was dying, I promised Rosemary that I wouldn't dance with another woman unless I planned to marry her. That time has not yet arrived."

Something in Philip's voice made Charles stare at the older man. "I had no idea you were considering marrying again." It had been ten years since Rosemary's death. In Charles's experience, widowers who remarried did so quickly.

"A man gets lonely," Philip said. "If the right woman will have me, I may reenter the state of marital bliss this summer."

Charles tried to mask his surprise that, not only was Philip planning to marry, but he had already chosen his bride. "And who might that woman be?"

The older man wagged his finger. "That, my boy, is something I'm not at liberty to disclose."

It was, Charles reflected, a night for strange revelations.

Chapter Eleven

"I wish you hadn't moved so far from Boston." It was mid-morning, only a few minutes before Anthony had to leave for the train station. Though Susannah had offered to drive him, Anthony had told her that he would prefer to say good-bye in private, and so he had come to Pleasant Hill. Brad Harrod was waiting outside in his motor car, and to Susannah's surprise, her mother had joined him and appeared to be discussing the vehicle's features.

"I had to come here for Dorothy's sake." Susannah spoke softly. Though they were alone in the parlor, the door was still open and Susannah did not want their conversation overheard.

Anthony's smile brightened as he reached for Susannah's hands. "I know. It was the right thing to do. It's simply that I miss you when we're apart." He leaned forward and kissed her. It started as the softest of caresses, a gentle touching, but then Anthony dropped Susannah's hands and drew her into his arms. "All I've been able to think about is how beautiful you looked in that ball gown." And then he lowered his lips to hers again. This time there was nothing gentle about his kiss. His lips moved greedily, devouring hers, forcing them to part; then he nipped her lower lip so sharply that Susannah almost cried out in pain. Anthony tugged her closer, one hand cupping her neck, while the other squeezed her breast.

"Anthony!" Susannah jerked away, shocked. Never before had he taken such liberties. Never before had he hurt her. Why was he acting this way? Although he had kissed her many times, they had always been soft, almost chaste kisses, never stirring passion and never, ever causing pain.

Blood drained from Anthony's face, and his expression filled with contrition. "I'm sorry, sweetheart. It's just that you're so beautiful that you make a man lose control." He ran a hand through his hair in apparent frustration. "Maybe it's better if we remain apart until the wedding. That may be the only way I can withstand the temptation." He gave Susannah one of his most persuasive smiles. "The trouble is, I'll miss you, you little temptress."

No one had ever called Susannah that before. But, then, she had never worn clothing like the ball gown before. To the dressmaker's dismay, the gown's cut had been conservative, displaying far less flesh than the current style demanded, but the peach silk had clung to Susannah's curves, and even she had not denied that the gown had made her feel both feminine and attractive. Perhaps it was at least partially her fault that Anthony had lost control of himself. Perhaps the sober clothing she had always worn had served more purposes than she'd realized.

"I'll miss you, too," she told Anthony. He was an important part of her life, and one day he would be her husband. Of course she would miss him when they were apart.

When the automobile had disappeared from sight and Susannah's hand was tired from waving, she walked back into the house.

"Has your gentleman caller left?"

Susannah managed a small smile for her mother, who was now pacing the length of the hallway. She had come back into the house when Susannah and Anthony had walked toward the car. "Anthony went back to Boston," Susannah reminded Dorothy as she steered her into the parlor and rang the bell.

When Megan delivered a pot of tea and some of Moira's freshly baked muffins, Dorothy settled back in her chair and regarded Susannah steadily. "Are you sure he's the man you want to marry?"

Dorothy's question startled Susannah almost as much as Anthony's display of passion had. Her father had introduced her to Anthony, and Dorothy had encouraged the match from the beginning. Why was she questioning it now?

"We have so much in common," Susannah told her mother, echoing the words Dorothy had used when she'd first voiced her approval of Anthony. "We read the same books and enjoy the same music."

Dorothy listened, then set her teacup on the table. "Do you love him?"

That question was easy to answer. "Of course." Of course what she felt for Anthony was love. How else would you describe the sense of comfort, the camaraderie she felt with him? No other man she knew inspired those feelings in her. And if their relationship had seemed a little strained these past few days, it was only because they were in a new setting, meeting new people and dealing with new situations. Even the best of marriages had its difficult times. There was no reason to worry.

Dorothy's face brightened. "Then it will be all right." She took a bite of muffin, chewing thoughtfully. "I want you to have the kind of marriage your father and I did," she said at last. A brilliant smile crossed Dorothy's face. "I knew from the first time I met him that Louis was the only one for me."

Susannah sipped her tea and hoped her curiosity was not too obvious. Though she had never doubted her parents' love for each other, she had not known that the attraction had been immediate, for love and other emotions were not topics of conversation in the Deere household. "What made you so certain?"

Dorothy's eyes were clear. For the moment at least, there was no sign of the confusion that disturbed Susannah so often. "It's difficult to explain other than to say that I felt there was a magnet pulling me to him. I couldn't have resisted, even if I had tried. Which," Dorothy said with a chuckle, "I did not." She leaned forward, taking Susannah's hands in hers. "When I was with him, I was complete. When we were apart, I felt this emptiness deep inside me, and I knew that the only way it would be filled would be by Louis." The happiness she saw on Dorothy's face brought tears to Susannah's eyes. How wonderful it must have been to have known a love like that!

"I would have done anything to be with him," Dorothy continued. "That's why I didn't even mind giving up my pretty hats and dresses when he told me he didn't like frivolous things."

Another mystery had been solved.

"All that mattered was making Louis happy. That's what made me happy." Susannah's mother took a deep breath. "And when he died, I felt as if my world had ended."

Her words confirmed what Susannah had guessed, that Dorothy had never recovered from her husband's death. "I wish I could do something to help you."

"But you did, my dear." Dorothy squeezed Susannah's hands. "You brought me home."

The light was perfect. Susannah stared at the apple tree, watching the way the rising sun changed the color of its bark. That was it! That was what she wanted to capture. She turned to her palette and began to mix paints. It was wonderful, being able to paint outdoors again. Though Susannah enjoyed her aerie, now that Dorothy was aware of her pastime and did not disapprove, she had decided to put the final touches on the painting in the orchard. The light was better here, and the scent of apple blossoms and the bees' faint droning served as inspiration.

"This is your last chance."

Susannah turned, startled by the man's voice. This early in the morning, she had not expected anyone else to be awake. When she recognized Rob, she stepped in front of her easel, hoping that by some miracle he wouldn't ask what she was doing in the orchard before breakfast. "Last chance to do what?"

"To change your mind about letting me borrow one of your horses."

She shook her head, relieved. If Rob hoped to ride before he began work, he would have no time to ask about the easel. "I'm glad you want to ride. My mother and I haven't gone out yet, which means that the horses are what Brian O'Toole calls an expensive nuisance." Brian had laughed as he'd made the comment and had laughed even more heartily when Susannah had asked whether he was suggesting she sell the horses and dismiss him. There was, of course, no need to repeat Brian's words, other than to keep Rob's attention diverted.

The diversion failed.

"I didn't know you painted." He came closer to the easel, his curiosity evident. "I hadn't realized you were an artist. No wonder you did so well with the hedgehog."

Susannah had finished the small carving, and it now sat on the bureau in her bedroom. She was sure that the fact that the wood bore some resemblance to a hedgehog was the result of Rob's assistance, not her own skill.

"I'm not a real artist. All I do is dabble." Why wasn't he in a hurry to reach the stable? The horses were more important than her painting.

"Let me be the judge of that." Without waiting for her consent, Rob stepped behind the easel and stared at it. He tipped his head to one side, and she saw his eyes narrow. Though he was the picture of concentration, his expression was inscrutable. Susannah's pulse raced, and she tried not to hold her breath. For a moment, he stood silently as he inspected her work. She bit her lip, anxious to hear what he thought at the same time that she was afraid of the verdict. What would she do if he hated it?

It felt like hours before he turned to her, a smile lighting his face. "It's as I thought," he said at last. There was a hint of satisfaction in his voice.

"What do you mean?"

Gesturing toward the easel, Rob said, "You have an excellent eye. Your technique could benefit from some polishing, but you've captured the emotion."

He didn't hate it! "I told you I wasn't very good."

Rob shook his head, and his blue eyes sparkled. "I didn't say that. The truth is, you have the talent to be a fine painter."

His words set her spirits soaring. Not only did Rob not hate her painting, but he'd used the magic word: talent. Though he

145

might not be a painter, he was an artist. His opinion mattered. "I've always dreamed of studying with a master," Susannah admitted.

"I'm certainly not a master, but I can show you a couple of things that might make a difference." Rob took a step backward and studied the painting again. She saw him squint, as if he were focusing on one part of the picture.

"I don't want to impose on you. Your time is valuable."

He shrugged. "So are your horses, and you're willing to share them."

"That's different."

Ignoring her protests, Rob took the brush and palette. "If you mix a little ocher with the brown here, the face will look more realistic." He pointed to a spot on the painting, then suited his actions to his words, combining the two colors on the palette. "Try this," he said as he handed the brush to her. He was right. Though the difference was subtle, the shading brought the man to life.

"Excellent." Rob narrowed his eyes again. "It's odd, but I feel as if I've met this man."

As Rob strode toward the stable, Susannah stared at the canvas. Once more, Rob was right, although this time, she wished he weren't. She had done it again. She had made the man in her painting look like Charles.

It was absurd, totally absurd, and she had to stop it. She shouldn't even be painting, much less painting Charles Moreland's face. If she had something useful to do with her life, there wouldn't be time for such nonsense.

She had put it off for too long. Today she'd go into town and see whether she could help at the school.

"We've completed our investigation into the fire."

Charles nodded at the man who sat on the opposite side of the desk. Though Charles had associated this office with unpleasant memories, perhaps today the jinx would be broken. It had been a long year waiting for George Fields to finish, but at last it was over. The insurance adjuster was back in Hidden Falls, and if all went well, the thick stack of papers he held would include a bank draft for the full amount of the claim.

"I don't mind admitting that I'm glad you're done," Charles said with as much warmth as he could muster. George Fields was a large man with a ruddy complexion and features softened by good living. He bore absolutely no resemblance to a ferret, and yet that was how Charles viewed him. "It's hardly a secret that I can use the settlement." Just as it was hardly a secret that he had found the long delays and the man's refusal to discuss the progress of the case infuriating.

Fields nodded, his expression as impassive as it had been throughout his investigation. Charles wondered if the adjuster was capable of displaying any emotions. "That's the reason I came to Hidden Falls rather than simply posting a letter." Fields laid the sheaf of papers on Charles's desk, then placed what appeared to be a protective hand on top of it.

"I imagine you get some satisfaction out of closing a claim in person, particularly one that's been open as long as this one."

Fields regarded him steadily, and if he hadn't known it improbable, Charles would have said there was a hint of sadness in his eyes. "There's no satisfaction in this case. Quite the contrary."

Charles blinked. He must have misunderstood the other man. "What do you mean?"

"Your claim has been denied." Twin furrows appeared between Fields's eyes.

For a long moment Charles stared at the adjuster in disbelief. "Denied?" It couldn't be. Not even in his worst nightmares had he considered this possibility. He had thought there might be quibbling over the amount of the settlement, but never that the claim would be denied. "On what grounds?"

The ferret pointed to his stack of papers. "We had our suspicions from the beginning," he said. That was hardly news to Charles. Why else would the investigation have taken so long? "We now have proof that the fire was caused by arson."

Charles leaned forward, wanting to learn more but needing to resolve the financial issues first. "Arson is covered." He had scrutinized the insurance contract so often that he doubted there was a clause he couldn't quote practically verbatim.

Fields shook his head slowly, and this time it was clear that he disliked the message he had to deliver. "Not under these circumstances."

"And what would those circumstances be?" It was enough of a shock to realize that the insurance company did not believe the fire was an accident. What more could Fields say?

The ferret rifled through the papers, pulling one from the middle. He laid it in front of Charles. "We have cause to believe your father set the fire, because he needed the insurance money to pay his debts. This is a report of your father's financial condition at the time of the fire."

Charles had thought the worst of the pain was over. He had thought that nothing about that horrible night could surprise him again. He had been wrong.

"That's ridiculous!" Though he felt as if a horse had kicked him in the stomach and he would never be able to breathe again, somehow his voice sounded normal. "He and my mother were killed in the fire." John had been many things, but he was not a murderer, and he was not suicidal.

The ferret shifted in his chair. Though his face remained impassive, his posture betrayed his discomfort. "We believe that was an unplanned side effect. The blaze spread more quickly than he'd expected."

The allegations were patently absurd. The insurance company did not want to pay the claim and was grasping at straws. "I know my father," Charles insisted. "He would not have set the fire."

Fields's expression was somber, as if he had expected Charles's denial. "There is no question that it was arson and not an accidental fire. We found traces of the gasoline that was used to set it."

Charles took a deep breath, trying to accept the adjuster's words. For a year, he had believed that the fire had been accidental, caused by an overturned lamp. But the presence of gasoline changed everything. Fields was right. That pointed to arson. Charles's parents had not owned an automobile, and even if they had, there was no reason gasoline would have been stored inside the house. Someone had set the fire deliberately.

"The only person who stood to gain was your father." The words were as damning as the traces of gasoline. But these words were not true.

Charles gripped the chair arms. What he wanted was to wrap his hands around the ferret's throat and force him to recant. Though there would be an undeniable pleasure in watching Fields show some emotion, Charles kept his hands firmly planted on the chair. "No matter what, he would not have endangered my mother and sisters."

Fields shook his head slowly. "Desperate men will take desperate actions."

Philip had said the same thing about Ralph when he'd accused him of stealing from his clients. But Charles would not believe that either man was that desperate.

"What recourse do I have?" he asked.

"You'll have to prove me wrong." Perhaps it was Charles's imagination, but he thought he saw a hint of approval in the adjuster's eyes. If the man had expected him to accept the verdict without a protest, he didn't know Charles Moreland very well. "If you can prove that someone other than your father set the fire," Fields continued, "we'll pay the claim. Gladly."

It was ironic, Charles reflected when the adjuster had left. To save his sisters' inheritance, he would somehow have to demonstrate that a guilty man was innocent. John Moreland was both guilty and innocent. Though he had been guilty of a heinous crime, he was innocent of the one that George Fields and the insurance company claimed.

Charles crumpled a sheet of paper and tossed it onto the floor. Damnation! He ought to be relieved. Though he had no way of knowing it, Fields's investigation had absolved Charles of responsibility for the fire. If it was indeed arson, Charles's fears were baseless. The fire had not been caused by his parents' fighting and accidentally overturning the lamp. His accusations that afternoon had not precipitated the tragedy. That was good. Charles should be rejoicing. But this was much worse, for if what the adjuster claimed was true, someone hated John Moreland enough to kill him.

An hour later Charles shook his head in disgust as he realized he had been pacing the floor. He was accomplishing nothing here. Perhaps if he went home and looked through the wreckage, he might find something the investigators had overlooked.

As he opened the door, Charles saw the production supervisor approaching him.

"Mr. Moreland." The man's voice was deferential.

"Yes, Mike?" Charles said a silent prayer that he was not delivering more bad news. A man could only handle so much.

"The towels are finished," Mike said, pride evident in the way he thrust his shoulders back. "We done started the sheets."

Charles nodded his approval. Now that all the looms had been repaired, production was back to normal. "Any problems?"

"Thank the Lord, no." Mike knocked on the door frame.

Charles was thoughtful as he walked into the bright sunshine. Could there be a connection between the fire and the incidents in the mill? It made no sense that the arsonist was the same person who'd sabotaged the looms. After all, John Moreland had died in the fire. If the fire had been motivated by hatred of John, surely his death—his murder—had been enough. Why would someone continue to wreak havoc? And yet it was difficult to believe that there were two people in Hidden Falls whose minds were so twisted.

Philip's and Fields's words reverberated in Charles's mind. *Desperate men will take desperate actions.* Who could be so desperate?

Charles strode briskly down the street, as if the simple action of pounding his feet against the cobblestones would relieve the tension that had settled in his neck and shoulders. But nothing could stop his thoughts from whirling. Who? Who was so evil?

Charles frowned. His frown turned to a scowl when he glanced across the street and saw them. She held a parasol over her head, and even though it shaded her face, he could see the way she was smiling. She was looking at the man as if he were some sort of hero, one of those knights in shining armor who'd just slayed a dragon to save her.

Her smile was more than sweet; it was radiant. She had never given Charles a smile like that. He didn't want one, of course.

Smiles like that would give a man ideas that he shouldn't be entertaining, not with her.

Damn it all! Susannah was engaged to Anthony. Why the hell was she smiling at a despicable piece of humanity like Matt Wagner?

Chapter Twelve

It was a glorious day, far too nice to spend in the shadows. Susannah gave the puppies a wry smile as she tied leashes around their necks. "I'm being silly, aren't I?" she asked. Predictably, the dogs responded with a wag of their tails and eager barking.

There weren't really shadows at this time of the day. It was only Susannah's imagination that imbued the damaged wing of the house with a dark aura. Though Charles did not appear to notice it, she found the sight of boarded-up windows and scorched brick depressing. And on a beautiful June afternoon like this, she wanted no reminders of unpleasantness. She didn't want to think about Dorothy's problems or the fact that, since school would soon end, Susannah was not needed there. She didn't want to think about the fact that she had not received a letter from Anthony in a week, although she had written him daily. She most certainly did not want to think about the fact that she still continued to dream of Charles and the way it had felt to be held in his arms.

"Okay, boys, which way should we go?" Normally, she would

take them either through the woods to Pleasant Hill or along the road toward the falls. Today, however, neither destination appealed to her. As if they understood her ambivalence, the dogs began to tug on their leashes, leading her behind the house. A tall hedge broken only by an iron gate marked the edge of the lawn. Though Susannah had never been through the gate, the dogs appeared to be no strangers to the area, for they jumped on the wrought iron, barking furiously. Susannah grinned. It was difficult to resist the puppies when they were in their playful mood, and that was the majority of the time.

As she closed the gate behind them, Salt and Pepper yanked the leashes with so much enthusiasm that they started to propel Susannah forward along a well-worn path. She looked around. On this side of the gate, the carefully mown lawn gave way to dense brush. Had it not been for the path, Susannah might have believed the area to be undisturbed by humans.

She let the dogs lead and watched, amused when they failed to chase a sassy squirrel. Whatever was at the end of the path must be special if they ignored a chance to follow one of those furry rodents. As the path veered sharply to the right, the puppies renewed their barking.

The brush ended suddenly, opening onto a large clearing. Salt and Pepper continued to tug on their leashes, but Susannah stopped abruptly, her face flushing with embarrassment. The dogs had led her to the swimming hole . . . and to Charles.

She ought to study the swimming hole that Charles's grandfather had commissioned fifty years earlier. At the time it had provoked criticism because the town was excluded. Although half a century had passed, the criticism had not completely disappeared, for Susannah had heard some grousing on one of her trips into Hidden Falls. She should look at the pond to see whether the water was as clear as the townspeople claimed. But all she could see was Charles.

His arms cleaved the water with such grace that Susannah caught her breath. Not even the statues she had seen in museums had been so beautiful. Though she had watched him working and had known his shoulders were broad and powerful, a shirt had camouflaged the true magnificence of Charles's body.

His skin was shades darker than hers, perhaps because it had been exposed to the sun. His muscles were clearly defined, the sinews rippling with each stroke. And his back . . . Susannah swallowed deeply. Although she had been pleased with it at the time, it was now evident that the painting she had done of the centaur had captured only a fraction of the power and the vitality that this man exuded. Charles was pure male, and oh, so very attractive.

Afterward she was not certain how long she stood there, staring. It might have been minutes. Perhaps it was only seconds before the reality of two eager puppies intruded and she realized that the man she had been observing so intently might not appreciate her presence. The pile of clothing at the edge of the water and the brief flashes of skin she'd seen left no doubt that he was naked.

Though she would not have believed it possible, Susannah's blush deepened. She should turn around. It was the decent thing to do. She would turn around. Soon. But her body refused to obey her thoughts, and she stood on the edge of the pond, her eyes riveted to the sight of the most beautiful man she had ever seen.

Charles reached the opposite bank. Making a quick turn, he headed toward her. She saw the moment when he became aware of her presence, for a mischievous smile crossed his face. The dogs renewed their yipping, tugging so hard on the leashes that Susannah could barely restrain them. She didn't blame them for their enthusiasm. As wrong as it was, she too wanted to be with Charles.

"I'd invite you to join me," he said when he was close enough to be heard, "but I'm afraid I might shock your delicate sensibilities." He stopped swimming and appeared to remain upright in the water by swirling his arms slowly in front of him. Though his arms and those magnificent shoulders were exposed, the rest of his body was concealed below the water. The water was as clear as the townspeople had claimed; it was only the motion of Charles's arms and the ripples it caused that kept her from seeing the rest of his torso.

Susannah flushed again. If she were fortunate, Charles would attribute her rosy hue to the sun. But Susannah suspected fortune was not on her side today. Charles was laughing at her. He had to know that she had remained there, watching him, and that if she had truly possessed delicate sensibilities, she would have run at the first hint of his presence instead of standing, staring. If she had had delicate sensibilities, she would not find herself lamenting the fact that she was unlikely to catch any further glimpses of his body.

"I'm sorry." It was a lie. She did not regret a single second. It was purely as an artist, of course, that she had studied Charles's form. Susannah had heard that art students had live nude models and did not have to rely, as she had, on statues in parks and museums. Since it was unlikely that she would ever realize her dream of studying in Paris, she would have been foolish not to seize this unexpected opportunity to study a male form. That was the only reason she had stayed. It was surely not because her heart had pounded as fiercely as if she'd run a mile or because the sight of Charles's arms and back had sent tingles through parts of her body whose existence no woman with delicate sensibilities would acknowledge.

At the sound of Charles's voice, Salt and Pepper renewed their tugging on their leashes, standing on their hind legs as they lunged toward the water and the man they so patently adored. "Come, boys." Susannah tried to pull them back. She needed to leave. Now.

"Don't go on my account," Charles said. He had come far enough that his feet touched bottom, and he started to walk toward her, then stopped, another smile lighting his face. "If you'll turn your back for a few seconds, I'll soon be ready for polite company."

Susannah shook her head. This was insane. She needed to leave. "I didn't mean to disturb your swim. I'll take the dogs back to the house." If her voice sounded strained, perhaps he would believe it was from the effort of holding Salt and Pepper.

As if they understood her words, the puppies lunged forward again, their tongues hanging out as they panted.

"I'd rather talk to you than swim," Charles said. He nodded toward the dogs. "Why don't you let them go?" Bowing to the

155

inevitable, she released them and watched as they launched themselves into the water. After a moment of sputtering, they began to paddle toward Charles, their excited yips telling Susannah that they enjoyed swimming. Though they possessed none of Charles's grace, their flailing paws managed to transport them to him, making her suspect they'd done this before.

Charles patted their heads, suffered a few licks on his face, then started walking again. "You'd better turn around now," he said when the water lapped his waist.

Susannah did. For good measure, she moved a few feet back on the path. Not so far, though, that she could not hear the rustling as Charles donned his clothes. Not so far that she could not imagine how he looked standing there, rivulets of water gliding down that magnificent chest, making their way to his waist and then . . . Susannah blushed. She fanned her face with one hand, even as she wondered what it would feel like to be held in his arms, to press her fingertips against his skin, to see if it was as firm as it appeared.

"All right."

She turned and caught her breath again. Though he was dressed, his hair was wet, his shirt clung to his chest, and his feet were bare. Never in her life had she seen a man in such dishabille. There was something oddly, disturbingly intimate about it. He looked the way Susannah imagined a man would if he were about to enter his wife's bedroom and . . .

She forced those thoughts aside. "You made it seem so easy," she said in a desperate attempt to think of something other than Charles's blatant masculinity and the warmth it sent coursing through her.

"What?"

The dogs emerged from the water, shaking vigorously. Susannah jumped back as the spray hit her skirt. "Swimming. I wish I knew how. Then I could swim with Anthony on our honeymoon." It was important to think about Anthony. After all, he was the man she was going to marry. If she thought about him, those disturbing images of herself in Charles's arms would disappear.

Charles's face darkened, and he reached for Salt, rubbing the puppy's fur. "I'm surprised you never learned. Boston's not too far from the ocean."

"Dorothy couldn't swim, and my father didn't like the sand, so we never went to the beach." Anthony had told Susannah that was one of the reasons she would enjoy Cape Cod, that it would be a new experience for her. The sun and sand, he had assured her, were very romantic. Though there was no sand here, Susannah could not deny that she found the location enticing. But that, she feared, had more to do with the man who'd been swimming than the water or the shady glade.

Pepper nudged Susannah's leg, apparently asking her to rub him. She sank to the ground and gathered the now damp puppy into her lap.

"I can teach you, if you really want to learn." Charles's blue eyes were serious as he made the offer. He sat only a few feet away under the shade of an oak tree.

"I do want to learn," Susannah said. It would please Anthony if she could swim. That was the only reason she cared. She was not—she absolutely was not—looking for an excuse to see Charles again or to return to this spot.

He nodded. "We can start tomorrow if it's sunny."

Pepper squirmed, anxious to join his brother in a game of tag. Susannah squirmed, but for a different reason. "We'd probably better wait until next week," she said. "I need a bathing costume." And some time to forget just how alluring she had found Charles.

Another mischievous smile crossed his face. "It would be more fun without one."

Susannah couldn't help it. She blushed. Dipping her head so that her hat shaded her face she said, "Now you've embarrassed me." For Charles's suggestion had fueled her imagination, that traitorous imagination that had no difficulty picturing herself standing close to him, his arms around her as he showed her the proper strokes.

Charles laughed. "You know I was only joking." He leaned forward and touched her chin, turning her face so that she had to look into his eyes. "You're good for me, Susannah Deere. You give me a reason to laugh."

Something in his expression told her that not only had there been few such opportunities over the past year, but also that something unpleasant had happened recently. "Have you had more problems at the mill?" Though she hoped there had been no further sabotage, Susannah welcomed the change of subject.

Charles shook his head slowly. "Not exactly, although it's related. The insurance company denied my claim for fire damage on Fairlawn." Although it appeared involuntary, he glanced in the direction of the house. Fairlawn was not visible from here, but Susannah knew the responsibility weighed heavily on him and that he was unable to ever completely forget it.

"That's awful!"

It certainly was. Charles leaned back against the tree, watching Susannah's expression change from mirth tinged with chagrin to concern. Did she have any idea just how attractive she was, or how endearing he found her blushes? It was ridiculous to be thinking of her that way, just as it had been ridiculous the way his body had responded to the knowledge that she had been staring at him while he swam. Oh, he knew she would deny it, but she had been blushing. Perhaps it was simply maidenly modesty, the delicate sensibilities he'd teased her about having. After all, he doubted she'd encountered many naked men in her life. Perhaps, though, it was something else. Perhaps she found him as attractive as he did her.

Absurd! Charles dug his fingers into the tree bark. It was rough and could abrade his fingertips, unlike Susannah's skin. That was softer than a rose petal. *Stop it!* Susannah was going to marry Anthony. It was Anthony who would receive those beautiful smiles and who would have her in his bed each night. Lucky Anthony!

Charles forced his thoughts back to the mill. "I could have used the insurance money to pay off some of the mill's debts." He couldn't ignore the irony that that was exactly why Fields had thought his father had set the fire.

"There must be other ways to reduce the debt," Susannah said. She looked up at the cloudless sky, as if it would provide some inspiration, and lines formed between her eyes. "I have an idea that might increase your profits. It wouldn't happen overnight, but it might help."

The dogs returned, exhausted from their games, and flopped on the ground in front of Susannah. She reached a hand out and stroked first one head, then the other. Charles tried to force back the image of that hand stroking his arm, moving slowly upward, caressing his chest, then gliding lower.

"What do you suggest?" *Please,* he implored, *say something . . . anything that will help me corral these traitorous thoughts.*

"Have you considered specialty prints?" There was a note of hesitation in Susannah's voice that told Charles she wasn't sure of his reaction. Did she think he was some kind of ogre? Charles smiled, trying to reassure her. "The only colors I've seen used in Moreland fabrics have been the woven patterns and stripes," she continued. "They're beautiful, but you might expand to silk-screening."

Again, she sounded diffident. She shouldn't, for she was right. Though Moreland prided itself on the quality of its weaving, the mills had never produced prints. "Do you think there's a market for that?"

Susannah nodded, and her brown eyes sparkled. "I know there is, especially for good-quality Chinese designs. If you can capture the colors—those special shades of blue and jade green—you should be able to charge a premium." Charles wondered if there was a market for that special shade of chocolate brown that was Susannah Deere's eyes. If Moreland Mills could capture that, surely every man in America would buy it.

"Will you sketch the designs?"

Those lovely brown eyes widened with surprise. "I'm not that good an artist."

"That's not what Rob says." Charles knew he shouldn't care, but it was maddening that Susannah would show Rob her paintings when she hadn't let him see them. It had taken an hour of tussling with the dogs before he'd calmed down enough to eat supper the day he'd learned that Rob had seen Susannah's work.

As Susannah shrugged, her dress stretched across her breasts. Charles tried not to groan. "I'm surprised Rob would even mention my painting." It was fortunate Susannah had no idea the direction Charles's thoughts had taken. "It was only half done when he saw it. It still needs a lot of work."

"And I'm still waiting for an invitation to see it."

Though he hadn't meant for his words to sound chiding, Susannah flushed. "I'll tell you when I've finished. It was only by accident that Rob saw it."

Somewhat mollified, Charles rose and extended a hand to Susannah. They had best return to the house before he said or did something he would regret.

Screen printing was a good idea, Charles reflected as he left the mill the next day. He had spent the day deciding which floor could be converted to a screening area and considering which weaves would be most suitable for the initial products. As for designs, he intended to ask Anne and Jane to bring samples home from Europe. Susannah was probably correct that there was a demand for oriental patterns, but Charles knew that the women in New York would also purchase European designs. Maybe even some in what he thought of as Susannah Deere brown. Yes, it was a good idea.

Just as he hoped the carousel would prove to be. The sound of men's voices drifted onto the spring afternoon, reminding Charles that he had not visited the workshop for several days. He was nearing the former stable when a woman emerged from the woods.

"Oh, Charles!" Megan's face was white with strain, her eyes red rimmed as if she'd been crying.

"What's wrong?"

"It's me da."

Charles suppressed a sigh. "What has Brian done?" He glanced at the sky, looking for smoke. Thank God, there was none. Brian hadn't set anything on fire.

Megan's eyes filled with tears. "I can't find him. We don't know where he's gone."

"Have you tried Schultz's?" If he were a betting man, Charles would have wagered that the tavern was Brian O'Toole's destination.

Megan shook her head. "He wouldn't go there. He promised me mam he wouldn't touch a drop."

"I don't want to sound skeptical, Megan, but it is possible he broke his promise."

She shook her head again, more violently this time. "He wouldn't. I know me da."

It was, Charles realized, the same thing he had said in response to Fields's allegations. "All right, Megan," he said, not bothering to hide his sigh this time. "I'll help you search for him." And the first place he would look would be Schultz's.

Her face brightened. "Thank you, Charles. Thank you." Before he knew what she intended, Megan flung her arms around him and kissed him.

Susannah sneezed. Though she and Megan had started cleaning the attic the previous week, there was still a heavy coating of dust on the trunks in this corner. She opened the lid to one and began to remove the items inside. Somewhere there had to be a bathing costume. Even though Dorothy had never swum, Susannah was certain that her grandmother had. This trunk, which bore her grandmother's initials, was the logical place for a bathing costume to be stored.

Susannah lifted the wooden tray and laid it on the floor, sneezing again. Though the items on it drew her interest, particularly the small leather-bound books and the strands of beads, she would look at them later. Today she needed to find clothing. But by the time she reached the bottom of the trunk, Susannah knew her search was futile. Though she had found frocks and delicately tucked chemises, there were no bathing costumes. The only remaining item was large and square and too heavy to be a garment.

Susannah pulled it out and removed the paper wrapping, exposing a portrait of a young girl. Smiling, Susannah realized that the girl was her mother as a child. She carried the painting to the window. Though the artist was clearly not a master, he had captured Dorothy's smile perfectly. Even at four or five, her smile had been fully formed.

"What are you doing, dear?" As if Susannah's thoughts had

conjured her, Dorothy entered the attic. She looked in all directions. Susannah wasn't certain whether her mother was searching for something or whether the attic seemed foreign to her today.

"I thought there might be a bathing costume in one of these trunks." Susannah gestured toward the row of steamer trunks.

"Oh, no, dear." Dorothy shook her head. "There aren't any." She smiled, the same smile that the artist had immortalized on canvas.

"Look what I did find." Susannah turned the painting so that her mother could see it.

Dorothy took a step forward and stared at the portrait. Her head was tipped to one side the way Rob's had been when he'd studied Susannah's painting. "Very pretty, my dear, but I'm afraid I cannot tell you who it is," Dorothy said at last.

Blood drained from Susannah's face, and she reached behind her to grasp the windowsill for support. How could it be that Dorothy had not recognized herself? Horrified but not wanting to alarm her mother, Susannah took a deep breath, then exhaled slowly. When she had her emotions under control once more, she said, "Why, Dorothy, I believe this pretty young girl is you."

Her mother peered at the painting again. "Of course she is. That's what I said, isn't it?" She laid her hand on Susannah's arm. "Now, come downstairs. Moira made some of those delicious cakes."

Though she doubted she would be able to swallow a crumb, Susannah followed her mother to the parlor, where Moira had placed a tray of tea and small cakes. While Dorothy chattered happily about the cakes and the weather, Susannah tried to smile. And all the while her heart thudded with the realization that she could not deny it. Her mother was not improving. To the contrary, her condition appeared to grow more serious each day.

There had to be something Susannah could do to help. Filled with a desperate need to confide in someone, she fled from the house as soon as Dorothy was settled in the kitchen, talking to Moira. Charles would be home soon. He would listen. He would understand. And this time she would ask him about the doctors he'd consulted for Anne's injuries.

Susannah's heart lightened at the thought of seeing Charles again. He was no stranger to problems. Even if he was unable to provide a solution, just talking with him would help. Charles was the friend she had always longed for, almost as dear to her as a sibling would have been. How lucky she was to have him!

She descended the hill, her feet moving quickly now. She was close to the stable when she saw them. Charles had his back to her, but there was no mistaking him, just as there was no mistaking the fact that a woman had her arms around his neck and that they were pressed together in a passionate embrace.

For a second the world turned black and Susannah gasped for air. Her step faltered as she forced herself to take a deep breath. And then he moved, and she recognized the woman. *No!* Instinctively, Susannah recoiled. *Not Megan!*

Gathering her skirts in one hand, Susannah raced up the hill, heedless of the brambles that tore at her hair or the branch that scratched one cheek. Nothing mattered except blocking the memory of Charles and Megan.

Ridiculous. It was ridiculous to remember how good it had felt to be kissed by Charles. It was even more ridiculous to care that he was kissing Megan. He had every right to kiss anyone he chose. Susannah knew that. Just as she knew that whatever she had felt when she had seen Megan in Charles's arms was not jealousy. Susannah wasn't certain what it was, but it most definitely was not jealousy. There was no reason to be jealous. Charles was her friend. That was all.

Chapter Thirteen

"It would be faster if I went alone." Charles stared into the distance, not wanting to meet Megan's gaze. He knew what he would see if he looked at her: an inviting smile and green eyes that implored him to help her. He would help her. Damn it! He had agreed to that. But agreeing to help a woman in distress didn't mean he had to take her with him. Especially not when he confronted her father. The last thing on earth he needed was Megan O'Toole at his side, those red lips pursed as if she were planning to kiss him again, when he dealt with a drunken and probably cantankerous man.

Charles shook his head and started walking. The afternoon that had seemed so promising a few minutes ago had lost its luster. Now, instead of seeing the progress Rob and his assistants had made on the carousel and then joining Susannah for a romp with the dogs, he was engaged in a wild-goose chase with a woman he wished he had never met.

Charles increased his pace. Maybe Megan would take the hint. Maybe she would understand that he was better equipped to find her father alone. Maybe she would realize that he hadn't welcomed her kiss. Charles balled his hands into fists. Why the hell had she done it, anyway? Surely he had done nothing to invite her embrace. He frowned, not just at the memory of how her lips had felt pressed to his but also at his reaction.

It wasn't natural. For Pete's sake, she was an attractive woman. Most men would have been thrilled to have a woman who looked like Megan throw herself into their arms. Most men would have taken what she'd offered and counted themselves lucky. Most men would not have compared her kiss to Susannah Deere's and found it wanting. Charles, it appeared, was not most men. And that disturbed him as much as Megan's kiss had.

He had been certain that whatever else he had inherited from John Moreland, it had not been the man's dubious sense of loyalty. Charles had been convinced that he could withstand temptation, that he had conquered his tendency to covet his friend's betrothed. He had not—he absolutely had not—inherited John's belief that there was nothing wrong with adultery. And yet how else could he explain the fact that, though he knew Susannah was engaged to his friend, Charles still continued to dream of her kiss and how good she had felt in his arms? How could he explain that, even though it was for Anthony's sake that he'd agreed to teach her to swim, Charles's blood heated every time he thought of Susannah at the swimming hole?

"He's me da." Megan's words brought Charles back to the present. Though her face was flushed, perhaps with the effort of matching Charles's pace, she uttered no complaint. "Sure and he wouldn't go home with a Moreland."

Especially not this Moreland. Accepting the validity of Megan's assessment, Charles nodded. "All right."

If she noticed that his tone was less than gracious and that he walked a bit more quickly than he would normally have in a lady's company, Megan said nothing. Instead, as they descended the hill toward River Road, she spoke only of her father. "He hasn't been the same since your da let him go."

Charles felt the blood rise to his face. "Nothing has been the same since then." Involuntarily, he turned and stared at the burned wing of his home. Though ivy had begun to grow again, it would be years before the blackened bricks were hidden. It would be longer than that before the remaining Morelands were freed from the memory of that night. Charles took a deep breath, trying to clear his head. Despite the insurance adjuster's claims, he was certain his father had not set the fire. If Charles wanted to clear the family name, not to mention easing their financial difficulties, he would have to discover who had.

As they passed Brad's house, Charles glanced at Megan, wondering whether Brian O'Toole had been changed by more than the loss of his job. Could Brian have set the fire at Fairlawn and now be suffering remorse? The man had certainly had the motivation. Though Charles had not been in Hidden Falls when his father had thrown Brian off the estate, the townspeople had been more than willing to recount all the details, including the threats that Brian had made while downing a pint or two.

Those tales had been tempered with reminders of how Brian liked to boast when he was in his cups. But what if the threats had been more than the ranting of an angry, intoxicated man? What if the grudge Brian had harbored had been strong enough to cause him to act on it? Could Brian be the man Charles sought?

"It's strange, it is, working at Pleasant Hill," Megan said. Though Charles would have preferred to walk in silence, Megan insisted on talking. "Me mam and da like being there. Meself, I think it's spooky. Mrs. Deere is a little daft, you know."

Charles had paid scant attention to Megan's rambling, preferring instead to consider the ramifications of Brian O'Toole as an arsonist, but when he heard Megan mention Susannah's mother, Charles was jolted back to reality. That was one story he didn't want bandied about. Though in her current condition Dorothy Deere might never be aware of the gossip, it would hurt Susannah, and that was something Charles would not allow. The woman had enough problems; she didn't deserve to be the brunt of Hidden Falls' speculation.

"That's not the sort of tale I'd advise you to carry if you value your family's position," Charles said sharply. "I don't imagine Susannah would appreciate your betraying her trust." Though he was a fine one to be talking about betrayals.

Megan laid a hand on Charles's arm, and her eyes filled with tears, her sorrowful expression reminding him of the puppies when they'd chewed one of his boots. "I meant no harm." Perhaps not, but harm, Charles knew, could be inflicted innocently. Tonight he was in no mood to be tolerant of O'Tooles.

When they crossed the bridge, though Charles intended to continue up the street to the tavern, he glanced toward the mill. It was instinctive, the action of a man who worried about his business. At this time of day, he expected to see an empty street. The mill had not yet closed, but it was late enough that casual pedestrians would have gone home. Charles gave the street a cursory look, then stopped, startled. Not only was a man striding down Mill Street, but it was the man he sought.

"There's your father." Brian O'Toole's walk was unmistakable, a combination of swagger and the slightly bowlegged stance of a man who'd grown up on a horse. To Charles's surprise, today Brian's gait was steady. Whatever he'd been doing, it had not involved excessive amounts of whiskey. Brian strode quickly and purposefully, though he shot a furtive glance or two over his shoulder, as if he feared someone was trailing him.

"I told you he wasn't at Schultz's," Megan crowed. She turned onto Mill Street, and this time it was Charles who lengthened his stride to keep pace with her. When they reached her father, Megan stopped, put both hands on her hips and demanded, "Where were you? Sure and you had us worried."

Brian narrowed his eyes as he frowned at Megan. "Just like your mam, always nagging." He glanced backward. "Truth is, missy," he said in a voice that resonated with anger, "I don't owe you any explanations. You, on the other hand, had better have a good reason for being with *him*." He jabbed a finger in Charles's direction. Though Brian's anger was palpable, his words were distinct, confirming Charles's earlier thought that wherever Brian had been, he had not been drinking.

"Tell me, missy, what it is you're doing with that one."

Without posing a single inquiry, Charles had the answer to one of his questions. The animosity he had seen that day in the Deeres' stable had not been an aberration. Brian hated him. The question was, had he hated John Moreland enough to kill him?

Megan gave her father a conciliatory smile. "I was worried about you, Da. Mr. Moreland was simply being neighborly by escorting me into town." It was the first time Charles could recall Megan referring to him as Mr. Moreland. Somehow, the formal title appeared to soothe Brian. He smiled at his daughter, then turned to Charles.

"You keep your hands off me girl." Brian's stance had changed; now he stood with his weight balanced on the balls of his feet, ready to strike. "She's a good girl, me Megan is. Too good for the likes of you. Of course," he said, his lips curling contemptuously, "you Morelands like to take what you please whether it belongs to you or not."

Charles tried not to flinch at the thought of what his father had taken in the gazebo. It had been a June afternoon, a day much like today and yet very different, just as he was very different from John.

"Now, Da." Megan took another step toward her father.

"It appears we've accomplished what we set out to do." Charles nodded at Megan. "You found your father. Now, if you'll excuse me, I have a few things to see to at the mill." He didn't. That was why he had returned home early, but this was clearly not the time to question Brian about his actions the night Fairlawn had burned.

As Charles strode toward the mill, he looked up Rapids Street. It was another automatic glance. Though he expected to see the street deserted, two men stood near the doctor's office, their heads bent as if they were deep in conversation. Charles stared, surprised when he recognized them. The taller man was Matt, the other one of the mill workers. The older man should have been at work, and Matt—Matt should have been anywhere else. Why were they together? Was one of them the person Brian had thought might be following him? Charles shook his head, trying to dismiss his uneasiness and wishing he could recapture the elation he'd felt as he had planned Moreland Mill's foray into silk-screening.

When Charles awoke the next morning, his head throbbed, the result of a night of troubled sleep. Though he was rarely plagued with nightmares, he had wakened several times, his heart pounding with fear. The dreams had been so vivid. A home—his home—in flames. A woman fleeing, her gown on fire, her face contorted in pain. It was a dream he'd had before, the logical aftermath—or so he believed—of the fire. But this time when the woman turned and he could see her clearly, Charles realized that it was not his sister Anne who fled the house.

It was Susannah. Susannah who had been hundreds of miles away that horrible night. At the sight of her face enveloped in flames, Charles had bolted awake. Even Salt's and Pepper's attempts to comfort him by licking his face had been in vain, for each time he had fallen back to sleep, the dream had recurred.

Charles's mother had believed that dreams were symbolic, that they held hidden messages. It wasn't difficult to understand why he had dreamt of fire again after months without a nightmare. Though he had tried to put the fire behind him and focus on rebuilding the family fortune, the insurance company's verdict of arson had changed everything. Charles could no longer be single-minded. He had to discover who had set the fire. The irony that he had to prove his father's innocence was a nightmare in itself. But why had Susannah been part of the dream? Surely she had no connection to the tragedy.

Charles's heart skipped a beat as he remembered his mother's words. Dreams, she had claimed, could be either a reliving of the past or a portent of the future. *Please, God, no!* Susannah did not deserve that kind of pain. But, no matter how he tried, Charles could not shake the feeling that Susannah was in danger.

It was only a dream, he reminded himself as he walked to the mill. There was no reason to have this sense of foreboding. When Charles reached his office, he found one of the supervisors waiting, his expression glum.

"What's wrong, Hedley?" Charles tried to suppress a sigh. Though Hedley was known for his dour mien, today he looked as if he were chewing on a lemon peel. Had he spent a night trying to shake off the terror of a nightmare? Reality was far worse.

"It's the loom harnesses, sir. Someone smashed three of them."

With a muttered expletive, Charles took the stairs to the drawing-in room two at a time. Here skilled operators threaded the harnesses with the warp. Although the actual weaving was done by machine, with bobbins shooting back and forth hundreds of times a minute to produce the finished cloth, the harness threading—or drawing—was done by hand. It was painstaking work, for if the tension was incorrect or the yarn twisted, the entire bolt would be ruined.

The drawing-in room was one of the quietest spots in the mill, a fact that many workers appreciated. This morning, however, the silence was almost eerie. Though several of the drawers stood next to their shattered equipment, no one spoke, and no one met Charles's gaze.

He strode to the first of the harnesses, trying to marshal his fury when he saw the extent of the damage. Unlike the loom belts, which could be repaired, the harnesses were smashed beyond all hope. They would have to be replaced. Charles did some rapid mental calculations. The cost of the new harnesses would wipe out any chance of a profit this quarter. Even more disastrous, the Catskill resort's shipment was in jeopardy. Whoever had done this had been thorough in his destruction, waiting until he could cause maximum disruption to the mill's production.

Charles stared at the splintered wood, looking for a clue. Whoever the saboteur was, he was clever, but eventually he'd slip and leave a trace. Charles looked at the shattered equipment. The beautifully crafted wood was useless now, fit for nothing more than kindling. Then he saw it, a piece of mustard-colored leather caught on the edge of one harness. Charles reached forward, plucking the scrap from the wood. Though he could not positively identify it, the leather appeared to have been part of a man's glove. Charles frowned. Was it only coincidence that Matt Wagner had been wearing that same shade of gloves yesterday?

When he had arranged for the debris to be carted away, Charles returned to his office. Somehow he would have to find the money to buy three replacement harnesses. And until they arrived, somehow he would have to find a way to keep production levels constant.

How he wished he were back in New York! Life had been simple there. No mill, no worries, no Susannah. Charles blinked. Where had that thought come from?

Susannah leaned back in the chair and drew the sheet of paper from its envelope. Today, at last, she had received a letter from Anthony. Though she opened other mail in the parlor with Dorothy, Susannah had brought Anthony's letter to the library where she could be alone. *Dear Susannah,* she read, forcing her eyes to move slowly, savoring each word. It was silly to wish he had started the letter with *darling* or even *dearest.* What mattered was that he had written.

"I finished me cleaning." Susannah looked up, startled by Megan's voice. Though it was no secret where she'd gone, Susannah had not expected to be interrupted. "I'm ready for the attic."

Susannah nodded. She and Megan had agreed that they would spend one morning each week trying to clean the attic. "I'll meet you there in just a minute," she said, glancing at the letter.

But Megan did not take the hint. "Is that from Mr. Anthony?" She leaned against the door frame, apparently content to wait for Susannah.

Susannah nodded again, her eyes scanning the page, looking for an endearment. When she reached the end, she slid the letter back into the envelope, telling herself that it was foolish to be disappointed that there were no words of love. Men were different from women in so many ways. Perhaps they didn't put as much store in words as she did. Anthony had asked her to marry him. He'd given her his ring. That was what was important, not a few pretty words on a piece of paper.

"He's a fine man, Mr. Anthony is," Megan said as they climbed the stairs to the attic. "I reckon his family don't have dark secrets like the Morelands."

Susannah stared at Megan. "What do you mean?" She had

not forgotten Megan's claim that the Morelands were cursed. While Susannah did not believe in curses, she wondered if the secrets—whatever they were—were the reason Charles felt responsible for the fire.

Megan narrowed her eyes and shook her head. "Sorry, miss. I spoke out of turn." And though Susannah tried to convince her to finish her thought, Megan would say no more.

That afternoon Susannah found her mother dressed in her favorite lilac frock and an elaborate hat. She was buttoning her gloves when Susannah entered her room.

"Are you going out, Dorothy?"

The bird that decorated her hat brim appeared to bob for food as Dorothy nodded. "It's time I returned some calls. Mary Moreland has left her card here on at least four occasions. It would be a dreadful lapse of manners for me not to call on her."

Susannah tried not to sigh. Today was obviously one of her mother's bad days. "Mary doesn't live at Fairlawn anymore," she said as calmly as she could.

"Are you sure, dear?" The lines that formed between Dorothy's eyes mirrored her perplexed tone, and she abandoned her attempt to button her right glove.

"Yes." Though she had had little success reminding her mother of recent events, Susannah tried again. "There was a fire last year. Mary and her husband died in it." Susannah finished buttoning Dorothy's glove, although she hoped to persuade her mother to nap rather than make afternoon calls.

Dorothy reached for a parasol, apparently unconvinced by Susannah's words. "Now, dear, that doesn't sound right. I know I saw John just yesterday." She gave Susannah a sly look. "I can't tell Mary, of course, but he was kissing that dark-haired woman. She's a shameless hussy!"

Susannah's heart sank. Her mother was obviously speaking of Charles, since she frequently confused him with his father. The dark-haired woman was Megan; Susannah knew that. Just as she knew she shouldn't care. But the realization that Charles and Megan had stolen kisses here at Pleasant Hill wrenched Susannah's heart.

"That's a pretty locket you're wearing." Susannah pointed at her mother's necklace, trying desperately to change the subject.

Dorothy fingered the gold oval that Susannah had found in her grandmother's trunk. When she had brought it and the books downstairs, meaning to look at them later, Dorothy had pounced on the locket and fastened it around her neck. "It is pretty, isn't it? My mother had many jewels, but she liked this the best, because my father gave it to her on their wedding day."

Dorothy opened the locket and showed Susannah the photographs of her grandparents. Though she had been confused only a minute earlier, now her mind seemed lucid. "I imagine my mother had the same sentimental feelings for this that you do for the ring Charles gave you."

Susannah glanced at her left hand. "The ring is from Anthony," she said, gently correcting her mother. Even when her memory seemed clear, Dorothy was having increasing difficulty with names. "Anthony's the man I'm going to marry."

Dorothy reached for Susannah's hand and stared at the sparkling diamond. "Are you sure, dear? Sometimes I worry about you and wonder if your father and I did the right thing, raising you the way we did." Dorothy's frown deepened, and Susannah saw concern reflected in her eyes. She put her parasol aside and sank onto one of the two Queen Anne chairs. Though she fumbled with the buttons on her gloves, apparently planning to remove them, she kept her gaze focused on Susannah. "I've always wanted you to be happy," Dorothy said, "but sometimes it's difficult to know what brings joy to another person."

Her legs suddenly weak, Susannah perched on the edge of the other chair. It was the first time her mother had ever voiced such concerns, and the words brought tears to Susannah's eyes. "Oh, Dorothy, all I want is to make you happy."

Dorothy patted Susannah's hand in a gesture she remembered from her childhood. "You've done that, dear. Now it's time to think about yourself."

But that would mean treading on dangerous ground. If she worried about making herself happy, Susannah would have to confront her dreams. She would have to admit how often memories of Charles intruded into her life, how often she thought of the way his arms had cleaved the water, of how wonderful it had felt, being held in those arms and of how sweet his lips had tasted pressed against hers.

She couldn't—she wouldn't—think about that.

Chapter Fourteen

It was a good thing he wasn't trying to restore the Moreland fortune by working as a detective, Charles reflected as he watched the dogs run. Though it was one of his most important tasks, he was proving to be a failure.

He'd spent more time than he cared to think about combing through the ashes and debris in the south wing of the house, searching for clues, but he'd found none. As if that weren't frustrating enough, his interview with the worker he'd seen with Matt the day before the harnesses had been destroyed had revealed nothing of interest. The man had claimed that he'd been consulting Matt about arranging for a cousin to emigrate from Italy. Though it was possible the man had lied, his words had carried the ring of truth.

Matt, of course, had laughed at the notion that he'd left a piece of his glove in the mill. "I keep telling you," he said with one of those condescending looks that Charles hated, "that when I make my move, you won't have to ask who was responsible. You'll know."

And then there had been Charles's conversation with Brian

O'Toole. Not only had the man flatly denied he'd been any-where near Fairlawn the night of the fire, but he'd also retaliated by warning Charles that if he valued his pretty face—Brian's term, not Charles's—he had best keep his hands off Megan.

All told, it had been a highly unsatisfactory experience.

"Okay, boys. Time to go inside." The two balls of fur that had been racing back and forth, apparently reveling in the wet grass that was long enough to tickle their bellies, ignored him. "C'mon."

Most mornings Charles let the dogs outside only long enough to ensure that they did not incur Mrs. Enke's wrath by soiling one of the carpets, but today something—perhaps it was the pink hue that the rising sun cast over the trees, perhaps the scent of roses that wafted through the open window, perhaps nothing more than the desire to have a few minutes of simple pleasure—had brought him outdoors with the puppies. They had gamboled for a few minutes, chasing their tails as they cir-cled his legs, yipping with glee. Though their energy was still unabated, it was time for Charles to eat breakfast and go to the mill.

"Now!" he said as sternly as he could. The dogs continued to ignore him. Charles took a step forward, intending to grab their collars. Apparently convinced he wanted to play a new game, Salt and Pepper charged in the opposite direction, barking fu-riously. "Come back!" But they continued racing toward the woods as if dinner were waiting for them among the trees.

With a resigned sigh, Charles sprinted after them. He couldn't blame the dogs for thinking he wanted to play. They knew the routine. He was the one who'd changed it, confusing the pups. Charles's lips curved in a wry smile. You'd think he'd learn. Look what had happened the last time he'd changed his routine and come home from the mill early. He'd ended up accompa-nying Megan as she searched for her father.

"Salt! Pepper!" They continued to ignore him. Charles laughed as he realized he'd been bested by two puppies. That's what came of wanting to enjoy a beautiful June morning.

The dogs stopped just out of Charles's reach. He lunged, trying to grab them, and his boots slid on the damp grass. Instinctively, he reached out for a tree, and as he did, the memories came flooding in. It had been a June morning long ago when he and his father had crept from the house, taking care not to don their boots until they were outside so that Anne and Jane would not waken and demand to accompany them. It was, John Moreland had said, to be a men's day out, one of the rare occasions when he did not go to the mill but instead spent the morning teaching his son to fish.

When they had planned the excursion, Charles's chest had puffed with pride both at being referred to as a man and at having his father as a conspirator in the effort to escape his all too often pesky little sisters. For days before the grand event, Charles had hugged the prospect to himself, delighting in the knowledge that he'd be alone with his father.

They had caught only one fish that morning, a puny specimen that they had quickly tossed back into the river. And yet the memories of dappled sunlight and camaraderie had lingered. *Damn it!* Charles didn't want to remember those days. They had simply been part of the web of lies John had spun, pretending to be a fond father and a loving husband when all the while he was deceiving them. There was nothing good or true about John Moreland. Nothing.

"Salt! Pepper! Get back here!" Charles's pleasure in the morning evaporated faster than June dew. The dogs turned and stared at him for an instant. Then their ears perked and they cocked their heads as if they heard something. Without a backward glance, they shot into the woods, veering left when they reached a small clearing. Charles followed, expecting to see them taunting a squirrel. What he saw made him stop abruptly.

Good Lord, she was stunning! Though she was wearing a dress that even he knew was woefully out of fashion and had her hair tied back in a simple knot rather than arranged in the intricate pompadour that she normally wore, there was something breathtakingly beautiful about Susannah Deere. The sun glinting on her hair gave her an almost otherworldly look, but there was nothing otherworldly about the way she made Charles feel. She was quite simply the most alluring woman he'd ever seen.

Dimly Charles registered the sight of an easel. Though that was what had brought her to the forest, now she knelt on the grass, rubbing the puppies' heads.

"You're out early." The words were inane. Charles knew that, and yet he could think of nothing else to say. Surely he could not begin a conversation with Anthony's fiancée by saying, "You're the most gorgeous creature I've ever seen."

Her smile was as radiant as the sun. "I needed to capture the light," she said, still fondling the dogs. Charles felt an ache deep within him as he imagined how those fingers would feel threaded through his hair or tracing the outline of his ears. *Damn it!* It was absurd to be jealous of two rambunctious pups.

"It changes almost minute by minute."

For a second Charles wasn't sure what she meant. The light. Of course, she was speaking of the sunlight. "I hadn't realized that. It makes sense, though." Charles made a show of staring at the sun in an effort to marshal his thoughts. The last thing on earth he wanted was for her to realize that he was thinking about her smile and how it sent a warmth shimmering through his veins.

It was bad enough that he possessed an imagination that had somehow conjured the picture of Susannah standing behind the easel, slowly unbuttoning her dress, then unfastening the ribbons of her chemise, letting the garments slide ever so slowly to the ground until every soft curve, every delicious inch of flesh was revealed. *Thou shalt not covet,* Charles reminded himself. But it was more difficult than he had ever dreamt to turn away, to stare at a birch tree's silver-white bark instead of Susannah's golden skin.

She rose and shook her skirts as Salt and Pepper flopped onto the grass, apparently exhausted by their previous antics. "I never really noticed light until I started painting." Susannah glanced at the easel, and a flush rose to her cheeks. How she would flush if she knew how he'd imagined her and that easel.

Charles repressed his traitorous thoughts. "Will you let me see the painting now?" It wasn't important, he told himself. It didn't matter if she refused. But, though he tried to convince himself that he didn't care, he failed. It was a matter of trust, and today more than ever he needed to know that Susannah trusted him enough to show him her painting.

She pleated her skirt between her fingers in a nervous gesture he'd never seen before. When her gaze met his, Charles saw uncertainty reflected in her eyes. For some reason, she was as fearful of his viewing the painting as he was that she would refuse. It wasn't as if he were an art critic whose opinion could affect her career. He was only a man, wanting to learn more about the woman he . . . Charles stopped abruptly, refusing to complete the sentence. He wanted to learn more about his friend and neighbor, he amended his thoughts.

He gave her a smile that was meant to be reassuring.

"All right," she said at last. ·

Before she could change her mind, Charles moved behind the easel. Though he had meant to do no more than glance at Susannah's work, he found himself staring, amazed. Susannah had mentioned that she painted landscapes, but nothing she had said had prepared him for this. A couple clad only in rags leaned against the door frame of a tumbledown shack at the edge of a forest, staring at the storm clouds that darkened the sky. Though there were no crops in sight, Charles had the impression that the storm would destroy the couple's livelihood. It should have been a depressing painting. And yet somehow it was filled with hope. He wasn't sure how she had done it, but somehow Susannah had imbued the painting with promise rather than despair.

"You hate it." Susannah's voice jolted him from his reverie. To Charles's astonishment, her lower lip was trembling. Salt, apparently sensing Susannah's distress, bounded to her side and yipped. Though she patted the dog's head, she kept her eyes fixed on Charles, waiting for him to speak.

"I don't hate it. Not at all," he assured her. It was Charles's turn to hesitate. "Rob was right; you're very talented. It's just . . ."

"Just what?"

Charles paused, not sure how to explain his reaction, even less sure how she would respond to it. Would she recognize him for what he was, a very flawed man? And if she did, would

179

she flee in disgust? He took a deep breath, then said, "I guess I don't see the world the way you do."

Susannah closed her eyes, and pressed her lips together as if she were trying to hide her pain. "Are we dealing with that matter of perspective again?" she asked in a surprisingly light voice. When Salt yipped, Pepper abandoned his hunt for a chipmunk and came to stand next to Susannah. The dogs were obviously trying to protect her. Equally obvious, they viewed Charles as the threat.

He managed a smile. "I suppose you're right," he said. He knew his expression sobered as he continued, "You've painted what could have been a bleak scene, and yet I'm left with a feeling of optimism."

"Of course." This time there was no doubt that her smile was genuine. "Even when things look impossible, there's always a silver lining." Susannah shrugged, as if trying to minimize the depth of her feelings. "That's what I was going to title the painting, *Silver Lining*."

Charles stared, not certain what had amazed him more, the painting or her explanation. "You're a dreamer, Susannah." He hadn't meant it to sound like an accusation, but the way she flinched told him his words had wounded her.

"You act as if that's wrong." She shook her head, then put a protective arm over the top of the easel. The dogs growled. "I don't know how I could face each day if I didn't believe there would be something good in it. That's not wrong, Charles. It's not."

He softened his voice, not wanting to hurt her any more. "You misunderstood me." The truly miraculous part of Susannah's declaration was that she could remain so optimistic when each day she faced her mother's illness and the knowledge that Dorothy's condition would not improve. "I'm not saying it's wrong to dream. The truth is, I envy you, Susannah. I wish I still had some dreams."

Susannah laid her hat on the bed, then rummaged in her bureau drawer for a hat pin. Where was that long one? The porkpie hat needed the extra length of pin securing it if it was going to remain perched on top of her head.

She frowned as she jabbed the pin through her hat and hair. She didn't understand the man. How could Charles claim that he had no dreams? What else would you call the carousel? Only a man who dreamt of making his sister's life better would commission one, and yet when she had told him that, Charles had dismissed his actions as simple necessity. Balderdash! Charles was too caught up in his problems to realize that he still had dreams.

As the carriage crossed the bridge, Susannah looked up the river at the mill, wondering where Charles was. Was the mill part of whatever had caused that sadness that—try though he might—he could not disguise? Even when he appeared to be relaxed and laughing, Susannah had seen the underlying sorrow. It could have been the result of the fire and his parents' death, and yet Susannah sensed that it was caused by something else. It was almost as if he was disillusioned, and that disillusionment had brought him great sorrow. But what could have happened to make him so cynical? She wished she knew.

What else could go wrong? Charles frowned as he stared at the sheet of paper in front of him. Mrs. Enke had threatened to quit when the dogs tracked mud inside the house; another worker had cut her hand on a loom, and now this. Jane's letter was the proverbial icing on the cake.

"Am I interrupting at a bad time?"

Charles looked up, startled by the sound of Philip's voice. It had been several weeks since Philip had visited him at the mill. "Come in," he said, rising and gesturing to his old friend. "I'm happy for the diversion."

When Philip had taken a seat on the opposite side of the desk from Charles, he leaned forward. "What's wrong?" the former banker asked. "Are your creditors harassing you again?" It was probably only Charles's imagination that Philip's voice sounded strained and that the furrows in his brow were deeper than before.

"No, thank God." Charles gestured toward the envelope that

lay on the desk between them. "I received another letter from Jane. The doctor says Anne will be ready to come home in August."

Philip appeared to relax. "That's not bad news."

"It's not all good, either. Jane says Anne won't look into mirrors. She's convinced she's ugly." Unable to sit still, Charles rose and walked to the window. The mill yard was almost empty now. The earlier flurry of activity as workers loaded bolts of fabric onto railcars was over, leaving only the two men who guarded the gates.

"That's absurd. Anne could never be ugly." Charles turned and saw Philip shake his fist for emphasis. His friend's blue eyes were filled with an intensity that surprised Charles. Normally Philip was almost phlegmatic. "Some beauty is only on the surface," the older man declared, "but hers is innate."

At Philip's words, some of the tension that had caused Charles's neck to knot began to subside. Philip was right. "You and I know that," he told Philip. "I'm afraid that convincing Anne will be more difficult."

Charles leaned back against the wall. He wasn't sure what Philip was thinking, but the distant look on his face told Charles his friend was pondering something.

"Why don't you plan a small party for her when she returns?" Philip said at last. "When Anne sees that all the young swains accept her, she'll realize her fears were groundless."

On the surface, it was not a bad idea. But it was also fraught with risk. "What if they don't?" Unlike Philip, Charles was not sure he could trust the young swains of Hidden Falls. "I couldn't bear to see her be a wallflower."

Philip shook his head emphatically. "She won't lack for partners. If no one else fills her dance card, I will."

It was a day for surprises. "I thought you promised Rosemary you wouldn't dance with anyone other than your next wife."

With a shrug, Philip dismissed Charles's concern. "Rosemary would understand if I made an exception for Anne. Now," he said, obviously anxious to change the subject, "tell me that the stories I hear of Matt Wagner trying to organize the mill workers are false."

The day had just gotten worse. Charles strode to the other side of the office, trying to compose himself. Though he had not heard these rumors, he did not doubt their veracity. Matt had warned him that he was going to make the mill his business, and he'd boasted that when he took action, Charles would know he was responsible. This, then, was what he had meant.

Charles clenched his fist as he stared out the window. A second later his eyes focused on two people standing on the street corner, and he felt rage begin to boil within him. For it was Matt who stood next to Susannah, far closer than any gentleman should be to a lady. And it was Matt who raised his hand to touch her hair.

Charles had said nothing when she had smiled at Matt. There were, after all, no laws against smiling. But there *were* laws against touching. Only one man had the right to touch Susannah, and that was . . . Anthony. Of course it was Anthony.

Susannah was tossing the ball for Salt and Pepper when Charles appeared in the yard, the set of his shoulders and the scowl on his face telling her more clearly than words that he was angry. She rose and forced herself to smile, wondering what had happened at the mill to disturb him. Had there been another accident?

"If I were painting you, I'm afraid I'd have to put storm clouds over your head, and these might not have a silver lining in them." Though the brief afternoon thunderstorm had cleared the air, it was obvious that Charles's mood was far from pacific. He glared at Susannah, those beautiful blue eyes radiating fury.

"If there's a storm, it's because you caused it." Charles's words were little more than a snarl.

The dogs whined, not understanding why their master refused to acknowledge them. "What do you mean?" she asked, bewildered by his anger.

Charles took another step toward her. The dogs yipped and jumped, begging for attention, but he ignored them. "The least you could do is behave with a little more circumspection."

"What are you talking about?" He was close enough now that she could smell his breath, and it held no hint of whiskey. What possible reason could there be for his strange behavior?

Grabbing her left hand, Charles pointed toward Susannah's engagement ring. "Doesn't that mean anything to you?"

He was making no sense. "Of course it does."

"Then why the hell were you letting Matt Wagner paw you where every busybody in Hidden Falls could see you?"

Susannah jerked her hand out of Charles's grasp. "Whatever do you mean?" Matt paw her? She wasn't certain which shocked her more, the accusation or Charles's profanity.

"Don't try to deny it. I saw you two." Charles took a step forward. The dogs ran between them, barking furiously. Both Susannah and Charles ignored them.

"What are you talking about?" she demanded.

"He had his hands all over your hair." Charles's own hands were clenched in anger.

As comprehension dawned, Susannah shook her head. "It was a windy day," she said as evenly as she could. "My hat blew off. Matt caught it and helped me put it back on. That's all."

Charles's eyes narrowed. "Then he wasn't—"

Suddenly Susannah's own anger erupted. "What did you think?" she cried. "Did you imagine that we were engaged in a passionate embrace on Mill Street?" When Charles did not respond, she took a step toward him, poking her finger at his chest. "That's absurd, Charles Moreland, and if you'd used your brain, you would have known that. Matt's my friend. Nothing more. I feel about him the way I do about . . ."

The blood drained from Susannah's face. *Anthony.* She had almost said "Anthony." It couldn't be. It was a slip of the tongue, nothing more. She *loved* Anthony. Of course she did.

Chapter Fifteen

He was an idiot. Charles tried not to stare as Susannah emerged from the makeshift cabana he'd erected near the swimming hole. Why had he ever agreed to this? Agreed? Hell, he'd suggested giving her swimming lessons, and if that wasn't sheer idiocy, he didn't know what was. He hadn't been thinking that day. That much was clear. Just as he wasn't thinking now. No, indeed. His brain was not the active organ right now. Charles was re-acting, and—worse than that—he was reacting in a manner that was totally, completely inappropriate.

He should have rescinded his offer, particularly after the day he'd seen her with Matt. In the dark hours of the night Charles had replayed the scene when he'd confronted Susannah and could no longer deny it. He had been jealous. It was totally absurd, of course. Charles knew she was going to marry Anthony. Just as he knew that the only reason he'd suggested teaching her to swim was to help her please Anthony. Those were facts. Unfortunately, logic and rational thought had the most disturbing habit of disappearing when Charles was close to Susannah.

Damn it all! He hadn't realized just how alluring she would be in a bathing costume. She moved as gracefully as ever, but now there was more of her to admire. Though her ball gown had revealed her arms and that lovely throat, Charles had never had more than a glimpse of an ankle. Until this afternoon. He groaned. Whoever had devised women's bathing suits hadn't been thinking any more than Charles was, or he would never have created a skirt that ended at the knees, displaying shapely legs and the most beautiful ankles God had created. How was a man supposed to keep his mind on swimming lessons when the student was almost unbearably attractive?

Charles looked at the big oak tree, trying to focus on its shiny leaves. The ploy was futile, for his eyes refused to obey the command to look at something—anything—other than Susannah. In desperation, Charles closed his eyes, praying for the strength to resist her. It wasn't as though she was deliberately casting lures the way Charles and his father had when they'd gone fishing. No, the problem wasn't Susannah. It was Charles. He knew that just as he knew he was a louse to even notice how alluring she looked. If he weren't utterly despicable, he would realize that Susannah was simply his friend and neighbor, not an incredibly desirable woman.

With his eyes closed, Charles's other senses were heightened, and he was aware of her perfume as she came closer, a blend of lilacs and carnations and some other sweet-smelling flowers. Was there to be no relief? It was bad enough that his eyes were being tempted, but now his nose was joining the rebellion, refusing to see Susannah as nothing more than Anthony's fiancée. Charles opened his eyes.

Susannah shivered.

"Cold?" Though Charles knew he was grasping at straws, perhaps this was the excuse he needed to end the torture. Perhaps she had realized that the lessons were a bad idea. After all, most ladies didn't learn to swim. They might wade into the water to cool their feet, but generally they did not actually immerse themselves. Even Charles's sisters, who had grown up with the swimming hole behind the house, rarely visited it . . . and then only when Charles had promised to stay away and to keep his friends from spying on them.

That was it! Charles smiled with relief. Susannah was having cold feet. The cold snap that had postponed their lessons had finally ended, but if Susannah was cold—either literally or figuratively—Charles would consider it a well-deserved reprieve.

"No, I'm not cold." Susannah's folded arms gave lie to her words. "I'm just nervous. I've never done this."

"Me, neither." She had never swum. He had never taught swimming, and he most certainly had never had to clench his fists to keep them from reaching out to touch that soft hair or the skin that looked even silkier. God willing, he would never again be in this situation.

"But you know how to swim." Though Susannah had a smile fixed on her face, it appeared strained. "I doubt the thought of going into the water is alarming to you. I, on the other hand, am sure I'm going to sink like the proverbial rock."

Charles shook his head. Rocks were hard and heavy, whereas she was soft and looked almost delicate in that short skirt. He tried to avert his eyes. "You won't sink." Charles managed a short laugh, though his eyes refused to remain focused on the grass. "At least not often."

There was still time for a reprieve. Maybe she would decide this was not a good idea. Maybe she would turn around and go back into the cabana. But Susannah took another step toward the water. "I've never taught anyone anything," Charles told her. "Truth is, I never thought I'd be a good teacher."

She shrugged, obviously not discouraged by his self-disparaging comments. "I may not be a good pupil, but we won't know unless we try."

She wasn't going to give up. He should have known that. One of the things Charles admired about Susannah was her determination. Unfortunately, today he wished that determination were fixed on something—anything—else.

When she reached the edge of the pool, Susannah gave Charles a smile that elevated his pulse to alarming rates. "I'm ready," she announced.

So was he, although not for swimming lessons. He was ready

to turn and flee before he said or did something that would embarrass both of them.

Apparently oblivious of his consternation, Susannah dipped her foot into the water, shivered, then continued walking with the same determination she applied to everything. When the water lapped around her calves, she turned and smiled at Charles. "It's warmer than I expected."

He was warmer than he'd expected, though he had no intention of telling her that. With a sigh, he waded in to stand beside her. It seemed there would be no reprieve. He would have to teach Susannah to swim. "We need to keep walking until the water is about waist deep," he told her. At least then those lovely legs would be hidden. Charles frowned at the realization that once she started to swim, he'd see them again. Worse yet, the wet fabric of her bathing costume would cling to her curves.

"The first thing is to learn to float," he said, trying to focus on swimming lessons rather than his alluring pupil. "Once you realize that the water will hold you up, the rest is easy." Susannah stared at him, those warm brown eyes registering alarm when she realized that he meant for her to put her face into the water.

"Let me show you." Charles stretched out and floated for a few seconds, then lowered his feet to the bottom. "Your turn."

Though he could see that she was wary, she managed a small smile. "You make it look easy." Gamely, she stretched her arms out in front of her, placed her face in the water, kicked her feet up and sank. Sputtering, she rose and faced Charles. "It's not easy!"

Even dripping wet, she was the most beautiful woman he'd ever seen. "The trick is to relax," he said when she had tried and failed more times than he could count.

"That, as you can see, is easy to say but not so easy to do." Susannah tried again, and again she sank.

It wasn't going to work, but Susannah, being Susannah, wasn't going to stop trying. And Charles, being Charles, wasn't going to stop gritting his teeth in frustration until this lesson had ended. There had to be a way to teach her to float. Once she mastered that, Charles was certain she'd learn to swim. And then this torture would be over.

He thought back to the day his father had taught him to swim. They'd come here. Unlike Susannah, Charles had felt no apprehension, only anticipation. Swimming would be like fishing, just another skill to learn. Once he had accomplished that, he would be one step closer to being a man. At first Charles had sunk and sputtered like Susannah, but then his father had tried another tactic. That had made the difference between Charles sinking like a rock and floating like a leaf. It had worked, but . . . Charles tried not to frown as he thought of what it would be like to teach Susannah that way.

"Let's try a different approach," he suggested. The sooner she could float, the sooner he could end the lesson. "I'll hold you up until you get used to the feel of the water." Charles extended both hands, forming a shelf. "I'll hold up your . . . er . . . middle." Susannah's eyes widened when she recognized the implication of his proposal. He would be touching her in a most unseemly manner. "I'll keep you suspended," Charles said. *And I'll pretend I'm holding one of those blocks of wood Rob turns into horses.*

"When you need to breathe, just turn your head to the side." Charles took a deep breath as he demonstrated the technique. Regular breathing filled his lungs but did nothing to slow the racing of his heart. Nothing could change the fact that it was Susannah, beautiful, tempting Susannah, he would be holding, not a chunk of basswood.

"Relax, Susannah. That's what's important." Not that he was relaxed. Far from it. *This is no different from dancing,* he tried to tell himself. *You've touched her before. You've had your hand on her waist.* But this *was* different, and no amount of rationalization could convince him otherwise. When they had danced, they had been in a crowded ballroom, chaperoned by dozens of Hidden Falls' residents. Here they were alone without so much as the puppies for company. When they had danced, they had been dressed in formal clothes, clothing that covered far more than either Susannah's or his bathing costumes did. When they had danced, he had not been plagued with the traitorous thoughts that, despite his valiant efforts, would not disappear. It would take so little effort to bring her upright, to pull her body close to his, to touch those luscious lips with his.

As Susannah lifted her head out of the water to breathe, her legs began to descend. "Sorry," she said and kicked her feet upward.

Sorry. That was one way to describe his own state of mind. Charles looked down at the beautiful woman he now held suspended on one hand. Being so close to her was sheer torture. Was it also poetic justice? Perhaps this was his just desert, a graphic example of how powerful temptation could be. Charles had accused his father of weakness, insisting that a strong man could withstand temptation. Was this his own test? He would pass it. He would, he would, he would. He was not like John. He would not succumb. But, oh, how difficult it was to resist.

When he felt Susannah begin to tremble, Charles lowered her feet to the pond's bottom. "Enough for today?"

"Maybe." The trembling intensified.

A shaft of guilt shot through him. "You're cold! I should have gotten you out sooner."

Though she continued to tremble and wrapped her arms around her waist, Susannah shook her head. "I'm not really cold. It's mostly nerves." Her laugh was weak. "I know it's silly, but I'm still afraid I'll drown. I shouldn't be. After all, I trust you."

Maybe you shouldn't.

"I think you're ready to boast."

Susannah stared at Rob. He looked perfectly serious, his expression apparently sincere. What did he think she'd boast? That she had spent an hour in Charles's arms? That she couldn't forget the way Charles had looked in his bathing suit? That she had found floating far more difficult than she'd dreamt because, instead of concentrating on swimming, all she could think about was how good it felt to be touched by Charles?

Surely Rob didn't know about the swimming lesson. Susannah had told no one other than her mother. Dorothy's reaction had surprised Susannah. Though she had thought her mother might have remarked on the dubious propriety of being alone with Charles, Dorothy had nodded her approval, saying only that she wished she'd learned to swim.

Moira and Megan couldn't help being aware that Susannah had worn the bathing costume, since she had hung it out to dry afterward, but they had no way of knowing that she had been with Charles.

"I beg your pardon." Susannah hadn't meant her words to sound so haughty. That they had slipped out with more fervor than she'd intended simply bore witness to the fact that she was disturbed by the thought of boasting about Charles.

Rob scratched his head, then grinned sheepishly. "Sorry," he said. "I forget you don't know the lingo. To a carver, 'boasting' means cutting the rough shape." On the other side of the workshop, Mark and Luke chuckled. Susannah started to relax. They didn't know how she and Charles had spent yesterday afternoon. "You're ready now that you have the blank." Rob handed her a gouge.

"Should I assume that 'blank' has a second meaning to you?"

One of the assistants laughed, while the other called out, "Hey, Rob, why don't you speak English?"

Rob shot his helper a quelling look. "Why don't you finish that body?" He turned back to Susannah, an apologetic smile on his face. "A blank is the block of wood you made by gluing all those pieces together." Rob gestured toward the wood Susannah had glued and clamped earlier that week and where she had traced the outline of the horse's tail two days ago.

"You called it a lingo, but I'm beginning to think carvers have more than a specialized vocabulary. It seems like it's almost a language."

Rob shrugged. "In that case, you should be a natural at it. Didn't you tell me you spoke German?"

Susannah picked up a mallet and positioned it over the wood, trying to decide where to make the first cut. The wood was perfect now, unmarred by mistakes. She doubted she'd be able to say that in an hour. "My parents spoke German at home as well as English, so it would have been difficult not to learn it."

"I imagine you'll find that valuable when you go to Europe."

Susannah looked up, startled. "How did you know that I wanted to go to Europe?" Not even Dorothy knew that she dreamt of studying in Paris. Charles was the only person Susannah had told. She stared at Rob in alarm. If Charles had told him that, what other confidences had he shared? Had he mentioned that he was giving Susannah swimming lessons?

Rob shrugged. "I didn't know," he said. "I just guessed you'd want to travel. After all, a lot of people do."

"Including us." Mark—or was it Luke?—turned from the drawing he'd been studying and grinned at Susannah. "If this man paid us more, we'd be in Seville next month."

Rob laughed. "If these men carved faster, I'd have taken them with me on my last trip."

"When were you in Europe?"

"About three years ago. I spent a year studying carving."

Susannah's pulse leapt, and she almost dropped her mallet in excitement. Rob was an artist. He would answer her questions from an artist's view. "Were you in Paris?"

Rob nodded. "For about a month."

A month. Though Susannah wanted to spend at least a year there, she would settle for a month. "Was it as beautiful as I've heard?" The pictures in the book Charles had given her had shown a city of great beauty, but it was impossible to determine whether that beauty was only superficial or whether the city's charm extended beyond the magnificent architecture. Charles himself had spent only a few days in the City of Light and hadn't been able to answer all Susannah's questions.

Rob pointed to a spot in the middle of the block of wood that she was supposed to transform into a horse's tail. "Start here," he advised. "It's easier to round the piece if you begin in the middle instead of at one end." When she had made the first tentative cut, he nodded his approval. "As for Paris, yes, it's beautiful, but I prefer other places."

"Such as . . . ?"

Rob's answer came automatically. "In Europe, Bern—or almost anywhere in Switzerland. In the States, Philadelphia."

Susannah couldn't help it. She frowned. "You sound like Anthony. He claims that Cape Cod is more beautiful than Paris."

The sound of snickering could be heard over the soft scratching of gouges on wood. Mark and Luke, it seemed, did not share Anthony's opinion.

Rob shrugged. "You know the adage about beauty being in the eye of the beholder. It's true, but for a painter, Paris stands alone." He pointed toward the block of wood in front of Susannah. "Now, you're ready to release that."

She reached for the clamp, then stopped when Rob shook his head. "In carousel lingo, 'release' means to set the animal free from the blank. In plain English, continue your carving."

As Rob returned to his place, working on the lead horse's head, Susannah tried to fashion a tail. Even though she doubted her skill with wood, she had been thrilled when Rob had asked if she would like to carve a piece of one of the horses. But, though she tried to concentrate on the carving, today she felt jittery. She dropped her chisel every time the stable door opened and flinched when one of the carvers let out a peal of laughter.

With the easy grace that characterized all of his movements, Rob came to Susannah's side and inspected the tail. "He's a lucky man," he said softly.

She looked up, as startled by Rob's words as she had been by Luke's laughter. "Who?"

The smell of sawdust and wood shavings was stronger than normal today, perhaps because the air was heavy with moisture. Susannah wrinkled her nose as she stared at Rob. He chuckled. "Why, Anthony, of course."

Anthony? What did Rob mean? When Susannah raised an eyebrow, he continued his explanation. "I have three sisters, so I've seen the symptoms dozens of times. You can't disguise it, Susannah. You're a woman in love."

Charles was whistling with happiness as he closed the iron gate behind him. Though it was earlier than normal for him to be leaving the mill, the excitement that bubbled up inside him kept him from doing anything productive in his office. He needed to go home. He needed to see Susannah. The reason was inside the brown-paper-wrapped package he carried under his arm.

Today they had finished the first trial of silk-screening, using

193

one of the designs that she had approved. Though there were minor flaws in the process and the dye wasn't exactly the shade Charles had specified, he was pleased with the results, and he wanted to share them with Susannah.

Charles gave the sky an appraising glance. It was apparent that Mrs. Enke was right in predicting rain. If luck was with him, it would hold off until he saw Susannah. It was a simple matter of courtesy. After all, she was the one who had suggested silk-screening in the first place. That was why Charles wanted to show her the cloth. As if that weren't enough, she was an artist. That made her opinion of the designs valuable. There was no other reason Charles wanted to see her. None at all.

He turned at the corner and was striding toward the bridge when he heard a woman call to him. Charles turned, surprised to see Megan O'Toole, her face flushed, as if she'd been hurrying.

"Good afternoon, Megan." Charles tipped his hat. "Did Mrs. Deere send you into town?" Though he suspected that Dorothy Deere had little to do with the running of the house, he would not ask about Susannah.

"Sure and she did not." Megan tossed her head, her smile bright and saucy. "It's me half day off. A girl likes to go for a stroll sometimes, you know."

Though it was not a day that Charles would have considered ideal for a stroll, he said nothing lest he encourage Megan's garrulity. Courtesy demanded that he greet her, but it did not require him to engage in a lengthy conversation. What he wanted was to see Susannah. But Megan continued her explanation. "Me timing was perfect. When I spotted you leaving, didn't I realize that I never did thank you properly for helping me find me da?"

"No need for thanks. I'm glad you found him." Charles started to tip his hat again in farewell, then, remembering the furtive glances Brian had given that day and the sense Charles had had that Brian was afraid of being followed, he asked, "Did Brian ever say where he'd been?"

Megan shook her head. "I heard him telling me mam he went to see an old friend, but even me mam couldn't coax a name out of him." Megan's green eyes sparkled with mirth as she smiled up at Charles. "Me mam can be mighty persuasive, you know."

Despite himself, Charles chuckled. "And your father can be just as stubborn."

"Sure and that's the truth." As Charles pulled out his watch and consulted it in a less than subtle indication that he was in a hurry, Megan asked, "Is it home you're going?" When Charles nodded, Megan flashed him another smile. "Then surely you won't object to me walking with you."

He did object. However, it would be rude to refuse, and Charles had been taught the importance of courtesy, particularly to women. "I'm in a bit of a hurry," he said, hoping Megan would take the hint.

She did not. "I can keep up with you. Me legs are long." She lifted her skirts, revealing trim ankles and shapely calves.

Charles tried to mask his surprise, not just at the unseemly display but also at Megan's frank words. How many times had he heard his mother admonish his sisters that ladies did not speak of legs? The most they did was refer to limbs, and then only when there was no polite way to avoid the topic. Megan had no such maidenly reserve.

"I wouldn't want you to forfeit any of your time in town." He was grasping at straws again, and he knew it.

Megan shook her head, setting the wax fruit on her hat to bobbing. "I'd rather be with you."

What could he say? Accepting the inevitable, he held out his arm for Megan's hand. "Were you visiting the mercantile?" Charles lengthened his stride. He wanted to see Susannah, not stroll with Megan.

She shook her head again. "I came to see you."

This time Charles was unable to hide his surprise. His mother would have been aghast had Anne or Jane spoken with such directness. "A lady must never, ever do or say anything that would lead a gentleman to believe she is 'fast,' " Mary Moreland had decreed. *Fast,* the girls had learned, was an epithet to be avoided, almost as bad as the forbidden word *bastard*. While

Megan wasn't a lady like Charles's sisters, surely her mother had taught her the rudiments of social behavior.

"You think I'm being forward, don't you?" There was a slightly defiant note to Megan's voice. "It was only the truth I was tellin'. I thought men valued honesty."

As they crossed the bridge, Charles glanced back at the mill. Whoever had sabotaged the belts and harnesses had been far from honest. "I do."

"Then what's wrong with a girl speaking the truth?"

Charles tried not to squirm. "Nothing," he admitted. The truth was, he wasn't used to such candor, and it was making him uncomfortable. He had the feeling that Megan wanted to use what his mother had called female wiles to convince him of something, and that added to his discomfort.

"Well, then, perhaps you won't mind if I ask a favor."

Charles gritted his teeth, wishing he had not been right. "That depends on the nature of the favor," he said warily.

Megan tightened her grip on his arm. "Susannah told me you were teaching her to swim."

Forcing himself to continue to take slow, even breaths, Charles remained silent. There was no reason to tell Megan that he wished she were unaware of the afternoon he and Susannah had spent together. Anything he said could be construed as encouragement, when the last thing he wanted was to encourage Megan O'Toole.

"I've always wanted to learn to swim," she announced. "Will you teach me, too?"

Charles looked up the hill at Brad's house, wishing his friend would suddenly appear and diffuse the tension. Teaching Megan could be the answer to Charles's problem. If Megan accompanied him and Susannah, perhaps his wayward imagination would cease conjuring pictures of Susannah in his arms. Perhaps he would be able to regard her as nothing more than a friend. There would be another advantage. He and Susannah would be properly chaperoned. Not even the most avid gossip in Hidden Falls could object to the fact that they were spending time together if Megan were there. It was a good solution.

He should agree. He would agree. But the words that came out of his mouth were, "I'm sorry, Megan. I'm afraid I can't do that."

Chapter Sixteen

Susannah rose, placing one hand on the small of her back. A morning of bending and lifting as she and Megan attempted to clean the attic had taken its toll on her. "Where did your family live before they worked for the Morelands?" Susannah knew that while they had been employed by Charles's family, the O'Tooles had lived above the stable in the rooms that Rob and his assistants now occupied, but she had no idea what their lives had been like before that.

Megan brushed back a lock of hair that had tumbled from her cap. "Me parents were at Fairlawn before I was born. Sure and it was my home until last year."

"Where did you go then?" Since she had seen the deplorable conditions that some of Hidden Falls' residents endured, Susannah had begun questioning where others lived. Megan and her family were comfortable here, and they had had excellent accommodations with the Morelands, but what about other times in their lives?

Frowning as she shook the dust rag out the window, Megan said, "Me mam's sister has a farm. We stayed with her." Megan wrinkled her nose. "I hated it. It's happy I'll be if I never gather another egg or milk another cow. Those must be the most ornery critters God created, and the smell . . ." She pinched the tip of her nose. "They stink worse than a dead groundhog."

Though Susannah suspected Megan was exaggerating, she couldn't help smiling at the young woman's descriptions of her former accommodations. Susannah wished that cows and chickens were the worst experience anyone had. "You were lucky," she told Megan. "Matt Wagner was showing me around town this week, and some of the houses we saw were worse than barns. I can't imagine how people live in them."

Megan's green eyes narrowed. "Where were you? On Forest past Falls?" When Susannah nodded, Megan continued, "Those girls were dumb."

Dumb was not an adjective Susannah would have thought to apply to the people who lived in such squalor. "What do you mean?"

Her lips tightening in obvious disgust, Megan said, "They had good jobs in the mill until they broke the rules." She leaned against the windowsill. "Old Mr. Moreland was a real stickler for what were proper. Everyone knew that unmarried girls in the family way couldn't work at his mill."

Dust motes danced in a ray of sunshine. Susannah stared at them for a second, unsure what Megan meant. Then she realized that she was referring to unwed mothers. Apparently Charles's father thought that unplanned pregnancy was a crime. How different from Susannah's own parents' beliefs. They—especially her mother—had worked to improve the conditions of what they referred to as "unfortunate women."

"How did they provide for their children?" she asked.

Megan shrugged as if the answer should have been obvious. "They had to find themselves a man, and then they had a passel more babies, 'cause they didn't know no better."

Susannah shuddered and reached for her mop, wishing she could wash away the memory of the hovel on Forest as easily as she banished dust from the attic. "That seems unfair."

"Old Mr. Moreland weren't wrong. It was the girls what were dumb." Megan removed a dust cover from a large piece of furniture, folding it carefully to keep the dust trapped inside. "Mighty nice bureau," she said, running her hand over the intricately carved mahogany. "I aim to have one of these in my house one day."

They cleaned in silence for a few minutes. Then Megan said, "You sure won't catch me in the girls' predicament. I'm smarter than that." She tugged on one of the bureau drawers. "I know what men want, and I'm not giving it away for free."

Susannah blinked in surprise. Surely Megan wasn't planning to . . .

"You needn't look so shocked, miss." Megan's lips curved in a grin. "I ain't aiming to be a soiled dove. No, indeed. I'm holding out for a wedding ring, just like you." She stared pointedly at Susannah's left hand, where Anthony's ring sparkled. Megan's smile shone as brightly as Susannah's diamond. "He's gonna marry me. I'm sure of that."

Susannah felt as if a hand had grabbed her heart and was squeezing it. She didn't believe that Charles would marry Megan. He might be attracted to her. After all, Megan was a beautiful woman. He might kiss her. Susannah knew he had done that. But marriage? Though Dorothy might deplore what she called the American caste system, in a town as small as Hidden Falls it was unlikely that a man in Charles's position would marry a servant. And, despite her beauty, that was Megan's status.

There was little chance that Megan's dreams would come true. That thought disturbed Susannah at the same time that it set her heart soaring. When she realized that though Charles might dally with her, he had no plans for marriage, Megan would be hurt. Susannah hated to see others hurt. But if, by some chance, Charles did marry Megan, then the person who would be hurt would be . . .

Susannah refused to finish the thought.

"I'm glad you came today," Rob said as Charles walked into the stable. His face lit as he smiled. "There's something I wanted to show you."

Charles closed the distance between them, pleased that he

had obeyed his instincts and come to the carvers' workshop. Today he needed enthusiasm and good news more than normally. He had spent a particularly frustrating morning sifting through the rubble in the burned rooms, searching for clues, finding nothing.

Charles tried not to frown at the thought of his mission and the failure he had experienced. No matter how often he looked through the debris, he found nothing unusual. Charles wasn't sure what he had expected. Whoever had started the fire had obviously been clever and had left no traces. Still, there had to be a way to prove that John hadn't set the fire. The man had been many things including a hypocrite, but he was not an arsonist. Charles was certain of that. Of course, he reflected ruefully, there was the question of how accurate his own instincts were. After all, he had once believed John to be a good, loving father and a devoted husband. He'd been wrong about that.

"What do you think?" Rob pointed to a detailed carving behind the saddle of the lead horse. He had completed the horse's head two days earlier and was now working on the body. Though Mark and Luke would carve the bodies for the other animals, Rob had explained that he wanted to do the lead horse himself. It would be the most elaborate of the animals and the only one to bear his signature.

Today was supposed to be the carvers' half day off, but while Mark and Luke had taken advantage of Susannah's offer of real horses, Rob had remained in the workshop. Charles wasn't sure the man ever rested. As much as Charles himself, he seemed driven to complete his work.

Charles looked at the object that appeared to be hanging from the saddle. Though it was not yet finished, he could see that eventually it would be a satin bag, holding a child's doll.

He smiled. "That's hers, all right." Charles had found his sisters' dolls when he had been sorting the few things that he could identify in the rubble. Though Anne and Jane were long past the age for toys, their mother had kept their favorite dolls in a cabinet in her sitting room. Apparently the glass front of the cabinet had protected them from the worst of the fire, for although their dresses were scorched and their faces covered with soot, they had sustained remarkably little damage. When Rob had told Charles that he wanted to personalize the lead horse by adding details that were unique to Anne, Charles had brought the blond doll to the carver, telling him it had been one of his sister's most prized possessions.

"Do you think she'll like it?" To Charles's surprise, there was a hint of vulnerability in Rob's voice, as if he were uncertain of Charles's response.

Charles ran a finger over the delicate carving. The horse was magnificent. Even without the addition of the doll, it appeared to be the finest animal Rob had ever created. And that, Charles realized, was saying a great deal. As he had told Brad, Rob was a master. He routinely carved almost unbelievably beautiful horses. But this one surpassed the others. If Charles had had to explain the difference, he would have said that Rob had been inspired by this horse.

"The Anne I knew a year ago would love it," he told Rob, thinking of the lovely young woman whose life had been altered so dramatically. "I can only pray that she hasn't changed too much after all that she's endured."

Rob's blue eyes were serious. "My experience is that people are stronger than we think." He reached for a piece of sanding paper and smoothed an edge of the bag. "The picture I have of your sister is of a beautiful, strong woman. If I were fanciful, I'd describe her as one of the Greek goddesses. Maybe a combination of Aphrodite and Hera." His voice was wistful, and Charles stared at him, startled by Rob's reference to the goddesses of love and marriage.

"You sound like a man in love." The instant the words were out of his mouth, Charles regretted them. It was absurd. Just because Rob had mentioned Greek goddesses didn't mean he was in love. It was Charles who was obsessed with the concept. Why did he continue to think about love? It must be because it was spring and all the animals were mating. It surely had nothing to do with himself and the way he felt about . . .

Rob looked directly at Charles, his expression inscrutable.

"That could be," he admitted slowly. "You've made Anne seem very lovable."

Rob and Anne? That was a thought Charles did not want to pursue. No man wanted to think of his younger sister with a man. "Have you finished the plans for the carousel?" he asked in a deliberate attempt to change the subject. Love and his sister were not things he wanted to consider.

Rob nodded as he pulled out a piece of paper. "We'll have the twelve animals you and I agreed on. Eight will be horses," he said, pointing to a number of the circles on the drawing. "I thought we'd also have a giraffe, an ostrich and a monkey. That leaves one animal." Rob showed Charles a circle with a question mark in it. "I considered a fish, but those puppies of yours made me think about a dog."

Charles cocked an ear. The dogs in question were in the yard, tied to trees. Though they had protested the restraint, preferring to be with Charles, he knew they'd only disrupt the workshop.

"A dog would be fine," Charles agreed, relieved when he heard no whining. Perhaps Salt and Pepper had fallen asleep. He looked at Rob's chart. "I'm not sure about the monkey. I remember one frightening Anne when we went to the zoo."

"No monkey then. Which animals did she like?" Rob picked up another sheet of paper, drawing a line through the rough outline of a monkey.

It had been a bright summer day when the family had visited the zoo. Though Charles had tried to pretend that he was too old to care about animals and had insisted that his enthusiasm was feigned to make the day more enjoyable for his sisters, he remembered that his heart had raced when the lion had roared, demanding his food, and that he had joined Jane in coaxing the kangaroo to waken. That had been one day when Jane had been the more adventurous of the twins, once even trying to climb into a cage. Anne had hung back, clinging to their mother's hand, until they had reached the elephant. Only then, and when they had visited the black bears' cage, had she crowed with glee.

"Elephants and bears," Charles told Rob, smiling at the memory of his sister's pleasure.

Rob looked at the drawing and squinted as if he were envisioning the finished carousel. "Why don't we have both an elephant and a bear instead of the monkey and dog?"

Charles nodded, pleased with the idea. "Two dogs are more than enough trouble." He grimaced at the memory of one of his canine companions gnawing his favorite slippers. "I ought to get rid of them."

Though he laughed, Rob's voice was serious as he suggested that Charles give one to Susannah. "She seems to enjoy them," he pointed out.

That she did. It seemed that Susannah was happier playing with the puppies than doing anything else. "Maybe I will." The idea had merit, although Charles wasn't certain how the dogs would react if they were separated. As if they somehow sensed that he was thinking of them, they started barking frantically. "The pests," he muttered as he walked toward the door. "I wonder what they're up to now."

Somehow they had loosened their ropes and were running in circles around the floor of the former gazebo. The reason was not difficult to find, for in the center sat Dorothy Deere.

Charles tried not to sigh at the thought of how worried Susannah must be. This was the time of day when Dorothy was supposed to be napping. He sprinted across the grass, gave the dogs a quick pat and shooed them away. Though the sun had probably made the gazebo floor uncomfortably warm, Susannah's mother was sitting cross-legged, her skirts hiked up well above her ankles. It was only as he came closer that he saw the tears that streamed down her cheeks.

"Is something amiss, Mrs. Deere?"

She turned her tear-streaked face toward him. Though he saw a glint of recognition in her eyes, it was clear that she hadn't realized he was addressing her. "Mrs. Deere?" She shook her head. Charles tried not to frown. Why didn't she recognize her own name? Then he remembered that Susannah normally called her by her first name. A small quirk he'd always assumed stemmed from the fact that Susannah was an only child.

"Can I help you, Dorothy?"

This time she reacted. Brushing the tears from her cheeks, she said, "I lost it. I lost the locket. Mama will be so angry."

Tears began to course again, and Dorothy sobbed, "Mama loves that locket. She only let me play with it."

Charles tried not to let his dismay show. Though Susannah had told him that some days her mother appeared to be more of a child than a parent, he had not realized how serious the condition was. "Perhaps you left it at home. Why don't we go back and look there?" The lost locket did not concern him. What did was getting Dorothy Deere back to Pleasant Hill. He extended his hands and helped her stand.

She looked around, her eyes as blank as if she had never seen the yard before. "I thought I knew where I was," she said slowly. "It doesn't look the same. I remember a white . . ." She paused, and lines formed between her eyes as she appeared to concentrate. "A white . . . you know." She gestured toward the cement foundation.

"A gazebo?"

"Yes." She nodded. "That's right. There was one here."

"Let's go home, Dorothy." He cupped her elbow and began to lead her away.

"Yes, John."

Charles winced at the name but realized there was no point in correcting Dorothy. He needed to get her back to Susannah.

As they walked toward the path, the puppies returned and began to circle Charles and Dorothy. She knelt on the ground. "Oh, aren't these pretty dogs?" Dorothy stroked Pepper's head and let Salt lick her fingers. "I like dogs, but Mama won't let me have one."

Charles raised Dorothy to her feet again. "Please wait just a moment," he said as he tethered the dogs. It would be difficult enough getting Dorothy home without having to worry about the puppies being underfoot or racing off to chase a squirrel.

"Yes, John." And she said nothing more as they walked through the woods that separated their homes. When they reached Pleasant Hill, Susannah came rushing to the door, her face lined with worry. Though Charles gave Susannah a reassuring smile, he kept a firm grip on Dorothy's elbow.

"Oh, Susannah," her mother cried, "look who brought me home. Isn't John a gentleman?"

Susannah shot Charles a quick look of dismay at the misnomer. He shook his head slightly. That was unimportant. Keeping a smile fixed on his face, he led Susannah's mother into the large entry hall. "The pleasure was all mine, Dorothy." Charles bent his head in farewell.

"Come, Dorothy." Susannah took her mother's arm and began to walk toward the staircase. "It's time for you to rest."

But Dorothy refused to move. "I can't. I lost Mama's locket. She'll be angry with me." This, then, was the reason Dorothy had run away from home. For some reason, she must have thought the locket was in the gazebo.

"Let's look in your pocket," Susannah suggested. "I saw you put the locket there this morning."

"Really?" Dorothy slid her hand into her pocket and withdrew a piece of jewelry. "You're so clever, Susannah!"

As the women walked toward the stairs and Charles turned to leave, Susannah mouthed the word *stay*. He paced the floor of the parlor, wishing there were something he could do to lighten her burden. Poor Susannah! If it had been difficult for him, seeing a woman who looked like an adult but acted like a child, how much more difficult must it be for Susannah to confront the changes in her mother each day? There must be something they could do to help Dorothy.

When Susannah entered the parlor, her face was ashen, and her shoulders were shaking. "Thank you for bringing her home."

Charles reached out and grasped her hands. "It's all right, Susannah. It'll be all right."

Tears welled in her eyes. "No, it won't be all right. You've seen her, Charles. Dorothy's like a child." She shuddered. "Dr. Kellogg was right. She just keeps getting worse, and I don't know what to do."

"Let me help you."

Susannah stared at Charles for a long moment, and he could see the indecision on her face. Though it was apparent that she needed help, for some reason Susannah was reluctant to ask for—or accept—it. At last she nodded.

"Dr. Kellogg doesn't know everything," Charles said, remembering how the doctor had admitted there was nothing he could do to help Anne. "There are other doctors." There had to be one somewhere who could cure Dorothy's illness.

"I know. I wanted to ask you to help me find one."

"Why didn't you?" The words came out more harshly than he'd intended, and a tear escaped from Susannah's eye.

"You had so many problems that I didn't want to burden you. Besides, I thought I ought to be able to solve the problem by myself."

She was wrong. Even the strongest of people needed help occasionally. Another tear stained Susannah's cheek. It was more than Charles could bear. Impulsively, he pulled her into his arms. "Don't cry, Susannah," he murmured. "I'm here. You can lean on me."

Perhaps it was his words, perhaps his embrace. All Charles knew was that something released the torrent of Susannah's emotions, and she began to sob. He drew her closer, letting her tears soak his shirt, hoping that the horrible shudders that racked her frame would subside when she realized she was not alone. Poor Susannah, having to be both parent and child, afraid to admit to any weakness. Gradually the spate of crying subsided.

"Thank you, Charles." Susannah turned a tearstained face toward him and tried to smile, then laid her face back against his chest, wordlessly seeking comfort.

Charles closed his eyes, wishing the moment would never end. It was wonderful, so very wonderful, having Susannah in his arms! He could feel the beating of her heart and the soft puffs of breath as she struggled to control her tears. He could smell the sweetness of her perfume and the clean scent of her hair. She was soft and womanly and, oh, how he longed to cup that delicate chin in his hand, to turn her face toward his, to once again taste the nectar of her mouth.

Charles shuddered. He was despicable! Susannah had turned to him as a friend, and how had he reacted? Like an animal. Nothing more. For only an animal or a man without a shred of morality would have forgotten for even a second that the woman he held belonged to his friend. Though he wanted to deny it,

Charles could no longer ignore the evidence. He was no better than his father.

The church bell was pealing, reminding the townspeople that today was the Sabbath, as Susannah and her mother walked down the aisle. Susannah blinked, trying to let her eyes adjust to the darkness. She had been surprised when Dorothy had come to breakfast, dressed in one of her favorite gowns, a hat on her head. When Susannah had asked where she was going, Dorothy had looked startled.

"Have you forgotten that it's Sunday?" she asked, her tone more than a little reproachful. "You know that we attend services each week."

That was not true. They had not been to church since they had returned to Hidden Falls, although Susannah had reminded her mother each week. Something was different today. Since it appeared that Dorothy was determined to go to church, Susannah asked Brian to harness the buggy. She herself had changed clothes quickly and accompanied her mother.

If the usher was surprised to see them, he gave no indication, merely offered Dorothy his arm and led them toward the front of the church. The Ashton pew, Susannah had been told, was the third on the right, directly behind the Morelands' and the Harrods'. Custom dictated that no matter how crowded the church might be, those three pews remained empty unless the families were in residence.

As she slid in next to her mother, trying to ignore the soft murmuring that their presence had generated, Susannah saw that Brad Harrod and his parents were seated in front of her and that Charles had joined them, leaving his family's pew empty. Susannah was puzzled. Was it that Charles disliked being alone? That seemed unlikely, and yet she could think of no other reason why he would flout convention.

As the service began, the murmuring subsided, and Susannah began to relax. Though the sanctuary was simpler than the ones in Boston, and no stained-glass windows cast rainbows on the floor, she was filled with the same peace she always found when she worshiped.

That peace was shattered a few minutes later. When the last notes of the second hymn faded, Reverend Collins climbed into the pulpit and addressed the congregation. "This morning we are going to speak about temptation. It is with us constantly, ready to lure the unwary from the path of righteousness. Think, my friends, of the words we utter each time we repeat the Lord's Prayer. 'Lead us not into temptation.' Think of the temptation the prophets endured. Think of the way Satan tempted the Lord himself."

Susannah stared at the man sitting in the row in front of her. His shoulders were broad, and though she could not see them, she knew that his hands were gentle. How wonderful it had felt, being held in those arms, having those hands touch her! When she had been in Charles's embrace, she had felt safe. For a few moments, her problems had disappeared, and nothing had mattered other than being close to Charles, hearing his heart beating, feeling his comfort surround her like a downy pillow. For a few moments, she had believed that all was well with the world. He had been her friend, her comforter, and she had gladly accepted all that he had offered.

But that hadn't been enough. When they had stood there, so close that their breaths mingled, she had wanted more. She had wanted him to kiss her. And that would have been wrong. She had been tempted. Sorely tempted. Somehow Reverend Collins had known. That was why he had chosen temptation as the subject of his sermon. Susannah felt her face flush with shame.

That afternoon when Dorothy was resting, Susannah climbed to her studio. She needed—oh, how she needed—the escape that painting always brought her. But today, though she mixed paint on her palette and stood in front of the easel, she found herself unable to relax. The landscape that she had begun two weeks earlier looked as strange as if it had been painted by someone else, and she could not force herself to put another dab of paint on it.

What was wrong? Laying her palette aside, Susannah moved to the window and stared outside. She could hear songbirds trilling to each other, and in the distance a raptor soared. It was a beautiful afternoon, one that should have set her heart to singing with joy. Instead, she stood at the window, her thoughts confused and her heart heavy.

Dorothy was worse. Each week the woman Susannah had once known seemed to fade a little more. Oh, there would be moments when her mother would return and would seem almost normal. But those moments were fewer, and each lasted a shorter time. In place of the Dorothy Deere whom Susannah had known was a child in a woman's body. This Dorothy needed to be reminded of basic things, and she was frequently as willful as a child. Charles might claim that everything would be all right, but Susannah knew better.

And then there was Charles, the man who tempted her. Susannah wished she understood what there was about him that made her enjoy his company so much. She had never met anyone like Charles. She had never longed to be with anyone the way she did with Charles. She had never wanted to kiss a man the way she did Charles.

She was going to marry Anthony. Why, then, did it feel so wonderful to be held in Charles's arms? Why did she dream of his kiss and not Anthony's?

The world was upside down, and Susannah had no idea how to right it.

Chapter Seventeen

"Are you sure you want to go inside?" Matt stopped at the iron gate that led to the Moreland Textile Mills. "You may not like what you see."

Susannah nodded. The day was perfect. A few fluffy clouds floated in a sky that was almost as deep a blue as Charles's eyes. Dorothy was resting, and Moira had promised that she would keep her from leaving the house. There would never be a better time. And, no matter what Matt said, it was time for Susannah to see the place that was such an important part of Charles's life.

"I'm ready," she said. Though Matt had told her the conditions inside the mill were worse than the cavelike houses she had seen, Susannah believed that he was exaggerating. Surely Charles would not permit truly deplorable conditions within his mill. Even if they had been there when his father was alive, Susannah was certain that Charles would have improved them. He was a man with a conscience, and his conscience would not let him place others in danger if he could prevent it. Susannah remembered the day the young mill worker's fingers were amputated and the sorrow Charles had shown.

Matt was wrong. Charles was not a monster. The mill was not a horrible place. Susannah needed to convince herself.

"I want to see how that beautiful fabric is made," she told Matt. It was not a lie. Charles had shown her the silk-printed cotton he had made using one of the designs she'd suggested, and it had been magnificent. After only two tries they had captured the exact shade of China blue that the pattern deserved, and now the mill was producing a few hundred yards a week. Although Charles had told her he could easily switch one loom's entire production to the print, he explained that he would be able to charge a higher price if he kept the production limited. "It's one of those basic laws of supply and demand," he had told Susannah, the rare smile that lit his face confirming that her suggestion had been a good one.

"Mornin', miss, Matt." As they approached the guardhouse, the watchman tipped his hat to Susannah, then nodded at Matt. "Reckon I'd take the back stair if I was you."

"Thanks, Wilson." As Matt led Susannah into the redbrick building, he said, "Wilson knows that Charles doesn't approve of my being here, so he tells me how to avoid him." Though it was clear that neither Charles nor Matt would tell her, Susannah wondered what had caused the enmity between them. By Charles's own admission, it was of long standing.

Susannah and Matt climbed the back stairs to the second story. "I thought you ought to see the weaving room first," Matt told her as he opened the door.

For a long moment Susannah stood motionless as her senses were bombarded with new experiences. Though she had read about the mills in Lowell, the descriptions had always focused on the town's cultural attractions and the betterment of the workers' lives. For Susannah, accustomed to a quiet house, the reality of the weaving room was shocking.

She clapped her hands over her ears, then forced herself to let them drop to her sides. The pounding of the looms was louder than even a cannon shot, and unlike the thunder of a cannon, it seemed incessant. The air, heavy with cotton dust and overheated from a hundred bodies, swirled around her. Susannah reached out a hand to steady herself while she tried to ease her breathing. But the air was so moist that she could hardly draw a breath, and the light from the few gas lamps seemed to cast eerie shadows on the floor. It was, she thought, a scene from Dante's *Inferno*, sinners condemned to endless toil near the fires of Hades.

Matt took her arm and led her back into the stairwell. "Seen enough?" he asked.

She nodded and leaned against the wall for a second. "How can they work there?" she asked. "I could hardly breathe, and I couldn't even hear myself think." Mill wages were good. Susannah knew that. But surely farming was easier.

Matt nodded slowly, his dark eyes filled with concern. "The workers tell me you get used to that. What they complain about is pain in their backs from standing all day. That and the constant fear of losing a finger. It's dangerous work, Susannah," Matt added with a frown.

"Can't anything be done?" Though she could not imagine spending entire days in the mill, she was certain that conditions could be improved. The noise and the heavy air had been a shock. She would not deny that. But Matt had been wrong. The mill was not worse than the hovels he'd shown her. His feelings toward Charles influenced his view of Charles's business.

Matt waited until they were outside the mill and back on the street before he spoke. Here the air was fresh, and though a wagon rumbled down the road, it seemed almost silent compared to the incessant pounding of the looms. "Nothing can be done without Charles Moreland's consent," he said, not bothering to hide the bitterness in his voice. "And Charles doesn't care about anything other than money."

Though Susannah was appalled by the conditions in the mill, she would not believe Matt's accusation. It was what she had surmised. The years of enmity between Matt and Charles had colored his thoughts. "I think you're wrong about Charles."

Matt shook his head, his expression tinged with what appeared to be regret. "I wish I were, Susannah. I truly do. But I've known the Morelands my whole life, and money is the only thing that matters to them."

Though the sky was still as clear as before, Susannah felt as if a storm were imminent. "I can't believe that. Charles cares about his sisters. That's why he's building the carousel."

Matt led her up the short hill to Main Street. Although it was not the most direct route home, Susannah suspected he realized she wanted to distance herself from the mill, at least for a few minutes.

"I'll concede that one point," Matt said as they passed Dr. Kellogg's office, his words reminding Susannah that he was an attorney. "Morelands care about money and their families. The rest of the town exists only to serve them."

There was such bitterness in Matt's voice that Susannah stopped. She put her hand on his arm and gazed at him. "Aren't you being a bit harsh?" Charles was not the monster Matt believed him to be. Oh, he wasn't perfect, but who was? She herself was not, and she suspected Matt had flaws beside his distorted view of Charles.

Charles cared about others and was not motivated solely by money. She knew that as well as she knew Matt was unlikely to believe her. Though he had no hope of financial gain and they were not his family, Charles had been unfailingly kind to her and Dorothy. He'd brought Dorothy home when she wandered and had offered to contact doctors on her behalf. If that weren't enough, he'd taken time from his own busy schedule to teach Susannah to swim. She tried not to blush at the memory of those lessons and how wonderful it had felt to have Charles touch her. "I think you've misunderstood Charles."

"Have I?" If Matt noticed Susannah's heightened color, he was polite enough not to mention it. "You raised the carousel in his defense. You probably realize that everyone in town knows he's having it built and is anxious to see it." Susannah nodded. Though speculation had dwindled somewhat, it was rare for her to enter an establishment on Main Street without hearing someone discussing the carousel. "How do you think they'll feel when they learn they'll never ride on it?" Matt demanded.

Susannah's eyes widened in surprise. "What do you mean?"

"They may believe that it's going to be set up in the park, but that's not so. Charles is leaving it on his property where no one except his sisters can ride it."

Surprise turned to shock. "Are you certain?" Though she had never asked Charles, like the townspeople, Susannah had believed that the carousel would be moved to the park.

"Rob told me they would build it on the site of the old gazebo."

Susannah took a deep breath, trying to slow the pounding of her heart. "That's terrible."

"No, Susannah. That's a Moreland."

Though Salt and Pepper raced after balls with the same enthusiasm they displayed each afternoon, Susannah could hardly muster the energy to throw the toys. She had debated coming to the house, knowing she would see Charles if she did, knowing she would ask him about the carousel if she did, not wanting to hear his response. But staying at home, she realized, was the act of a coward and—whatever else she might be—Susannah Deere was not a coward.

It was odd. When Brian had driven her into town, Susannah had been prepared to be disturbed. She had known that the conditions in the mill might upset her. What she had not anticipated was that she would be more distressed by Charles's plans for the carousel than by anything she had seen at the mill.

Desultorily, she tossed the ball again. This time, though, the dogs did not respond. Ignoring her, they raced toward the house. The reason was not hard to divine. Charles had arrived. Susannah rose to face him, still not certain how she was going to broach the subject of the carousel.

But Charles gave her no opportunity to even greet him. "I heard you went visiting today," he said without preamble. There was no mistaking the anger in his voice, though it was tinged with something else, something Susannah could not quite identify.

"Do you object?" How could a man's eyes be both hot and cold at the same time? Somehow, Charles's were.

"As a matter of fact, I do." His words were clipped, the harsh tone causing both Salt and Pepper to cock their heads. "If you wanted to see the mill, you should have asked me. I'd have shown you around."

Amanda Harte

The blood drained from Susannah's face as she realized what had overlain Charles's anger. Disappointment and pain, and she'd been the cause. Susannah lowered her eyes. Though she had believed she'd planned today's excursion carefully, she had never considered that she might hurt Charles. "That's true, but . . ."

He took a step forward. She stood her ground, unwilling to back away from a problem she'd created. "What's the matter? Were you afraid I wouldn't have the same—let's use your favorite word—perspective as Matt?"

"It's true Matt's views are different," Susannah said as evenly as she could, hoping he'd understand. "He does have a different perspective. But that wasn't the reason I went with him. I know that you're busy, and I thought I had already infringed on enough of your time."

There was one other reason, one she would not admit to Charles. She had been afraid that Matt might be right, that the mill was worse than the houses on Forest, and she hadn't wanted Charles to see her reaction. Though she had wanted to spare him pain, her plan had backfired.

He stared at her for a long moment, as if he were trying to assess her sincerity. At last he said, "So tell me, what do you think of my albatross?" His voice was normal now, no longer cold and angry.

Susannah took a deep breath as she started to relax. "Is that how you see the mill?"

"What else would you call something that takes you away from everything you love and drags you down?"

The anger might be gone, but it had been replaced by cynicism and something else, something so dark she thought it was despair. Perhaps anger was preferable. It dissipated more quickly. "I might call it a challenge or a trust," she told Charles. "You don't just make cotton textiles there. You change people's lives."

Charles looked up from petting the dogs, and those blue eyes that somehow found their way into each of her paintings widened in surprise. "What makes you say that?"

216

Carousel of Dreams

"People who used to work on farms come here, hoping for something better."

"And they find it." Charles rose to face Susannah. Though his voice was even, she saw the challenge in his eyes. "They earn more money in the mill than they could farming."

"Correct. That's one way you've changed their lives." Susannah picked up Pepper, who'd been whining at her feet, then handed him to Charles so she could hold Salt. Though what she had to say was important, she wanted to couch her words carefully, lest Charles feel she was criticizing him. The dogs would help. In Susannah's experience, it was difficult to be angry with a squirming puppy in your arms. "There are other changes," she said. "For one thing, there are dangers to working in the mill."

Charles's eyes flashed with anger again. "Now you sound like Matt. My mill is as safe as any." Pepper licked his face, and though Susannah could tell that he was trying to resist, Charles smiled.

"I don't doubt that," she agreed, stroking Salt's head, "but it could be better. You probably can't reduce the noise, but you could improve the lighting."

As they stood here in the bright sunshine, it was hard to imagine working all day in the poorly lit mill. Charles shook his head. "Lights take money, and that's one thing I don't have."

Susannah was not going to give up, not now that she had Charles's attention. "I think the improvements would pay for themselves over time. If the workers had more light, they would have fewer accidents, and they'd produce more yardage. That would increase your profits."

Slowly Charles nodded. "That's possible. The simple fact is, I don't have any money to invest. Maybe in another year."

It was a concession. Susannah decided to change her tactics. She placed the squirming puppy on the ground, then looked up at Charles.

"If you can't add lights, what about the carousel?"

He looked as if she had suddenly started speaking a foreign language. "What about it?"

"I heard you were planning to keep it here." She gestured

217

toward the place where the gazebo had once stood, the place she had first met Charles, the place he had kissed her. It would be a beautiful spot for a carousel, but there was a better one.

"That's right."

Susannah spoke slowly, trying to keep her tone casual. He had accepted other suggestions she'd made. Perhaps he would be receptive to this one. "If you put it in the park, everyone could enjoy it, not just your sisters."

The way Charles's shoulders stiffened told Susannah she was wrong. Charles did not like this idea. He shook his head, and the anger she thought gone flared in his eyes. "What kind of a man do you think I am?" he demanded. "Do you think I'd expose Anne to the town's stares and their pity? If the carousel were in town and she had to go there to ride it, that's exactly what would happen. They'd stare, and they'd talk, and they'd make her miserable." Charles clenched his fists. "I want Anne to have some happiness in her life. She's the one I care about, not the town of Hidden Falls."

Charles wasn't sure what wakened him. His head was groggy with sleep, and the crescent moon was still high, telling him dawn was hours away. Perhaps it had only been a dream. His watchdogs slept, undisturbed on the foot of his bed. Perhaps he had imagined the sound of footsteps in the hall. But then the soft shuffling was repeated, and this time the dogs stirred.

Sliding his arms into a robe, Charles walked to the door. Was it possible that whoever had set the fire had returned to finish the destruction he'd begun a year before? Shushing the dogs and moving as quietly as he could, Charles entered the hallway. The light was dimmer here, barely enough to distinguish forms. He looked both directions, then saw her. She stood at the top of the stairway, clad only in a white nightdress, her hair unbound.

What on earth was Dorothy Deere doing in his home in the middle of the night? Hastily Charles lit one of the gas lamps.

Dorothy blinked and shook her head, as if to clear it. "John?" She took a step toward him, her face reflecting her confusion. "Where's Lucy? I need to see Lucy." She looked around, apparently searching for the woman named Lucy. "It's important."

Charles tried not to frown at the name that had disturbed him from the first time he'd heard her utter it. Dorothy might believe it was important to see Lucy, but Charles knew that what was important was getting Dorothy back to Pleasant Hill.

"Come, Dorothy." He held out a hand. "Let me take you home." He wouldn't try to convince her that he was Charles and not John. Not tonight.

"But . . . Lucy . . ."

He shook his head. "Lucy's not here." He spoke slowly, calmly, as he guided Dorothy down the stairs.

As they walked across the grass, Dorothy stopped. "Lucy must be here," she insisted. "I saw you with her in the . . . the white building." She pointed toward the spot where the gazebo had once stood. "You're a sly one, John. I know you didn't want anyone to know, but I saw you. I saw you kissing her."

It was nothing more than the ramblings of a confused woman. Her words meant nothing. They couldn't. Though Charles had thought that Lucy might be the dark-haired woman he had seen with his father in the gazebo, he knew that Dorothy hadn't been in Hidden Falls last year when John and Lucy had had their assignation. She couldn't possibly have seen them together. Unless . . .

Susannah had said that the last time her mother had been home had been a brief visit for his parents' wedding. Was it possible? Were there two dark-haired women that his father had kissed in the gazebo, or had Lucy been part of his life for all those years? Charles shuddered, not certain which prospect was worse.

"Let's go home, Dorothy. Let's get you back to sleep."

And then Charles could return home to his own nightmares: the mill, his sister, the letters he had to write about Dorothy. He could deal with them. What he wouldn't think about were his father, a woman named Lucy and trysts in the gazebo.

Chapter Eighteen

Normally Susannah liked rain. Although the light on a wet day was not conducive to painting, she enjoyed the sound of rain-drops pelting against windowpanes, and she found the sharp crackle of thunder and lightning invigorating. But today the rain brought no joy. She sat in the library, trying to focus on the pictures of Paris that Charles had given her, but found herself listlessly turning the pages, her mind whirling.

Although the picture in front of her showed a group of tour-ists riding donkeys to the base of the Eiffel Tower, when she closed her eyes, Susannah saw Charles, his face suffused with anger at the thought of opening the carousel to the town. And yet as she looked more closely, Susannah realized that his anger was underlain with sorrow and frustration. Charles was angry, not with her for suggesting that he move the carousel into the park, but with himself, because he felt powerless to help his sister.

How well she knew the feeling! Like Charles, Susannah needed to believe that she was doing something constructive, that in some small measure, she was making a difference in others' lives. Charles might not recognize the need in himself, but it was there. It was the reason he had come back to Hidden Falls and why he worked so hard to make the mill profitable. It was instinctive for Charles. Susannah had been taught.

For years, her parents had preached the importance of helping others. For years she had focused on helping groups of people in unfortunate circumstances. Now her focus had changed, narrowing. Today Susannah wanted nothing more than to be able to help two people: her mother and Charles Moreland. Even the mill workers' plight paled compared to those two. Though there was nothing Susannah could do to restore his sister's beauty, she could help Charles make the mill more profitable. That would not solve all his problems, but it might give him the time he needed to spend with his sister when she returned, and it could give him enough money to improve the mill.

Her motives were not completely altruistic, Susannah admitted. Yes, she wanted Charles to be happy, and yes, it would be good if she could help the mill hands. That was important. But Susannah was also selfish. She needed to feel useful; she needed to know that she could still make a difference. Sadly, when she dealt with Dorothy, all she felt was helpless.

She wanted, oh, how she wanted, to believe that Dorothy would get better. But the truth was, her condition continued to deteriorate. At first her mother would hesitate over an occasional word; now she had difficulty completing whole sentences, as if she forgot what she was going to say before she had a chance to express the thought. And this morning at breakfast, Dorothy had stared at the saucer as if it were a foreign object. It had taken all of Susannah's strength not to cry at the sight of her proud, independent mother reduced to asking what she should do with a piece of china. With every fiber of her being, Susannah wished she could help Dorothy. And because she could not, she sought a substitute.

Susannah looked down at the book in her lap. She turned the page, revealing a photograph of the *Arc de Triomph*. What a beautiful monument! While a fire crackled in the stove, chasing the unseasonable chill from the room, Susannah stared at the picture, trying to imagine herself in Paris, strolling the length of the Champs Elysees from the Place de la Concorde with its huge obelisk toward the triumphal arch. It would be a warm, sunny May day. The famous chestnut trees would line the boulevards. She would stop at a small café for a cup of coffee and a pastry. She would . . .

"Mr. Anthony's here." Megan's voice broke Susannah's reverie. Susannah looked up, startled by the sight of her fiancé. It had been several weeks since she'd received a letter from him, and he'd said nothing of another visit to Hidden Falls. Had he somehow known that she was in the doldrums and had come to cheer her the way he'd cheered her father during his final illness?

Susannah rose, extending her hand to Anthony and giving Megan a nod of dismissal.

"Come in, Anthony." Susannah's smile faded when she looked at her fiancé's face. For the first time since she had met him, his eyes were lined with fatigue, and he hesitated to meet her gaze. The rain pelting the window and the gray sky looked cheerful compared to Anthony's expression.

"Is something wrong?" Susannah asked. Not even when her father had died had Anthony been so solemn.

"No . . . yes." He kept his eyes fixed on the carpet, seemingly fascinated by the pattern of the Persian rug. Though she could see him swallow as if trying to form words, he said nothing more. The vague malaise Susannah had felt turned into full-fledged dread. "I don't know how to tell you this," Anthony said at last.

Something was terribly wrong. Susannah could see it on his face and hear it in his voice, but she had no idea what had caused Anthony's distress. Taking his hand, she guided him to one of the settees that flanked the stove and took a seat on the one opposite him. Ordinarily she would have sat next to him, but today she wanted to see his face.

"What is it?" she asked, keeping her voice soft.

For another long moment, the only sounds were the raindrops on the glass and the crackling of the fire. Anthony swallowed again, then looked at Susannah. "I'm in love." The anguish she saw on his face gave the lie to his gentle words.

Susannah blinked in confusion. Of course Anthony was in love. So was she. That's why they were marrying, wasn't it? But why was he so distressed? Love should not cause pain. "Love is an important part of marriage," she said as calmly as she could.

"That's the problem." Anthony's eyes searched her face for a moment, then resumed their study of the rug. "There's no easy way to say this."

Susannah leaned forward and touched his hand, uncertain whether she sought to comfort him or to assure herself that this was not some hideous dream. "You're worrying me, Anthony. I've never seen you like this."

He met her gaze, and she saw pain reflected in his eyes along with something else, something that could have been chagrin. "I've never been in a predicament like this."

Susannah shook her head slowly. "Being in love isn't a predicament."

"It is for me." Anthony took a deep breath and straightened his shoulders. He stared at her for a long moment, then nodded, as if he had made a decision. When he spoke, the words tumbled out in a torrent. "Susannah, I love someone else, and I want to marry her. I've come here to ask you to release me from our engagement."

The blood drained from Susannah's face, then rushed back. She gripped the arm of the settee for a second to regain her balance. Someone else. Break the engagement. It couldn't be. Susannah took a deep breath, willing her hands to stop trembling. Though Anthony's words came as a shock, at some deeper level she realized that she was not totally surprised. This was the reason his letters had seemed so distant. This was the reason there had been no words of love in them. This was the reason he had been reluctant to set a wedding date.

"Are you certain?"

Anthony nodded. "I've never been so certain of anything in my life." He leaned forward, laying his hand on Susannah's as if it were his turn to comfort her. "I'm sorry, Susannah. I admire you greatly, but I don't love you the way I do Gracie. She's the woman I want to marry." If Susannah had had any doubts about

Anthony's sincerity, the smile that lit his face when he spoke Gracie's name destroyed them.

She looked down at her hands. They were perfectly still now, adorned only with Anthony's magnificent diamond. It was odd, but though the ring was beautiful, Susannah realized she had never felt comfortable wearing it. At first, she had believed it was only because she was unaccustomed to jewelry. But perhaps the reason had been deeper. Perhaps her heart had known what her head had not, that she and Anthony were not meant to be together.

She slid the ring off her finger and handed it to him. "Perhaps it's for the best."

Anthony shook his head and refused to take the ring. "Keep it," he said. "You can sell it and use the money to go to Paris." A faint smile crossed his face. "I would like to think you got something good from our engagement." His expression was earnest as he said, "I don't want you to hate me."

"I don't."

When Anthony left, Susannah returned to the library and stared out the rain-streaked window. She hadn't lied when she had told him that she felt no hatred for him. The truth was, she felt nothing other than empty. When the shock had faded, it had been replaced by a faint sense of relief.

Susannah laid her forehead against the windowpane, letting the glass cool her skin. There must be something terribly wrong with her. Her dream of marriage had vanished. The man she had expected to spend the rest of her life with had told her he loved another. And she could feel nothing. No anger, no pain, not even disappointment.

What kind of a woman was she?

Charles hated rain. He had ever since he'd been a child, for then rainy days had meant that he had had to stay indoors, reading a book or playing with his sisters, instead of going fishing or riding with his father. Since he'd taken over the mill, rain had begun to symbolize trouble. Today was no different. There had been another accident this morning, another man's hand cut by a rapidly flying shuttle.

Charles looked down at the papers on his desk. There was no need to read the report his foreman had given him. He knew it by heart. The man had said he couldn't see properly, and that was why he hadn't moved out of the shuttle's path. As he had paid the injured mill hand for a whole day's work and sent him home to recuperate, Charles had sighed. Susannah was right. He did need more lights in the weaving room. The problem was, he had no money to buy them, and he knew without asking that the banks would not lend him another cent.

Charles had hated the look of disappointment on Susannah's face when he had explained that he could not afford to install more lamps. If he had had it in his power, he would have agreed, simply to see her smile. How he loved to see her smile! It wasn't only that Susannah was breathtakingly beautiful then. It was more than that. For when Susannah smiled, Charles felt as if she had realized one of her dreams.

If there was anyone who deserved to have her dreams come true, it was Susannah. Unfortunately, they showed no signs of becoming reality. Happy endings, trips to Paris, even well-lit weaving rooms were elusive. Charles's heart ached at the knowledge that he was powerless to turn those dreams into reality. What a useless man he was! He couldn't even help Susannah with Dorothy. That was another reason Charles scowled at the rain pelting the window. The last of the doctors' responses had come in this morning's mail. To a man, they had all concurred with Dr. Kellogg's diagnosis. There was no cure for Dorothy's brain fever. It would only get worse.

How, oh, how was he going to tell Susannah that?

Though the hinges had been oiled only last month, a slight squeak told Charles that someone had opened the door to his office. He turned, then stopped, surprised by his visitor.

"Anthony! What are you doing here?" Charles grinned, thinking that his day had just improved. Anthony could be what he needed to cure his doldrums. When they'd been in school together, Anthony had always been able to coax Charles and Brad out of foul moods. He had always been the one with a joke and a ready smile.

But today Anthony was not smiling. "Can't a man visit a

friend without being subjected to an inquisition?" he demanded in a voice that was so devoid of humor that Charles almost recoiled.

"I didn't realize one question constituted an inquisition," he said as calmly as he could. If Anthony was bringing bad news, he could leave. Charles had reached his quota of problems for the day.

"Bad day, huh?" This time Anthony sounded more like the man Charles had known at college.

"I've had better," he admitted.

Anthony pulled Charles's hat from the coat tree and handed it to him. "Can I persuade you to leave this fine establishment and join Brad and me for a drink?" It must have been Charles's imagination that had made him think Anthony was the bearer of bad tidings, for his mocking tone was one Charles knew well. "Demon Whiskey may not solve any problems," Anthony continued, handing Charles his umbrella, "but even those temperance ladies can't deny its power to help a man forget them . . . at least temporarily."

Charles shrugged as he opened the door. "Why not? The day can't get any worse, and it just might improve."

He and Anthony walked quickly, their umbrellas unfurled against the rain that came down in torrents. It was a day when no one was outside for pleasure. The few other pedestrians on Mill Street scurried from one doorway to the next, trying to dodge both the raindrops and the splashes from the horse-drawn wagons.

Charles kept his head bent and his eyes on the street in front of him. It was only by chance that he happened to look up and see a familiar figure dart into a doorway, a doorway that appeared to be occupied by another. What was Brian O'Toole doing in town today? And who was the man he was meeting? For the way the two bent their heads together told Charles this was no chance encounter. It was none of his business, he reminded himself. This was, as Susannah would undoubtedly be quick to point out, a free country. Brian O'Toole could meet whomever he pleased. And, Charles reminded himself, so long as he did not set foot on Moreland property, he had no cause to question him. Charles increased his pace, anxious to leave Brian O'Toole and the rest of the day's problems behind.

"It's good to have the ABCs together again." Brad was waiting for them at the tavern, a half-empty glass of whiskey in front of him. When Charles and Anthony had ordered their drinks, Brad tipped his head toward Anthony. "What brings you to Hidden Falls on a rainy day, other than the desire to share a whiskey with your friends?"

The room was dark. It might have been Charles's imagination that Anthony appeared uneasy with the question. But when he spoke, the wariness in his voice told Charles it was more than imagination. Anthony was uneasy with the question.

"Some business with Susannah," he said.

"So you finally set the date!" Brad practically gloated. Charles tried not to flinch. There was no reason the thought of Anthony and Susannah's wedding date should disturb him. It wasn't as if he hadn't known for months that they were planning to marry. It wasn't as if he begrudged his friend happiness.

Anthony took a long swallow of his drink, then fixed his gaze on the far wall. The tavern had been built without windows. Though the original intent had been to provide the patrons with privacy, today the absence of windows meant that not even the sound of rain intruded. The ABCs' corner of the room was silent as Brad and Charles waited for Anthony's response. "Not exactly," he said at last.

That was not the answer Charles had expected. "Then what exactly was the nature of your business?"

Again, Anthony stared at the wall, refusing to meet either of his friends' eyes. "We ended our engagement." He spoke so softly that for a moment Charles thought he had only imagined the words. Brad's gasp told him he had not.

"I won't believe that Susannah cried off," Brad said. Charles agreed. If there was ever a woman in love, Susannah was it. And even if she weren't in love, Charles knew that her sense of loyalty would keep her from breaking the engagement.

Anthony ran his finger around the top of his glass in a nervous gesture that Charles remembered from college. "She didn't cry off," he admitted.

For a second, Charles refused to believe what he had heard. He plunked his glass onto the table and leaned toward his friend. Before he could speak, Brad drawled, "If I apply my finely honed power of deductive reasoning, that must mean you jilted her."

Charles felt rather than saw Anthony flinch. "That's not the word I'd have used." True to form, Anthony was trying to avoid taking responsibility for his actions. That had been one of his least admirable characteristics when they'd been in school together. Charles had believed that the intervening years had matured him; apparently he had been wrong.

"Tell me, Anthony," Charles demanded, "what word would you use to describe breaking a lady's heart?" His own heart ached for Susannah and the pain she must be feeling over Anthony's desertion, yet at the same time, he felt an unexpected lightness.

"It was hardly that dramatic," Anthony insisted. "If anything, I would say that she was relieved."

Charles knew otherwise. "You're deluding yourself, Anthony. That woman loves you." As Anthony started to take another drink, Charles pushed the glass out of reach. The man was going to listen—really listen—to what Charles had to say. For once in his life, he was going to accept responsibility. "I can't say I ever understood it, but she would do anything to make you happy. Why, she was learning to swim just so you could have the honeymoon you wanted." Anthony stared stonily at the table, apparently unmoved by the proof of Susannah's affection. "She loved you so much that she never even told you she dreamed of a honeymoon in Paris. No, she was going to the cape, because that would make you happy."

Anthony motioned to the bartender to bring him another drink. "There you have it. I'm clearly the wrong man for Susannah. She's better off without me. Now she can go to Paris."

He was excusing himself again. In the past, though he had recognized Anthony's weakness, it had never affected anyone Charles knew. Now he realized just how destructive Anthony's insouciance could be, and he could tolerate it no longer. Not when it was Susannah that Anthony was hurting.

"What a selfish bastard you are!" Leaping to his feet, Charles hauled Anthony out of the booth and landed a fist on his face. "You don't deserve Susannah!" He punched Anthony again, then ducked a blow.

The other patrons of the tavern stared, astonished at the sight of the normally controlled Charles Moreland pummeling a friend.

"Stop it!" Brad yanked Charles away from Anthony, then stood between the two men. "No woman's worth destroying a friendship."

His fists still clenched, Charles turned to Brad. "You're as bad as he is." He shot a contemptuous look at Anthony, who was mopping blood from his face. "Susannah is worth a hell of a lot more."

Charles wasn't sure what ached more as he climbed the hill to Susannah's house: his fists or his heart. It had been a long time since he had tried to settle an argument with force. As a child, he'd resorted to violence to get his way, until his father had shown him how diplomacy could gain him far more than a quick right hook ever would. Loyalty, his father had told him, was infinitely more valuable than fear. But today those lessons had paled beneath the all-encompassing white-hot fury that had swept through him when he'd learned what Anthony had done to Susannah. Susannah, beautiful, wonderful, lovable Susannah, had been dealt a blow far worse than any he'd given Anthony.

And now Charles was on his way to Pleasant Hill, unsure of the reception he'd receive. It was possible that Susannah would be so distraught that she'd refuse to see him. Charles hated the prospect of being unwelcome as much as he did the thought that she might be crying. He never had been able to adopt his father's cool attitude toward a woman in tears. Rather than offer her his handkerchief, Charles's first reaction was always to flee from a crying woman. But that was something he could not do today. Susannah might need a friend. That was why he forced his feet to continue up the path to the fanciful house on the hill.

"Good day, Charles." Megan's smile was as perky as ever. She looked behind him, as if expecting to see someone else. "Isn't Mr. Anthony with you?"

Charles felt a brief flash of annoyance that Anthony—the selfish bastard—rated a "mister," while he was plain Charles. He was also surprised that Megan asked about Anthony. If her father had returned from town, he undoubtedly knew of the scene in the tavern and the fact that Anthony had left Hidden Falls soon after that. But perhaps Brian was still in town and Megan had not heard the tale.

Charles had no intention of fueling gossip, even to set the record straight. He said only, "Anthony took the last train home." *And he won't be back.* Though he had not voiced the words, Charles knew that no matter what Brad said, the ABCs' friendship was destroyed. Charles could not condone a man's causing such pain, especially when it was Susannah who'd been hurt.

"Is Susannah home?"

"Yes, I am." She emerged from the small library so quickly that Charles guessed she had heard him arrive. Though she was not smiling, Charles noted that her eyes were not red rimmed. That was a good sign. A very good sign. He felt himself begin to relax.

"I wanted to thank you again for the book about Paris," Susannah continued in what sounded like her normal voice. "It must be a beautiful city."

He nodded. "It is. You'll enjoy it when you get there." No matter how calm she appeared on the surface, Charles knew that she must be hurt. It was important to remind her that the future would be happier. Anthony was right. He was not the man for Susannah. The only problem was, Susannah might not agree with that. It was his—Charles's—responsibility to convince her that she was better off without that sneaking, lying bastard.

From the corner of his eye, Charles saw Megan standing inside a doorway, obviously listening to their conversation. What he had to say to Susannah should not be overheard. "Would you like to take a walk?" he asked. "The rain has stopped."

Her lips curved slightly. While he wouldn't call it a smile, it was better than tears. "Let me get my bonnet." Another positive omen. Susannah must not be too distressed if she could think about a hat.

Moments later, they were outside. The air was still heavy as it tried to absorb the water that lay in puddles on the ground, but Susannah took a deep breath as if it were fresh spring air that she was savoring. "No puppies?"

Charles shook his head. "They're probably chewing my slippers in retaliation for being locked indoors, but I didn't want the distraction of chasing them today."

They walked down the long driveway, by unspoken consent ignoring their usual path through the woods. It would be too muddy to be enjoyable, and the trees would still be dripping rain. As Susannah gave him a long appraising look, Charles wondered if she knew that he was aware of what had transpired today. "I never did thank you for bringing Dorothy home that night," she said. "I hadn't realized that she wandered at night."

The almost eager way Susannah seized on a subject that had to be painful for her told Charles she wasn't ready to discuss Anthony. But she had to. Holding the hurt inside would only make it fester. Charles knew that, just as he knew he'd do anything in his power to ease her pain.

"I'm glad I could help, but that's not why I came today." As they approached a large puddle, Charles held out his hand to guide her around it. "Maybe it is," he said, reconsidering his words. "I do want to help you." They had reached the road. When Charles gestured to the right, Susannah nodded, agreeing with his suggestion that they walk toward the falls. Though the path to the falls themselves would be treacherous, at least this stretch of the road should be empty.

Charles stopped and turned toward Susannah, her hand still clasped in his. "Susannah, I know why Anthony came here today, and I'm sorry. He's worse than a cad. For an educated man, he's surprisingly ignorant."

Those lovely brown eyes widened, and he saw incredulity in them. "What do you mean?"

"Only a man who's both blind and dumb would give up a woman as beautiful and desirable as you."

Though she had met his gaze a moment ago, Susannah now stared at the ground. "It wasn't Anthony's fault."

Her voice was low, her words barely audible, as if she spoke of a shameful secret. This was what Charles had feared, that Anthony's rejection had made her feel that she was unworthy. The bastard! Charles should have hit him harder.

"Of course it was Anthony's fault." He couldn't let her believe that she had failed in some way or that she was less than a woman. He would not let Anthony destroy Susannah the way his father had destroyed his mother. There had to be something he could do or say to show her how special she was.

They had given up all pretense of walking and stood in the center of the road. It was an odd place for a conversation like this, but then today had been an odd day. Anthony had done his best to ruin it. Now it was up to Charles to salvage Susannah's pride.

He took a deep breath, hoping that she would listen. He wasn't Anthony. She didn't love him the way she loved Anthony. But he was her friend. Perhaps that would count for something. Perhaps she would believe him. If there was any justice in this world, she would believe him.

"Anthony is an idiot. Every other man on this earth recognizes that you're the most desirable woman God created." As Susannah raised her eyes to his, Charles saw disbelief reflected in them. He continued. "Every other man spends his nights dreaming about holding you in his arms." Her eyes widened, and this time he thought it was in surprise. "Every other man longs to kiss those sweet lips of yours." A flush colored her cheeks, and she dropped her head in confusion.

In the distance songbirds trilled. Susannah tipped her head to the side, as if listening to them. "Oh, Charles. You didn't have to say that." He heard the embarrassment in her voice. She thought he was telling her lies, feeding her compliments to soothe her after the pain that Anthony had inflicted.

Charles put his hand under Susannah's chin and raised it so that she would meet his gaze. She had to believe him. Somehow he had to convince her. "Do you think all I'm doing is trying to make you feel better?"

She nodded. "Why else—"

He wouldn't let her finish the sentence. "Because it's the truth. Because I meant every word that I said."

A hint of sadness filled her eyes, telling Charles just how badly her confidence had been shaken. Damn Anthony! A black eye and some bruises weren't nearly enough payment for what he'd done to Susannah.

"You're a good friend, Charles," she said, her voice as sad as her eyes. "I appreciate what you're trying to do."

"But you don't believe me." He completed the thought. "No, don't deny it. I can see it in your eyes." Charles gritted his teeth in frustration. "What do I have to do to convince you?"

When words failed, there was only one recourse.

Quickly, before she could guess what he intended, Charles pulled Susannah into his arms and lowered his lips to hers. Actions, his mother had told Charles and his sisters, spoke more clearly than mere words. Since his words were having no effect, he would act.

Charles had meant it to be a light kiss, little more than a friendly caress. It was to be proof that he—a man—found Susannah a desirable woman. That was all. A simple demonstration, nothing more. But Charles had not reckoned on the sheer magic of holding Susannah in his arms or the force, a force stronger than the most powerful magnet, that drew him to her. She was irresistible. And, if truth were told, Charles did not try to resist. Her lips were so sweet, and they felt so good beneath his that Charles pulled her closer.

How many nights had he dreamt of holding her in his arms, of kissing her, of feeling the warmth of her breath on his? How many nights had he wakened, aching to touch her? Charles had thought his dreams were vivid. He had believed that he remembered every detail of the kiss they had shared. He had been wrong. Nothing—not his memory, nor his dreams, not even his hopes—had prepared him for the wonder of holding Susannah in his arms.

Impatiently, he tugged her hat from her head and let one hand touch the softness of her hair. It was as silken as he had imagined it. His fingers gloried in the sensation of twisting a strand, imagining how it would look unbound, how it would feel against his bare chest.

She sighed, her lips moving ever so softly against his, and as she did, Charles slid his hand lower, caressing the base of her neck, allowing his fingers to move slowly down her spine, tracing the delicate curve, imagining how soft her skin would be. And as his hands navigated the uncharted territory of Susannah's back, his lips began an exploration of their own, feathering kisses on her eyelids, then moving to press a kiss on the tip of her nose.

Though her eyes remained closed, Susannah's lips curved in the sweetest smile he had ever seen. It was more than he could bear. With a groan, he recaptured her lips, coaxing her to part them, then savoring the sweetness within.

Susannah moaned and pressed closer to him, igniting new fires deep inside him and a longing that would not be quenched. He wanted her. Oh, how he wanted her! But it was more than simple desire. Susannah, he realized with a sense of wonder, meant much, much more to him.

He had been such a fool. Why had he never realized how right she felt in his arms? Susannah embodied everything he had ever dreamt of and more. Why had he never realized just how wonderful she was, this woman of his dreams? She was perfection, pure and simple perfection, and what he felt for her was deeper and stronger than any emotion he had ever known.

Chapter Nineteen

Perhaps it was a minute. Perhaps it was an hour. Susannah lost all sense of time. All that mattered was being held in Charles's arms, feeling the warmth of his lips on hers, hearing his heart beat so close to hers, smelling the crisp, woodsy scent that was his alone. Never in her life had anything felt so wonderful. Nothing, not even that first kiss they had shared, had felt so perfect, so close to heaven on earth.

It was magic. That was the only way she could describe being kissed by Charles. How else could she explain that, although the sky was still cloudy, she felt as if the sun had suddenly burst through, filling the world with its bright radiance? How else could she explain that, although they were standing in the middle of a muddy road, she felt as if she were in an enchanted land where mythical creatures like unicorns could appear at any moment? It was magic, and the magic was Charles.

"Thank you," she said, her voice husky with emotions that she would not attempt to hide. She stood in the circle of his arms, feeling at peace at the same time that her senses tingled, longing for the touch of Charles's lips and fingertips. He was the kindest, most wonderful man on earth. Somehow he had known how much she had needed a friend, and he'd come at exactly the right moment. He had done more than put soothing salve on her wounded pride; he had healed the lacerations. And if that wasn't magic, Susannah wasn't sure what was.

"I feel better."

"So do I." Those lips that had wrought such magic on hers curved upward. "That felt a whole lot better than smashing my fist into Anthony's face."

A gust of wind sent water spraying from the trees. Susannah recoiled instinctively, moving out of Charles's embrace. Then as his words registered, she gasped. "You didn't!"

"I did."

There was such satisfaction in his voice that she couldn't help smiling. "You make me feel as if we're back in medieval times, and you're a knight defending a damsel's honor." Though she had been taught to abhor violence, a shaft of primitive pleasure shot through Susannah at the realization that someone cared enough to defend her. Not just anyone, she amended, but Charles.

" 'Twas my pleasure to be at your service." Charles sketched a low bow. "Alas, milady, I hope you have no need for me to slay a dragon, for I regret to say that I've neglected to bring my dragon-slaying mace . . ." Apparently unable to continue his courtly dialogue, Charles resumed his normal voice. "Mace or whatever barbaric weapon knights resorted to when confronted with green-scaled, fire-breathing creatures."

As he had intended, she laughed. Her imagination had conjured unicorns, his dragons, but it seemed as if—at least for a few moments—they had both escaped to a magical place. If only they could remain there, in the land where there were no cares, no problems, only joy and happiness.

"You need to laugh more often." Though Charles smiled as he spoke, there was an underlying firmness to his words.

Susannah couldn't dispute his reasoning, but she wasn't the only one who needed laughter in her life. "You, too," she said.

For a second Charles stared at her, and she thought he was

going to object. Then he grinned. "Touché. Let's make a pact to laugh together every day."

What a wonderful thought, laughing every day. But even more enticing was the prospect of being with Charles each day. "Agreed."

As the wind sent another shower from the trees, Charles raised one eyebrow in a quizzical gesture. "Don't I get a kiss to seal the pact?"

It was so tempting. Susannah started to move back into his arms, then stopped, feeling as if somehow the ground under her feet was no longer steady. It was an illusion, nothing more. Though the road was muddy, it was not slick, and the earth was not moving. There was no reason to feel this way, and yet the fact that she did made her pause.

Perhaps it was time for caution. While it would be an exaggeration to say that the foundations of her existence had been shaken, much had changed today. Her future was suddenly uncertain, for she was no longer engaged to Anthony. That should have been the most important event of the day, and yet it had been eclipsed by the fact that she had kissed—really kissed—Charles. And now it felt as if she were riding a carousel that was out of control, spinning faster and faster with each revolution. Everything was moving far too quickly, and if she wasn't careful, she'd be too dizzy to stand. She took another step backward.

As if he sensed her hesitation and the reason for it, Charles shrugged. "All right. I can wait for my kiss."

Though he pretended to pout, he could not hide the mischievous twinkle in his eyes. Susannah smiled as the ground stabilized. Everything would be all right. "We should probably go back," she told Charles, suddenly aware that they had been gone for over an hour.

Charles nodded and placed her hand on his arm as they started to walk. "The important thing is that you're not devastated by Anthony's idiocy."

Was that what he had expected? If so, it was no wonder Charles had come to comfort her. "No," she said slowly, "I'm not devastated." How could she be when the broken engagement had led to the most wonderful moment of her life? "What surprises me is that I feel so little regret. It makes me wonder why I wanted to marry Anthony in the first place."

Charles gave her a long look, his blue eyes serious. "Why did you? Even though Anthony was my friend, and I thought I knew him well, I never could picture you with him."

Susannah was silent for a moment, trying to marshal her thoughts. She wished they would clear as easily as the sky had after the rain. "I met Anthony when my father was ill," she said, remembering how difficult those months had been. "We had a lot of visitors, but Anthony was one of the few who could take Father's mind off the pain." And for that she and Dorothy had owed him a huge debt of gratitude. Somehow Anthony had succeeded in entertaining Father when Susannah and her mother had been unable to focus on anything other than the doctors' grim prognoses.

"I never asked why, but Anthony kept coming, even after Father died." Susannah laughed, a little self-conscious over the seemingly haphazard way her romance had begun. "I guess you could say one thing led to another. I enjoyed Anthony's company. I liked the idea of marriage. Perhaps it was inevitable that I imagined myself in love."

Susannah was conscious of Charles watching her face carefully as he listened to her tale. They had stopped walking and were once more standing in the middle of the road facing each other, their lips only inches apart. Susannah tried not to stare at Charles's mouth.

When she finished speaking, he quirked an eyebrow. "You say you imagined love, but I think you must have loved Anthony if you agreed to marry him." Though Charles's voice was even, it held an intensity that surprised Susannah.

"I did. I do." When Charles's face darkened ever so slightly, Susannah hurried to clarify her statement. "You're right. I do love Anthony, but not the way I should have. Today, while I was pacing a track in the carpet, I realized that the love I feel for Anthony is what I would have for a brother, not a husband."

Susannah swallowed, thinking of the day Charles had accused her of being overly friendly to Matt. That day she had almost blurted out that her feelings for Matt were similar to those she held for Anthony. That should have told her that something was wrong. She should have known then that marriage to Anthony would be a mistake. Perhaps it was blindness, perhaps stubbornness. The fact was, Susannah hadn't been willing to give up the idea of a husband and happily ever after so easily.

She gave Charles a wry smile, relieved to see that something about her explanation had erased the lines between his eyes. "The odd thing is, Dorothy must have sensed my true feelings. She asked if I was sure I wanted to marry Anthony." Susannah shivered, more from the realization of how close she had come to making a serious error than from the light breeze that had tugged a strand of her hair loose. "I thought I was sure," she continued. "Fortunately, Anthony recognized the mistake before I did."

"Don't give him so much credit." Charles's voice was harsh, and Susannah saw sparks of anger in those beautiful blue eyes. "Anthony falls in and out of love twice a year, as regular as clockwork. Brad and I used to tease him about changing women with the seasons."

Susannah could not hide her surprise. This was a side of Anthony she had never seen. It was true, though, that they'd been engaged for less than six months.

Charles frowned again. "Brad and I never thought Anthony would actually marry. That's why we were surprised when he announced his engagement." As if suddenly reminded, Charles stared at her left hand. It was a measure of Susannah's distress that she had left the house without her gloves. "Where's your ring? Did he take it back?" The ferocity in Charles's voice told Susannah he was ready to punch Anthony again.

She shook her head. "Anthony told me to sell it and use the money for a trip to Paris."

A look of faint pleasure crossed Charles's face. "That's the only intelligent thing that man said today. Will you go?"

"Yes." That was one of the decisions Susannah had made while she paced the library floor. "I'll go when Dorothy's . . ."

Her voice trailed off, unwilling to put words to what she knew would happen.

". . . Better." Charles completed the sentence.

"Yes." Though she knew it would take a miracle to cure Dorothy, Susannah was not ready to give up hope. Not today.

The days began to form a pattern. Susannah had arranged with Brian to have the horses saddled early each morning so that she and Rob could ride before they both began their normal day. Although his assistants preferred to ride in the evening, she and Rob insisted that dawn was the best time. For Susannah, the hour that she spent in the saddle gave her day a peaceful beginning. She and Rob rarely spoke, although they'd exchange smiles when they managed to clear a hedge or when the sunrise was particularly beautiful. Unlike even the time that she spent painting, the hours on horseback seemed to grant Susannah inner peace, renewing her spirit and giving her the energy she needed for the rest of the day.

For when she returned, it was time to join her mother for breakfast. Mornings with Dorothy were the most difficult and yet, at the same time, the most rewarding part of the day. At first Susannah despaired of all the things her mother could no longer do. Choosing the correct piece of silverware had become a challenge, she appeared to have forgotten her German vocabulary and now she had difficulty reading even simple books.

But Susannah soon realized that there were many things Dorothy could enjoy, and they were things they could do together. Although her mother had never had a garden in Boston and had never expressed any desire for one, now that she was back at Pleasant Hill her face would light with pleasure at the flowers that had somehow survived the years of neglect, and she was content to spend hours weeding the extensive gardens. Susannah and Dorothy would work side by side, sharing the satisfaction of a garden whose beauty increased daily.

Though Dorothy retained few memories of their efforts from day to day, Susannah cherished each hour that they were together. As she told Charles one afternoon, she felt as if she were storing memories, putting them in a safe place for the time when she would need them. And that time, they both knew, might not be far away. Charles had confessed that the physicians he had consulted had agreed with Dr. Kellogg. Though it was not the answer she sought, Susannah had begun to accept the inevitability of her mother's decline.

In the afternoons while Dorothy rested, Susannah would go to the carousel workshop. She couldn't help smiling when she thought of how her role had changed. At first she had been a spectator. Now she was a participant, although not in the way she'd anticipated. The tail she had been carving had not been a success. Though he had continued to encourage her, at length even Rob had admitted that the tail was not good enough to be part of one of his horses. But Rob was nothing if not persistent, and he had insisted that Susannah could contribute to the carousel.

"You're a painter," he told her, "and I need one." He had explained that none of his carvers would have enough time—or the talent, Rob claimed—to paint the rounding board. When Susannah had raised an eyebrow, silently telling Rob that he had used another term from his specialized vocabulary, he had explained that the rounding board was a series of panels that covered the mechanism at the top of the carousel. Normally these were flat, rectangular panels joined by carved shields. Typical rounding boards of commercial carousels might have advertisements painted on them; private ones frequently featured landscapes. "That's why I thought of you," Rob said. "You're a natural." But Susannah, who had heard Rob use the same adjective to refer to her carving skills, was skeptical and had agreed only to try one panel. "I'm afraid it will be as awful as my horse tail."

That panel was now almost completed, and even Susannah had to admit that it was not awful. She had chosen the falls for her subject and had—according to Rob and his assistants—captured the beauty and the mystery of the site. She was pleased with the painting, but even if it had been a disaster, Susannah would have enjoyed her afternoons in the workshop. It was fun being with the carvers, joining in the gentle teasing and the occasional practical jokes that contributed to their camaraderie.

And then as the shadows lengthened, she would leave the workshop, play with the dogs and laugh with Charles. They both had abided by their pact to laugh together each day. There were days when Susannah saw lines of fatigue and worry on Charles's face. There were days when she knew he sensed her frustration. But each day, no matter how grim their experiences had been, they found a reason to laugh. And then, when they both wore smiles, they would talk about whatever had bothered them. It was more than catharsis; for Susannah, her time with Charles brought healing, and she would return home, ready to face her problems.

The one thing they had not done was resume swimming lessons. Charles had asked if she wanted to continue, but Susannah had declined, telling him she no longer needed to know how to swim, since she would not be honeymooning by the sea. Though that was true, Susannah's reasons were more complicated. One of the reasons involved her mother. The last few times she had seen Susannah's bathing costume, Dorothy had pleaded to accompany her. Susannah could not imagine Dorothy, who had forgotten such basic things as how to fasten her tea gown, learning something as difficult as swimming. And the pond was a far too dangerous place for her mother to be.

The dangers were not confined to Dorothy. Susannah feared what she might do if she were in Charles's arms again, clad only in a bathing costume, knowing no one was likely to interrupt them, no matter what they were doing. For in Susannah's imagination, they were doing far more than swimming.

If it hadn't been for Dorothy's illness, Susannah would have said that she was happy. But that and her dreams disturbed the fragile peace that she worked so hard to reestablish each day. The knowledge that Dorothy would never be well again haunted Susannah during her waking hours, while dreams haunted her nights.

The dreams were always the same. She and Charles were in the pond the way they had been that first time when he had taught her to float. His hand was at her waist, supporting her, and she was drifting effortlessly. She could feel the sun on her back, warming her. Then she would turn her head to breathe, her eyes would meet his and the sun's warmth would pale in comparison to the heat that flowed from his gaze.

For a long moment, neither of them would move. They would look at each other, their eyes asking questions their lips dared not form. Then slowly, as if he had all the time in the world, Charles would lift her into his arms. She would wrap her arms around his neck and smile up at him as he carried her from the water. He would walk for what felt like hours, and as he did their eyes remained locked, promising each other that this was only the beginning, that soon—soon—they would share delights they had only dreamt of.

When at last they reached the grass, he would lay her on a blanket, treating her so gently that she felt as if she were a piece of the most fragile crystal. Then and only then would he lower his lips to hers, and the heat she had seen in his eyes would be transferred to his lips, searing her with its intensity. For another seemingly endless moment, they would kiss, and the fire that started where their lips were joined would race through her veins, heating each inch of her body.

When she was certain the pleasure could not possibly increase, Charles would pull away from her, leaving her cold, alone and bereft. But only for a second. For then he would smile again, and this time he would begin to remove her clothing, teasing, tantalizing, touching and then kissing each inch of flesh that he revealed. First her neck, then her shoulders and then when her pulse began to pound with anticipation, when her nerve endings ached for him to continue, she would waken. It was always the same. She would lie in her bed, filled with a longing so strong that it was a physical ache.

Susannah knew it was nothing more than lust. She wouldn't make the mistake of calling it love, for it wasn't. But why, oh why, if it was only lust did the thought of being held in Charles's arms fill her with such longing? Why did the memory of their kisses fill her with such joy? And why, if it was nothing more than a physical urge, did they call it making love?

Charles slid the library ladder to the right. Where was that book? He was certain he had another book about Paris somewhere. It might not have such pretty pictures, but surely Susannah would enjoy reading more about the city of her dreams. Though it might be years from now, when she finally got there, Charles wanted it to be a visit she would never forget.

Unlike the kiss they had shared. That was something he wanted to forget. That was something he needed to forget. Charles shook his head and reached for a slim volume. There was no point in trying to lie to himself. Even though he knew he ought to, he did not want to forget the kiss. Far from it. He wanted to repeat it, and then he wanted to do more, much more. He wanted to make love to Susannah—not once, not twice, but as many times as it took to quench the fire those kisses had ignited. But no matter what he wanted, Charles could not take advantage of Susannah. For that's what it would be, preying on an innocent and confused woman.

Susannah was still vulnerable. It was too soon after Anthony's rejection for her to think rationally about another man. If she turned to Charles, it might be only because she feared no other man would find her desirable. Charles knew that. He also knew that no matter how much he wanted Susannah, he wanted her only when she could come to him with a whole heart. That was why he was going to pretend that he didn't remember their kiss and that he didn't dream of it each night.

He was also going to try his best never again to think of Anthony Borman. Anthony had known better than to send him the news, but Brad had received a letter, announcing that Anthony had married his Gracie. Though he'd been incredulous over the news, Charles had told Susannah of the wedding. He thought he owed her that much. If she was still harboring any lingering feelings for Anthony, she needed to know that he was now married. But, though he'd told her of the nuptials themselves, Charles had not—and would not—tell her that the newly wed Mr. and Mrs. Borman had gone to Europe for their honeymoon. It was, Charles realized, a measure of Anthony's insanity that he would insist that Susannah spend her honeymoon on Cape Cod rather than in the city of her dreams while the unknown Gracie was taken to Europe. The man was certifiably crazy. But at least he was no longer part of Susannah's life.

Charles looked at the book he'd selected. Though it was the size and color he remembered, it was not the one he sought. He stared at the shelves again.

Other than his worries over Susannah, Charles had to admit that his own life was more peaceful than it had been since he'd returned to Hidden Falls . . . perhaps even longer. The mill no longer dominated his thoughts, for it seemed to be running smoothly. Not only had there been no further accidents, but for the first time since it had become his responsibility, the mill had generated enough of a profit that he was able to repay part of the debt.

The reason for the increased solvency was easy to find: Susannah. The screen prints that she had suggested were selling well, so well in fact that buyers were bidding up the price of the limited supply and clamoring for more. Though Charles had refused to increase production of the first print, he had agreed that they could expand their product line and had asked Susannah to select a second design. At this rate, the mill might be solvent in a year.

There it was! Charles plucked the book from the shelf and riffled the pages. Yes, Susannah would enjoy this. He would give it to her when he saw her this afternoon. Satisfied now that he had found the book, he could return to his search of the south wing. Today, Charles had resolved, would be his final attempt. Though he had looked through the rubble more times than he could count, he had found nothing that would exonerate his father.

It was strange. At one point, clearing their father's name before the twins returned home had been his highest priority. Charles had told himself that he wanted to keep the girls' illusions intact. But as the days passed and he found no proof, he had gradually accepted the fact that although he would never believe that John Moreland had set the fire, he might be unable to prove that. And, he reflected, he would have to be satisfied with that.

Perhaps it was more important to focus his energy on the mill than to continue to search for clues. If he could improve the mill's profitability, he could protect Anne's and Jane's inheritance. Reputation was important, but they couldn't live on it. Fortunately, though there had been speculation about the fire, no one other than that ferret George Fields seemed to believe that John Moreland had set it. The insurance investigator might be one of the lowest life-forms, but Charles had to admit that he had acted honorably, apparently not confiding his suspicions to anyone. Perhaps Anne and Jane need never know what the ferret believed. More at peace than he'd been since the day of the fire, Charles left the library.

He had entered the hallway when he heard someone knocking at the front door. Without waiting for Mrs. Enke to admit the visitor, Charles flung open the door. "Philip!" he cried as he recognized his old friend. "It's good to see you. Come in and have a drink."

Philip removed his hat and ran a hand through his thinning hair. "Don't mind if I do. I heard you have something to celebrate."

"And what would that be?" Charles asked as he showed Philip to a comfortable chair and reached for the decanter. He was never certain what news spread through the town or what would be considered cause for celebration. All he knew was that for the last year, there had been precious few reasons to rejoice.

"I heard you repaid the first of your father's loans," Philip said, leaning back in the chair. With his legs crossed at the ankles and his eyes slightly hooded, he appeared the picture of a man at ease.

Charles nodded and handed Philip a glass of whiskey. "Susannah's responsible for my good fortune."

"Susannah Deere?" Philip's light blue eyes reflected such surprise that Charles started to bristle. Did Philip believe Susannah incapable of helping with the mill? If it hadn't been for her ideas, Charles would still be where he was a year ago, struggling to survive rather than finally believing there would be an end to the long nightmare.

"She's the only Susannah I know," Charles said as mildly as he could. "She told me there was a market for silk-screened prints, and she was right. She was also right," Charles added, "that the profits would be good."

Philip took a deep swallow, then set the glass on the table next to him. "Glad to hear that, my boy. Glad to hear it. Now maybe you'll have an easier time selling the mill."

Charles, who had taken a swallow of his own drink, sputtered. He hadn't thought of selling the mill in weeks. Though the thought had once obsessed him, it no longer seemed like a good idea. "I don't know that I will," he told Philip, surprised that the place he'd once considered an albatross now seemed more like the trust Susannah had called it. What was happening to him that everything seemed to revolve around Susannah?

Charles looked at Philip, startled when a flash of something that he could not identify lit Philip's eyes. The former banker lowered them quickly and said, "Hmmm . . . I hope you're not basing your decision on advice from Ralph Chambers. The rumors about his conduct persist." When Charles started to protest, Philip continued, "I know you don't want to believe them, but where there's smoke . . ." Charles stiffened. "Sorry, Charles. That was a poor analogy."

It was, indeed. Charles did not want to talk about the mill or the fire. "Would you like to see the carousel?" he offered.

"Of course, my boy." Philip swallowed the last of his drink and rose. "I've heard so much about it."

The awkward moment was over. Charles led the way to the stable, telling Philip of the progress the carvers had made and how he still hoped that the carousel would be completed before Anne and Jane returned.

They were nearing the stable, discussing the right way to tell Anne about her gift, when a woman emerged from the woods. Charles tried not to sigh at the thought that Dorothy Deere was wandering again. Somehow she had eluded Moira's watch, and if Susannah discovered her missing, she'd be worried. "Just a minute," he said to Philip, gesturing toward the woman. He greeted Dorothy warmly before suggesting she return home and pointing her in the right direction. Dorothy was pleasant and seemed amenable to heading back to her house, waving as she left him.

Charles was surprised to find Philip watching him with glazed eyes. Though his friend had not moved, his expression indicated his mind was miles away. Philip made a soft choking sound when Charles reached his side and his face was pale as he pulled out his watch. "It's later than I thought," he said a bit shakily. "I'd best be on my way." Alarmed, Charles started to accompany him toward his automobile, but Philip shook his head. "No need. No need, my boy."

Though Philip continued to insist that he required no assistance, Charles took his arm and guided him to the front of the house. It was, Charles realized as his friend drove away, the first time Philip had seemed old.

Susannah ran her hand over the smooth wood. "It's beautiful, Rob." He had completed the carving of the lead horse the day before and was now preparing to paint it. "Have you decided on the colors?"

Rob nodded as he opened a jar of white primer. "The horse itself will be a palomino with a gold leaf mane and tail."

The odor of oil paint filled the workshop, overpowering even the smells from Susannah's palette. "I never saw a horse with a gold mane."

"You will if you wait a week. I'd like to tell you it was my invention, but the Coney Island carvers started using gold leaf, and I liked the look. Some people call it flamboyant. I prefer to say it's special."

Rob gave Susannah's painting an appraising look, then nodded his approval. "Charles was a little skeptical about the gold, so I agreed to use it on only the lead horse. The rest will have ordinary painted manes."

"But not a tail carved by the famous Susannah Deere." She couldn't help teasing him.

Rob grinned. "You made a noble effort. I'd even say you have potential."

"But . . ."

Rob's grin turned into a full-fledged laugh. "But you're a better painter than carver. That's why I asked you to help with the rounding boards." He dipped his brush into the primer and began to paint the steed he had so meticulously carved.

"Are you sure it's not because the rounding board is so high off the ground that no one will see it?" Susannah continued her teasing.

"Now, Susannah . . ."

"Now, what?" Charles asked. Somehow he had entered the workshop so quietly that she had not heard him.

Susannah smiled. She knew her grin probably looked foolish, but she couldn't help it. Whenever she saw Charles, her heart turned over with pleasure, and she had to smile. It was always the same. No matter what the weather might be outside, when Charles arrived she felt as if the sun had suddenly emerged from behind a dark cloud.

"Rob was about to admit that no one would look at my rounding board," she told Charles.

"I will." He strode to her side and began to inspect her work. "Nice," he said.

"Your loyalty is admirable," Susannah said with a short laugh. "The truth is, we could have a Rembrandt on the rounding board, and no one would notice it. Rob's horses will outshine everything else." Her pulse had begun to race as it always did when Charles was near. Fortunately, her voice did not betray her excitement.

"That may be true," Charles admitted, "but your painting of the falls is beautiful."

"It's a special place." Susannah had given the falls an almost mystical atmosphere, trying to recreate the wonder she had felt the first time she'd seen it. With Charles. Rob's assistants had watched as the painting developed, saying little until she was putting the finishing touches on it. Then Mark had told Luke that Susannah must have seen the falls on a different day than he had, for he had never noticed that it was so beautiful.

"I told you she had a good eye," Rob had said.

"A true romantic," Luke had muttered, while Mark had said something that sounded like "woman in love."

"Have you decided which place you're going to put on the next panel?" Rob's words brought Susannah back to the present.

"The next one? What do you mean? I thought I was doing only one."

"Now, Susannah . . . you didn't think I'd want to mix artistic styles, did you?" He winked at Charles. "Especially when my patron likes your work."

"Patron?" Charles laughed as he shifted his weight, moving a little closer to Susannah. "I never thought of myself in quite those terms."

He was so close that she could feel his breath on her neck. If she turned, would his lips touch hers? Susannah forced herself to concentrate on what Rob was saying. "Patron's an appropriate term," she agreed.

"I thought I was a knight in shining armor."

Rob laughed as Mark and Luke shot each other oddly conspiratorial glances. "It's as I thought. A bad case."

Susannah blinked, unsure what he meant. Charles wheeled around and faced the carver. "What are you talking about?"

Rob feigned innocence, though his eyes flashed with mischief. "Nothing. I was simply wondering if either of you had any suggestions for the designs on the shields," he said, referring to the plaster pieces that connected the sections of the rounding board.

As a faint acrid smell drifted through the half-opened door, Susannah wondered who had lit a fire on such a warm day.

"Since it appears that we're going to have scenes of Hidden Falls on the rounding board," she said, "what about carving Charles's parents on two of the shields? We could put his grandparents on the other two."

To Susannah's amazement, Charles clenched his fists. "Absolutely not!" The amusement he had shown only a moment before was gone, replaced by white-hot fury.

"Why not?" Susannah persisted. It was unlike Charles to be angered without a reason. "They would tie the scenes together and make it truly a Moreland carousel."

"No." Charles's face was rigid with disapproval. "Find another design or leave the shields blank. I don't care. But you will not put John and my mother on display."

On the other side of the room, all activity ceased as Mark and

Luke stared at Charles. Though she still had no idea why he was so adamant, Susannah refused to stare at him. Instead, she watched Charles from the corner of her eye. His parents were obviously a sensitive subject. Knowing Charles, it would be days—if ever—before she learned why.

"Maybe faces aren't a good idea," Susannah said, trying to diffuse the tension that was almost palpable. She turned to Rob. "Didn't you say some carousels used designs from Greek pottery?"

"That's true, but what would the connection be to the rounding board?"

"I was thinking . . ." She sniffed again. This time the smell was unmistakable. "What's burning?"

Charles's face paled. "Oh, my God!" He raced out of the stable, returning a second later. "There's a fire at the mill!"

Chapter Twenty

Had it been only a week since he'd thought his life was on track, moving as smoothly as one of Brad's father's trains? That had certainly been an illusion. Charles gripped his walking stick with more force than necessary as he strode up Falls Street. Damn it all! He hated what he was about to do.

Tipping his hat to two of the matrons whose names he never could remember, Charles continued across Main. If only he could forget the events of the past week as easily as he did the women's names. He supposed he ought to be grateful. Susannah had told him that he'd been lucky. Perhaps she was right, but at the time it had seemed that he had more cause for regret than jubilation. Lucky was not a word he would apply to himself.

It had been a quirk of the weather that had brought the smell of smoke across the river. Normally the wind blew in the opposite direction, and the big houses on the hill were not troubled with the odors from the mill. But that day, the wind had come from the north, and that had saved him. On a still day, he might not have known of the fire until it was too late to salvage anything. As it was, the damage was serious. Two bales of cotton were completely destroyed, and three others were left smoldering. The bottom line: A full week's profits had gone up in smoke.

Charles thumped his stick against the cobbles. It had not been an accident. Though no one admitted to having seen anyone near the mill, the culprit had left a can of kerosene next to the cotton. That was not happenstance or even forgetfulness. Charles suspected it was a deliberate move, as much an act of defiance as the fire itself. The perpetrator was taunting Charles, goading him with the knowledge that until Charles discovered his identity, the destruction would continue.

It hadn't stopped with the fire. The next day, four belts in the weaving room snapped. There had been no question that they'd frayed and broken from age, for the damaged belts were among those that had been replaced only a few weeks earlier. It didn't take Sherlock Holmes's deductive powers to see that the clean slits had been caused by a knife. Someone—and Charles was confident it was the same someone who had set the fire—had sliced the belts halfway.

Again, he had been fortunate. Although the belts had broken and gone flying across the crowded weaving room, by some miracle no one had been injured. But the workers were understandably nervous. They had begun a deliberate slowdown, checking each piece of equipment carefully each morning, taking more time than usual to replace bobbins, moving with less speed than normal. The result was predictable: lowered production.

Charles could not afford that, any more than he could afford to keep the mill running if the slowdown continued as threatened. He had to stop the dissent, and there was only one way he knew to do that, which was why he was on a section of Forest Street that he rarely frequented, going to visit a man he had no desire to see.

Charles tried not to wrinkle his nose in distaste as he turned toward the house that was his destination. Though marginally less dilapidated than its neighbors, the small building was in need of paint and, unless he was mistaken, the roof probably leaked during heavy rainstorms. No plants softened the foundation, and the one scrawny tree provided no shade from the midday sun. It was not the typical abode of a Harvard Law School graduate. But then, Matt Wagner was not a typical anything.

Charles rapped on the door. Though he'd have walked directly into Ralph Chambers's law offices, the protocol was less clear when a man's home was also his office. Matt Wagner might be despicable, but he was still entitled to a modicum of courtesy.

Hidden Falls' newest attorney did not appear to share Charles's sensibilities. "Let me guess," Matt said, scowling as he assessed Charles's dark suit and the gold-headed walking stick that had been his grandfather's. "This is not a social call."

Nodding tersely, Charles followed his reluctant host into the building that served as both his house and his office. A scarred desk that looked suspiciously like one that had once graced Hidden Falls' school stood in one corner of the main room. It and a shelf of books were the sole signs that the town's junior attorney practiced his trade here. The rest of the room was furnished like the others on the street, with an ancient stove, a battered table and four mismatched chairs. Why on earth had a man who could be practicing law anywhere chosen to come here? The answer was simple and unpalatable: revenge.

"You're damn right this is not a social call," Charles said, not bothering to hide his anger. "I'm not feeling too sociable these days."

Though Matt gestured toward the single chair in front of the desk, Charles preferred to stand. He had no intention of prolonging this visit. Just the sight of his childhood nemesis raised memories that should not have been revived.

Matt perched on the edge of the desk, apparently at ease, and gave Charles another of those penetrating looks he so disliked. "What brings you to my humble abode?"

"I want it stopped."

Matt reached for a pouch of tobacco and busied himself rolling a cigarette. Odd. The Matt Charles had known hadn't smoked. Though that man hadn't had enough money to buy even the cheapest tobacco, the label on the pouch Matt held proclaimed it to be the most expensive available at the mercantile. Charles wondered what other changes the years had wrought. It was disconcerting to think that this man might be more stranger than familiar foe.

"You'll have to be a bit more specific," Matt said, not bothering to look at Charles. "I'm afraid 'it' is too enigmatic, even for a man with my superior intellectual capabilities."

This was the Matt Charles remembered, quick with verbal jabs. "Is it simply for my benefit, or are you always this insufferable?" he demanded.

Matt moistened the cigarette paper. "It's you, Charles. You always did bring out the worst in me." He held the cigarette between two fingers, studying it as if it were more interesting than his visitor. "Now, what is it you believe I have the power to stop?"

"The damage to my mill."

Leaning forward slightly, Matt raised one eyebrow. "You think I was responsible?"

As if he'd be here otherwise! "I know of the meetings you've had with the workers. I also know you've told them to slow down their work."

Matt reached for a match. "I can't fault your sources. They told you the truth." He started to strike the match, then stopped. This time he stared directly at Charles, his brown eyes serious. "Unlike you, I worry about the people who work in the mill. I want them to live long lives, and I don't want them maimed. So, yes, I told them to make sure they were safe, even if that meant working more slowly."

Grudgingly, Charles gave the man credit for honesty. That was another thing that had not changed. Matt had always been honest, almost to a fault. That's what made his involvement in the mill accidents so improbable. As Matt himself had once said, skulking was not his trademark.

"I don't understand your logic." Charles never had. "If the workers follow your advice, they'll produce less and earn less."

As Matt shrugged, the fine wool of his suit rippled across his shoulders. Harvard had certainly improved Matt's sartorial taste. "Money isn't everything," said the man whose tailor would have been appalled by the surroundings in which his suit was now housed. "If they're injured, they won't earn anything at all."

The logic was irrefutable, but so was Charles's problem. "I need the mill running at full capacity."

"Then make it safer. Stop the accidents."

Charles looked at the man who had once stared at a whirling carousel, open longing on his face. Today Matt's expression was impassive, either because he felt nothing or because he was now more adept at concealing his emotions. "That's why I'm here," Charles said. "To get you to stop the accidents."

Matt jumped down from the desk, his expression no longer bland. "If you remember anything from our childhood," he said in a voice that was low but venomous, "it should be that I'm not a man you want to anger. This is twice now that you've accused me of culpability in what you apparently believe to be sabotage." The fire in Matt's eyes was hotter than the summer sun. "I am many things, Charles, but I am not a saboteur, and I don't like the accusation." He strode to the door and opened it. "It would serve you well to remember that."

It was time for Charles to leave, and not because Matt was ushering him out. If there had been anything to be gained by remaining, Charles would. The fact was, he had learned all he could here. "Then who the hell is responsible?" Charles demanded as he plopped his hat on his head.

The look Matt gave him was filled with contempt. "I'd suggest you consult your list of enemies."

Susannah patted her hair as she descended the stairs. She had been late returning from her ride with Rob and had hurried as she changed into her day gown. Though a few locks had loosened and she had wanted to redo her pompadour, she had settled for pinning the wayward locks and hoping they would hold while she and Dorothy ate breakfast. Afterward, she would have time to freshen her hairdo.

"Good morning, Dorothy," Susannah said as she entered the dining room. The drapes were drawn wider than usual, and to Susannah's surprise, her mother had begun eating. Normally, even when Susannah was delayed, Dorothy waited.

Dorothy turned and stared at Susannah with eyes that held

not even a glint of recognition. "I beg your pardon, miss. What are you doing in my mother's house?"

The sun was shining. The rational part of Susannah's brain knew that. But the other part, the one that relied on pure emotion, was certain there had been an unexpected eclipse, suddenly darkening the room. Dorothy's words slammed into Susannah with the force of a blow, and for a second, she could not breathe. How could it be that her mother did not recognize her? Dorothy frequently confused Charles with his father and Moira with the long-departed Norma, but she had never, ever failed to recognize Susannah. "I'm Susannah," she said firmly. Maybe the sun was in Dorothy's eyes. Perhaps this was only a momentary confusion.

But Dorothy's expression remained unfriendly. "Then state your business, Miss Susannah." Her voice was crisp, as if she were addressing a recalcitrant pupil.

Susannah took a deep breath as she tried to steady herself. The pain was more than a blow now. It was as sharp as if a knife had been thrust deep inside her. Nothing in her life, not even her father's death, had hurt as much as this. "I'm your daughter, Dorothy."

As her words registered, Susannah saw a veil of confusion cloud her mother's eyes. Though she said nothing, Dorothy stared at her for a moment, then turned and picked up her coffee cup. As if she were alone in the room, Susannah's mother sipped her coffee, broke a piece of toast and began to butter it. Only when she had swallowed the toast and taken another sip of coffee did she turn toward the door, where Susannah gripped the door frame, trying desperately to remain upright and to control her tears.

"Good morning, dear," Dorothy said in her normal voice. "I'm sorry I started without you, but I was hungry."

Her legs no longer able to support her, Susannah sank into her chair. The moment was past. Dorothy recognized her. But what if it should return? What if the confusion should last? Susannah was not sure how she would bear a world where her mother did not know her.

That afternoon, for the first time in several weeks, Susannah did not go to the carvers' workshop. Though the rest of the morning had passed uneventfully as she and Dorothy gardened together, she could not forget the pain of breakfast and those moments of sheer horror when Dorothy had stared at her as if she were a stranger. Her tears were so close to the surface that she was afraid to be with Rob and his assistants, lest something trigger a spate of crying. She would see Charles, but no one else.

Now, though the dogs ran in circles, yipping with eagerness for her to toss a ball for them, she found herself unable to do even that. The morning had drained her, both physically and emotionally, and all she wanted to do was collapse. Susannah sank to the ground, spreading her skirts around her.

"Sorry, pups," she said as they deposited their balls in her lap. As if they understood, they climbed into her lap and began to lick her face.

"You look like you need a friend."

Susannah looked up, trying to blink back her tears. "I do," she said as she shooed the dogs away and rose. This was why she had come to Fairlawn, to be with her friend. "Oh, Charles," she said, still blinking furiously, "I can't think of a single thing to laugh about today."

The dogs barked, then jumped into the air. Normally their antics made her smile. Today she hardly saw them. Charles put his arm around her shoulders and gave her a quick squeeze. "There must be an epidemic of gloom, because I can't find anything to laugh about, either." His blue eyes were serious as he asked, "Do you want to talk about it?"

"I'm not sure." What had seemed like a good idea—confiding in Charles—was no longer such an obvious solution. He looked as if his day was as bad as hers. Though it might help Susannah to discuss her pain with him, she wouldn't do that if it meant increasing his burdens.

"Sometimes it helps to talk." Charles picked up the dogs and carried them inside the house. When he returned, studiously ignoring the puppies' cries of frustration, he led Susannah to the verandah at the back of the house. Here they would be out of sight of the workshop. "Now, tell me what's wrong."

Though he gestured toward the wrought-iron chairs that

lined one side of the verandah, Susannah shook her head. She couldn't explain why, but for some reason she wanted to remain standing. Susannah laid her hand against one of the columns, and as she did, the memory of standing in the dining room, braced against the door frame while Dorothy stared at her, came rushing back.

She blinked, but the tears that had hovered at the back of her eyes spilled forth. "Dorothy's worse. Much worse." Susannah swallowed deeply, not wanting to put words to what had happened. Charles said nothing, but waited patiently until she blurted out, "This morning, she didn't recognize me."

There was a moment of silence, as if Charles was as disbelieving as Susannah had been. Then those cerulean eyes that haunted her dreams darkened with pain. "Oh, Susannah." He opened his arms and drew her into them, pressing her head against his chest. "I'm so sorry."

A blue jay uttered his raucous cry as a squirrel tried to invade his nest, and in the distance the church bells chimed the hour. It was an ordinary day in Hidden Falls. There was nothing to mark the devastation Susannah had felt or the way she had despaired of the world ever being right again.

"It was horrible," she told Charles. "My mother stared at me as if I were a stranger."

Though Susannah kept her face pressed against Charles's shirt, he placed a finger under her chin and tipped her face upward. "Susannah." It was one word, and yet it was much more, for he had filled the syllables with such emotion that Susannah raised her eyes to meet his. His eyes were serious but not sorrowful. Susannah stared, not quite believing what she saw. There was sympathy and something more, something that made her catch her breath, in Charles's expression. "I can't even imagine how distressing that must have been," he said softly. "I wish I could do something to help you."

The pain that had surrounded her heart, squeezing it until she had feared that it would burst, began to subside. "You already have," she told Charles. "Just listening and caring helps."

He stroked her cheek. "I've been told that I'm a good listener, and I certainly care about you."

259

There was such warmth in his voice that Susannah felt herself begin to relax for the first time since breakfast. "I wish I could promise you that it would never happen again," he continued. "But I can't. The only things I can promise you are that I'll always listen and I'll always care."

His words and the expression she saw reflected in his eyes lightened Susannah's heart. This was Charles, her friend, and he'd somehow managed to give her hope.

She laid her hand against his cheek in a gesture that she hoped would give him comfort. His skin was slightly prickly against her palm, the unexpected roughness reminding her how different they were.

"Do you want to tell me why you're not laughing?" she asked. Perhaps they were more similar than different. Perhaps listening and caring would help him, too. "Were there more problems at the mill?"

Charles nodded, his eyes darkening once more. "That's only part of it. I'm beginning to wonder if the gossips aren't right. Maybe there is a Moreland curse."

Susannah laid a finger over his lips, trying to stop the flow of words. "You don't really believe that, do you?" He couldn't. The fire and the accidents at the mill all had logical, physical causes.

Charles managed a small shrug. "It's preferable to the alternative, which is that my family has enemies who hate us enough that they'll kill us and risk innocent lives."

Though his words were matter-of-fact, they sent a shiver of fear through Susannah. She kept her gaze fixed on Charles, trying to understand. "What do you mean?"

Tightening his grip on her, as if he were afraid she would flee when she heard his story, Charles nodded at the burned wing of his house. "The insurance investigator doesn't believe that the fire was an accident. He thinks my father set it."

The shiver turned into a tremor, and Susannah felt the blood drain from her face. This was far worse than anything she had imagined. "How could that be? Your father died in the fire."

A light breeze tousled Charles's hair. It should have given him a casual look, but there was nothing casual about Charles.

Susannah could feel the tension of coiled muscles in his arms.

"According to the investigator, that was the result of a miscalculation on John's part." Charles shook his head slowly. "I don't believe my father was responsible. What I do believe is that whoever burned the house is responsible for the sabotage at the mill."

If he thought that, it was no wonder Charles put credence in the existence of a curse. "Why would anyone do that?" Susannah could not imagine who would perpetrate such horrors and what could have motivated them.

"I wish I knew." Charles's gaze strayed to the blackened bricks of what had been the bedroom wing. "If I knew the reason, I'd probably also know who's behind the accidents that aren't accidents."

Susannah's thoughts whirled. "It's difficult to believe anyone in Hidden Falls would be that evil. As you said, whoever it is is putting innocent people at risk." Though she could not claim to have met all the townspeople, those she did know did not seem to be malefactors. And surely no one who worked in the mill would endanger the others.

"One of the lessons I've learned," Charles said, "is that people can wear masks. You may not really know them."

Anthony's image flashed before Susannah. While it was true that she hadn't really known him, perhaps the fault was not Anthony's. Perhaps she hadn't made the effort. Or perhaps she had deluded herself. "Sometimes I think we see what we want to see."

Charles looked down at her and managed a small smile. The way the lines between his eyes had disappeared told her that Charles had begun to relax. When he spoke, his voice was light. "I like what I see. And what I want to see is more of you." He kissed the tip of her nose.

It was a playful gesture, making Susannah smile.

"Do you suppose if I tried again, you'd laugh?" Charles kissed her nose a second time, then drew back slightly and smiled at her. This time it was a real smile. "We never did seal our laugh-a-day pact the way I thought we should have. What do you think, Susannah? Wouldn't this be the right time?"

She nodded, remembering that he had proposed a kiss. She needed, oh, how she needed, to kiss Charles. Maybe his embrace would chase the last of the doldrums away. Maybe being held so close that she could feel his heartbeat would remind her that the world was still a wonderful place.

As he lowered his lips to hers, Susannah realized that, despite his seemingly light words, Charles was filled with the same despair she was. She could taste it on his lips, feel it in the way he held her, as if he, too, sought comfort. She moved her hands to cup the back of his neck, her fingertips stroking him ever so gently as she tried to ease his pain.

For a long moment they stood there, two wounded people seeking comfort. And then his kiss changed. Charles's lips softened, and though his breathing quickened, it was with passion, not fear or sorrow. She could taste the difference, just as she could feel her body soften as she pressed against him. Charles's hands, which had gripped her in desperation, now moved slowly, caressing each inch of her back. In response Susannah slid her arms around his neck and drew him closer. And as she did, feelings of peace and joy coursed through her.

Charles was right. This was the right time. This was the right place. And he was the right man.

At length they broke apart, smiling as fatuously as children on Christmas morn . . . or adults who had discovered magic in the everyday world. Susannah slipped her hand in Charles's, and they strolled slowly back to Pleasant Hill. Though the pain of the day was not forgotten, the embrace they had shared had tempered it, reminding each of them that there was hope.

"I wish I could help you discover who's behind the accidents," Susannah said as they crested the hill. "Perhaps I could ask some questions—discreetly, of course. I might be able to learn something." More than ever, she needed to help him.

Charles nodded his agreement. "It was only a week ago that I told myself it didn't matter who burned the house. Now it does, because more than my family's reputation is at stake. Now it's the mill and everyone who works there."

Susannah squeezed his hand, trying to give him a measure of comfort. "I'll talk to Megan. She mentioned the Moreland curse the first day I met her. It may mean nothing, but she might also know something."

Charles raised Susannah's hand to his lips and kissed her knuckles. When she smiled at him, unable and unwilling to hide how much Charles's caresses thrilled her, he smiled. "I'd be wary of what she says. Megan's family has reason to hate mine."

"But Megan doesn't hate you." Though she had never pronounced Charles's name, Susannah believed that Megan still had illusions of marrying him.

"Perhaps not, but I'd weigh the O'Tooles' words carefully."

As they climbed the front steps of Pleasant Hill, still holding hands, Susannah saw Megan standing at the window of the parlor staring outside. Though she gave no sign that she saw Susannah and Charles, Megan turned abruptly. A second later, Susannah heard china shattering.

"What happened?" Susannah asked as she entered the parlor. The remains of Dorothy's favorite china figurine spattered the floor near the fireplace.

Megan's lips tightened in anger. "Sure and it was an accident. It slipped out of me hand."

But it was not an accident. The Dresden shepherdess had been on a table near the window. The only way it could have broken against the mantel was for Megan to have picked it up and hurled it across the room.

Susannah gave Megan a long, appraising look. Perhaps Charles was right. Perhaps she could not trust an O'Toole.

Chapter Twenty-one

It was dusk, that hour of lengthening shadows when, though the sun had not yet relinquished its power, nocturnal creatures had begun to stir, and the birds chattered as they sought their nests, giving one final burst of song before they slept. And so it was for him. He walked slowly, aimlessly wandering across the thick grass. At a time as beautiful as this, there was no need for a destination. Simply being outdoors was reward enough, for all too soon the sun would set and he would retreat to the house. Like the birds, he would enjoy these final moments of light.

He whistled softly, imitating the birds, and chuckled when a chipmunk stared at him, apparently bemused by his song. It was one of those times when the world was at peace and even the woodland creatures lived in harmony. And then he saw it. At first he stared, as bemused as the chipmunk by the tendrils of fire that sent tiny plumes of smoke dancing on the breeze. At first he saw only the beauty, his eyes noting the way the smoke curled around the edge of the gazebo. Then as his mind registered the danger, fear swept through him. Fear and the realization that he was not alone. The animals had fled, but inside the airy structure sat a woman, so engrossed in the book she held that she appeared oblivious to the danger.

She was young; she was beautiful; and unless he did something, she would die. He tried to move, but his legs refused to respond to his brain's command. The woman leaned farther back in the wicker chair, curling her legs under her, smiling as she turned another page. And still he stood, frozen in place.

The flames grew, licking the edge of the building. The smoke was darker now, blotting out the last of the sunlight as the woman continued to read. He started to run, but no matter how he forced his limbs to move, he came no closer. He ran and ran and ran. His heart pounded; he was breathless with the effort, and yet the gazebo remained the same distance from him. The woman turned another page, tilting her head to the side. And as she did, he recognized her.

"Run, Susannah!" She had to leave. It was her only hope. "Run!" Though he shouted the words, cupping his hands around his mouth to make them carry through the air, she gave no sign that she heard him.

He ran, taking huge strides that stretched his legs to their limits. He shouted warnings until he was hoarse. And yet, though his heart pounded with exertion and fear, he came no closer. The flames were higher now, surrounding the gazebo, crackling as they consumed the delicate structure.

"Fire!" he cried. "For God's sake, Susannah, run!"

But she only closed the book and smiled as the flames engulfed her. He stared, unable to believe the horror he had witnessed.

"Happy now, Charles?" Though he could not see the man, his voice was familiar. "You've lost the woman you loved."

Charles woke with a start. His mouth was dry, his limbs trembled, his heart overflowed with a fear greater than any he had ever known. Racing to the window, he yanked the drapes away and stared outside. The night was peaceful, undisturbed by even a breeze. There was no gazebo, no woman, no flames. It was only a dream.

And yet it had felt so real. Charles sank onto the edge of the bed and stared at the window, trying to understand why, though the dream had ended, he could not banish the terror it had engendered. His heart continued to pound as his mind replayed the horror of the fire. Was it a premonition? *Please, God, no!* he prayed silently. Surely he had endured enough. He had lost his parents and his old life. He could not bear to lose Susannah, too. Surely if there was any justice in this world, he would not lose the woman he loved.

The woman he loved. The thought slammed into him with the force of a runaway train. Was it possible? Charles rose once more and gripped the windowsill as he stared into the distance. Why hadn't he recognized what was happening? Of course. Charles managed a wry smile. He had been like the woman in the dream, unaware of what was happening around him, unable to see even when the flames engulfed him.

He loved Susannah! At first he had denied his feelings, knowing they were wrong. How could he love the woman his friend planned to marry? Even when Anthony had ended the engagement, Charles had been slow to recognize the strength of his emotions, telling himself that what he felt was friendship. He could deny the truth no longer.

He loved Susannah! The thought filled Charles with exultation. The feelings he had for her were not friendship. Oh, no. Far from it. What he felt was stronger than mere friendship. It was stronger even than the love he felt for his sisters. What he felt for Susannah was the deepest emotion known to mankind, the love of a man for a woman.

And now that he recognized it, he wouldn't—he couldn't— lose her.

"Is Susannah home?" Charles tried to mask his surprise when Dorothy opened the door. Although he had wanted to see Susannah last night in the aftermath of the dream, if only to assure himself that she was not in any danger, Charles had forced himself to wait until morning. It would have been unseemly to have stormed up to Pleasant Hill in the middle of the night, declaring his love for Susannah. But once daylight had broken, it had been difficult to restrain himself. For once he had not gone to the mill. This was far more important. He needed to talk to Susannah, to tell her he loved her and to learn whether she might return that love.

"She and Megan are doing something in town," Dorothy said. That explained why Dorothy and not Megan was greeting him. Charles cursed himself for waiting until what his mother would have called a "civilized hour" before coming. He should have arrived while they were still at breakfast. That way he would have seen Susannah. He had waited his whole life for this moment. Another hour should not matter. But it did.

"I expect them to be back soon," Dorothy continued. She inhaled deeply, seeming to enjoy the clear morning air. "Would you like to wait?" To Charles's relief, Dorothy sounded normal today. Susannah had told him that on good days, it was difficult to believe that Dorothy was ill, for she acted almost the way she had two years ago. The problem, of course, was that the good days were becoming less frequent.

Charles nodded and removed his hat as he followed Dorothy into the house. "If it would not be too much trouble for you." He didn't want to risk missing Susannah.

"Not at all." Dorothy's eyes twinkled with what appeared to be pleasure, perhaps because visitors were a rarity. "Come into the parlor." The heavy velvet drapes had been opened, and sunshine flooded the room. It was, Charles hoped, a good omen. But his hopes were quickly dashed, for when he had taken the seat opposite Dorothy, she leaned forward. "You remind me so much of your father." Dorothy smiled, and her eyes continued to twinkle. It was obvious she had no idea she had said exactly the wrong thing.

Charles was *not* like John Moreland. Not at all!

Undaunted by his silence, Dorothy persisted, "You have the same hair, and from what Susannah says, you've inherited more than John's looks. You've been blessed with his goodness, too."

It was too much. Though the last thing he wanted was to discuss his father, Charles could not let the ridiculous allegation stand. "Goodness is not a word I would have associated with him," Charles said as mildly as he could. His hands gripped the chair arms, and he wished it were John Moreland's throat they encircled. Dorothy was wrong. An adulterer was not a good man.

"Why ever not?" Dorothy appeared bewildered by Charles's

words, and he feared that he might have said something that would trigger one of her bad days. Susannah had explained that she was never certain what would transport Dorothy to a previous era. Today Susannah's mother stared at Charles, her eyes apparently clear and lucid. "John was one of the kindest, most generous men I've ever met. I don't know many who would sacrifice their own happiness for another."

Charles stared out the window for a moment, trying to decide how to respond. Somehow the day had turned upside down. He had come here to speak to Susannah, and now he found himself embroiled in a conversation with her mother about— of all things—her deluded opinion of his father. Despite earlier evidence to the contrary, this must be one of those days when Dorothy was confused. How else could you explain her praise of John?

"I beg your pardon, Mrs. Deere." Charles used the formal name deliberately, testing her reaction. Unlike other days when she had not responded to anything other than "Dorothy," today she nodded slightly, acknowledging Charles. Charles tried not to sigh. It appeared that his initial impression was accurate; this was one of Dorothy's good days. But why was she saying such nonsensical things?

"Are you sure we're speaking of the same John Moreland?" he asked. The grandfather clock chimed. Surely Susannah would soon be home. Surely this bizarre conversation would soon end.

Dorothy straightened her back and stared at him, her expression stern enough to quell even a recalcitrant pupil. "We most certainly are speaking of John Moreland." She waved a hand in a dismissive gesture. "You children are all the same. You don't appreciate true goodness of spirit."

"I'm afraid I didn't see a great deal of that." If it hadn't been the height of rudeness, Charles would have stormed out of the room. As it was, he gripped the chair arms more tightly.

"Nonsense!" The light in her eyes told Charles that Dorothy was warming to her subject. She was, he suspected, prepared to give him a lecture as if he were a student and she once more in her classroom. "As dearly as I loved my husband and as highly as I regarded him, I don't believe he would have been capable of the same self-sacrifice. John was as close to a saint as I've had the privilege to meet."

A saint! Charles closed his eyes and prayed for patience. Perhaps this was a nightmare and he would soon waken. John a saint. How absurd! "Mrs. Deere, I assure you that you're the first person who's called him that." Charles forbore from mentioning that someone apparently hated John Moreland enough to burn his house, sabotage his mill and kill him.

She was silent for a long moment, her eyes searching his face as if evaluating his sincerity. "Is it possible your parents didn't tell you what happened?" she asked at last. Without waiting for a reply, she continued, "Yes, I suppose it is. Perhaps they saw no need to dredge up the past."

Charles shifted in the chair, as uncomfortable with the speculative look on Dorothy's face as he was with the seat that did not fit his frame. "It is safe to say that I know of no reason why anyone would consider John Moreland worthy of sainthood." And at least one fact that ensured he had never entered the pearly gates.

Dorothy glared. "There's no need for sarcasm, my boy. It is most unbecoming in a gentleman. Still, I can see it's time you learned what happened all those years ago." She leaned forward, clasping her hands in her lap. "Were you aware that your father was in love with another woman before he married your mother?"

Charles shook his head slightly. Love was not a subject that had been discussed in the Moreland household. If he had thought much about it, Charles would have said that his parents were childhood sweethearts. Yet there was no denying that there had been another woman, at least once. Was this the Lucy to whom Dorothy kept alluding? At first Charles had thought the incident with the dark-haired woman in the gazebo had been a onetime event. Then he had begun to wonder. Was it possible John had known the woman for many years and that they had had an affair because they loved each other? That would have been consistent with the other comments Dorothy had made.

"You only had to see John and Lucy together to know that

they were perfect for each other." Dorothy's eyes crinkled as she smiled. "I never saw anyone, not even you and Susannah, who looked so in love."

Charles felt the blood drain from his face. How had Dorothy guessed that he loved Susannah? Had it been obvious to others when he himself had not known? He would ask Dorothy, but that could wait until later. Right now he needed to learn about the mysterious Lucy. "Who was she?"

Dorothy smiled as if the memory was a pleasant one. "She was a beautiful woman. I can still see that dark, dark hair and those brown eyes. Lucy was the belle of Boston society, but she still had time for Louis and me." Dorothy's shrug said she didn't understand the reason for the beautiful Lucy's attention. "I don't believe she ever came to Hidden Falls." If Charles was correct—and Dorothy's description made him believe he was—Lucy had come to Hidden Falls at least once, and that visit had triggered a series of events he doubted she or his father could have imagined. "John courted her in Boston," Dorothy continued. "I remember hearing that his own father was vexed that he would leave the mill so often just to woo a woman. Mind you, few outside the family knew that was what he was doing. John was secretive that way."

Charles wondered how Dorothy had heard that part of the story. She had obviously seen John and Lucy in Boston. Perhaps his mother had told her what was happening in Hidden Falls. Mother had mentioned that she and Dorothy were regular correspondents.

"John and Lucy were on the verge of announcing their betrothal when the calamity occurred."

Charles stared at the rug. A ray of sunshine shone on one corner, highlighting the intricate design. He wished he knew whether Dorothy's story was lighting the past in the same way. It was possible she was inventing the tale. Charles shook his head slightly. Susannah said Dorothy would forget events, but she didn't appear to create fictitious ones.

"What happened?" he asked.

Dorothy narrowed her eyes and regarded him for a long moment before she spoke. "That, my boy, is what I was trying to tell you. Your father gave up the woman he loved to help another. He said 'good-bye' to Lucy and never saw her again." A shadow crossed Dorothy's face. "After that, Lucy was a changed woman. She rarely smiled, and no matter how many offers she had, she refused each of the eligible young men who tried to court her. And then last year . . ."

Last year she had come to Hidden Falls. Charles knew that. What he didn't know was why.

"You were saying something about last year," he prompted.

For a second Dorothy's expression was vacant, and Charles feared that she had disappeared into another time. But when she spoke, her words rang true. "She met a man who made her happy, and she moved to California to be with him. But first, she told me she was going to see John one last time."

Charles closed his eyes, remembering the scene in the gazebo. Thank God it had been a single aberration and his mother had not been subjected to a constant string of infidelities!

Dorothy placed her hand on Charles's, as if she somehow sensed his distress and wanted to comfort him. "Poor Lucy. She suffered so much, and yet John did what was right. He was such an honorable man."

Charles was not convinced of that. "What happened?" he asked. Now that Dorothy had opened Pandora's Box, surely she wouldn't stop until she had described whatever calamity it was that had ended John's courtship of Lucy.

Dorothy stared at the carpet, then as she raised her eyes to Charles's, a sweet smile crossed her face. "John and Mary had been friends from early childhood." That much, Charles knew, was true. "They were closer than most siblings. Closer, I dare say, than you are to your sisters." Charles had no response. What mattered was not his relationship with Anne and Jane but whatever it was that Dorothy was calling a calamity.

She leaned forward, and Charles saw that her lips were pursed, as if whatever she had to say disturbed her. "John and Mary shared a deep love," Dorothy said, "but not the kind that leads to marriage. They would never have wed if Mary hadn't been . . ." Dorothy hesitated, and a faint blush stained her cheeks as she said, *"enceinte."*

271

The clock chimed again, reminding Charles of the passage of time. He knew he had been born almost exactly nine months after his parents' marriage, but he had never known it had been a forced wedding. Charles shook his head, then crossed and uncrossed his legs, trying to find a comfortable position. "I don't understand. You said they were like brother and sister. How did that lead to Mary's pregnancy?" Though Dorothy winced, Charles saw no need for euphemisms, especially since they were speaking of his own conception.

"Oh, my boy, you misunderstand." Her face crumpled, and for a second Charles was afraid she would cry. He leaned forward and patted Dorothy's hands, returning the comforting gesture she had offered to him. She gave him a tremulous smile. "Don't you see, my boy? The baby wasn't John's. It was another man's."

The sun was still shining. The birds were still chirping. Why then did the world suddenly seem dark, and why was the only thing he could hear the roar of blood in his ears? Charles forced himself to look at Dorothy. What was she saying? John Moreland wasn't his father?

As if she could read his thoughts, Dorothy nodded. "Mary would never say who the man was. All I know is that he forced himself on her. The baby was the result."

Oh, God! Charles closed his eyes, trying to block out the pain. Not only was he a bastard; even worse, he was the result of rape.

Dorothy settled back in her chair, apparently unaware of the empty cavern her words had left deep inside him. "Mary was distraught. She didn't know what to do. She couldn't stay in Hidden Falls. You know what it's like in a small town." Dorothy clenched her hands. "The shame would have been too great, and Mary would never again have been received in polite society. So she turned to her dearest friend." The look Dorothy gave Charles left no doubt who that friend was. "She asked John to help her go away. Mary wanted him to find her someplace where she could have the baby without anyone knowing."

Though Dorothy told the story dispassionately, Charles's imagination pictured his mother's anguish. First rape and then

272

an unwanted pregnancy. She could have hated him, and yet never had he felt anything other than love from his mother.

"John knew Mary would never have been able to forgive herself if she gave up her child. So he did the only thing he could. He married Mary and claimed the baby was his."

With just a few words, Charles's world had been shattered.

Susannah gripped the door frame to keep herself from falling. She hadn't meant to eavesdrop. When she and Megan had returned, Susannah had heard her mother's voice and had headed for the parlor, planning to join whoever was there. But as she grew closer and heard Dorothy say, "The baby wasn't John's," Susannah had stopped, frozen in shock by Dorothy's words and her own reaction to them.

Poor Charles! Susannah saw his face, white with anguish and bewilderment when he ran from the parlor, rushing blindly toward the door. She reached out a hand, wanting to touch him, to comfort him, then drew back into the shadows. His pain was too raw; she would only worsen it. Charles was like a wounded animal. He had been dealt an almost mortal blow, and he needed time to heal. He needed time to be alone. Susannah would give him that time, for she needed it, too. She needed time to think, to reflect on what she had learned in the instant she had seen Charles's face.

Grabbing her hat and jamming it onto her head, Susannah fled the house by the back door. Instinctively, she turned away from town, wanting to avoid meeting Charles. She craved solitude, and so she headed for the falls. Though she went there only occasionally, the water never failed to soothe her. Today she needed its healing.

But when she reached the cataract, Susannah found that the sound of falling water did not soothe her. Instead, she saw only the turbulence of the river before it tumbled over the precipice, a turbulence that mirrored her thoughts.

How had it happened? When she had seen Charles's face, not only had she *seen* his pain, but she had felt it as if it were her own. Susannah had felt the blood drain from her face, just as she had seen it drain from his. She had felt her heart thud as she was sure his had thudded. She had felt the anguish that was sharper than the thrust of a knife. And as she had felt the agony that Charles was enduring, she had prayed that somehow she could take it from him. She would gladly bear the pain if only he could be spared. In that moment, Susannah had known that she would do anything—anything at all—to help Charles, for he was the man she loved.

She stared at the falls, trying to make sense of her tumultuous thoughts. Charles was her friend. She had known that for a long time, and it had filled her with joy. But love? That was something different, something she had never expected. Was it possible that she loved Charles?

Susannah gripped a branch to steady herself. The water below the falls swirled, churning into a white froth, just as her thoughts continued to churn against the rocks of logic. Had her brain finally admitted what her heart had always known?

She took a deep breath and closed her eyes, remembering. There had been something special, something magical, between her and Charles from the very beginning. Susannah smiled, remembering the attraction she had felt toward the man she had once believed to be a common laborer and the very uncommon kiss they had shared that day. It had been love from the beginning. Susannah nodded, recognizing the rightness of her discovery. That was why she dreamt of Charles so often. That was why his lightest touch set her senses to humming. That was why the thought of his pain wrenched her heart so deeply. She loved Charles!

Charles strode down the road, barely aware of the direction his feet were taking him. By some instinct, he had chosen the road rather than the path through the woods, and now he was walking beside the river. His feet moved mechanically while his mind whirled, trying to accept all that he had learned.

John Moreland was not his father. He said the words aloud, hoping that would make them seem more real. But though he repeated the words as if they were a mantra, the simple syllables held no meaning for him. They were little more than gibberish.

He stared sightlessly at the trees his grandfather had planted.

No! Not his grandfather. Anne's and Jane's grandfather, but not his.

Charles clenched his fists, trying to marshal the emotions that roiled within him. The day had been filled with promise, and now . . . In just a few sentences, Dorothy Deere had destroyed the very foundation of his life. He was not John Moreland's son. He was not a Moreland.

Charles might have dismissed the story as the ramblings of a confused woman, but the chords rang true. He remembered the day of the fire and the final words he had spoken to his parents. "You don't understand," his mother had said. No wonder she had defended John! He had saved her and her child from a lifetime of shame. "Be careful who you call a bastard," his father had shouted. No, it hadn't been his father who had flung those words. It had been John, the man who was *not* his father, the man who was not a bastard. It was Charles who was the bastard.

Charles squeezed his eyes shut, trying to block out the pain. It was surprising how much it hurt knowing that John was not his father. How bitter the irony! For a year, he had denied that John Moreland was his father, preferring to believe that he had nothing in common with the man who had betrayed Mary. He had thought he was disowning a parent, when the truth was, there had been no father to disown. The man who had sired Charles Moreland was long gone, and it was John who had been a hero, forfeiting his own love to protect an innocent, wronged woman.

Charles's face twisted at the irony. After graduation, he had moved to New York because he had wanted to establish himself in the business world as himself, not as John Moreland's son. At the time, Brad had been envious, telling Charles he was lucky to have such a lenient parent. His own father had insisted that he return to Hidden Falls. But John wasn't Charles's parent. Was that why he had let him go? Was his generosity merely the result of knowing that he was permitting a stranger's child to make his own way in the world?

As he approached the mill's iron gates, Charles stopped. He had been so lost in his thoughts that he hadn't realized he was heading this way. His feet had brought him to yet another thing he could no longer claim. He should be relieved. The albatross that had hung so heavily around his neck was his no longer. He need not worry about Moreland Mills. Legally it might be his, for in the eyes of the world he was still Charles Moreland. But morally, he had no right to it.

Charles winced at the wave of pain that swept through him. He wasn't sure when it had happened, when he had ceased dreading the responsibility for the mill, when he had actually begun to enjoy the challenge. That no longer mattered. Knowing what he now knew, he felt there was only one honorable thing to do. He would ask Ralph to draft the papers, deeding his share of the mill to Anne and Jane when they returned from Europe. In the meantime, he would see if Philip knew anyone who could run the mill. And then as soon as he could, Charles would leave Hidden Falls, never to return.

Though the watchman nodded at Charles, he did not turn into the mill. He couldn't face anyone right now. He couldn't pretend that today was an ordinary day. He could think of nothing other than Dorothy's revelations. Who was his father? Charles tried not to shudder at the thought of a man who would rape a woman, taking advantage of his superior strength to force himself on her. That was heinous, and yet this was the man who had sired him. A rapist. What kind of man would do something so despicable? And if he would do that, what else might he do? As an ugly thought crossed his mind, Charles clenched his fists. What if his father was involved in other criminal activities? A thief or a murderer's blood might flow through his veins.

The plume of smoke rising from the mill's chimney reminded Charles of his dream. Perhaps it was fated that he met Dorothy this morning before he could speak his heart to Susannah. Perhaps he had been spared an even greater pain than the one he'd endured. At least he had not held Susannah in his arms, thinking one day she might be his. That would never be, for he had nothing to offer her now—not even his name.

The dream had been a portent, and the man had spoken the truth. Charles had indeed lost the woman he loved.

Chapter Twenty-two

He was avoiding her. Susannah reached for a hat pin, wincing when it scraped the back of her head. That pain was insignificant compared to the knowledge that Charles did not want to be with her. She could deny it no longer. The first day, she had thought it was because he was so distressed by the news that John Moreland wasn't his father that he did not follow his usual schedule. That day Susannah had played with Salt and Pepper until suppertime, hoping Charles would come. But he did not appear that day or the next or the next.

Mrs. Enke, grousing over dinners that dried out before they were eaten, told Susannah that Charles appeared to return from work well after nightfall. As far as Susannah knew, there were no new problems at the mill that required him to stay so late. The only explanation she could imagine for his prolonged absence was that he was avoiding her. Somehow—and she had no idea how—he must have realized that she believed herself in love with him. And, being Charles, rather than hurt her with the knowledge that he felt nothing more than friendship for her, he was avoiding the subject.

What he didn't know was how much that hurt. Susannah wanted more—much more—than friendship, but she would settle for less. If all Charles could offer was friendship, that would have to be enough. Surely she didn't have to lose everything just because she'd been foolish enough to fall in love.

She had to see Charles. Susannah pulled a pair of clean white gloves from the bureau and began to draw them on. She would stop at the workshop on her way into town. Perhaps Charles would be there, checking the progress Rob had made on the carousel. But Charles was not there and hadn't been for several days, a fact that obviously annoyed Rob.

"Doesn't the man care about the carousel?"

As much to assuage Rob's pride as anything, Susannah examined the carvers' most recent work. The carousel would be beautiful. Even though they were only half done with the animals, Susannah had no doubt of that. The six horses that were complete were magnificent, their manes and trappings worthy of a king or, as Rob would say with a smile, a Moreland princess. While his assistants completed the remaining two horses, Rob had begun to carve the elephant. Though it would never have the majesty of the steeds, the large pachyderm had already added a note of whimsy to the workshop.

Susannah had started the second rounding board panel, this time choosing to depict a scene from the town. This one would feature Hidden Falls' church with a bride and groom emerging from it. Though Rob and the other carvers had teased her about the subject, demanding to know whether she was planning to paint herself as the bride, Susannah had refused to rise to the bait. "It's romantic," she told them. "Just like carousels. Besides, I'm certain that Anne Moreland dreams of her wedding." The truth was, it wasn't difficult to guess why Susannah wanted to paint the happy couple, for thoughts of love and marriage seemed to fill her head.

It was odd. She had never felt that way before, not even when she had been engaged to Anthony. Then, though she had thought of marriage, she had been unable to form a clear picture of it. When she thought of living with her husband, she conjured images of her parents' faces, not hers and Anthony's. But now it was not difficult to imagine herself living with Charles. What was difficult was forcing herself to think of anything else.

When she left the workshop, Susannah continued into town, her sketchbook under her arm. Today, instead of running errands, she wanted to make some preliminary drawings of the church. Once they were complete, she would be able to begin the actual painting.

Though Dorothy would deplore the dirt it left on her skirts, Susannah sat on the steps of the bank, looking across the street at the church. According to town lore, the wedding cake bell tower was not part of the original building. The simple square tower had housed the bells until the mill was built. Then the townspeople had added the fanciful octagonal tower and positioned it on top of eight columns so that it stood higher than the mill. It was only fitting, Moira O'Toole had told Susannah, that the church was closer to heaven than a cotton mill.

Sketching was, Susannah discovered, a slow process, for almost every passerby stopped to see what she was doing, then inquired about the carousel's progress and when it would be moved to the park. Though she enjoyed the camaraderie and the townspeople's interest, Susannah did not have the heart to tell them that Charles was keeping the carousel on his property.

"You must be working on something for the carousel."

She looked up, surprised that someone required no explanation, then smiled as she recognized the man whose auburn hair set him apart from the rest of the town.

"Yes," she told Charles's friend Brad, "but how did you know? Did Charles tell you I was painting the rounding boards?"

Brad settled his hat back on his head. "Charles? Not hardly! I haven't spoken to the man in ages. As far as I can tell, all he does is work. Why, the man practically lives at the mill."

A glimmer of hope ignited deep inside Susannah. Perhaps Charles was not avoiding her; perhaps there were reasons why he spent so much time at the mill. It was clear, though, that if she wanted to see him, she would have to go there. When Brad left, Susannah packed up her sketch pad and headed for the corner of the mill where she had been told Charles had his office.

"Hello, Charles," she said, finding herself unexpectedly shy when he opened the door. It was one thing to imagine talking to him, asking him why she hadn't seen him since the day Dorothy had revealed the secret of his birth. It was quite another to actually do it.

"Susannah!" Charles rose from behind his desk, and for an instant, those deep blue eyes sparkled with happiness. The tiny flicker of hope grew, only to be extinguished a second later when Charles's eyes clouded with pain, a pain that was echoed in the lines etched next to his mouth. "Is something wrong?"

Suddenly unable to meet his gaze, Susannah glanced around the room. The furniture was large and old-fashioned, the colors dark. These were not the surroundings she would have expected Charles to have chosen. But he had not selected them. The office had undoubtedly been decorated by his father or grandfather. A flush colored Susannah's cheeks as she realized that those men were not Charles's relatives. How painful it must be for him, knowing that he was not a true Moreland.

"Is something wrong?" So many things were wrong. Although Dorothy had sounded perfectly normal when she was speaking to Charles that day, by the time Susannah returned from the falls, Dorothy had forgotten that she had had a visitor. Since then she had seemed to dwell almost constantly in the past, though she had never again failed to recognize Susannah.

And then there was Charles's unexplained absence. Susannah forced a small smile, trying to keep some semblance of normality. "I came to ask you that," she said. It wasn't as though she could just blurt out that she loved him. First, she had to learn why she hadn't seen him since that day. "Salt and Pepper have missed you," she said. *I've missed you.* But of course she could not say that. A lady didn't make such improper advances.

"I knew you'd take care of the dogs. They accept me, because I'm the one who feeds them, but you're the one they love."

Susannah tried not to flinch at the word. It wasn't the puppies that she wanted to love her. It was Charles. And if that wasn't possible, she wanted his friendship back. For, though Charles had greeted her with a brief smile, his face was now solemn, almost cold, as if he were wearing a mask.

280

He picked up a letter opener and twirled it between his hands. Susannah stared, remembering how wonderful those hands had felt touching her, yet surprised by the apparently nervous gesture. This was not the Charles she knew.

He continued speaking. "I've been busy here—too busy." A haunted expression crossed his face. "I have to catch whoever's been setting those fires."

Though the sabotage had taken various forms initially, now it seemed to have concentrated on fire. Each of the floors of the mill had been targeted, and though they had been able to stop the fires before they consumed the building itself, there was no doubt that the destruction of yarn and finished goods was taking it toll, not just on Charles's profits but also on the morale of the workers. Susannah had heard more than one person mutter that the Moreland curse was starting to affect everyone in Hidden Falls.

"I wish I could help." And not simply with finding the arsonist. She wanted to help Charles regain his smile. She wanted to help him discover how wonderful love could be. "Unfortunately, I haven't learned anything." Susannah had tried subtle probing when she'd visited the various shops in town and again today when so many passersby had stopped to admire her sketching. But no one appeared to know any more than Charles did about who was causing the fires . . . or why.

"Whoever it is is clever," Charles said. "He knows the mill schedule and just where to strike to cause the maximum disruption."

Susannah noticed that Charles kept his eyes focused on the floor rather than meeting her gaze. Like fiddling with the letter opener, avoiding eye contact was unlike him. Normally he would look directly at her, smiling or frowning, depending on what they were discussing. But nothing had been normal since the day Dorothy had revealed the Moreland family secrets.

"Is there anything I can do? I want to help you, Charles."

His head jerked up, and the expression she saw in his eyes made Susannah's heart contract. Was this why Charles had not met her gaze? His eyes were not cold or expressionless. Instead, they were filled with the most heart-wrenching pain she had ever seen. Dear God, what could have caused that anguish?

"There's nothing you can do." Charles shook his head for emphasis. "This is something I need to do myself."

As he returned his gaze to the papers on his desk, Susannah realized she had been dismissed as surely as if he'd opened the door for her and ushered her outside. Why? her heart demanded. What had she done? Surely she hadn't imagined that he cared for her. But perhaps she had. Perhaps she had repeated the mistake she had made with Anthony, seeing what she wanted to see rather than what was really there.

Would she never learn?

Why had she come? Charles clenched his fists in frustration. When he had seen her walk through the door, it had taken every ounce of control that he possessed to keep from pulling her into his arms, from kissing those sweet lips and running his hands along those curves that seemed created for no reason other than to tempt a man. And when she had offered to help him, those lovely brown eyes overflowing with compassion and something else, something he could only dream of, Charles had struggled to keep his face impassive. He wanted her help. Oh, yes, he did. Not for the mill, but for himself. She was his one hope for happiness.

Charles strode to the window and stared outside. At least there was no chance of seeing Susannah from this window, for it overlooked the river. He would think about the trees, the rocks in the river, anything but Susannah. As if that would help! Thoughts of her kept him awake at night and haunted his days. Everywhere he went, memories of Susannah accompanied him. His only respite had been his office, the one place she'd never been . . . until now.

He had tried to stay away from her, though it had been one of the hardest things he had ever done. He knew she would wonder why; he knew she would be hurt; he knew he ought to explain. But how could he when his own pain was so raw, when the knowledge that he would never have the one thing he most wanted in life gnawed at him like a ravenous beast?

As his stomach growled, Charles grabbed his hat and headed

outside. If only that were the only hunger he felt! It was easy to satisfy his stomach; Mrs. Enke's meals did that regularly. But his hunger for Susannah—ah, that was different. Charles wanted her so badly, it was an actual physical pain. He had scoffed at the poets' tales of aching hearts. Hearts didn't ache; that was nothing but literary exaggeration. Charles would scoff no more, for it was not only his heart that ached, but also his arms and legs, even his fingertips. All of him craved Susannah, and the craving only deepened with the realization that he would never be able to satisfy it.

Dorothy Deere's revelations had taken away more than his name. They had destroyed his dreams. No matter how much he wanted to, he couldn't have Susannah, not for the lifetime he craved, not even for a single night. He couldn't risk hurting her that way, for he knew that Susannah wanted children. She had told him how much she had longed for siblings and how she longed to have three or more babies of her own.

The ache deep inside Charles intensified as he pictured Susannah holding a chubby, dark-haired baby with her mother's smile. Susannah would be a wonderful mother; Charles had no doubt of that. Just as he had not the slightest doubt that he would never father a child. Perhaps another man could ignore his unknown lineage, but Charles could not. He couldn't do that to himself or Susannah or the child. He could not risk passing on tainted blood.

His feet moved mechanically, following his normal route, while his thoughts whirled. It was with mild surprise that Charles realized he had reached Fairlawn. As he strode into the house, intending only to eat and then return to the mill, two balls of fur launched themselves at him, barking furiously, jumping off the floor in their eagerness to greet him. Charles knelt and let them lick his face. Poor puppies! Susannah was right. He had neglected them, and they didn't deserve that, any more than she did. He might not be able to resume his friendship with Susannah, but there was no reason Salt and Pepper had to suffer.

"Want to play in a new place?" he asked them. "You can be watchdogs at the mill." Not that Charles had any illusions that the dogs would be any more effective than the men he had hired to guard the mill, but at least he would assuage some of his guilt by spending time with the dogs. Tonight, though no one knew it, he planned to stay at the mill all night.

For the past few days, he had varied his schedule, arriving at and departing from the mill at unusual times in hopes of discovering who was behind the sabotage. He had failed. Perhaps tonight would be different. Perhaps he would be able to do what the guards could not. Perhaps he could apprehend the man who was setting all the fires.

Charles had never realized how eerie his mill appeared at night. With only moonlight for illumination, the looms looked like ghostly contraptions, mechanical monsters poised for flight. At first the dogs had cowered, intimidated by the looms' size, but once Salt and Pepper overcame their initial fear of the huge machines, they acted as if Charles had given them new playmates and proceeded to race in circles, trying to nip the wheels. If the situation hadn't been so serious, Charles would have laughed at the sheer idiocy of two mongrels attempting to herd a hundred looms.

Eventually the dogs tired of their game and flopped on the floor, content to sleep. Charles stretched out beside them, pillowing his head on some of the cloth that had been singed in one of the earlier fires. He wasn't sure why, but something—intuition, perhaps—told him that the saboteur would strike the looms. Though there was less to burn here, the equipment was the most costly.

Somehow, someway he would catch the man who was wreaking such havoc on the mill. And then he would learn who hated the Morelands and why. The possible motives bothered Charles almost as much as the actual destruction. Who—other than Matt Wagner and Brian O'Toole—had a reason to hate his family?

Though he had been certain he would not sleep, Charles felt his eyes grow heavy. It was Salt's whimper that wakened him. The white dog stood at the door, his ears perked, his tail sticking straight out.

"Good boy," Charles said as he rose. His dogs, who had barely stirred when Dorothy had wandered through Fairlawn, had somehow recognized that tonight's intruder was dangerous. When Pepper started to bark, Charles laid a hand on his head. "Not now." By some miracle, both dogs understood his desire for silence. "Stay!" he commanded.

He eased the door open. For a second, Charles stood motionless, not believing the scene in front of him. He tried to contain his horror but failed, for his worst nightmare had come true. The stairwell was filling with smoke, and above the crackle of the flames came the sound of a man's screams. The mill was on fire and someone was badly injured.

Thank God the dogs, with their more acute hearing and sense of smell, had alerted Charles before the destruction was complete. Thank God the man was still alive.

Charles gripped the rail as he descended the stairs. The smoke was thicker here, the cries louder. "Dear God, no! Not again!" Scenes of the ruined rooms at Fairlawn flashed before him, and for an instant Charles thought it was his father's shouts he heard. Then he recognized the voice. He narrowed his eyes against the smoke as he raced toward the man whose agony sent shafts of pain through his heart. No man, not even this one, deserved to suffer so. "Wilson!" Charles shouted, hoping to rouse the watchman. "Help me!"

There at the bottom of the staircase, his legs twisted at an impossible angle, his body engulfed in flames, lay the man who had once threatened Charles. The puddle of gasoline on the stairs and the overturned flask of whiskey bore mute testimony to the cause of the fall. The fire that surrounded him told Charles the man had intended to burn the entire mill. Instead . . . Charles shuddered at the sight and smell of charred flesh. He stripped off his coat and flung it over Brian O'Toole, hoping to stamp out the fire.

"Ow . . ." The word was little more than a howl. Though Charles was able to suffocate the flames, they had already worked their evil, eating clothing and flesh.

"Wilson!" Charles shouted again as he dragged Brian toward the door. The man needed fresh air. Perhaps he'd be able to breathe outside. But when the watchman joined Charles, the

285

look he gave him confirmed Charles's worst fears.

"Call the doctor," he said to Wilson.

Brian managed to shake his head. "Too late." Though Brian's eyes were dulled with pain, Charles knew he would never forget the anguish he saw in them. "Tell Moira," the dying man said. "Tell her I'm sorry." Then with a shudder, he closed his eyes for the last time.

By the time the sheriff arrived, Wilson had put out the fire in the mill and rescued the dogs while Charles had arranged Brian's body as best he could.

"Poor bastard," the sheriff said as he looked at the still figure. "I reckon he was the one behind all the mischief. 'Pears to me to be an open and shut case."

Charles nodded. Though he doubted that Brian was clever enough to have masterminded the sabotage at the mill, there was no doubt about his culpability tonight. And, though there was no proof that Brian had set the fire at Fairlawn, circumstantial evidence was strong enough that Charles's father would be exonerated. Tonight's fire would convince the insurance company to pay the claim on Fairlawn.

He ought to be glad about that, and yet all Charles could think was that another man had died, another young woman was bereft of a father, and another woman would grow old without the man she had loved so dearly. That was far too great a price to pay to restore one family's fortunes.

Wearily, Charles rose to his feet. Though the sheriff had offered, he knew that he should be the one to tell Moira and Megan O'Toole what had happened. And he would be the one who would arrange for the funeral and provide the family with an annuity.

It was early morning by the time Charles reached Fairlawn. Stripping off his smoky clothes, he splashed water on his face, then dressed hurriedly. He was in the front hall, his hand on the outside door, when he stopped. Charles couldn't explain what compelled him to turn around. He needed to return to the mill to reassure the workers. Instead, he found himself climbing the stairs to the ruined wing of his house. There was no need to look for clues again, for he knew who had set the fire. There was no reason to set foot in the deserted rooms. Charles's mind told him that; his heart refused to listen.

He pushed open the door to his parents' room and looked around. Nothing had changed. The charred remains of furniture still littered the floor; a few shreds of fabric hung from the window. Everything looked the same as it had the last time, and yet something felt different. For the first time since the fire, Charles felt as if he were not alone in the room.

He walked slowly to the window, and as he did, he felt the presence behind him. He pivoted and stared. There was no one. Of course there wasn't. But as he turned back to the window, he could hear his father's voice. "It's difficult to be a parent. You want to protect your children, but at the same time you know that they need to learn lessons on their own. Sometimes, Charles, the hardest thing is to do nothing. To let go."

A shudder rippled down Charles's spine, and he closed his eyes, trying to block out the image of John Moreland's face and the sound of his voice. There was no voice, just as there was no one else in the room. Charles knew that. But there was a warmth in the room that defied rational explanation. John had pronounced those words the day that Anne had insisted on raising the bar too high for the horse and had taken a serious fall. At the time Charles had asked his father why he hadn't stopped Anne, why he had let her be hurt.

Charles leaned out the window and took a deep breath. Had his father been speaking of more than Anne that day? Though he had never considered it, perhaps it had been difficult for John to watch him move to New York rather than stay in Hidden Falls and help run the mill. Yet John had never held him back. From early childhood, he had encouraged Charles to make his own decisions, so long as he was willing to accept the consequences.

The scent of roses filled the air, reminding Charles of the day his father had picked a bouquet for his mother. Though Jane had snickered at the fact that the stems were too short and he'd bruised the leaves, his mother had looked happier than Charles had ever seen her as she buried her face in the fragrant blooms.

"It's the thought that ladies appreciate," John had told him. "Never forget that."

Charles blinked rapidly, trying to hold back the moisture that insisted on filling his eyes. He had been so wrong! Though John may not have sired him, he had been a father in every other sense of the word. He had taught him to fish and swim and ride a horse. He had taught him how to run a cotton mill. He had taught him the difference between right and wrong. Most importantly, he had taught him the meaning of love.

Charles spun around and looked at the room his parents had once shared, the bed where he had been born and where Anne and Jane had been conceived.

"I failed you, didn't I?" Though there was no one else in the room, Charles spoke the words aloud. "I didn't trust you, and I wouldn't listen to you or Mother. If I hadn't been so hot headed, maybe you'd both be alive. Maybe if I had been here the night of the fire I could have saved you." He clenched his fists, trying to ease the pain.

Tears streamed down his cheeks, and for a moment Charles could not see. Then, brushing the tears aside, he made his way toward the door. He was halfway across the room when he stopped. The presence was closer now. Though he knew it was impossible, Charles would have sworn that he felt a hand on his shoulder.

"Let go, son. Let go." The words echoed clearly in his mind. Though the presence began to fade, in its place a deep sense of peace invaded his heart. Charles nodded. That was the answer. He could not change the past; there was no point in continuing to try to do the impossible. His father was right. He needed to let go.

That night for once Charles's sleep was dreamless and undisturbed.

Susannah wasn't certain what had wakened her. All she knew was that she woke suddenly, certain that something was wrong. She lay quietly, listening. Though she could hear crickets chirping and the sound of nocturnal animals scurrying in the garden, there were no unusual noises. It was the middle of the night, and the house was silent, as it should be. Was it too silent?

With a feeling of dread, Susannah hurried to her mother's room. It was empty. This was why the house was too quiet. Ever since the night that Dorothy had wandered down the hill to Charles's house, Susannah had slept with her door open, hoping she would waken if Dorothy should leave. Tonight she had slept soundly.

Susannah took a deep breath, then exhaled slowly as she reminded herself that Dorothy might be in another room. But by the time she had searched the house from her tower room to the cellar, Susannah knew that Dorothy was gone. Grabbing a torch, Susannah checked the garden; Dorothy was not there, either.

Oh, dear God, where could she be? Biting her lips to control their trembling, Susannah reached for the phone. Thank goodness it had finally been installed. She needed help, and this was the quickest way to summon it. *Please answer, please answer, please answer.* He did.

"Charles, it's Susannah. I hate to waken you, but . . ." She spoke quickly, hoping that despite the way he had dismissed her the other day, he would still help her. "Dorothy's gone. I've looked everywhere, and I can't find her." Unbidden, a sob escaped. "Did she come to you?"

"She's not in the house." Though the message was not the one Susannah wanted to hear, Charles's voice was warm and comforting. "I'll be there as fast as I can. I'll check the stable and the gazebo first. If she's not there, we'll search together." His words were like a warm blanket, helping to ease the trembling in her limbs. "Don't worry, Susannah. We'll find your mother." Susannah wished she were so confident.

When Charles arrived, telling Susannah he had not seen Dorothy anywhere along the way, he asked if she had any idea where her mother might have gone.

Susannah shook her head. "It's never the same place twice. Once I found her sleeping in my grandparents' room. Another time, she was lying on the couch in the parlor. Still another, I found her curled on the kitchen floor."

"We'll find her," Charles repeated.

As they searched the grounds beyond the garden, Susannah saw a scrap of white cloth on one of the bushes. "It's Dorothy's nightdress. She must have come this way." Susannah's heart sank, for the path led to only one destination: the falls. "What if . . . ?" Though she couldn't finish the thought, her mind reeled with the image of Dorothy slipping on the path and tumbling into the river.

"We'll find her."

If only it were true! As they descended toward the falls, picking their way along the narrow, rock-strewn path, Susannah caught her breath. It had been difficult walking, even with the torches Charles had brought. "How did Dorothy find her way without a light?" For there was no doubt that Dorothy had come this way. Susannah had found a second piece of lace on another bush.

"Maybe the moonlight was enough." The night was darker now, the moon's rays obscured by a heavy cover of clouds.

They walked in silence for a few minutes, then Susannah cried. "Look!" It was Dorothy. It had to be. Susannah began to run toward the still white form curled under a tree. *Please, God, let her be alive.* Kneeling beside her mother, Susannah laid a hand on Dorothy's shoulder. It was warm. Susannah's prayers had been answered. "Wake up, Dorothy."

Her mother blinked her eyes open. "It's not morning," she protested.

"No, it's not, but you need to come home." Susannah put an arm around Dorothy's waist and helped her to her feet.

"All right," she said, surprising Susannah with her docile reply.

An hour later, when Dorothy was back in her own bed and sleeping peacefully, Susannah descended the stairs. It was, she knew, a delayed reaction to the strains of the night, but her legs were trembling, and she clutched the railing, desperate to keep from falling.

"Thank you, Charles," she said when she reached the parlor. Though she had told him there was no reason to wait, Charles had insisted. Now she was glad he was here. "I don't know what I'd have done without you."

He rose and smiled. "That's what friends are for. I told you I'd always help you."

One good thing had come from this dreadful night: The cold and distant Charles of the mill office had been replaced with Charles, her friend. She had told herself she would be content with that. It should have been enough, but it was not. As he moved toward the door and reached for his hat, Susannah extended her hand. "Don't go. Please, Charles."

He stared at her for a moment, and she could see the indecision on his face. Was she so unlovable that he wouldn't hold her, just for a moment? Then he opened his arms. Susannah ran into them. It might be shameless, but she didn't care. She wanted Charles. She needed him.

"Oh, Susannah!" As she wrapped her arms around his waist, she could feel his breath on her hair. He was warm and wonderful, and she never wanted to let him go. "You're stronger than you know," he said.

She shook her head, feeling his heartbeat as her ear brushed against his chest. "I don't feel strong."

Charles laid one hand under her chin and tipped her face up. For a long moment, he looked at her, his eyes filled with an emotion she had never seen. Could it be the same one she was feeling? Was it possible that he loved her the way she loved him? Perhaps this was wrong. Perhaps she should send him away. But all she wanted was to keep him close to her, to feel his healing warmth, to revel in the sensation of being safe and the illusion of being loved.

Slowly, ever so slowly, Charles lowered his lips to hers. His mouth was gentle, his kiss slow and sweet. Susannah felt a languor steal over her as the fear that had consumed her while they searched for Dorothy subsided. This was wonderful. She wanted to stay in Charles's arms forever. She never wanted the kiss to end. And yet she wanted more—much more.

Susannah stretched until her hands were behind Charles's neck. Slowly but steadily, she pulled him closer. There was no hesitation. As if her touch had ignited something deep within him, Charles's kiss changed. It became strong and deep and urgent, and the languor that had filled Susannah disappeared, replaced by a vortex of emotions, swirling, spiraling and threatening to overwhelm her. This was what she wanted. This was what she had dreamt of.

"Oh, yes!" she breathed.

"No!" Charles dropped his arms and took a step away from her. "I'd better leave before I do something we'll both regret."

And without another word, he strode from the house, leaving Susannah feeling emptier than ever before.

Chapter Twenty-three

Once again, her days had fallen into a pattern, but this time the pattern was not of her choosing. Susannah brushed her hair vigorously, wincing as her brush caught a snarl, then smiling ruefully as she realized that she was taking out her frustrations on her hair. Since Brian's death, so much had changed. Though Susannah hadn't been sure how she would care for the horses, fortunately Matt had found a boy who loved horses. While Frederick might not have Brian's years of experience, he was willing to learn and didn't balk at tasks as menial as feeding the horses and mucking out the stalls.

Susannah laid down the brush and began to coil her hair. The horses were well cared for, although there were days when Susannah wondered why she bothered to keep them. It had been Dorothy who had insisted on having them, yet she had not ridden since they had returned to Hidden Falls. And since the night when her mother had wandered toward the falls, Susannah had not taken a morning ride, for something—perhaps it was the sadness that clung to Moira and Megan O'Toole, perhaps something else—had affected Dorothy, and she wandered

293

more often. Susannah had continued to sleep with her door open so that she would hear Dorothy when she stirred, and more nights than not, she had to return her mother to her room at least once. Even if she had wanted to ride with Rob, Susannah found herself too tired most mornings.

Her time away from Pleasant Hill was now reduced to the afternoons when Dorothy napped and she hurried to the workshop to help with the carousel. The animals were almost finished, and she was working on the third rounding board. Even the carvers had laughed when they'd seen the completed wedding scene on the second and recognized Rob as the groom. Susannah had painted him, as much to prove to herself that she could make a male figure look like someone other than Charles as to give Rob a lasting part in the carousel.

This third painting, though, would have Charles in it, for the central building was the mill. Susannah had sketched it at noon, when the workers were hurrying home for dinner, and she'd put Charles in one of the windows, looking out at the mill hands, a smile on his face. He might not be willing to share the carousel with the townspeople, but Susannah had resolved that they would play a role in it. By the time Charles realized what she was doing, it would be too late to change it.

Susannah had had to paint his face from memory, for she had not seen Charles since the night they had found Dorothy at the falls. Susannah tried not to cringe at the realization that he had kissed her so tenderly, then pulled away. At the time, she had thought that he had enjoyed the kiss as much as she had. She had thought that maybe—just maybe—he had felt a little of the love that she had for him. But she had been wrong. Perhaps he had kissed her because he had realized she needed comfort. Perhaps it had been nothing more than lust. The one thing it had not been was love, for if he had loved her, he would not have walked away—and stayed away—as he had.

She was truly the most foolish woman on earth. She kept repeating her mistakes. When would she learn that Charles wanted nothing more than friendship from her? It was obvious that while Susannah Deere might be many things, she was not a lovable woman.

Susannah slid the final pin into her pompadour. It was silly for her to dwell on her failings. What mattered was helping Dorothy. They still worked in the garden most mornings, and although Dorothy no longer seemed able to distinguish between weeds and flowers, and her attention span was greatly diminished, she still appeared to enjoy digging in the dirt. That was what was important for Susannah, not the fact that Charles did not love her.

If only she didn't dream of him! The dreams that had tormented her had grown more detailed. Now she dreamt not just that they were together but that they were in Paris. They would stroll along the banks of the Seine, laughing, holding hands and occasionally stopping to share a kiss. Sometimes it would be daylight, and the sun would sparkle on the water, reflecting their images. Other times, it was night, and they would joke about a lover's moon before their lips met. No matter the time of day, they were young and happy and in love.

It was all a dream, nothing more.

What a fool he was! Charles tossed the ball with more force than usual, sending the dogs running across the lawn. He should never have kissed her. He had known that before he started, but once his lips had touched hers, he had been lost. She had felt so good! Her body fit his as perfectly as if she had been fashioned for him, and when their lips had met, he had never wanted to stop kissing her.

Charles frowned as Pepper deposited a soggy ball at his feet. Susannah was everything he had dreamed of: warm, wonderful and utterly desirable. Oh, how he desired her! And that was the height of insanity, wanting a woman he could never have.

He tossed the ball again, watching the dogs try to outrun each other. They might never learn, but perhaps he could. Since that day in his parents' room, Charles had felt different. He had made peace with his father and was doing what John had advised, letting go of the past, focusing on the future. That felt right, and so too did his decision about the mill. Although he knew there would be an emptiness inside him once he had done it, Charles had resolved that he would deed the mill to Anne and Jane as soon as they returned.

Ralph was working on the legal papers, and Philip had begun looking for a manager. Though Ralph had been open in his disapproval of Charles's plan, Philip had merely nodded when Charles had explained what he wanted to do and had agreed to help. He had even offered to serve as an interim manager if he couldn't find a replacement soon enough. It had been a generous offer, though it was one Charles could not accept. Philip, as he had realized the last time his friend had visited Fairlawn, was no longer a young man. It would be unfair to expect him to come out of retirement to run the mill, for the mill required a substantial amount of time and energy.

Thank goodness, it was now running smoothly. The destruction had ceased with Brian O'Toole's death, and with each day that passed without an incident, the workers' morale improved. The mill was now back to full production. That combined with the profits from the new silk screen prints was helping Charles repay the debt his father had incurred.

Salt and Pepper whined, begging Charles to play a new game. He reached for a rope and began a match of tug-of-war.

He should be content. The mill was running smoothly. His life was running smoothly. He had made his decisions. He knew what he would do, and he knew what he would not do. He would leave Hidden Falls. He would not let himself care for Susannah. The one was easy, the other impossible. The simple fact was, it was too late. He already cared for her.

Admit it, Moreland. You don't just care for Susannah; you love her. He did, and loving her meant he wanted to spend the rest of his life with her. He wanted her face to be the first thing he saw each morning and the last thing each night. He wanted to laugh with her and cry with her. He wanted Susannah in every way a man could want a woman.

But loving Susannah was a dream. And that dream, Charles knew, would never come true.

Susannah was smiling as she returned from the workshop. The third panel was completed, and everyone agreed that it was the

296

best yet. She had been so pleased with the results that, rather than take the path through the woods, she had walked along the driveway and out to the road. It was silly, of course, to think that Charles might be on his way home from the mill and that she might share her pleasure with him. But, though she had lingered on the road for a few minutes, her eyes searching the distance for the sight of his familiar figure, she had seen no one. It was disappointing, but even that couldn't diminish her sense of satisfaction that her painting was improving.

She was still smiling as she entered the house. There were no lights on in the parlor, a sign that Dorothy was still asleep. To Susannah's surprise, Moira hurried from the kitchen. She looked at Susannah, then stared at the space behind her. At the sight of Moira's expression, Susannah caught her breath. "She's gone, isn't she?" Somehow Dorothy had managed to elude Moira's watch. Susannah swallowed deeply, trying to contain her fear. They would find Dorothy, and she would be all right. Of course she would. "Where have you looked?"

Moira held out her hands, palms up. "Everywhere except the Morelands'. When we couldn't find her, we figured she was with you."

The fear that was never far from the surface threatened to engulf Susannah. She sank onto a padded bench and tried to think. Panic would solve nothing. "Look again," she said. "Megan can take the buggy into town; send Frederick to the falls; you check the house again."

Susannah took a deep breath, willing her heartbeat to return to normal. "I'll go back to the workshop. She probably took the path there." That had to be what had happened. Dorothy had wanted to watch the carvers at work. She must have been coming down the path while Susannah was on the road. Oh, why had Susannah decided to take the long way home?

There was no time for regrets. What she needed to do was find Dorothy and bring her home. Susannah ran through the woods, heedless of the branches that caught on her hair and skirts. Though she was breathless when she reached the workshop, she raced inside, calling out Dorothy's name.

"What is it?" By some miracle, Charles was in the former

stable, inspecting the carousel animals. When Susannah explained, he sent the carvers in different directions. "You stay here," he told Susannah, "in case Dorothy comes this way."

And so Susannah sat outside the stable, her hands pleating and unpleating her skirt as she waited, silently praying for her mother's safety. Afterward, she could not have said how long she sat. All she knew was that when she heard Charles calling her name, the plaintive note in his voice made her legs tremble so much that she could barely stand.

She heard his voice and then she saw him as he rounded the corner of the house, carrying Dorothy in his arms. Thank God he had found her! Her heart pounding with a dread she did not want to acknowledge, Susannah raced across the lawn. It was only as the distance narrowed that she saw that both Charles and Dorothy were dripping wet. Dear God, no! There was only one place Dorothy could have gotten so wet.

Susannah stared at her mother. Dorothy was still. Much too still. Reluctantly, afraid of what it would tell her, Susannah raised her eyes to Charles's face. What she saw made her step falter, and for a second the world began to turn black. Susannah took a deep breath and swallowed.

"Is she . . . ?" Though she tried, she could not pronounce the word. Dimly Susannah heard a chipmunk chatter and the dogs bark. Dorothy made no sound.

Charles nodded. "I'm afraid so." He looked down at Dorothy, his expression filled with compassion. When his gaze met Susannah's, she saw tears in his eyes. "I'm sorry, Susannah."

His words and the kindness she heard broke through the wall of denial she had erected around her heart. Tears began to stream down Susannah's face as she realized that she would never again hear Dorothy's voice or touch her hand or see her smile. Her mother was gone.

Afterward, Susannah was never sure how she and Charles got Dorothy home. All she knew was that Charles called Mrs. Harrod, and before Susannah knew what was happening, her neighbor had arrived. There were decisions to be made, clothes to be selected, hymns to be chosen. Somehow Susannah did what was needed, but through it all, she felt as if she were standing in the corner, watching a woman who looked like her go through the motions of planning her mother's funeral.

It was late and the sun had already set by the time the good women of Hidden Falls left. Though Mrs. Harrod and the minister's wife had offered to stay with Susannah, she had refused, insisting that she needed to be alone. Perhaps then she would begin to believe that it was true.

She was sitting on her front porch, staring sightlessly at the stars when she heard his footsteps. "Dorothy never learned to swim," she said, blurting out the thought that had haunted her all afternoon. "Why did she go to the pond? Why, Charles? Why?" The night was warm and redolent with the scents of summer flowers, flowers that Dorothy had helped plant, flowers she would never again smell.

Without waiting for an invitation, Charles sat next to Susannah on the swing. "I wish I had answers, but I don't." Though Susannah had been unable to muster the energy to propel the swing, Charles set it in motion.

They sat for a few minutes, rocking in silence. Somehow he knew that she didn't want to talk, that all she wanted was the comfort of having him with her. Then Susannah said, "I can't believe she's gone."

Again, Charles spoke softly, his words little more than a murmur. "I know. I felt that way when my parents were killed. I was numb at first; then the pain came crashing in."

Somehow the knowledge that she would eventually feel pain helped. It seemed so terribly wrong that her heart hadn't yet registered what her mind knew. She was thinking of trivial things, like whether she should leave Dorothy's wedding ring on her hand, rather than admitting that the future stretching before her looked like a string of empty days. "It's my fault. I should have stayed with her."

This time Charles reached out and took Susannah's hand in his. "You mustn't think that. I used to blame myself for the fire and my parents' death." His hand was warm and comforting. Though Susannah suspected the terrible cold that had settled on her when she had seen her mother's lifeless body in Charles's arms would never recede, at least her fingertips no longer felt frozen.

"It took a long time before I learned the futility of blaming myself, and I wasted a lot of energy that could have been spent on better things," Charles said. "What I know now is that you can't change the past. You need to remember the happy times you shared with Dorothy and then think about the future."

But the future was bleak. Susannah shook her head. "When I think about Dorothy, I feel so alone."

For the first time in her life, Susannah had no reason to live. There was no one who needed her. Today she was the needy one, and nothing in her past had prepared her for this. She needed help, but it felt wrong—so very wrong—to ask for something for herself.

"You're not alone." Charles squeezed her hand. "I'm here."

The breeze was warm, reminding Susannah of the night she and Charles had found Dorothy by the falls. He had said he would always be there for her, and then when she had kissed him, he had fled. It could happen again.

Susannah thought she had shed all the tears her eyes could make, but she was wrong. As the tears began to fall, she sobbed. "I'm so selfish. My mother is dead, and all I can think about is that I'm alone and there's no one left on earth who loves me."

"That's not true."

Susannah turned and faced Charles. His features were the ones she loved, but in the moonlight they looked different. There was a softness and at the same time an intensity she had not seen before. "Yes, it is true. Anthony pretended that he loved me, but it was Gracie he loved. And you . . ." She couldn't tell Charles how much it hurt that he didn't love her.

He reached forward and cupped her chin in his hand. His fingers were firm, the skin slightly rough against hers as he forced her to look at him. For a long moment he said nothing, merely stared at her, his expression serious. Even in the dim light, Susannah could see the indecision on his face. Whatever he was about to say weighed heavily on him.

When he finally spoke, his voice was low but fervent. "Don't ever—ever—doubt that I love you."

Susannah caught her breath as she felt the blood drain from her face. Was it possible? Had she been wrong? Charles's fingers were warm on her face, but it was the heat she saw in his eyes that began to thaw her heart.

"I never thought I'd feel like this," Charles continued, his voice harsh with emotion, telling Susannah this was not an easy confession. "The truth is, I never thought I could feel like this. But I do. I love you, Susannah, with my heart, my soul and every fiber of my being."

These were the words she had wanted to hear, the ones she had dreamt of her whole life, and he was the man she had dreamed would say them. Susannah stared at Charles, wanting to believe him but not daring. It couldn't be true. This was all a dream, and she'd waken in a minute to find that she was alone and unloved. But Charles did not move. He sat next to her, those blue eyes that she loved so much serious, a little smile curving the corners of his mouth.

She had needed those words and the assurance that she was loved. But she needed more than words. She needed tangible proof of Charles's love. She needed his kiss, his touch, all of him to dispel that horrible feeling of emptiness that had settled on her this afternoon. He would give her what she needed. All she had to do was ask. But that was wrong. It was selfish.

"What is it, Susannah?" Somehow he had sensed her dilemma.

"I . . ." No. She couldn't do it.

"Susannah?"

She stared at Charles, wanting him, needing him. All she had to do was ask. That was all. Susannah swallowed deeply and gathered every shred of courage she possessed. Slowly she rose, then tugged him to his feet. "If you love me, Charles, show me." She gestured toward the front door. "I need your love."

He pulled his hands from her, then gripped her shoulders, forcing her to look directly at him. "Are you sure?"

Susannah nodded. Her earlier indecision had faded. "I've never been so sure of anything in my life."

As they climbed the stairs, neither of them spoke. Susannah's heart pounded, and for a second her step faltered as she thought of the enormity of what she had done. She—sensible Susannah Deere—had asked a man to make love to her. Perhaps she was shameless. Perhaps she was foolish. Perhaps she would regret it in the morning. All she knew was that nothing had ever felt so right. She loved this man with all her heart and soul, and she wanted—oh, how she wanted—to love him in every way possible.

When they reached the landing, Susannah hesitated for a second, then turned to the right. Her room and Dorothy's were to the left. The only room in this direction was the big bed-chamber that had been her grandparents'. Perhaps she was being fanciful, taking Charles to the room where her grandmother had come as a bride, but though no vows had been spoken, Susannah felt as though she were a newlywed, and so she led Charles to what had once been a bridal suite.

Susannah pushed the door open. It was only when they were inside that she faltered again, suddenly unsure. This time her hesitation was caused by fear of the unknown. What if she did something wrong? Charles had said he loved her, but what if she was awkward? Would he turn from her in disgust?

As if he understood, Charles lit the lamps. As the shadows dissipated, so did some of Susannah's fears. Though the four-poster bed dominated the room, Charles led her to the small settee next to the window. He sat, then pulled her onto his lap. For a long moment he stared at her, his eyes blazing with warmth, his lips curving into a smile. Though he said not a word, his smile reassured Susannah. This was Charles, the man she loved. Everything would be all right.

Then he leaned forward and pressed his lips to hers. It was a gentle kiss, a tentative exploration. Susannah sighed with pleasure. How could she have doubted even for a moment that this was right? And then Charles deepened the kiss, his lips devouring hers, driving all thoughts from her mind save the wonder of being in his arms, sharing his embrace. Susannah reached her arms around his neck and clung to him, returning kiss for kiss, caress for caress.

At length, Charles pulled away. "Your mouth is so sweet," he said, his voice husky. "I can't stop dreaming of how it tastes—just like honey."

Though her heart was beating faster than a hummingbird's wings, Susannah forced her hand to move slowly as she traced his lips with a fingertip. "From the first day, I dreamed of your lips and that kiss we shared." Was that her voice? Even to her ears, it sounded strange, so low and sultry. Was this how a woman in love sounded? "I believed it was only because the kiss was stolen that it tasted so sweet, but I was wrong. It was sweet because it was yours."

Charles smiled and though she hadn't thought it possible, the warmth in his eyes intensified. Had she thought she was cold? The fires she saw reflected in Charles's expression would thaw even solid ice. Reaching his hand behind her head, Charles began to unpin her hair. "This is another one of my dreams," he confided. "I've always wanted to see what your hair looks like spread out over your shoulders." Suiting his actions to his words, he fanned her hair and stroked it. "It's as soft as silk."

Her head tingled with pleasure from his touch. Who would have dreamt that something so simple could feel so wonderful? Wanting to share the pleasure with him, she ran her fingers through his hair. To Susannah's surprise, the pleasure she received from Charles's caress paled compared to the delight of being able to touch him. "Your hair is springy. It's as if it had a life of its own."

Susannah wasn't sure whether it was her words or her touch. All she knew was that Charles's eyes darkened. "Oh, Susannah!" He leaned forward, capturing her lips again. "You're wonderful!" Charles stroked her cheek. Then his hand moved to unfasten the hooks on her collar and spread it, exposing her neck. Bending his head, he kissed the nape of her neck. "Your skin is even softer than your hair," he murmured. His lips were firm and warm, sending shivers of delight down her spine.

Following Charles's lead, Susannah unfastened his cravat and pulled it away. "Oh!" she said as she pressed her lips to his throat. "You taste like salt." It was wondrous, exploring his body, discovering how different it was from hers. This was what she had dreamt of doing from the first time she'd seen him. But,

303

vivid though her dreams had been, they could not compare to the reality of touching Charles, of being touched by him.

"Sweetheart, you're driving me crazy." With a groan, Charles finished unfastening her bodice and slid it from her shoulders. He set her on her feet, then unhooked her skirt and petticoat. Susannah shivered.

"Are you cold?"

Cold? Oh, no. She was burning with heat. Susannah blushed as she looked down. Never before had she stood before a man clad only in her chemise and pantalets. "I'm a little scared," she admitted. She glanced at the bed, then blushed again.

Though he had been stroking her shoulders, Charles's hands stilled. "We can stop."

The room, which had felt so warm, suddenly grew cold. It was, Susannah realized, because Charles was no longer sending warmth coursing through her. "No!" As Susannah shook her head, her hair tumbled forward, brushing the tops of her breasts. Charles's eyes widened, and she heard him catch his breath. "I don't want to stop," she said. "I'm just afraid that I won't please you."

Charles chuckled. "Sweetheart, that's one fear you can dismiss right now. You can't possibly not please me." He continued to stroke her shoulders, sending shivers of delight through her arms and tingles all the way down her spine. "You look like a goddess."

His words and the look he gave her dispelled the last of Susannah's doubts. Unable to stop herself—and not wanting to—she ran her hands along Charles's arms, smiling as he shuddered. "I painted you as a Greek god."

Charles's laugh was oddly, endearingly shaky, as if he were as overcome with emotion as she. "I assure you, my dearest Susannah, that I'm no god. I'm one very human man who wants you so badly he's about to burst."

The fire she had seen in his eyes intensified, making Susannah wonder if she would combust from the heat. The room was warm, far too warm. As if he sensed her discomfort, Charles reached for the ribbons on her chemise. Susannah shook her head, suddenly shy. This was something she had to do. She had to show Charles that she wanted him as much as he claimed he wanted her.

Slowly, deliberately Susannah pulled the chemise over her head, then unfastened her drawers. As she stepped out of them, for a second, she was unable to meet Charles's eyes. Had she been too brazen? But when at last she raised her eyes to Charles's, the expression she saw on his face made her gasp. His eyes were darker than before, and the smile he wore was so filled with wonder that Susannah could hardly believe it was directed at her.

"Oh, my darling," Charles said, his voice low and husky, "you're even more beautiful than I dreamed."

And then, as if he could wait no longer, he drew her into his arms and lowered his mouth to hers. But Charles was not content to simply kiss her. As he pulled her close to him, his fingers slid down her back, caressing her.

It was more wonderful than anything she had ever dreamt, being held by the man she loved, being touched as if she were a priceless piece of porcelain. But porcelain was cold, and Susannah was not. Charles's touch was incendiary, intensifying the heat that had already begun to course through her. As he deepened the kiss and pulled her even closer, Susannah gasped.

He stopped and drew back. "Did I hurt you?" Charles's eyes darkened.

She shook her head, then nodded, afraid to shatter the spell he'd woven. "Your buttons." Susannah glanced down at the red indentations in her breasts.

Charles touched them gently. "I'm sorry," he murmured. Susannah was not, for her breasts began to tingle with the most exquisite pleasure she had known.

"Let's make certain I don't hurt you again." More quickly than she would have thought possible, he shed his clothes and stood before her. As he had done only moments before, she let her gaze roam from the top of his head down to his toes.

"Oh, Charles!" He was magnificent, more beautiful than she had imagined. She knew that his body was firm where hers was soft, but she had not known just how spectacular his muscles were or how the sight of his skin stretched over those muscles would stir her. Susannah wanted to explore each inch of him and let her fingers revel in the sensation of touching him just as her eyes had feasted on his beauty. She reached out and stroked his chest hair, laughing at the way it curled around her pinkie. "It's just the way I thought it would feel."

He chuckled. "So you did look that day at the pond."

Susannah's blush deepened. "I couldn't look away. I told myself I should." As her fingers traced the lines of his chest and began to move lower, Charles gasped. "I tried not to look, but I was mesmerized. All I wanted to do was stare at you."

Charles's gaze moved slowly down her body. Then he smiled. "I want to do more than look. I want to let my fingers learn the way you feel. Then I want to taste you. And then . . ." He let his voice trail off.

Charles scooped her into his arms and placed her on the bed. Once again his gentleness made her feel treasured, for the harshness of his breathing told Susannah how difficult it was for him to restrain his desires. A second later, he lay next to her. His lips descended to hers, and this time there was no gentleness in his kiss. It was hungry and demanding, and she loved it. Though Susannah's hands moved to his shoulders and she began to explore the muscles of his back, Charles contented himself with kisses. When they were both breathless, he wrenched his lips from hers and slid back an inch. "Are you sure?" he asked, his eyes meeting hers.

Susannah nodded. This was what she wanted. This was what she had dreamed of for so long. "Yes, yes, a thousand times yes." And she pulled him back into her arms.

Charles touched and tasted and taught her the mysteries of love, his fingers and lips caressing her, sending sweet sensations spiraling through her. It was everything she had ever imagined and more, much more. For the way Charles moaned told Susannah that her own touches were bringing him the same measure of joy.

The pleasure grew, more powerful, more wonderful than anything she had ever dreamed. And then when Susannah was certain she could bear no more, he touched her again and the world shattered into a million sparkling pieces. Slowly, ever so slowly, she drifted back to earth, wrapped in the arms of the man she loved.

For a moment when she wakened, Susannah was not certain where she was. This was not her room; it was not her bed; and she did not feel like herself. She closed her eyes once more as the memories came rushing in, a kaleidoscope of black and white and a thousand brilliant colors. There had never been a day like yesterday, where tragedy mingled with the greatest pleasure she had ever known.

She had lost Dorothy.

She had found Charles.

Susannah stretched her hand out, reaching for him, finding nothing. She was alone in the bed. The ache that had filled her heart at the thought of her mother overflowed as Susannah looked around the room. Charles's side of the bed was cold and the room was empty, devoid of any sign that he had ever been there.

Susannah shook her head, trying to clear the cobwebs. She hadn't imagined him. The fact that she was naked and the memories that were more vivid than any dream told her that. She rose and began to throw on her clothing. And as she did, she looked around the room. Surely he would have left her a note, explaining where he had gone. But there was nothing.

Hastily she pinned her hair up, trying not to cry as understanding swept through her. The truth was as strong as the waves of pleasure he had given her last night. Charles Moreland did not love her. It was as plain as if he'd carved the words on the bureau top. If he had loved her, he would have stayed. He would have wanted, as she did, to spend every minute of every day with her. But Charles did not love her.

He pitied her. That's why he had spent the night with her. She had begged for comfort, and he had given it. As someone who had lost his own parents, Charles knew the pain and loneliness Susannah was feeling, and so he had provided what she needed to help her through the night. He had murmured pretty words; he had given her wonderful memories; he had not given her love.

Susannah stared at the bed and blushed as she realized that, though Charles had introduced her to the heights of passion, they had not actually performed what her mother had referred to as "the marriage act." Though she had trembled with ecstasy and tumbled over the precipice of her own climax, Susannah was still technically a virgin. Charles had given; he had not taken. And that, she knew, was proof positive that he did not love her. Men, her mother had explained, found it difficult to control their lust. That Charles had not even lusted after her confirmed what Susannah had feared: she was unlovable. He might deny it, but Susannah knew the truth. Actions, she had always heard, were more powerful than words. And Charles's actions had been unmistakable. He saw her as a friend, nothing more.

Susannah blinked back her tears. And yet she could not regret the night, for Charles's kindness had given her memories that would last a lifetime. They would have to, for they were all she would have to help her through the empty years that stretched before her.

Susannah was dressed in black, her hair neatly arranged, her face composed when he arrived. She greeted him as she would have any of the other townspeople. Though she had begged Charles last night, she would not embarrass him with a further display of need. He had once told her she was stronger than she knew. Today she would prove it.

"I came to see if there was any assistance I could provide." His voice was cool and formal, as if she were nothing more than a casual acquaintance. Though Susannah hated it, her eyes searched his face, looking for a hint that he remembered last night and that it had meant something to him. She found nothing more than polite concern. He stood in the foyer, his hat in his hand, looking the way he always did. Apparently she was the only one who had been changed by their night together.

"Mrs. Harrod and the minister's wife have made all the arrangements for the funeral." Susannah tipped her head toward the parlor door, silently inviting Charles to stay. He appeared not to see her gesture, nor did he make any effort to hang his hat on the tree.

"What will you do afterward?" Though his voice was even, the concern she saw in his eyes told Susannah that Charles cared, but only as a friend.

"I don't know." None of the women had asked her to plan anything beyond tomorrow's funeral, but none of the women believed as Charles did that it was vital to live for the future.

He nodded as if he understood her indecision. "You could go to Paris."

She could. Odd. For years, Paris had seemed like a beacon in the darkness, an almost unattainable goal. Now there was nothing to stop her from going, and yet she felt not the slightest excitement. "I suppose. Is that what you think I should do?"

"Yes." Charles answered without hesitation. "Make your dream come true." This time his voice was low and fervent, reminding Susannah of the passion she had heard in it only a few hours before.

"What if Paris isn't my dream any longer?" For the briefest of moments before she had fully wakened, her dream had been of a life with Charles. In that instant, she had been filled with happiness and an overwhelming sense of destiny, that this was what her life was meant to be. The dream of Charles was stronger, more powerful than any thoughts of Paris had ever been. If that dream of life with Charles wouldn't come true— and she knew it would not—there seemed no reason to dream of anything. The day was sunny and clear, yet it brought Susannah no happiness. For she had lost more than her mother. She had lost Charles and her dreams.

She stared at him for a second, wanting to speak but not daring to. As if he sensed her need and sought to help her, he started to reach his hand out, then pulled it back, seemingly afraid to touch her. "It's not surprising that you're feeling confused today." His eyes radiated some of the pain she knew must be reflected in her own. "This is a difficult time, but don't give up your dream, Susannah. Make it come true."

What about last night? Wasn't he going to say anything? Would he continue to pretend it hadn't happened? Susannah bit her lip again, then said, "About yesterday . . ." She wouldn't say "last night."

Before she could complete the sentence, Charles interrupted. "I'm thankful that I could provide some assistance." He spoke as if all he'd done was find Dorothy and bring her home, as if he had not given Susannah the most wonderful night of her life. "Please call me if you need anything else. Otherwise, I had best leave. I wouldn't want to start rumors by being here without a chaperone."

Was that the reason he had left this morning? It could be, Susannah admitted. Perhaps he had spoken so circumspectly because Moira or Megan might overhear him. All that was possible. But in the depth of her heart, Susannah knew that wasn't the case. Quite simply, Charles did not love her.

Charles watched as she walked from the grave site. Though she was dressed in black and her face was pale, Susannah looked more beautiful than ever. She moved with a quiet dignity and a new maturity. Though her grief was palpable, so was her strength. Thank God! This was the way he wanted to remember her, strong and brave.

It had been the most difficult thing he had ever done, leaving her bed before she woke. But he had had no choice. If he had seen her sweet smile one more time, if she had reached for him again with hunger in her eyes, he would have succumbed to temptation. He would have broken his vow. He would have loved her in every way he could. As it was, Susannah could go to her husband—if not untouched—still technically a virgin, and Charles need not fear that he had passed on tainted blood to an innocent child.

It had been so damnably difficult not to take everything she had offered. He had wanted to. Oh, how he had wanted to. Even now, he ached at the thought of Susannah's sweet body and how innocently she had opened it to him. It had required every ounce of willpower he had possessed not to take the gift she had offered. Somehow he had mustered that strength, but he had known his limits, and so he had left before she had wakened.

The truth was, he should not have gone back to her house that night. He had known she would be lonely. He had known she would need a friend. He could try to make excuses, to say that he had gone because he had known she would need him, but Charles couldn't lie to himself. He had gone because he couldn't resist her. He had gone, knowing full well what might happen. He had gone hoping that it would happen.

The reason was simple. Charles had wanted one night of memories to get him through all those years of empty nights that stretched before him. He had believed that he would be able to walk away with those memories, to keep them in a safe place and cherish them. He hadn't known that loving Susannah and then leaving her would break his heart.

Chapter Twenty-four

"Beggin' your pardon, Miss Susannah, but will you be wantin' me to help you?"

Susannah looked up from the pile of clothing she was sorting and shook her head. "No, thank you, Megan. This is something I need to do myself." She had put off the task for a week, but today she knew that she could delay no longer. She needed to clean out her mother's room, pack the few mementos she wanted to keep, give the rest away. Though Susannah had no doubt that the day would be fraught with painful memories, she knew that it was time. It wasn't simply that the day was cool and rainy, making her reluctant to go outdoors. Though she could not explain it, when she had wakened, she had been filled with a strange restlessness and the sense that it was somehow important that she sort her mother's possessions today.

Charles had been right. The horrible emptiness that had plagued her that first day had been replaced with a grief so deep that it made Susannah long for those few hours when she'd known only numbness. She grieved for Dorothy, for the woman her mother had once been and for the way that woman had gradually faded. It was terrible, losing her mother, and Susannah's pain was intensified by the knowledge that her future was bleak.

Now somehow it seemed right to be in Dorothy's room, handling her possessions one last time. With each dress that she folded, each pair of shoes that she stuffed with paper, Susannah felt as if she were saying farewell to her mother. Though she couldn't explain it, she felt as if Dorothy approved.

The clothing was easier than Susannah had expected. Even if she had been able to wear the garments, Susannah doubted she would, and so she planned to give them to the minister's wife. Mrs. Collins would distribute them to needy parishioners. The only item Susannah kept was the bonnet Dorothy had worn to church. Though it had clearly been a possession from her childhood, Dorothy had taken inordinate pleasure in wearing it, and Susannah could picture her mother's smile as she tipped her head to one side, accepting compliments. It was a happy memory, one Susannah wanted to cherish.

She saved the trunk for last. When they had moved back to Hidden Falls, Dorothy had packed it herself and had watched over its transport, as if it held prized possessions. And, unlike the other trunks that were stored in the attic, Dorothy had kept this one in a corner of her room. Susannah took a deep breath, then unlatched the heavy leather buckles, her heart pounding as she wondered what she would find.

There were surprisingly few things inside. Susannah pulled out a set of Goethe in the original German, a fragile china cup and saucer that had somehow survived multiple moves and a length of lace, now yellowed with age. Underneath the lace was a tarnished silver frame. As she pulled it out and held it to the light, Susannah saw that the photograph was of her parents. They looked so young and happy that Susannah caught her breath as an almost unbearable longing swept through her. Would she ever be blessed with that kind of joy?

The formal clothing and the brilliant smiles they both wore told Susannah that the picture had been taken on their wedding day. While most portraits had the subjects facing the photographer, Dorothy and Louis had turned toward each other, as if they could not bear to look at anyone else. Though the picture had faded, the love that flowed between them was almost palpable, and it brought tears to Susannah's eyes.

That was what she wanted, a love so strong that nothing could destroy it, a love that would fill her life with joy and give it meaning. Susannah knew that what she felt for Charles was that kind of love. She knew that if she were with Charles, her own expression would have the same almost luminous quality that Dorothy's did. But she also knew that she would never have a wedding day, and Charles would never regard her the way Louis had Dorothy. Charles had murmured words of love; he had given Susannah a night of unforgettable passion, but he did not love her.

Brushing aside her tears, Susannah laid the photograph down. Tears resolved nothing. She reached into the trunk and pulled out the remaining item. It was a packet of letters, tied with a simple cord. Susannah thought she might be holding her father's love letters until she realized that the handwriting was a woman's. Curious, she slid the first letter from its envelope and glanced at the date and signature. The letter was almost thirty years old; the author was Charles's mother Mary. Without reading it, Susannah returned it to its envelope and retied the string. She would give the letters to Charles. Perhaps he would find something of value in them.

Lightning split the sky, and seconds later thunder boomed. It appeared that the gentle morning rain was being replaced by a violent storm. As thunder cracked again, Susannah winced. She tried not to wince at the thought of Charles or the fact that she had not seen him since the funeral. Though she went to the workshop occasionally and played with the dogs each day, there had been no sign of Charles. Rob had shaken his head once, saying that he was concerned about Charles. "The man is unhappy," Rob said, "but he won't say why."

Susannah was unhappy, and though she wouldn't confide in Rob, she knew why. She rose, brushing the dust from her hands, and returned to her own room. There she settled the photograph of her parents on her bureau where she could see it from her bed, then picked up the envelope that contained her tickets for Paris. When she had made the arrangements, Susannah had felt a glimmer of hope that Charles was right, that going to Paris would bring her happiness, but it had quickly dissipated. Now her heart felt as heavy as it had the day Dorothy had died.

Susannah stared out the window, trying to make sense of her jumbled thoughts. The rain pelted the earth, puddling in the flower beds. Though the sky was gray, she knew that the rain would revive the flowers. Nothing, she feared, would revive her dreams. Susannah closed her eyes, remembering when she had first started dreaming of Paris. It had been the year she had turned ten, the year her parents had refused to let her paint, insisting that she spend her free time reading to children at an orphanage.

In retrospect, Susannah realized that what had drawn her to Paris had been not just the city's undeniable beauty and the opportunity to study painting with a master but also the fact that if she went to Paris, she would be alone. She would be responsible for no one other than herself. From that moment, Paris was more than a place. It became a symbol of Susannah's dream of independence, and as such, it had helped her through many difficult days.

But now . . . Now independence was not what she craved. Love was. Susannah wanted a love like her parents', a love that was shared, a love where the two people were complete only when they were together.

Susannah picked up her parents' picture and stared at it. Was this the reason she had felt compelled to open the trunk today? Did her mother want her to see what true love was like? Susannah shook her head. Dorothy had never willingly caused Susannah pain, and the knowledge that she would never know the kind of love her parents had shared could only bring pain. There must be another reason.

Susannah closed her eyes, and as she did, she could picture her mother handing her a book to take to the orphanage. "The most blessed thing is to give," Dorothy had said, "and the greatest gift is yourself."

As tears welled in her eyes, Susannah nodded. This was what her parents had taught her, that she could help others by giving of herself. She had not done that since Dorothy's death. It was time. Though Charles might not return her love, he could not stop Susannah from loving him. She would give him that love unconditionally, and maybe—just maybe—her love would help him.

As frequently happened, the rain ended by late afternoon, and the sun emerged, its warmth beginning to dry the puddles. It was, Susannah told herself, a good omen. Surely Charles would accept her offer. She waited until the sun was close to setting before she took the crooked path down the hill, picking her way along the still muddy trail. Though she tried to tell herself that this was no different from a hundred other times that she had visited the Moreland estate, Susannah's heart knew differently, and she gripped the packet of letters so tightly that the string dug into her fingers. So much depended on Charles's reaction!

"Susannah!" His eyes widened in surprise when he opened the door. "Is something wrong?"

His expression was guarded, so different from the smiling warmth that had once characterized their time together. Susannah tried not to let that discourage her. What was important was helping Charles. She shook her head. "I needed to see you, and this was the only time I was sure you'd be home."

He stepped outside, closing the door behind him. "I'd invite you in, but I won't risk your reputation."

He had spoken of reputations before. Perhaps it was wrong, but today Susannah cared not a whit for that. "What if I said I didn't care?"

Charles shook his head, his expression as stern as if he were dealing with a misbehaving child. "I care. I won't let you destroy your good name. Without that, a person has very little." There was such bitterness in his voice that Susannah flinched. Though Charles had never referred to it, she knew he must be remembering that he was a Moreland in name only. That and the knowledge that Brian O'Toole had sought to destroy the mill and discredit Charles obviously weighed heavily on him.

Perhaps there was some way Susannah could help him. She held out the packet of letters. "I found these when I was sorting

my mother's belongings. They appear to be from your mother."
Though his father might be unknown, Mary Moreland was his
mother. Perhaps he would find some comfort in her letters.

For a long moment, Charles stared at the envelopes. Then,
with obvious reluctance, he reached for them. When he spoke,
his question surprised her. "Are you packed for Paris?" Susannah would have expected him to say something about the letters
or even to ask about the carousel paintings. Instead, she had
the feeling that he was anxious for her to leave Hidden Falls.

Though the evening air was warm, Susannah shivered. This
was more difficult than she had anticipated. "I've decided I'm
not going." She watched Charles's reaction, and her heart thudded when she saw the narrowing of his eyes.

"Why ever not?" Though he kept his voice light, he could not
hide the way his eyes darkened or the lines that appeared between them.

Susannah took a deep breath. Somehow she had to make him
understand. "I believe I can do more good here," she said.
Thank goodness, her voice was steady, betraying none of the
fear that gripped her heart. "I know you're trying to improve
the mill's profits; perhaps I can help you find some new designs.
You told me that the last ones sold well."

Charles stared into the distance. Though the lines on his face
eased, Susannah saw that he was fidgeting with the cord on the
envelope. He was not as calm as he wanted to appear.

At length he shook his head and looked directly at Susannah.
Even the gathering darkness could not hide the disapproval in
his eyes. "You're not thinking clearly, Susannah. Your judgment
is clouded by grief." Charles took a step forward, and for a
second she thought he was going to touch her. Then he moved
back. "You need to go to Paris, and you need to do it now."

This time there was no doubt of the reason Susannah shivered. Charles's voice was stern, totally devoid of the warmth
that usually characterized it. Both his tone and his words chilled
her more than a winter wind.

"Listen to me, Susannah. You can't continue to go through
life putting your needs in second place. Paris is something you
have to do for yourself."

317

Susannah felt as if she were a student, listening to a professor's lecture. Though Charles's words made sense, she felt no emotion behind them. If she hadn't known better, she would have said that he was reciting from a text. He was trying to push her away, but she had no intention of going.

"I want to stay here," she said. "I want to help you."

A flicker of emotion crossed Charles's face, only to be extinguished before she could identify it. "That would be admirable, except that I don't need you." His voice was more than cool; it was icy cold, his words so firm there was no mistaking them.

Susannah gasped in disbelief. Never before had anyone refused her offer of assistance. "I beg your pardon."

Charles took a step backward, distancing himself from her physically as well as emotionally. "You heard me the first time. I appreciate the designs you chose." Though the words were polite, Charles's cold tone made them seem like an insult rather than a compliment. "Your ideas were fine for the pilot, but we've gone beyond them. I believe customers want modern patterns, not copies of classical designs."

Susannah blinked, not understanding why he was rejecting her. She could help him choose new designs. She could even create some. But his next words crushed that idea. "Jane will help me when she returns from Europe. She sent a few sketches, and I've already spoken to customers about them."

Susannah stared as the last of her illusions crumbled. Though she knew he didn't love her, she had believed he would want her to help him. "Then you don't need me." Somehow she managed to pronounce the words that wrenched her heart.

"That's right." Charles's face was as cold as the marble statues she had once studied. "There's no reason for you to stay in Hidden Falls. Go to Paris."

"I will." Susannah turned and fled, waiting until she was out of sight before she began to cry.

Had it only been a month? Charles didn't need to consult a calendar to know that it had been thirty-two days. Why did it feel like a lifetime since he had seen Susannah? He thrust his hands into his pockets to keep from balling them in frustration.

Thirty-two empty days; thirty-two nights filled with tortured dreams.

He strode from the house, trying not to think of the last time he had seen Susannah, but the memory of that evening haunted him. Though there were things in his life that he was ashamed of, never before had he been deliberately cruel. But that day he had been inexcusably cruel to a woman who deserved only kindness.

Charles gritted his teeth as he crossed the lawn. How he hated what he had done! He had hurt the woman he loved, inflicting wounds that might never heal. Lord knew he hadn't wanted to do it. Even to his ears, his words had sounded wooden, as if he'd had to force them through his teeth. Which he had. But there had been no choice. When he had realized that Susannah wanted to stay in Hidden Falls, Charles had known what he had to do. He couldn't let her give up her dream for him.

It would have been wonderful, having her here, seeing her every day. It would also have been sheer torture, having her here, seeing her every day but being unable to touch her, to love her the way he wanted. Most of all, it would have been unfair to Susannah. Charles had nothing to offer her: no future, no children, not even a name. Though he wanted her with every fiber in his body, even more than that, Charles wanted at least one of Susannah's dreams to come true, and so he had sent her away.

The afternoon was warm, filled with birds' songs and the scent of flowers. The perfect day should have filled him with gladness. Instead, Charles could think of nothing other than the pain he had seen on Susannah's face that night and the knowledge that he had been the one to cause that pain. John had been right; it had been difficult—incredibly difficult—to let Susannah go. But he had done it, and now he had to go on with his life. Yet that had proven almost as difficult as sending Susannah away.

No matter what Charles did, he could not forget her. Memories were supposed to fade with time; his did not. Instead, no matter where he was, he pictured Susannah there with him. She would be smiling, and then her eyes would fill with tears. And when they did Charles would remember how he had hurt her and how many times he had disappointed her.

Charles flung open the door to the stable in a vain effort to dissipate some of his frustration. Though the door slammed against the wall, Rob ignored the noise.

"I'm glad you came," he said, a satisfied grin on his face. Rob gestured toward the large bear and a horse that Mark and Luke had been painting on Charles's last visit to the workshop. "The animals are complete. Now all that's left is to build the platform and assemble the jumping mechanism."

It was good news. Rob had told Charles that this was the fastest part of the process. Unless a major problem developed, the carousel would be completed before Anne and Jane returned. Charles should be pleased. This was what he wanted. But instead of satisfaction, all he felt was emptiness and the sensation that something was very wrong.

Though he admired the animals, Charles knew his desultory comments disappointed Rob. "Sorry, Rob," he said, clapping the carver on the shoulder. "The problem is me, not your work."

At Rob's suggestion, he and Charles headed toward the site of the former gazebo to make a final decision about the carousel's location. Though Rob continued to speak about the animals, saying something about paint finishes and jewels, Charles's thoughts began to whirl. For the first time, when he looked at the spot where the gazebo had once stood, he saw not his father and Lucy but himself and Susannah. Why had he hated the site? This was where he had met Susannah, where he had first kissed her and where he'd fallen in love. Those were happy memories, thanks to Susannah. He owed her so much!

Charles frowned as he remembered Susannah's face the day she'd spoken to him of the carousel and her visible disappointment when she had realized that the carousel would remain at Fairlawn, open to no one other than his family.

"How long would it take you to make another twelve animals?" The words were out of Charles's mouth before he realized what he was going to say.

Rob, who had been pacing the site, stopped and stared at

Charles. "What do you mean?" The sun shone in his face, making him squint at Charles.

"I've changed my mind." Why hadn't he admitted it before? Susannah was right. She had always been right. Charles spoke quickly. Now that he'd made his decision, he was filled with a sense of urgency. Though Susannah might never know what he had done, the sooner his idea became reality, the better.

"I want to put the carousel in the park and let everyone ride it." Rob blinked in surprise. "The problem is, twelve horses won't be enough. People would have to wait too long."

Though a speculative light appeared in Rob's eyes, he asked only, "Do you want a second row of animals or a wider circle?"

"A second row," Charles said without hesitation. "That way courting couples can ride side by side."

Rob's smile could only be described as satisfied. "That's the right choice if you're in a hurry. Inside row horses are smaller and less elaborate, so we can finish them sooner."

His heart lighter than it had been in over a month, Charles nodded. "Let's do it."

That night when he had finished dinner, Charles paced the floor of the library, oddly restless. There was no apparent reason. From the moment that he had decided to expand the carousel, he had felt a deep sense of peace descend on him. He could almost feel Susannah smiling her approval. Why, then, did he feel as if he had forgotten something important? There was nothing waiting for him at the mill. The dogs were curled on the hearth, patently enjoying the feel of cool stone beneath them. Why did he have the sensation of something eluding him?

Charles walked to the window and stared outside. There was nothing unusual there. Pivoting on one heel, he resumed his pacing. It was only when he reached the small desk that he stopped. The letters. He had put the packet of letters Susannah had given him in one of the drawers. At the time, he had had no intention of reading his mother's letters, but something about them beckoned to him tonight.

Charles untied the string and slid the first letter from its envelope. Ten minutes later, his eyes widened with shock and he could feel the blood drain from his face. *Oh, my God!* Charles gripped the edge of the desk and read the words again and again. There was no mistake. It was true.

"No! No! How often must I tell you? Hold the brush thees way, Mademoiselle Deere."

Susannah felt the blood rush to her face. "I'll never learn." She had felt that way ever since she had arrived. Though Monsieur Beaulieu was reputed to be one of the best painting teachers in Paris, the only thing that she could vouch for was that he was the most critical man she had ever met. No matter what she did, he found fault with it. Susannah stared at the canvas in front of her, wondering why she even tried. None of the other students received this level of criticism.

"Nonsense." The voluble Frenchman shook his head as he positioned her hand on the brush. "Do you think I would waste my time if you had not the talent? Of course not! You have the talent, mademoiselle, but you must practice."

Susannah blushed again, this time from happiness. She felt like a flower receiving its first drops of rain after a long drought, for this was the only encouragement she had received in the three weeks that she had been in Beaulieu's class. Oh, how she needed it.

Paris was even more beautiful than she had dreamed. Walking the tree-lined boulevards, seeing Notre Dame's flying buttresses, marveling at the stained glass in the Ste. Chapelle, and spending days in the Louvre had been marvelous. And yet . . .

This should have been the happiest time of her life. Susannah was in one of the most beautiful cities in the world, responsible for no one other than herself. She ought to be enjoying every minute of every day. Instead, she was miserable. That was the only way to describe her feelings. Being in Paris was a dream come true. Unfortunately, that dream was no longer hers. Even the knowledge that her painting was improving brought no joy. Without Charles, her life felt empty and devoid of meaning.

"I don't understand him," the young painter who normally planted his easel next to Susannah's muttered. "Beaulieu demands more from you than the rest of us. He's a veritable ogre."

The man in question frowned. "I heard that, young man. The

reason I demand more from Mademoiselle Deere is that she has the talent. You do not."

Susannah flushed with embarrassment. "I'm so sorry, Henri." It was her fault that he was now bearing the brunt of Monsieur Beaulieu's scorn. Though even Susannah's untutored eye knew that Henri had no real talent, he had been kind to her, never failing to greet her with a smile or to commiserate when their instructor was unusually harsh.

"Don't feel sorry for me," Henri said. "He's not telling me anything I didn't know. But if you want to make amends, you can assuage my wounded spirits by joining me for a cup of coffee or a glass of wine."

Henri flashed her a smile so filled with charm that Susannah doubted any woman could refuse him. Since she had joined the class, he had invited her for coffee, pastries, dinner, dancing, a night at the opera—anything he could imagine. And each time she had refused. It wasn't simply that she had no interest in Henri; she also felt that spending time with another man would somehow be disloyal to Charles. But today, buoyed by Monsieur Beaulieu's praise, Susannah nodded. "I accept with pleasure." Though that was an exaggeration, she saw no reason to dash Henri's exuberance.

An hour later they were seated at a sidewalk café on the Boulevard St. Michel. Susannah stirred her coffee, trying to dissolve the sugar, while Henri raised a glass of wine to toast her health. As he started to say something, she heard the commotion. Glancing to the right, she blinked. It couldn't be. Her eyes were deceiving her, for what she thought she saw was not possible. And yet it was.

It was the dogs who found her. Though Charles knew he could have waited until she returned to the small apartment she had rented, that an hour or two more should make no difference when it had been so long since he had seen her, his heart would not believe that. And so when Susannah's landlady had told him that she was at class, Charles had charmed her into giving him the address. But he had been too late, the teacher had said, adding that she might be at a café somewhere on the Left Bank.

That hadn't narrowed the field very much. A wise man would have returned to her lodging and waited there. But Charles was not a wise man; he was a man in love, a man who had no desire to wait even one minute longer than he needed to.

And so he had wandered the streets, looking for the most beautiful woman in all of Paris. But it had been Salt and Pepper who had sensed her presence. Though they had been walking docilely, all of a sudden the dogs began to strain at their leashes, barking and making such a commotion that Charles had finally let them run. They'd leapt forward, darting between pedestrians, heedless of the leashes that trailed behind them. Charles, encumbered by human sensibilities, followed at a slower pace.

There they were, two dogs whose enthusiasm was even larger than their paws. Right now those paws were placed firmly on Susannah's knees. She had bent down, letting them lick her face, and those lovely long fingers that had once set his blood boiling were stroking the puppies' coats. Though Charles had told himself that this was a public place, that decorum was needed, he was practically sprinting as he approached Susannah. It was absurd to feel jealous of two dogs, to wish that he were the one kissing her, that he were the one her fingers were touching.

Charles glared at the bistro table. He ought not to be concerned about canine rivals when a handsome Frenchman was seated far too close to Susannah, his fond expression leaving no doubt that he sought more than mere friendship from her. Forcing his hands to remain at his side, Charles reminded himself it would do no good to pound the man's face.

"Hello, Susannah," he said when he reached her. Though she was still in mourning and wore a gown so simple it could have belonged to a nun, Charles was certain she was the most beautiful woman he had ever seen.

She looked up at him, and her expression, which had been filled with affection when she petted the dogs, grew wary. "Why are you here?" she asked. Though her words were not hostile, there was no warmth in them, and Charles could not help noticing that she gripped Pepper's fur as if for support. Susannah was obviously not happy to see him. It was, Charles knew, no more than he deserved. On the seemingly endless voyage from

New York he had reminded himself that she might reject him the way he had rejected her offer of help. It was a possibility he had not wanted to consider.

Why had he come? The reason was both simple and complex. "The dogs missed you." Though it wasn't a lie, it was far from the truth, but with that damnable Frenchman sitting there, Charles wasn't going to say anything more. "I couldn't put them on a boat by themselves."

"I see." This time Susannah's voice was distinctly frosty. The only encouraging omen was that she was still looking at him.

"No, you don't, but I hope you will." Charles gave the Frenchman a look designed to encourage him to leave. "I need to talk to you. Perhaps your friend would excuse us." The café's other patrons regarded the tableau with interest. Just what he did not need—an audience.

When her companion laid a hand on Susannah's arm, it was all Charles could do not to twist that hand until it broke. "Are you sure?" the man asked Susannah.

She nodded. Though she gave the Frenchman a parting smile, her face was solemn as she rose and took Salt's leash, telling Charles without words that he was being tolerated, not welcomed. He was not surprised. Indeed, he would have been surprised if she had greeted him eagerly. Quietly, Charles led the way to the banks of the Seine. Though there were always a few pedestrians strolling along it, the pace was slower, the noise less than on the busy boulevards.

For the first time since they had left the café, Susannah smiled. "I used to dream of walking here. Although I must admit that I never pictured Salt and Pepper being with me."

Though she hadn't said it, Charles wondered whether she had dreamed of walking with him. If she had, perhaps he still stood a chance.

"I couldn't leave the dogs at home," he admitted. It was the truth, although not for the reason he had given. When he had decided to come, Charles had realized that Susannah might refuse to see him. But he knew that she would have trouble ignoring the dogs. If he brought them, they might provide his only chance to get close to her. "Salt and Pepper are part of my dream." That, too, was the truth.

Susannah stopped abruptly and stared at him, obviously astonished by his declaration. "I didn't think you dreamt anymore." Was it his imagination that her voice trembled? And, if it did, was that a good sign?

"I dream. I guess I always have. It's simply that for a while I no longer believed they could come true." But now, if the Fates were with him, his fondest dream would become reality. Charles gave Susannah a sidelong glance, trying to read her mood. Would she listen to him? And if she did, how would she react?

Susannah tried to quell the pounding of her heart. If it weren't for the dog tugging on his leash, she would have believed she was dreaming. How many nights had she dreamt that she and Charles were strolling the banks of the Seine? That was one dream she had been certain would never come true. But here they were, together in the City of Light.

Why had Charles come to Paris? Susannah didn't believe that story about the dogs. Charles was not given to impulses, and only an impulsive man would have traveled such a distance because his dogs were lonely. That wasn't the reason he had come; Susannah knew that as surely as she knew that she would not ask him again.

Two boats passed, their crews calling greetings to each other, and in the shelter of a bridge, a couple embraced. Susannah closed her eyes for a second, remembering how wonderful it had felt to be held in Charles's arms, to have his lips on hers. That was part of her dream, sharing endless kisses with the man who now walked next to her.

If he saw the couple, Charles gave no sign. He gestured toward a narrow alley, then led her into a park that she hadn't known existed. At this time of day, it should have been filled with people enjoying the sunshine. But today it was almost deserted, and the row of black iron chairs that lined the walk was empty. Taking Salt's leash from her hand, Charles tied the two dogs to the iron fence, then motioned Susannah to one of the chairs. He had said he needed to talk to her; this apparently was where he planned to have that conversation.

When Charles tugged a chair out of the line and turned it so that he was facing her, Susannah was surprised. It was an almost unwritten law that the chairs remained where the grounds-keepers had placed them.

For a moment Charles said nothing. Susannah saw him swallow deeply, and she wondered whether he was as uncomfortable as she was, remembering the last time they had spoken. The memory of that night on his front porch and his rejection was still all too fresh in her mind.

Charles paused, swallowed again, then began to speak. "I've been such a fool." Susannah stared at him. Whatever she had expected him to say, it was not this. Part of her wanted to lean forward, to touch his hand and reassure him. The other part remembered how he had hurt her, and so she did nothing.

Charles's eyes darkened. "Can you ever forgive me?" Though his voice had been cold the night he had turned her away, it was now so filled with intensity that Susannah could almost feel the warmth radiating from him. Again, she wanted to touch him but held back, afraid of being rejected. "I thought I was protecting you, Susannah, but all I did was hurt you."

Susannah looked at the man she loved more than anything on earth. She wanted—oh, how she wanted—to believe him. "I don't think I could bear it if you pushed me away again," she said, trying to obliterate the memories of how she had felt, waking alone, then being told she wasn't needed.

Charles leaned forward, and there was no mistaking the pain that shone from his eyes. "Believe me, Susannah, pushing you away is the last thing I want to do. Will you let me explain?"

An elderly man entered the park. When he saw Susannah and Charles, he veered in the opposite direction. She nodded slowly in response to Charles's question. He had crossed the ocean to speak to her. The least she could do was listen.

"I loved you from that very first day." Perhaps it was foolish, for he had spoken of love before, but Susannah felt a tiny seed of hope begin to grow deep within her. She had loved Charles from that day, too.

"At first I didn't realize it was love," Charles continued. Susannah smiled, remembering how she had believed what she and Charles shared was friendship.

"I thought what I felt was nothing more than attraction," Charles confessed, "and I fought it because you were Anthony's fiancée. Even when I realized that the attraction was stronger than anything I had ever experienced, I knew I could do nothing. Anthony was my friend, and I wouldn't betray him."

Though Charles spoke calmly, the way he clutched the chair arm gave the lie to his composure. Oddly, that proof of his nervousness helped dispel Susannah's last fears that he might not be speaking the truth. She leaned forward, smiling slightly to encourage him. The seed of hope had sprouted.

"The day that Anthony broke your engagement, I was furious with him because he had hurt you. Then I realized that Anthony had done me a huge favor. He had removed the barrier that separated us. I could court you." But he hadn't. Charles had been her friend, and then he had pulled away. Surely that was not his idea of courtship.

A wry smile twisted Charles's lips. "I was so naive. I thought that my friendship with Anthony was the only thing keeping me from declaring my love for you. I didn't want to wait any longer, so I came to your house one morning, planning to ask you to marry me."

Susannah knew her eyes widened. "But you didn't." Never once had he mentioned marriage.

The elderly man walked past them, this time openly staring at Charles and Susannah. "May I be of assistance?" he asked, his eyes darting from Charles and Susannah to the two dogs who were now sleeping in the grass near the gate.

Charles shook his head but waited until the man had left the park before he spoke again. "For a while I thought no one could help me. By some horrible twist of fate, the morning I came to propose to you was the day your mother told me the circumstances of John and Mary Moreland's marriage."

This time Susannah obeyed her instincts. She leaned forward and laid her hand on Charles's, hoping to ease some of the pain she saw on his face. "In just a few sentences, the foundations of my life were destroyed," he said. "I wasn't John Moreland's child. I was the son of a rapist."

Susannah closed her eyes in a desperate attempt to block the images Charles's words had conjured. Though she had heard part of her mother's story, she had not known that Mary's child had been the result of rape. "Oh, Charles!" No wonder he had distanced himself from everyone. What a horrible burden to bear!

Charles gripped Susannah's hand as if it were a lifeline. "That changed everything. Though I loved you, I knew my love was doomed. I had nothing to offer you, not even a name."

That wasn't important. How could he have thought that she cared about social standing and proud names? She loved him because he was Charles, not because he was a Moreland. "But, Charles—"

"Please let me finish." Charles released his grip on her hand, then stroked her fingers gently. Even though they both wore gloves, the warmth of his hand sent shivers through her, reminding her of the night they had spent together. "I loved you so much, it hurt," Charles continued. "I tried to stay away from you, but I couldn't. Even though it was wrong of me to kiss you the day we brought Dorothy home from the falls, I couldn't resist. And once I kissed you, I didn't want to stop." Charles's eyes were dark and filled with remembered pain. "Susannah, it was horrible. I wanted nothing more than to hold you in my arms and beg you to love me, but I couldn't risk hurting you. That's why I tried to stay away."

Though she still didn't understand everything, Susannah realized that Charles had not meant to cause her pain. "I thought you didn't love me," she told him. No matter what his intention had been, that thought had hurt almost unbearably.

Deep furrows appeared between Charles's eyes. "I thought I was protecting you. Susannah, you must know that I didn't want to hurt you."

If they had any future—and how Susannah hoped they did!— it had to be based on truth and honesty. "You did, though. You hurt me that day and . . ."

". . . The morning I left your bed." Charles finished the sentence.

"Yes." Even now the memory of how lonely and abandoned she had felt when she had found herself alone wrenched Susannah's heart.

Charles's blue eyes darkened again. "Leaving you that morning was the second most difficult thing I've ever done. You were so beautiful lying there that all I wanted to do was hold you close and make love to you. But I couldn't. I was afraid that if I stayed, I'd lose control. I couldn't do that. I couldn't risk your becoming pregnant."

Susannah shook her head. For a smart man, he certainly had been ignorant when it came to her feelings. "I wanted your baby."

Salt and Pepper woke and began to tug at their leashes, whining when they could not reach Charles and Susannah.

"Later, boys." By some miracle, the dogs recognized the firmness in Charles's tone and quieted. "Don't you see, Susannah?" he said, gently pulling her glove from her fingers. "I couldn't risk that, not when I knew my father was a criminal. You deserved better than that; that's why I insisted you come to Paris."

Charles drew her hand to his lips and pressed a kiss on her palm. His lips were warm and comforting, far different than they'd been the day he had rejected her offer of love. Susannah closed her eyes, trying not to remember how her heart had ached at the knowledge that he hadn't wanted her. "You were so cold and heartless that day that I was certain you didn't love me."

Charles shook his head. "Telling you to leave was the hardest thing I've ever done. I knew I was hurting you, and I hated myself for doing it." His eyes were as warm as his lips, and the look Susannah saw radiating from them filled her with wonder. "I told you I was a fool," Charles continued. "Even when I knew my cruelty would hurt you, I was convinced that it was the right thing for you. The only thing I can say in my defense is that I was trying to protect you from me." Charles slipped to his knees and looked at her, his eyes imploring her to understand. "Can you forgive me?"

Susannah nodded slowly. The truth was, she had long since forgiven him, even when she hadn't understood why he had acted as he had. What she needed now was to understand why he had come to Paris. Surely it wasn't simply to explain his past behavior.

"What has changed, Charles?" Something must have, or he would not have traveled across the ocean, and he would not be kneeling at her feet, looking like a suitor.

"What changed is that I read the letters you gave me, the ones my mother wrote." Charles's gaze was steady, but to Susannah's surprise, his eyes filled with tears. "Mother told Dorothy everything that happened. You already know how John married my mother to save her from disgrace. That's what Dorothy told me. What I didn't know was that Mary lost the baby on their wedding night. Since there was no longer any reason for the marriage, she offered John an annulment." Charles blinked furiously. "He refused. He told Mary he wanted a real marriage." Charles's voice was husky as he said, "I was the result."

Though the sun shone brightly, turning Charles's hair to pure gold, nothing could match the brilliance of his eyes. They were filled with love and joy and a tiny shadow of doubt. As the implication of his words registered, Susannah found her own eyes beginning to tear. "So John is your father, after all."

He nodded. "That letter was one of the greatest gifts I've ever received. It gave me back my father. Even more, it gave me back my dreams."

Charles reached for Susannah's right hand, clasping it between his. "You accused me of not dreaming. The truth is, I didn't want to when there was no chance of them coming true, but I never, ever stopped."

The look he gave Susannah made her think that maybe—just maybe—her own dreams might come true. One already had. She was in Paris with the man she loved. As for the others . . .

"Do you want to know what I dream of?" Charles asked. The expression in his eyes made Susannah's pulse begin to race. Her heart so filled with emotion that she was unable to speak, she nodded.

Charles spoke slowly, keeping his gaze fixed on her. The

warmth that she saw radiating from his eyes brought a flush to Susannah's cheeks. This was the Charles she had seen in her dreams.

"I dream of a house with two very spoiled dogs," he said softly. "There are three children, and one of them looks just like her mother." He swallowed deeply. "Most of all, I dream of you and me and our life together."

Susannah stared, wondering whether she was the one who was dreaming. This was how each of her dreams had ended, but each time she had wakened to the reality of a life alone. Even now, Charles had not said the words that would make her dreams come true.

He pressed his lips to her hand, then raised his eyes to meet hers again. "Susannah, I can't promise that I'll never hurt you again. What I can promise is that I'll do everything in my power to make you the happiest woman on earth. Will you let me?" The joy that filled her heart was stronger and deeper than Susannah had believed possible.

Charles continued, "I love you, Susannah, more than I can ever say. All that I ask is that you'll let me show you."

Charles loved her! He loved her!

His voice was low and tender as he said, "My dearest, I beg you, if you love me even a little, marry me and make my dreams come true."

Charles loved her, and he wanted to marry her! Happiness swept through Susannah like a summer wind, warm and caressing, filling her with joy and deep contentment. "Oh, Charles, I love you more than I ever could have imagined!" Her smile matched the one she saw on her beloved's face. They had endured so much and traveled so far, but now the pain was gone, and in its place Susannah found pure happiness.

She smiled at the man she loved. "I want to be your wife and—if we're blessed—the mother of your children." When Charles grinned, Susannah pulled his hands to her and pressed a kiss on his knuckles. "Yes, my darling, I'll marry you."

He rose, drawing her to him. As Charles wrapped his arms around Susannah and lowered his lips to hers, the dogs raced in circles, yipping with glee.

Epilogue

Two months later

"Have I told you how much I love you, Mrs. Moreland?" Charles asked, pressing a kiss on Susannah's neck as she attempted to put the final pins in her coiffure.

The woman who filled his days with joy and his nights with passion chuckled. "Not recently. I believe it's been at least ten minutes."

"Are you complaining?"

"Indeed not." Susannah batted his hand away and reached for another hairpin. "But, my love, I suspect we have one very nervous carousel carver waiting for us." She started toward the door.

"You think Rob's more nervous than I am?" Charles couldn't imagine that. For weeks he had worried that Anne would not like the carousel. When she and Jane had returned from Europe only a few days after Charles and Susannah, he'd seen for himself the changes a year had wrought in his sisters. Jane was more self-assured than before, but—as he'd expected—Anne was the

333

most altered. Though she refused to believe it, she was once more beautiful, but it was a different kind of beauty—quieter and more mature. More than ever, she reminded Charles of photographs he'd seen of their mother as a young bride. But Anne was not a bride, and the sadness he saw in her eyes made Charles fear she never would be.

"Rob's nervous," Susannah confirmed. "He has a lot at stake."

"He must know this is the best work he's ever done. I've told him so a hundred times."

Susannah's brown eyes sparkled and she gave Charles what he had begun to call her wifely look, the one that said he was only a man and couldn't possibly understand some elementary concept that was immediately apparent to every female on the planet. "Maybe it's not your approval that Rob wants," Susannah suggested.

"What do you mean?"

"You'll see. Now let's hurry."

As Susannah had predicted, Rob was pacing the floor of Charles's study. "Do you think she'll like it?" he asked without bothering to greet either Charles or Susannah. His hands were fisted, and deep grooves had settled between his eyes.

Charles gave Rob a long assessing look. So that was what Susannah meant! "Anne?" he asked with as much innocence as he could muster, though he was hard pressed to hide his delight. A light flirtation with Rob might be just what Anne needed to regain her confidence.

"How could Anne not like the carousel? It's magnificent." Though Rob appeared to relax slightly, there was no mistaking the tension in his shoulders. "Let's do our final check, and then I'll get the guest of honor." There was no reason to keep the poor man in agony any longer.

As he and his wife walked hand in hand to the site of the former gazebo, Charles reflected that this was yet another way Susannah had brought joy to his life. Though he had not changed his mind about locating the carousel in the park where everyone could enjoy it, Susannah had remembered his concerns about Anne and had suggested that they have a dress rehearsal. They'd run the carousel at Fairlawn tonight with only family present. Then tomorrow it would be moved to the park. It was, Charles thought, a brilliant suggestion, yet another example of his wife's wisdom.

It had been Rob, though, who had insisted that while Anne might see the other animals, she could not view the lead horse until tonight. He had also forbidden her from watching the assembly of the carousel, insisting that that would spoil the unveiling.

Though the sun was setting and it was difficult to see the details of the horses, Susannah walked around the carousel. "Oh, Rob, it's incredible!" She touched each of the outer row animals as if she had never seen them before. It was true, Charles had to admit, that they looked different tonight. They'd been magnificent standing in the workshop, but that beauty paled compared to the sight of them here, part of a complete carousel.

"Anne will love this!" Susannah declared.

Charles nodded, sure that his wife was right. And when it happened, when he saw the expression of delight on Anne's face, all of his dreams save one would have come true. The other was in God's hands. "Let's get the girls."

While Rob stayed in the carousel pavilion, Charles and Susannah walked back to the house. "Anne, Jane," Charles called, "we're ready."

Seconds later, Anne hurried down the stairs. Throwing her arms around him and hugging him, she cried, "You're the most wonderful brother a girl could want."

To Charles's surprise, his face felt warm, and he heard Susannah chuckle. "Flattery will get you everything. Now, where's that sister of yours?" Though Jane had always been the tardy one, since they'd returned from Europe she was normally dressed and ready before Anne.

Anne shrugged one shoulder. "She said she'd be back."

"What do you mean? Has Jane gone somewhere?" Charles's tone was harsher than he'd intended, and Susannah laid a cautioning hand on his arm.

"She wouldn't say where she was going," Anne told him, "only that it was important."

Impatiently, Charles pulled out his watch. "We can't wait much longer." He and Rob had planned the evening so carefully. The moon would be full tonight, and they had both agreed that the perfect time to light the carousel would be as the moon rose behind it. Jane couldn't spoil those plans.

Susannah slipped her arm around Charles's waist as if for comfort. "If Jane doesn't come in time," she said, her voice calm and soothing, "we can delay the first ride until she arrives, but we can still turn on the lights the way you planned."

It was another of Susannah's perfect compromises. Charles kissed the tip of his wife's nose. "Trust you to find a way to make everybody happy."

Anne gave her sister-in-law a fond glance. To Charles's delight, both of the twins had welcomed Susannah to the family, and Anne appeared to have established a special bond with her. "You're a lucky man, Charles."

"Believe me, I know it." If it hadn't been for Susannah, none of his dreams would have come true.

Charles wrapped an arm around his sister's shoulders and the other around Susannah's waist as they walked across the lawn. The sun had set, leaving the pavilion in total darkness. Though the night was clear, the moon had not yet risen, and only stars lit the sky. As they approached the carousel, Rob joined them, taking his place on Anne's other side. Was it his imagination, Charles wondered, or had Anne placed her hand in Rob's? He wouldn't stare, not now when he was supposed to be watching for the moon.

An owl hooted; a small animal scurried through the leaves. And on the horizon, a silver glow signaled that the moment of truth had arrived.

"Now!" Rob called. A second later, the hundred tiny lights that lined the canopy of the carousel blinked on, and the Wurlitzer organ began to play.

"Oh, Rob." Anne slipped from under Charles's arm and ran toward the carousel, dragging Rob with her. "It's even more beautiful than I dreamt!" The fervor he heard in Anne's voice made Charles swallow deeply.

His sister climbed onto the platform and walked to the lead

horse. "It's incredible!" She stroked the gold mane. "And, look!" she cried in delight as her fingers touched the figure that Rob had carved next to the saddle. "You put my doll here!" Anne leaned forward, peering at the tiny letters on the doll's skirt. "My name! Oh, Rob, this is the most beautiful thing I've ever seen."

Rob cleared his throat. "It's no less than a princess deserves." His gaze remained fixed on Anne.

Anne blushed, and Charles thought he saw tears glistening in her eyes. "How can I thank you?"

Still not breaking his gaze, Rob gestured in Charles's direction. "Thank your brother. He commissioned the carousel."

Anne flashed Charles a smile before quickly turning back to Rob, her expression adoring. "But you're the one who made it."

Charles suspected the two of them would stare at each other like love-struck fools for the rest of the night unless he did something. "Why don't you try to ride one?" he suggested to his sister.

When Rob had helped Anne mount the lead horse, he stood next to it, apparently unsure what to do. Charles gave Susannah a conspiratorial glance. "I think Rob should ride next to Anne, don't you?"

His wife grinned. "Of course. I'm expecting you to ride a giraffe with me."

As they walked toward the tallest of the carousel animals, Charles saw a man and woman begin to cross the yard, hand in hand. The woman was Jane. And the man? Charles felt a knot of apprehension settle deep in his stomach as he recognized Jane's companion. Matt. The knot tightened. It was Matt Wagner Jane had gone out to meet.

Charles closed his eyes for a second, remembering the reason he'd come home early that fateful day more than a year before. Jane had written that she was in love and wanted Charles's advice. Was Matt the man? He had admitted he'd been in Hidden Falls that day and that he'd had a meeting with Charles's father. Had Matt come to seek Jane's hand in marriage?

Charles opened his eyes and stared at the man who had been his adversary for so long. Though his stance was defiant, some-

337

thing in the attorney's expression reminded Charles of that night long ago when his parents had hired a carousel for the twins' birthday. That night Matt had stood at the iron gates, his wistful look telling Charles that he longed to ride the carousel. Charles had glared at Matt that night and shaken his head. The boy from the wrong side of the tracks was not going to set foot on Moreland grass. It was a decision Charles had regretted many times.

He stared at Matt for a moment longer, then nodded. Though he could not undo the past, he would not repeat his mistakes. "Come on, Matt," he said. "We've been waiting for you and Jane." The grateful look Jane gave him was all the reward Charles needed.

When Matt and Jane were seated, Rob gave the command to start the carousel. Slowly at first, it began to revolve. Slowly, the horses began their rhythmic up-and-down motion. And then as the carousel reached full speed, Charles heard Anne's cry of delight. He grinned. This was what he'd wanted; this was why he'd built the carousel.

At Charles's side, Susannah gripped the brass pole and laughed as the giraffe moved up and down. "This is such fun!" she cried as she passed Charles.

"Anne's enjoying it."

Susannah nodded, her brown eyes sparkling with excitement. "In a few days, everyone in Hidden Falls will enjoy it, too. Oh, Charles, I'm so happy!" Something in her voice made Charles narrow his eyes. Was it possible that something other than the carousel was causing Susannah's happiness? As she had dressed this evening, she'd looked radiant. At the time, Charles had thought it was the excitement of the night to come. Now he wondered.

Susannah waited until they were next to each other again. Then she leaned toward him and, giving him a coy smile, said, "In a year maybe we'll take our daughter on her first ride."

Charles felt the blood drain from his face as the words registered. "Daughter?" he demanded when he could speak again. "Are you . . . ?" He still couldn't pronounce the words. "Are you sure?" he asked at last.

When Susannah laughed, it was the sweetest sound he'd ever heard. "Am I sure the baby will be a girl?" She shook her head. "No, I'm not. But I *am* sure we're having a baby."

As the carousel continued to revolve, Charles stretched his hand to Susannah. "Oh, my love!" The last of his dreams was coming true.

AUTHOR'S NOTE

I hope you enjoyed Susannah and Charles's story and that, like me, you're eager to return to Hidden Falls and the Moreland family.

I'm sure you noticed that although I usually tie up all loose ends by the last page of a book, this time there are a number of unanswered questions. Did you wonder what caused the enmity between Matt and Charles or whether Ralph was really cheating his clients? What about Philip's comment that he was planning to remarry? Who was the man who raped Mary, and if Brian wasn't the person behind the sabotage at the mill, who was . . . and why?

The reason for those unanswered questions is that *Carousel of Dreams* is the first of a trilogy featuring the Moreland family and their secrets. *Painted Ponies* tells Anne's story. Did you think she was going to marry Rob? That's possible, but there are complications, and Anne—who feared she would never marry—finds herself torn between two suitors. Speaking of complications, Jane has more than her share as she searches for true love in *The Brass Ring*.

The publication dates for these books haven't been established yet, but if you enter the carousel horse contest (which I hope you do!) or send your name and address to me either via e-mail or snail mail, I'll let you know when the next book is available. I promise that by the end of *The Brass Ring* you'll have all the answers to the questions that were raised in *Carousel of Dreams* as well as two love stories that I hope you'll find as heartwarming as Susannah and Charles's.

In the meantime, I wish you many hours of reading pleasure and many dreams come true.

Rainbows at Midnight

AMANDA HARTE

To inherit his father's legacy Sam Baranov needs a bride, a woman to keep house and bear children. He doesn't expect love; in fact, he doesn't believe in such a poetic notion. Which leaves him hard-pressed to explain why one glance from the new schoolteacher sets his pulse racing, or why her smile has him offering to teach the students woodworking.

Laura Templeton has traveled to Alaska to make a fresh start, not to find a husband. But after meeting Sam, matrimony occupies all her thoughts. Until Laura knows that in a land which boasts rainbows at midnight, they have discovered a love powerful enough to wash away the mistakes of the past, a love to light their future together.

Dorchester Publishing Co., Inc.
P.O. Box 6640   4953-8
Wayne, PA 19087-8640 $5.99 US/$7.99 CAN

Please add $2.50 for shipping and handling for the first book and $.75 for each additional book. NY and PA residents, add appropriate sales tax. No cash, stamps, or CODs. Canadian orders require $5.00 for shipping and handling and must be paid in U.S. dollars. Prices and availability subject to change. **Payment must accompany all orders.**

Name: _____

Address: _____

City: _____ State: _____ Zip: _____

E-mail: _____

I have enclosed $_____ in payment for the checked book(s).

For more information on these books, check out our website at www.dorchesterpub.com.
_____ *Please send me a free catalog.*

EXTREME MEASURES
RENEE HALVERSON

If André DuBois were a betting man, he would lay odds that the woman in red is robbing his dealers blind. He can tell the beauty's smile disguises a quick mind and even quicker fingers. To catch her in the act, he deals himself into the game, never guessing he might lose his heart in the process.

Faith O'Malley depends on her wits to succeed at cards, and experience tells her the ante has just been raised. The new gambler's good looks are distracting enough, but his intelligent eyes promise trouble. Still, Faith will risk everything—her reputation, her virtue—to save the innocent people depending on her. It won't be until later that she'll stop to learn what she's won.

OFFICIAL ENTRY FORM

Win a carousel horse music box! Just correctly answer the three following questions based on Charles and Susannah's story from *Carousel of Dreams* by Amanda Harte. Be sure to give your complete and correct address and phone number so that we may notify you if you are a winner.

(Please type or legibly print.)

1) What did Charles name the puppies he found by his back door?

_____

2) What is the name of the Moreland estate?

_____

3) Which style of carousel horse is the most elaborate?

_____

NAME: _____

ADDRESS: _____

_____

PHONE: _____

E-MAIL ADDRESS: _____

MAIL ENTRIES TO:
DORCHESTER PUBLISHING CO., INC.
COD CONTEST
276 FIFTH AVENUE, SUITE 1008
NEW YORK, NY 10001